Alexander McCall Smith is the author of over sixty books on a wide array of subjects. For many years he was Professor of Medical Law at the University of Edinburgh and served on nati— —nternational bioethics bodies. Then in 1999 he achieved —ion for his award-winning series The No.1 Ladie— —y, and thereafter devoted his time to the writi— —g the 44 Scotland Street and the Portuguese I— —s. His books have been translated into forty-fi— —ves in Edinburgh with his wife, Elizabeth, a doctor.

Praise for Alexander McCall Smith's writing:

'Perfect escapist fiction'   *The Times*

'There is a timelessness to the tales, yet they are also of the moment . . . His talent is to see the god in small things' *Sunday Times Scotland*

'Simple, elegantly written and gently insightful'   *Good Book Guide*

'Highly amusing, intelligent and heart-warming'   *Scotsman*

'A treasure of a writer whose books deserve immediate devouring'
Marcel Berlins, *Guardian*

'It is hard to think of a contemporary writer more genuinely engaging . . . his novels are also extremely funny: I find it impossible to think of them without smiling'   Craig Brown, *Mail on Sunday*

'Alexander McCall Smith's stories are subtle, gentle works of art'
Daily Telegraph

'Delicious, light-hearted stuff and I love it – my only criticism is that these books are just not long enough'   *The Lady*

ALEXANDER McCALL SMITH

THE UNBEARABLE LIGHTNESS OF SCONES

A *44 Scotland Street* Novel

Illustrations by
IAIN McINTOSH

ABACUS

First published in Great Britain in 2008 by Polygon, an imprint of Birlinn Ltd
First published in paperback in Great Britain in 2009 by Abacus

A CIP catalogue record for this book
is available from the British Library.

ISBN 978-0-349-12114-7

Typeset by Palimpsest Book Production Limited, Grangemouth, Stirlingshire
Printed and bound in Great Britain by Clays Ltd, St Ives plc

Papers used by Abacus are natural, renewable and recyclable
products made from wood grown in sustainable forests and certified
in accordance with the rules of the Forest Stewardship Council.

Mixed Sources
Product group from well-managed
forests and other controlled sources
www.fsc.org   Cert no. SGS-COC-004081
© 1996 Forest Stewardship Council

FSC

Abacus
An imprint of
Little, Brown Book Group
100 Victoria Embankment
London EC4Y 0DY

An Hachette Livre UK Company
www.hachettelivre.co.uk

www.littlebrown.co.uk

This book is for Jan Rutherford and Lesley Winton

1. Love, Marriage and Other Surprises

The wedding took place underneath the Castle, beneath that towering, formidable rock, in a quiet church that was reached from King's Stables Road. Matthew and Elspeth Harmony had made their way there together, in a marked departure from the normal routine in which the groom arrives first, to be followed by the bride, but only after a carefully timed delay, enough to make the more anxious members of her family look furtively at their watches – and wonder.

Customs exist to be departed from, declared Matthew. He had pointedly declined to have a stag party with his friends but had none the less asked to be included in the hen party that had been organised for Elspeth.

'Stag parties are dreadful,' he pronounced. 'Everybody has too much to drink and the groom is subjected to all sorts of insults. Left without his trousers by the side of the canal and so on. I've seen it.'

'Not always,' said Elspeth. 'But it's up to you, Matthew.'

She was pleased that he was revealing himself not to be the type to enjoy a raucous male-only party. But this did not mean that Matthew should be allowed to come to her hen party, which was to consist of a dinner at Howie's restaurant in Bruntsfield, a sober do by comparison with the Bacchanalian scenes which some groups of young women seemed to go in for.

No, new men might be new men, but they were still men, trapped in that role by simple biology. 'I'm sorry, Matthew,' she said. 'I don't think that it's a good idea at all. The whole point about a hen party is that it's just for women. If a man were there it would change everything. The conversation would be different, for a start.'

Matthew wondered what it was that women talked about on such occasions. 'Different in what way?' He did not intend to sound peevish, but he did.

'Just different,' said Elspeth airily. She looked at him with curiosity. 'You do realise, Matthew, that men and women talk about rather different things? You do realise that, don't you?'

Matthew thought of the conversations he had with his male friends. 'I don't know if there's all that much difference,' he said. 'I talk about the same things with my male and female friends. I don't make a distinction.'

'Well, I'm sorry,' said Elspeth. 'But the presence of a man would somehow interrupt the current. It's hard to say why, but it would.'

So the subject had been left there and Elspeth in due course enjoyed her hen party with seven of her close female friends, while Matthew went off by himself to the Cumberland Bar. There he met Angus Lordie sitting alone with his dog, Cyril.

'I suppose that this is a sort of stag party for me,' Matthew remarked to Angus.

Underneath the table, Cyril, who had long wrestled with

temptation to bite Matthew's ankles, suddenly leaned forward and licked them instead.

'There, you see,' said Angus. 'When a dog licks you, it confers a benediction. Cyril understands, you know. That's his way of saying that he's going to be sorry to lose you.'

'But he's not going to lose me,' protested Matthew. 'One doesn't completely disappear when one gets married.'

Angus looked at Matthew with his slightly rheumy eyes. 'Really? Well, we won't be seeing much of you here after the event.'

'We'll see,' said Matthew. He raised his glass of beer to his lips and looked at Angus. Angus was much older than he was and was unmarried, which meant either that there was some profound reason – lack of interest – or that he had been successful in evading commitment. Now, which of these was it?

'What about yourself, Angus?' Matthew asked. 'Have you ever thought of . . . tying the knot with anybody?'

Angus smiled. 'Nobody would have me, I fear. Nothing would give me greater pleasure, I suspect, but, well, I've never really got myself organised.'

'Of course, you'd need to find somebody capable of taking on Cyril,' said Matthew. 'And that wouldn't be easy.'

Angus shot Matthew an injured glance and Matthew immediately realised his tactlessness.

'Cyril is a slight problem,' said Angus. 'It's difficult being canine, you see. Lots of women turn their noses up at dogs. Particularly with Cyril being the sort of dog that he is. You know, a wandering eye and some unresolved personal freshness issues. But I wish people would see beyond that.'

Matthew nodded. Angus would be a task enough for any woman, and to add Cyril to the equation made it even more of a burden. 'What about Domenica?' he asked suddenly. 'I've always thought that you and she might make a good couple.'

Angus looked wistfully at the ceiling. 'I've thought that too,' he said. 'But I don't think there's much of a chance there. She can't abide Cyril, you see, and I can hardly get rid of him after all these years. His heart would break.'

3

'She'd get used to him,' said Matthew. 'And dogs don't last forever.'

Angus shook his head. 'No prospect,' he said. 'But let's not talk about me and my problems. What about the wedding? I hear you've got Charlie Robertson to do it for you. I knew him when he was at the Canongate Kirk. He does a nice line in weddings, and Her Majesty used to enjoy his sermons, I gather, when she was in residence at Holyrood. She must have had to listen to an awful lot of wheezy lectures from various archbishops of Canterbury – it must have been so refreshing for her to get a good-going, no-nonsense sermon from somebody like Charlie. You know where you stand with the Church of Scotland, although as an Episcopalian, I must say there's a certain folksiness . . .'

'We're making certain changes,' said Matthew. 'We're walking up the aisle together. And we're having a reading from Kahlil Gibran. You know, *The Prophet*. There's a chapter there about love and commitment.'

Angus began to let out an involuntary groan, but stopped himself. 'Sorry,' he said. 'Yes. Kahlil Gibran. I see. And the honeymoon?'

Matthew leaned forward and whispered. 'I haven't told Elspeth. It's going to be a surprise. Australia!'

Angus looked into his glass. For some inexplicable reason, he felt a sense of foreboding, as if a sinister angel had passed overhead and briefly looked down upon them, as one of those lumbering heavy bombers, laden with high explosive, may spot a target below – a quiet lane with lovers popular, the innocent going about their business, a farmer driving a truck along a winding lane; irresistible temptations for a sinister angel.

2. By the Side of the Bridal Path

Inside the church, three hundred guests – and a handful of regular members of St Cuthbert's, entitled in that capacity to attend any service – sat waiting for the ceremony to begin. Matthew had told Elspeth that she should invite as many friends as she wished. His father was paying for the wedding, and had imposed no limits; his own list, Matthew felt, was at risk of being embarrassingly small: a few old friends from school, his father and his new wife, a couple of distant cousins, Angus Lordie, Domenica Macdonald, Big Lou, James Holloway; that was about all.

Pat, Matthew's former girlfriend and occasional employee, had been invited too, and had accepted. Much to Matthew's relief it appeared that she bore no ill-will towards the woman who had supplanted her in Matthew's affections; and for her part, Elspeth, by nature, was not one to be jealous. Matthew had reassured her that although he had been serious about Pat, his seriousness had been a mistake; misplaced seriousness, as he described it. 'She was really more of a sister,' he said. 'I don't know why I . . .' he left the rest unsaid, and it was not referred to again. So many men might say 'I don't know why I . . .' when talking about the carnal, reflected Elspeth; all men might, in fact.

Elspeth had invited everyone in her address book and many who were not. All her colleagues from the Steiner School were there, her suspension having been formally rescinded after the evidence of the other children – prominent among them Tofu – that Olive's account of the incident in which the teacher had pinched her ear was at the very least confused, and more likely mendacious. But by the time her reputation was cleared she had already resigned, become engaged, and had decided not to go back to teaching.

As well as Elspeth's former colleagues, an invitation had been given to all the children in the class she had taught. They were to attend under the supervision of their new teacher, who had led them into the church as a group and taken them to the pews reserved for them up at the top on the left. Here they sat —Merlin, Pansy, Lakshmi, Tofu, Hiawatha and the rest, hair neatly combed, their legs swinging freely, not quite touching the floor, whispering to each other, awed by the solemnity of the occasion and the significance of what was about to happen to their beloved Miss Harmony.

5

'She'll probably have a baby in a couple of weeks,' said Olive knowingly. 'I hope it's a girl. It'll be a big tragedy if it's a boy.'

Tofu turned and sneered at her from the pew in front. 'Babies take time,' he said, adding, 'stupid.'

'What do you know about it?' hissed Olive. 'And anyway, no girl would ever marry you. Not in a hundred years.'

'You mean that nobody would ever marry you,' retorted Tofu. 'They'd take one look at you and be sick.'

'I'm going to marry Bertie,' said Olive smugly. 'He's already asked me. We're going to get married when we're twenty. It's all settled.'

Bertie, who was sitting a couple of places away from Olive, heard this remark and froze. 'No, Olive, I didn't say I would,' he protested. 'I didn't.'

Olive glared at him. 'You did!' she said. 'You promised! Don't think you can break your promises like that.' She snapped her fingers to demonstrate the speed of Bertie's broken promises, then looked at him and added, 'Especially in a church. God's really going to hate you, Bertie!'

This conversation was interrupted by the organist, who began to play a Bach prelude. Although the congregation was unaware of their presence, Matthew and Elspeth had already arrived and were sitting with Charlie Robertson in the chapel at the back of the church, a small, tucked-away room on the walls of which the names of the fallen were inscribed in lead, equal in death, with no distinction of rank, just men. Matthew, feeling awkward, gazed at the lists of names and thought: they were my age, or younger. Some were seventeen or eighteen, and were only in France or wherever it was for a week or two, days in some cases, before they died in that landscape of explosion and whistling metal. They didn't have a chance, and now here am I, whose life has been so easy, reading about them and their sacrifice.

It was as if Charlie Robertson had read Matthew's thoughts. 'We've been very fortunate, haven't we?' he said. 'Being born at the time we were.'

Matthew glanced at Elspeth. He reached for her hand.

6

'On a more cheerful note,' said Charlie. 'Did you know that it was in this chapel that Agatha Christie got married?'

Matthew showed his surprise. 'I would have thought that she would have been married in a sleepy little English village somewhere,' he said. 'In one of those places with an extraordinarily high murder rate.'

Charlie laughed. 'I see what you mean,' he said. 'But no. She got married here in Edinburgh. To her archaeologist husband. She said that an archaeologist was an ideal husband as the older the wife became the more interested he would be in her.'

Matthew smiled. It was difficult to imagine Agatha Christie as being young; some people were remembered as how they became, rather than how they were; it was something to with names, he thought. Agatha was not a young name. 'But didn't she run away?'

'That was earlier,' said Elspeth, who knew something about Agatha Christie. 'Her first, dashing husband fell in love with somebody else. So she disappeared, and was eventually found staying at a hotel in Harrogate.'

Charlie Robertson looked at his watch. 'Well,' he said. 'We should be thinking of starting. Are you two ready?'

Matthew rose to his feet. Their conversation, innocent enough, had nevertheless made him think. In getting married, he realised, he was giving a hostage to fortune. By taking Elspeth into his life, the chances that the world would hurt him were doubled. She might leave him; she might run away, like Agatha Christie. There was so much that could go wrong in life if you took on somebody else, and then there were children and all the worries and anxiety they brought. There were so many reasons, he thought, for remaining single.

He looked at Elspeth, who was adjusting the veil she had pinned to her hair. I don't want to hurt you, thought Matthew; that's the last thing I want. But should I really go through with this? Is it wise?

3. Wedding Daze, and a Hint of Doubt

Suddenly, though, there was the sound of bells, and Matthew found himself outside the church, with Elspeth beside him, arm linked in arm. There were people in the churchyard – people whom he did not recognise, but who were smiling at him. One woman, a visitor, had a small disposable camera, which she raised and pointed at them. Matthew smiled for the camera automatically, although he felt dazed. He turned to Elspeth, who was looking behind her now; the children had emerged from the front door and were jostling one another for her attention. She bent down and placed a kiss on the forehead of one of them, a small boy in a curious, rainbow-coloured coat. Matthew saw the boy's sandals, one of those little details one notices, and smiled again; he was proud of Elspeth. He was proud.

There were other guests now, stepping out into the light. The late afternoon sun was blocked from the church by the towering bulk of the Caledonian Hotel over the road, but it reached the Castle now, up above them, touching the walls with gold; and the sky was so empty, just blue. Somewhere behind them, a train moved through Princes Street Gardens, a clattering sound, and there were pigeons in the air, a sudden burst of them. The children pressed around Elspeth; Matthew found himself beside Gordon, his father, bekilted like Matthew himself. This unites us, he thought, father and son; this shared garb, this same tartan; and he reached out and took his father's hand in a handshake that became a semi-embrace and then reverted to a handshake.

'Well,' said Gordon, 'that's that then. You've done it, Matt. Well done, son.'

Matthew looked at his father. The little paternal speech, so apparently trite, seemed just right, so pre-ordained, just like the words he himself had uttered in the church, although he could hardly remember what he had said. Presumably he had done all that was expected of him, as Charlie had smiled throughout and had not corrected him. And what else could his father say? That he was relieved that Matthew had at last done something decisive? That he hoped that at least he would get marriage right, even if he had never got anything right with all the businesses he had been set up in? The gallery, though, was not a failure, and he wondered if his father knew that. But this was not the time.

Gordon leaned forward and whispered into his son's ear. 'When you walked up the aisle together, you know, I thought by the look on your face . . . I thought that you were having second thoughts! I was mighty worried!'

Matthew's smile was fixed. 'Me? Second thoughts?'

'Well, obviously not,' said Gordon. He glanced at Elspeth, who was surrounded by a group of women in elaborate hats who were having their photograph taken with her. 'You'll remember those people we knew in Kilmacolm? Well, she called it off at the very last moment, you know, and everybody had to traipse back to the hotel. It was over in Largs. And then she changed her mind and they sneaked into the register office two weeks later and did it. You were too young to know about it.'

Matthew listened to his father's story patiently, but he was really thinking of what his father had said about his expression as he had made his way up the aisle. Had it been that obvious? If it had, then he wondered if anybody else had noticed it. Of course nobody looked at the bridegroom; all eyes would have been on the bride, as was always the case at weddings.

His father was, of course, right. As he walked behind Charlie Robertson, he had been thinking of the consequences that would ensue if he were to decide not to go ahead with the wedding. It would be heartless in the extreme to let the bride down before the altar, but presumably that had been done before, on the very brink of the exchange of vows. And perhaps there were circumstances in which it would be the right thing to do – not an act of selfishness, or cowardice, but an act intended to prevent the other person from making the mistake of marrying somebody whose heart was not in it.

Well, he had not done it, and they had gone ahead with the ceremony. And now, he thought, I'm married! He looked down at his hand and turned the ring around on his finger. How strange it felt; how grown-up.

9

He glanced at Elspeth. She had moved away from the women in hats, and the children, and was talking to an elderly man wearing a soft brown hat and a pair of large sunglasses. That, he thought, was the Uncle Harald of whom she had spoken, her half-Norwegian uncle who had moved to Portugal with his friend of thirty years, a man who wrote books on china. The friend had drowned when their yacht had been swept onto rocks. Harald had remained in Portugal, alone. How many of us lead lives of quiet desperation, thought Matthew; we hope to be saved by one person, one thing; we convince ourselves that one thing can last.

Harald was making a point to Elspeth and reached out to touch her on the arm. Matthew heard what he was saying to her. 'I do so like weddings,' he said. 'I've always liked them.'

And Matthew thought: until a very short time ago, you could have been only a spectator. And now it's too late.

The car that was due to take them to the reception had turned round and was now pointing back up the driveway of the church. The chauffeur, wearing a smart black uniform and peaked cap, had opened one of the passenger doors and was standing by it. Matthew caught Elspeth's eye, and she nodded. She whispered something to Uncle Harald, and then came over to join Matthew. They climbed into the car.

As they turned out into King's Stables Road, the chauffeur turned to them and said, 'A busy day for me. I did an airport collection first thing and then I did a chap I used to know at the pub.'

'He got married?' asked Matthew.

'Yes,' said the chauffeur. 'A dreadful mistake.'

There was silence in the back of the car.

Matthew smiled. 'Do you mean it's a mistake to get married, or your friend made a mistake in his choice?'

'Both,' said the chauffeur.

Elspeth laughed. 'Very funny,' she said.

'No, I'm serious,' said the chauffeur.

4. Answers to the East Lothian Question

The reception was held in two large marquees pitched in Moray Place Gardens. After his own wedding to Janice, a second marriage that his son had found difficult to accept at first but to which he had eventually become resigned, Gordon had moved to a house in Gullane. This is pronounced Gillan, on the basis of the Gaelic etymology of the word, a matter which divides the population of the East of Scotland into warring factions every bit as much as heresies divided the population of early Christian Europe. Those early heresies had led to bloodshed, and so had the issue of the correct pronunciation of Gullane (which is, as has been said above, Gillan). In late 1973 a fight had broken out in the neighbouring town of North Berwick when a passing motorist had stepped out of his car and, innocent of the controversy, had asked the way to Gullane, giving the u an i value. The response of the person asked had been to punch the motorist squarely in the face, breaking his nose and a small bone below the right eye. The motorist had then hit his assailant with a golf club that he had extracted from the back of his car.

This unseemly incident had resulted in the appearance of both parties in Haddington Sheriff Court, where they were charged with assault and breach of the peace. In the course of his judgement, the sheriff, an erudite man, had commented on the *casus belli*, pointing out that arguments over place names were inevitable, but that they should never deteriorate into physical violence. That was a perfectly normal thing for a sheriff to say when dealing with immoderate behaviour, but he went further.

'The place name Gullane,' he pronounced, 'is, as we all know, shrouded in obscurity, and indeed controversy, as this unfortunate incident reminds us. The name comes from the Gaelic word *gollan*, meaning a small loch, or possibly from another Gaelic word, meaning the shoulder of a hill. If the derivation is from *gollan* then, in one view, the pronunciation should be o rather than u or i. However, it is likely, in my view, that if indeed the name comes from *gollan* then, for the sake of clarity, popular usage would have sought to differentiate the place name from the geographical feature word (small loch), and this differentiation would most naturally have been gill – rather than gull – the former being easier on the tongue. I myself have never doubted that the correct pronunciation is Gillan rather than Gullane. There are many reasons for this, one of which I have already animadverted to, but a particularly persuasive reason is that that is the way I have heard it pronounced by the Lord Lyon, Sir Thomas Innes of Learny, GCVO, WS. If there is a greater authority on names in Scotland, then let him step forward.' None did.

This is the only time that a Scottish court has ruled on the matter. Some have pointed out, of course, that the sheriff's remarks were *obiter*, and therefore not binding, but, in the absence of any more authoritative ruling, others have argued that we must accept ourselves as being bound by what was said in Haddington Sheriff Court. It may be, they say, that the Court of Session itself will rule on the matter – and indeed that would be helpful – but until the court does, those who have insisted on a u value should have the good grace to recognise that they are wrong.

When Matthew's father had moved to Gullane, he had discovered that the pronunciation of the town's name appeared to be determined by the side of an economic and social fault-line on which one dwelled. Those who lived in the large houses on the hill, great villas favoured by the Edinburgh haute-bourgeoisie, would never have said anything but Gillan, while those who lived on the other side of the High Street would choke rather than use that pronunciation.

Gordon considered the matter to be one of extreme unimportance. He had no time for such pettiness and for the verbal signals by which people set out to demonstrate that they belonged to this or that segment of society. What did it matter if one said table napkin or serviette? It mattered not at all, not in the slightest, although the correct word, of course, is napkin. But everybody knows what is meant by serviette, and that is the important thing, rather than the issue of getting it right and saying napkin.

Although they spent much of their time in their house in Gullane, Gordon and Janice kept a flat in Moray Place, which they used when they had something on at night and when it would have been tiresome or inconvenient to drive out to East Lothian.

This flat was on the north side, looking out over the Dean Valley towards the Firth of Forth and the hills of Fife, a city view of incomparable beauty; or, if comparisons were to be attempted, they would have to be with the views enjoyed by those with the good fortune to live on the Grand Canal in Venice or Fifth Avenue in Manhattan.

Gordon was not sure how far Janice appreciated the aesthetic pleasure of living in the classical New Town; she was not one to spend much time in the admiration of beauty, and when they had inspected the flat before buying it he had noticed her indifferent expression when he had first commented on the astragals. She had been more interested in the kitchen and in what would be required to bring it up to a satisfactory standard.

'Everything must go,' she said. 'We'll have to get rid of everything and start from scratch.'

'Everything?' Gordon had been surprised. Had she not noticed the lovely old Belfast sink? Had she not appreciated the ancient meat safe, half recessed into the wall? Janice had been adamant, though, and in due course men came round to take everything out.

'An awful pity,' said one of the men. 'This good stuff. This lovely old sink.'

Gordon had looked away, ashamed. I've married beneath me, he suddenly thought. It was an odd thought, the sort of thought that people now would never admit to thinking. And yet there were occasions on which people married beneath them – not in social terms – but in terms of intelligence or sensitivity. Why deny that such unions took place?

And this dispiriting judgement was later to be confirmed, when Janice had dropped a hint about a present for her forthcoming birthday. Had he heard correctly? Had she really said: 'I'd love something like that picture of the people dancing on the beach. You know the one I mean?'

5. *Almost a Perfect Summer Night*

Elspeth Harmony's parents were both dead and so there had been nobody to object to Gordon's offer to pay for everything connected with the wedding, down to the last canapé. Of course the custom that the bride's parents should pay for the reception had changed, although it was still sometimes defended by the fathers of grooms. It was common enough now for the couple themselves to pay, thereby relieving the parents of all costs, and Matthew would certainly have been in a position to afford anything (he had, after all, four million pounds; rather more, in fact, as the market had been kind to him). But Gordon had been insistent and Matthew had not argued.

The rental of the marquees, of which there were two, was expensive enough in itself, costing over two thousand pounds – and that was before anybody had so much as sat down at the tables at which they were to be served the menu that Janice had arranged with the caterers. This was Menu E on a scale that progressed from Menu A – the you'll-have-had-your-tea menu, at six pounds per head (inclusive of half a glass of champagne per guest) – through Menus

B, C and D, to the higher glories of Menu E, described in the brochure as a meal of which passing angels might well feel envious. But it would have been unlikely that any passing angel would have guessed at the cost of what was seen below – fifty-eight pounds per head.

The caterer, a short, stout man, had recited the delights of Menu E to Janice when he came to visit her with his illustrated brochure and notebook.

'We shall start,' he intoned, 'with the parcel of oak-smoked salmon, with fresh crab, bound in a lemon and dill mayonnaise.' He paused, watching the effect. 'And then,' he continued, 'there will be a gazpacho, over the surface of which a fine amontillado sherry has been dribbled.'

Janice raised an eyebrow. 'Dribbled? Or drizzled?'

The caterer had laughed. 'Drizzled. Of course. Silly me. It's just when talking about such delicious things, one's inclined to . . .'

'Of course.'

'And then, a *trou normand*, followed by loin of Perthshire lamb with mushroom mousse, wrapped in . . .' again he paused for effect, 'puff pastry.'

'Delicious,' said Janice.

The caterer agreed. 'Indeed.' He raised a finger. 'And to pile Ossa upon Pelion, if you'll permit the allusion, biscuits and cheese, rounded off with strawberries, meringues glacés and clotted cream.'

Menu E was chosen, as were wines – champagne, a good Pouilly Fumé, and an equally good, but considerably more expensive, Brunello di Montalcino.

Then there was the music, which was provided by the Auld Reekie Scottish Dance Band under the leadership of David Todd, an accomplished musician who was also the nephew of that great man, the late Sir Thomas Broun Smith, author of the *Short Commentary on the Law of Scotland*. Dancing would take place in the second of the two marquees, with the band at one end, heroically making their way through 'Mhairi's Wedding' and the like, and the dancers at the other, flinging each other about with all the enthusiasm which Scottish country dance music engenders in the normally sedate Scottish soul. Tribal memories, thought Matthew, as he watched the spectacle of the dancing that evening; distant tribal memories that were still there.

As Matthew surveyed the guests enjoying themselves, the reality of what he had done came home to him. It made him feel more adult than he had ever before felt. Now he was responsible for somebody else, and that somebody else, who was at that moment dancing a Gay Gordons with Angus Lordie, was responsible for him. He felt the ring on his finger, twisting it round and round – it was a strange feeling, a symbol of the profound thing that had happened to him.

Elspeth caught his eye from the dance floor and smiled. Angus Lordie nodded. And then they were swept away by the whirl of dancers. Matthew saw the children dancing too – he noticed Bertie with a rather bossy-looking little girl; Bertie seemed to be an unwilling partner and was grimacing, which made Matthew smile. What did little boys see in weddings? he wondered. The end of freedom? The end of fun? Or something simply inexplicable?

Matthew moved outside. The evening sky was still light and the air was unusually heavy for early June. He moved further away from the open sides of the marquee, from the light and sound that spilled out from within. There were days, he thought, which one was meant to remember in all their intensity; days such as this, his wedding day, which he should be able to bring back to mind years from now when the rest of this year would be forgotten. And yet he found that he could barely remember anything that had tran-spired within the church, and that even the journey from the church to the Moray Place Gardens, a journey of ten minutes at the most, seemed to have passed in a flash of . . . of what? Confusion? Elation?

He threw a glance back into the marquee. The band had started to play something slower now and the crowd of people on the dance floor had thinned. He should not stay out here, he decided; he should go back into the marquee and claim his bride.

He had reached the entrance to the tent when a figure came out – Elspeth's Uncle Harald, holding a glass of champagne in his hand.

'Are you enjoying yourself, Harald?' Matthew asked. It was a banal question, but he did not really know what else to say.

Harald nodded. 'Of course I am. And if I appear to be somewhat emotional – which I am – then that is purely because this music makes me pine for Scotland. I go back to Portugal tomorrow, but every time I return to Scotland it becomes more difficult to leave.'

'Then why don't you stay?' asked Matthew; if exile was a bitter fruit, it seemed to him, then end the exile.

Harald took a sip of his champagne and looked at Matthew from over the rim of his glass. 'It's the idea of Scotland that I like,' he said. 'The real thing is rather different.'

Matthew frowned. 'But this is the real thing,' he said. 'This is real.'

Harald looked at Matthew in what appeared to be astonishment. 'My dear chap,' he said, after a while. 'You're not serious, are you? Smoked salmon and Perthshire lamb in Moray Place Gardens? The real Scotland? Oh, my dear chap! My dear, dear chap!'

6. Still Life, with Cyril

Angus Lordie thought about Matthew's wedding as he laid out his palette and brushes in preparation for Monday morning's painting.

Angus had always been somewhat ritualistic in his approach to his work; the image of the bohemian painter in a chaotic studio may have fitted Francis Bacon (whose studio was a notorious mess) but it did not suit Angus. He dressed with care for the act of painting, usually wearing a tie which he fixed to his shirt front with a small gold tiepin – a practice which gave him a slightly raffish air. His shirts were double-cuffed, fastened with a pair of worn gold cufflinks on which his father's initials – HMcLL (Hamish McLennan Lordie) – had been engraved more than forty years ago. The cufflinks were something of a talisman, and Angus would have found it difficult to paint without them; a common concern of artists of all sorts: of the opera singer who cannot perform without a favourite teddy bear propped up in the wings; of the writer who cannot write without a statue of Ganesh on his desk; and so on. And lest any Freudian should mock such superstitious reliance, let it be remembered that the desk of Freud himself was covered with his Egyptian statuettes; his familiars.

Angus was working that morning on a still life – not a common subject for him, as he was principally a portrait painter. At that time, though, there were no commissions in hand, and rather than wait for something to turn up, he had decided to embark on this still life, which now sat on the table in front of him, perched on a blue gingham tablecloth of the sort that used to cover the tables upstairs at McGuffie's Tavern near the Waverley Station. As a student at the Art College, Angus had lunched at McGuffie's once or twice a month, in the days when Jimmy McGuffie himself was still the host. He remembered the courteous welcome that Mr McGuffie gave his guests as they came to the top of the panelled staircase which led up from the street, and the kindness of the ancient waitresses in their traditional outfits of black skirts and white bibs. And he remembered those tablecloths over which various journalists and politicians had exchanged information and anecdotes. There one might meet, as Angus had, the likes of Owen Dudley Edwards, the scholar and raconteur; or Stephanie Wolfe Murray, the publisher; as well as others who had books and ideas within them that they were yet to reveal. McGuffie's tables were always democratic.

That, of course, was a time when people still had lunch, and talked. Now, thought Angus, with a degree of regret, lunch as an institution was threatened. The world of work had become all-consuming, as fewer and fewer people had to carry out the jobs that used to be done by so many more. To have lunch now was an indulgence, a guilty pleasure, disapproved of by employers, frowned upon by colleagues, many of whom had, at the back of their mind, the unsettling thought: while I'm eating lunch, people like me in Shanghai or Bombay are working – such were the implications of globalisation, that paraquat of simple security. And so restaurants that had once been a hive of conversation at midday were now largely deserted, or spottily populated by tables of one or two people, largely silent, eating salads and drinking mineral water. Mr McGuffie, were he to come back, would be dismayed by the change, and would wonder what had gone wrong. Perhaps he would think that another Reformation had occurred; that the iconoclasts had turned their ire on restaurants, having destroyed all of Scotland's religious imagery in the previous show.

Angus smiled. The moral energy, the disapproval, that had fuelled Scotland's earlier bouts of over-enthusiastic religious intolerance were still with us, as they were with any society. It wore a different cloth, he thought, and was present now in the desire to prevent people from doing anything risky or thinking unapproved thoughts. Oh yes, he muttered, they're still with us, and they're still ready to carry out the burning of witches, even if we don't call them witches any more. All that moral outrage, that self-righteousness, that urge to lecture and disapprove – it's all still there.

He looked at the objects resting on the tablecloth that had triggered these thoughts. The real secret in a still life, he thought, is to give the painting the sense of there being something about to happen. The objects might be quite still, but there had to be in the painting a sense of suppressed energy, of expectation, as if somebody were about to come into the room, to render the still life living; or lightning was about to show through the window behind the objects.

He wondered how he could suffuse these few ordinary things

with a feeling of immanence. What were they? A blue jug of the sort painted by so many Scottish artists – a Glasgow jug, as it was called. Indeed, the presence of a blue jug was more or less a requisite of any echt Scottish still life; so much so, perhaps, that it might have been the same blue jug that appeared in all those paintings. One might imagine William Crosbie telephoning Alberto Morrocco and asking him if he had finished with the blue jug, as he wanted to start work on a still life. And Alberto Morrocco would have replied that unfortunately he had just passed it on to William Gillies, who said that he would need it for a week or so, until he had finished his current still life, but would a bowl, replete with apples, do instead?

There was the blue jug, occupying centre stage on the table-cloth. And beside it, a modest green glass Art Nouveau inkwell, with its top open, plus a small posy of dried lavender, and a bunch of over-ripe grapes on a Minton plate. The over-ripeness of the grapes could be remedied in the painting, Angus thought, but could he remedy the essentially static nature of the objects he had chosen?

He was searching for the answer to this unsettling problem when he heard the doorbell ring. His dog, Cyril, who had been sitting beside the table – although he would, by nature, have to be excluded from the still life – perked up his head at the sound. As he did so, he uttered a low growl, baring his teeth slightly; the sun, slanting down from the studio window, caught the dog's single gold tooth and flashed a tiny glint of light, like the warning of a minute Aldiss lamp.

7. *Art of the Matter*

Angus did not like being disturbed when painting, as it broke what he thought of as his train of artistic thought. In reality it was not so much a train of thought as a mood, since all manner of unconnected thoughts crossed his mind while painting; no train, real or metaphorical, would ever be so loosely organised as this. Some of the thought, indeed, was fantasy – mild, Walter-Mittyish (Waltermittilich, as the Germans now have it, or should have, if they don't) thoughts; imagined meetings with the Scottish Government in which he was asked to take over what the requesting civil servant described as 'the culture brief'. And Angus would laugh and say, 'Well, we'll start by avoiding terms like that!' But then, magnanimously, he would agree – subject to time being available – and he would announce the abandonment of the intrusive attempts by politicians to control cultural institutions or to use culture as an instrument of social engineering. There would be grants – large ones – available to those of real talent in the world of painting, particularly to those who showed some ability to draw, a skill notably lacking, Angus thought, in so many aspirants to the Turner Prize. He agreed with David Hockney that an artist really had to be able to draw before anything else could be achieved. Now, Hockney could draw, as Angus often pointed out in the Cumberland Bar.

Then there would be grants for portrait painters, or Civil List pensions, perhaps, of the sort awarded to MacDiarmid. The importance of the portrait would be stressed in his new arts policy, just as the utterly ephemeral nature of installation art would be made crystal clear. Those unfortunate gallery cleaners who threw expensive installations out in the belief that they were rubbish would be vindicated, perhaps even given the grants taken away from those of whose work they disposed. And as for portraiture – what a glorious age would begin for this unjustly neglected branch of painting! The spirit of Henry Raeburn would again make itself felt in Edinburgh, and people would once more take an interest in the human face, not under the false light of our vain contemporary quest for beauty, but as the incorporation of humanity's virtues and vices.

Look at Raeburn, Angus once remarked to Domenica Macdonald. Everything is there in those faces: wisdom, tolerance, learning.

'But not pride,' said Domenica. 'Raeburn's subjects don't look proud, do they?'

Angus mused for a moment. 'Is there no pride there?' He thought of some of the better-known portraits: Francis MacNab, the McNab, draped in tartan and wearing a muckle hairy sporran. Was the face not proud? Or was it just grim? To be an anything must be difficult; how much easier going through life being just a something. Scottish aristocrats, of course, were odd. They belonged to a national tradition that did not really approve of anybody getting too above himself, and yet there they were, genuine, twenty-four-carat toffs, and if you were too demotic then what was the point of being a toff in the first place?

'Henry Raeburn was a kind man,' he said. 'Some of his subjects may have suffered from pride, but it doesn't really come through in the paintings. He concentrated on other things. One has to be charitable as a portrait painter.'

Domenica raised an eyebrow. 'Does one? And why? Because the person you're painting is paying the bill?'

Angus had to concede that this might sometimes happen. 'Court painters, that sort of person does that, yes. And I suppose all those paintings of chairmen of the board – sometimes I think that those paintings are done to keep the share price up. If you had an honest portrait of the chairman, one showing him to be all worn out with care and heading for a heart attack, then . . . well, it wouldn't help.'

'Nor would portraits of military figures showing their gentle side,' suggested Domenica.

'No, that might not help one's defence posture,' agreed Angus. He paused. 'I painted George Robertson once, you know. It was while he was Secretary-General of NATO.'

'Did you make him look resolute?' asked Domenica.

'Reasonably so,' said Angus. 'But he looked fairly resolute anyway. He came out of it very well. I got on very well with him. He has a sense of humour, you see. And he's a great man. He comes from Islay, you know, and that's an island that always produces good men and good whisky.'

'Not a portrait to scare NATO's enemies?'

'My portraits don't scare anybody,' said Angus. 'Mind you, I did once, years ago, do a little picture of Margaret Thatcher – bless her – a tiny little miniature. Then I pasted it onto a matchbox.'

Domenica looked puzzled. 'Oh?'

Angus smiled. 'Yes. Then I stood the matchbox outside a mouse hole. The mouse had been bothering me – he had gnawed away at some canvas I had. So I used it as a mouse-scarer. It was more humane than a mouse-trap, you see. The mouse came out and saw this picture of Margaret Thatcher staring at him and he ran straight back into the hole. It was very effective.'

'Did she scare us that much?' asked Domenica, trying to remember.

'Yes,' said Angus. 'She scared everybody. She was nanny, you see. She was a stern nanny who marched into the nursery and read the Riot Act. She told us to tidy up our rooms, that's what she did.'

'I suppose she did,' mused Domenica. 'But did people listen?'

'At first they didn't,' said Angus. 'But then they realised how strict she was. Nanny had a hairbrush and she whacked people with it. The miners. The Argentines. The railways. The universities. Whack, whack!'

Domenica remembered. Yes, there had been a great deal of chastisement, and not everybody had enjoyed it. 'Didn't Oxford refuse her an honorary degree?'

Angus nodded. 'Yes, it was a bit petulant, I thought. Rather like a child saying, I won't invite you to my birthday party. You know how children are always doing that – it's their only little bit of power.'

'Yes. And what did Maggie say?'

'Oh, she was wonderful,' said Angus. 'She replied in kind. She said she didn't want to come anyway. Which is exactly what one child says to another when that particular threat is made.'

But now he had to go to answer the door. It was most tiresome.

And there was nobody there – just a note, which he picked up, unfolded and read. The puppies are downstairs, said the note. In a large cardboard box. Your dog produced them and you are therefore responsible for them. There really is no alternative.

Angus stared at the note. Margaret Thatcher herself could not have put it more succinctly.

8. *Puppy Facts*

Old friends, like old shoes, are comfortable. But old shoes, unlike old friends, tend not to be supportive: it is easier to stumble and sprain an ankle while wearing a pair of old shoes than it is in new shoes, with their less yielding leather.

In his despair, Angus decided that it would be Domenica to whom he would turn. He did not have much choice, of course; in recent years he had not paid as much attention to friendships as he should have done, and there were relatively few people with whom he had preserved a dropping-in relationship. And there are many of us, surely, in that category; we may feel that we have numerous friends, but how many can we telephone with no purpose other than to chat? Angus was aware of this. He had spent evenings on his own when he ached to talk to somebody and he had decided that he really should do something about acquiring more friends.

Fortunately, Domenica was in. She was due that morning to attend a Saltire Society meeting, but that was not until eleven, and it was barely half past nine when Angus knocked on her door. She immediately sensed from his expression that something was wrong, and invited him in solicitously.

'Something's happened?' She thought immediately of Cyril. To have a dog is to give a hostage to fortune, and Domenica had occasionally reflected on the fact that when Cyril went – and dogs do not really last all that long – Angus would be bereft. Yes, she thought; something has happened to Cyril – again. It was only a month or so ago that he had been arrested and had faced being put down for biting – an unjust charge which had in due course been refuted. And then there had been his earlier adventure when he had been kidnapped while Angus had been buying olive oil in Valvona & Crolla. Cyril, it seemed, was destined to bring drama to their lives.

'Cyril?' asked Domenica, putting an arm around Angus's shoulder.

Angus nodded miserably.

'Oh, dear Angus,' said Domenica. 'He was such a fine dog. One of the great dogs of his generation. An example to . . . to other dogs.'

The eulogy was premature; Angus was shaking his head. 'Is, if you don't mind. Is, not was.'

Domenica was momentarily taken aback. While she might have described Cyril in those glowing terms once he was safely dead, she was not sure if she would compliment him thus during his lifetime. In fact, she thought rather the opposite; Cyril, in her view, was distinctly malodorous and somewhat odd, with that ridiculous gold tooth of his and his habit of winking at people. No, there was something rum about Cyril; and I have to use the word rum, thought Domenica – there is no other word in the English language with that precise nuance of meaning. Cyril was rum and Angus was . . . well perhaps very slightly rum – sometimes. Perhaps we needed a word, she wondered, not quite as strong as rum, which might be used for people who are just a little bit . . . again the language failed, thereby underlining the need for the elusive word. The lexicon of drinks might be dipped into for this purpose: if not rum then gin? No. Gin already had its metaphorical burden, at least when linked with tonic. Somebody who was a bit G and T was the sort of person who hung about golf club bars, a bit flashy. Port? That was more promising perhaps.

Angus had politely shrugged her arm off his shoulder and was now sitting at her kitchen table, looking at the kettle.

'Coffee?'

'You're very kind. Thank you.' He paused for a moment before continuing. 'Cyril had an affair, you see.'

Domenica looked at Angus wide-eyed. 'Well, I suppose that these things happen. But what's wrong with that? Don't you approve of his choice?'

'A very brief affair,' said Angus. 'It lasted about four minutes. With a bitch he met in Drummond Place Gardens. I couldn't stop it, really. And then she became pregnant.'

Domenica suppressed the urge to laugh. 'Well, I suppose that's what happens. People have affairs and . . . well, biology takes the shine off.'

'Well, the puppies have been delivered to me,' Angus blurted out. 'In a box. Six of them.'

Domenica, who was in the middle of filling the kettle, stopped what she was doing. 'To you?' she asked. 'To the flat?'

Angus sighed. 'They're in my studio at the moment. I've put them in there. Cyril was delighted to meet them.'

Domenica reached for the coffee jar and ladled several spoonfuls into the cafetière. She tried to imagine what it would be like to have seven dogs in one flat, even in a flat the size of Angus's.

'Well I don't know what to say,' she said. 'You'll have to get rid of them. Obviously.'

Angus looked up from the table. 'How? How can I get rid of six puppies?'

'Put them in *The Scotsman*. You see dogs for sale there.'

It was clear to Angus that Domenica knew nothing about the world of dogs. 'Those are pedigree dogs,' he explained patiently. 'Cyril is, of course, a pedigree dog, but the mother . . . Well, she's multicultural. Half spaniel, I think, with a dash of schnauzer and goodness knows what else. Nobody wants funny-looking dogs any more.'

'Well, take them to the dogs' home then,' said Domenica briskly. 'That's why we have dogs' homes.' She paused. 'We do have a dogs' home in Edinburgh, don't we?'

'We do,' answered Angus. 'And I've already been in touch. I telephoned them straight away. They're chock-a-block full at the moment, and they told me that I should try to find homes for them myself. So that's not on.'

Domenica resumed her making of the coffee. Then, suddenly she turned to him and said, 'I don't want a puppy, Angus.'

He looked at her, wounded. 'I wasn't going to . . .'

'Well, I just thought I'd make that clear from the start,' she said. 'I don't actively dislike dogs, but I would have to draw the line at owning one.'

Well, that answers that, thought Angus. He had been planning to ask Domenica to take one, but that was not the reason he had come here. He had come here for sympathy and advice, and all he was getting was a warning and a cup of Domenica's coffee, which never tasted very good anyway and was certainly not as good as

the coffee made by . . . He stopped. Big Lou! Big Lou was all heart
and what heart would not be melted by a puppy . . . or perhaps
even two?

9. Scout's Honour

'You just sit there in the waiting room for a few minutes, Bertie,'
said Irene Pollock, adding, 'like a good boy.' Bertie said nothing,
but sat down on the chair that he normally sat on during their
weekly visits to Dr Fairbairn. He was not sure why his mother had
asked him to sit like a good boy; how exactly did a good boy sit,
he wondered, and, perhaps more puzzlingly, how did a bad boy sit?

Bertie was not sure if he was a good boy. He tried to do his
best, but he was not sure if that was enough. Did good boys go
out of their way to do kind things for other people, as cubs and
scouts were meant to do? Bertie was always picking up odd books
and he had found one in the school library that dealt with the life
of somebody called Baden-Powell. There was a picture of this
Baden-Powell in the front of the book and Bertie had studied it

with interest. Mr Baden-Powell was dressed in extraordinary shorts and a khaki shirt with a loop of thin rope tied round his shoulder and tucked into his top pocket. It was a very nice uniform, in Bertie's view, and he wondered what one had to do to deserve it. Mr Baden-Powell, the book explained, had written a book called *Scouting for Boys* and had invented an exciting movement called the boy scout movement. Now there were branches of this movement all over the world, with cubs for small boys and scouts for older boys. Girls had their own branches called brownies and guides, but now, Bertie read, that had all been mixed up. That was a pity, Bertie thought, as it meant that Olive could join as well, which would spoil everything. Why could they not have something that was just for boys?

He had borrowed this book from the school library and had taken it home to Scotland Street.

'What's that you're reading, Bertie?' his mother had asked when she had come into his room – without knocking, as usual – and had found her son stretched out on his bed, absorbed in a book.

'It's about Mr Baden-Powell, Mummy,' said Bertie. 'I've just got to the place where he's fighting in the Matabele War and he's thought it would be fun to make a club for boys who wanted to do that sort of thing.'

Irene walked over to Bertie's bed and took the book from him. 'Let me see this,' she said. 'Now, Bertie . . .'

She broke off as she read the offending text. 'Baden-Powell was a very brave man. While taking part in the action to suppress the uprising in Matabeleland, he developed a series of skills suited to fighting in the bush. He learned a great deal from the trackers that the British Expeditionary Force used to hunt down the last of Mizilikazi's warriors as they hid in the valleys and caves of the Matopos hills . . .'

Really! She would have to speak to the school about allowing such literature in the library. *Scouting for Boys* indeed!

'Now, Bertie,' Irene began. 'I'm going to have to take this book away. I'm sorry because, as you know, Mummy doesn't believe in censorship, but there are limits. This is awful nonsense, Bertie, and I don't think you should fill your mind with it.'

'But, Mummy,' protested Bertie. 'The book says that Mr Baden-Powell was a good man. He was brave and he liked to help boys have fun.'

Irene closed her eyes, a sign that Bertie knew well meant that her mind was resolutely made up. He had noticed it when she read something in the *Guardian* that she agreed with – which was the whole newspaper, he thought. She closed her eyes after reading the article.

'Bertie,' she began, 'you must realise that this book is very much out of date. Nobody today thinks that this Baden-Powell was a good man. *Au contraire*. He was an imperialist, Bertie, somebody who went and took other people's countries. Poor Mizilikazi had every right to rise up against people like Baden-Powell.' She paused. 'Of course these things are very complicated when you're only six, I know that. But an intelligent boy like you should be able to see them, Bertie. Scouting is a thoroughly bad thing. It's very old-fashioned.'

'But why, Mummy?' Bertie protested. 'All this happened a long time ago. And cubs and scouts have lots of fun – the book says so. Look, let me show you the bit.'

'Certainly not,' snapped Irene, and then, more gently, 'You see, Bertie, the problem is that these organisations appeal to a very primitive urge in boys. They make them want to pretend to be little hunters. They make them want to join together and exclude other people. They make them want to get dressed up in ridiculous uniforms, like *Fascisti*. That's why Mummy thinks they're a bad idea.'

Bertie said nothing. The more his mother denigrated the activities of the boy scouts, the more desirable they seemed to him. Hunters! Uniforms! It would be such fun, he thought, to dress up and make one of those circles that he had seen pictured in the book. And they went camping too, which must be the most wonderful fun. There were photographs of boys standing about their tent while others made a camp fire. And then there was a picture of boys, all in their uniforms, sitting about their fire singing a song. The book gave some of the words of the song, 'One man and his dog, went to mow a meadow . . .' That sounded like a very exciting song, thought Bertie, so rich in meaning; and for a moment he imagined the man and his dog setting off to cut the grass in Drummond Place Gardens. And the man was Angus Lordie and the dog was Cyril, whom Bertie had always liked.

But he knew that he would never be able to be a cub or a scout. There would not be time for it, for one thing, what with his Italian lessons, his yoga and his psychotherapy. Which was why he was now sitting in Dr Fairbairn's waiting room while his mother went through for her private chat with the therapist before Bertie was called in. He knew that they were discussing him, and he had once tried to listen through the keyhole while his mother and Dr Fairbairn had talked. He had not been able to make out what they were saying, though, although he did hear mention of Melanie Klein's name once or twice and something about avoidance, whatever that was. Then his mother muttered something about Bertie's little brother, Ulysses. This was followed by silence.

10. A Setback for the Bertie Project

In the consulting room of Dr Hugo Fairbairn, the distinguished psychotherapist and author of *Shattered to Pieces: Ego Dissolution in a Three-Year-Old Tyrant*, Irene sat on the opposite side of the desk, staring at Dr Fairbairn uncomprehendingly.

'A chair?' she said, eventually. 'A chair?'

Dr Fairbairn beamed back at her. 'I wanted you to be one of the first to know,' he said. 'I shall, of course, be writing to all my patients, and there may even be something in the press about it . . .' he broke off, smiling in a self-deprecatory way. 'Not that I'm newsworthy, of course, but the fact of the matter is that Aberdeen has decided to create the first chair of child psychotherapy at a Scottish university and, well, they've very kindly chosen me.'

Irene struggled to pull herself together. 'But why can't you do this here in Edinburgh? What's wrong with Edinburgh University or any of the other universities we've got here? Queen Margaret University – they go in for that sort of thing, don't they? Health sciences and so on. Why don't you be a professor there? Or Napier University? What about them? They've got that film school or whatever – they're forward-looking.'

Dr Fairbairn smiled. He appreciated such praise from Irene, but he wondered if she knew much about the mechanisms of getting a university chair. 'It's not that simple,' he explained. 'There's nothing available in Edinburgh at the moment. Maybe some time in the future, but now . . . Well, it's Aberdeen who have taken the step. And I must say I do feel somewhat flattered.'

Irene decided to change tack. 'Flattered by being offered a chair? Come now, Hugo, somebody of your eminence . . . A chair is not even a sideways move; you have far bigger fish to fry . . .'

Dr Fairbairn frowned. Was it possible that Irene did not know what a singular honour it was to be asked to become a chair? What did she think chairs were for? Sitting in?

'There will be a great deal for me to do in Aberdeen,' he said slowly. 'They would specifically like to raise their profile in psychotherapeutic studies. They know about . . .' he paused, as if modesty prevented the mention of his book, but decided to continue, '*Shattered to Pieces*. It has, I believe, been used as a textbook in Aberdeen.'

Irene snorted. 'Aberdeen! What do they know in Aberdeen?'

Dr Fairbairn's expression now began to show signs of irritation. 'A great deal, I would have thought,' he said. 'It is one of our most distinguished pre-Reformation universities. It is a very prestigious institution.'

'Oh, I know all that,' said Irene quickly. 'It's the place I was thinking of.'

'And the city too,' said Dr Fairbairn. 'As a city, Aberdeen has an illustrious history. It's a very significant place.'

'And very cold too,' Irene interjected.

For a few moments nothing was said. Irene reached out and picked up a pencil that was lying on Dr Fairbairn's desk. 'Of course there are other considerations,' she said, almost casually.

Dr Fairbairn watched her. He said nothing.

'I would have thought that you would have rather too many commitments in Edinburgh to leave,' she said.

He waited. Then, in a hesitant voice, 'Such as?'

'Oh, your practice?' said Irene airily. 'Your patients. Wee Fraser . . .' She was not going to mention Bertie . . . yet.

'Wee Fraser is no longer a patient,' said Dr Fairbairn defensively. 'He is a former patient with whom I have not had any dealings for some considerable time.'

That was not true, of course, and he knew it; but by dealings he meant professional dealings, and the punch to the jaw that he had administered – in a moment of madness, and in response to being head-butted by the now adolescent Wee Fraser – on the Burdiehouse bus did not count as a professional dealing.

Irene knew about his burden of guilt. She knew full well – because he had, in a moment of weakness, told her all about it – she knew of how he had gently smacked Wee Fraser when the boy, then three, had bitten him in the course of play therapy involving small farm animals. Dr Fairbairn had suggested to Fraser that the miniature pigs with which the small boy was playing (or, more correctly, enacting his inner psychic dramas) were upside down. Wee Fraser had obstinately insisted that the pigs' legs should point upwards and, when corrected again by Dr Fairbairn, had bitten the psychotherapist. Anybody, even St Nicholas of Myra, the patron saint of children, might be tempted to slap a child in such circumstances – and Irene conceded that; indeed there was an entire school of psychotherapy, Cause-Effect Theory, which held that people needed to know that unpleasant consequences flowed from unpleasant acts. This theory, however, had been widely discredited, and Dr Fairbairn should never have raised a hand to the biting child. That was crystal clear. Psychotherapists did not slap their patients, and the metaphorical rucksack of guilt that Dr Fairbairn carried with him was entirely his own fault.

'Well, Wee Fraser is neither here nor there,' said Irene, adding, 'perhaps.' Irene's knowledge of Dr Fairbairn's guilt gave her some leverage over him; she would not want Wee Fraser to be completely forgotten.

Dr Fairbairn said nothing. He was looking out of the window, in the direction of Aberdeen, which lay several hours to the north. There would be a great deal of psychopathology in Aberdeen, he imagined, but people might be unwilling to talk about it very much. If Californians were at one end of the spectrum of willingness to talk about personal problems, Aberdonians were at the other. It was a form of verbal retention, he thought; one did not want to part with the words unnecessarily. Words needed to be hoarded, at least in the verbal stage. He thought of a possible title for a paper, 'Verbal Retention in a Cold Climate'. That was rather good, even if not as good as *Shattered to Pieces*, a title of which he was inordinately proud. It was quite in the league of *Fear and Loathing in Las Vegas* or *Zen and the Art of Motorcycle Maintenance*.

Irene was watching him look out of the window. She had not imagined that Bertie's psychotherapy would come to a premature end and that she would be deprived of these comfortable conversations with this fascinating man in his wrinkle-resistant blue linen jacket. Suddenly she felt very lonely. Who would there be to talk to now? Her husband?

Her words came out unbidden. 'And what about Bertie? What about the Bertie project? Weren't you going to write him up?'

Before he could reply, she added, 'And then there's Ulysses.'

11. A Spoiled Secret

Matthew and Elspeth had left their wedding party in Moray Place Gardens not in a car, but on foot, which gave their going-away not only an intimate, but also a contemporary conservationist feel. Matthew, of course, was modest, and would have eschewed any ostentation; he ridiculed the appearance in the streets of Edinburgh of stretch limousines, and had no car himself, instead preferring to walk or take a bus wherever possible. For her part, Elspeth had a

33

car, but only a small one, which had a permanently flat battery and was therefore little burden on the environment.

They did not have far to walk. India Street, where Matthew – and now Elspeth – lived was only two blocks away, down Darnaway Street and along a small section of Heriot Row. They were to go there when they left the wedding party, now winding down after the ceilidh band had packed up their instruments and the dancing had stopped. Then, on the following day, they were to leave for their honeymoon, to a destination Matthew had kept steadfastly secret from Elspeth.

When they reached the front door of his flat on the third floor, he fumbled for the key in the pocket of his kilt-jacket.

'You should keep it in your sporran,' said Elspeth, 'along with all the other things that men keep in their sporrans.'

Matthew looked at her in surprise. 'But what do men keep in their sporrans?' he asked. He had no idea, but he knew that his was always empty.

'Oh, this and that,' said Elspeth. She had only the haziest notion of what men did in general, and none, in particular, of what they kept in their sporrans. Indeed, as she looked at Matthew standing before the door of her new home, it occurred to her that she had done an extraordinary thing – or at least something that was extraordinary for her – that she had married a man, and that this person at her side – much as she loved him – was, in so many important ways, quite different from her. He would look upon the world through male eyes; he would think in a masculine fashion; he was something else, the other.

'You could look in my sporran if you like,' Matthew said.

She looked down at the leather pouch and very gently reached down to touch it.

She said nothing; both were somehow moved by what was happening. This sharing of a sporran was an unexpected intimacy; ridiculous, yes, but not ridiculous.

'I've found my key,' said Matthew, after a while. 'Here.'

He slipped the key into the lock and opened the door. Inside, at Matthew's request, and placed there by his best man a few hours before the wedding, a large bunch of flowers dominated the hall table, red and white carnations.

'Thank you for marrying me,' Matthew said suddenly. 'I never thought that anybody . . .'

'Would marry you? But there must have been lots of girls who . . .'

'Who wanted to marry me?' Matthew shook his head.

She said, 'I don't believe that.'

'It's true. Nobody. Until you came along and then we knew, didn't we? We just knew.'

Elspeth smiled. 'I suppose that's right. I thought that I was on the shelf. I thought that I would spend the rest of my days teaching Olive and Bertie and . . . Tofu.' She gave an involuntary shudder: Tofu. 'But you took me away from all that.'

Matthew took her hand, moved by the frankness of what she had said. These words, he felt, were like an act of undressing. 'You took yourself away.'

He dropped her hand and walked across the hall to switch on a light. 'Is your suitcase all ready?'

She nodded.

'And your passport?' Matthew asked.

She laughed. 'Do we need that for Arran?'

'I wouldn't mind going to Arran,' said Matthew. 'We used to go over there when I was a boy. My uncle had a house near Brodick and we would go there in the summer. It was mostly Glasgow people and there was a boy there whom we called Soapy Soutar who threw a stone at me because I was from Edinburgh. He said I deserved it and that if I came back next summer it would be a rock. I remember it so clearly.'

'So it's not Arran. Why don't you tell me?'

'Because I want it to be a surprise.'

She reached out and slipped her hand back into his. 'You're a romantic.'

'If you can't be a romantic about your own wedding,' he said, 'then what can you be romantic about?'

'So no clue at all?'

He thought for a moment. 'A tiny one . . . maybe. All right. A tiny clue.'

She looked at him, searching his expression. She hoped that it would be Italy; that he would say something like 'where there's water in the streets' or 'the Pope lives nearby' or 'hum a few bars of "Return to Sorrento"'.

'It's a big place,' said Matthew at last.

So they were going to America (or Canada, or Russia, or Argentina).

'You've got to tell me more than that. You must.'

Matthew looked at her teasingly. 'I really want it to be a surprise. So that's all I'm going to say.'

'Texas. Texas is big.'

Matthew frowned. If she insisted on guessing, sooner or later she would come up with the right answer and he was not sure that he would be able to remain impassive when at last she did.

'So it's not Texas.'

'No. It's not Texas.'

She moved forward and kissed him gently on the cheek. 'It's Australia, isn't it?'

She knew immediately that she was right, and at the same time she immediately regretted what she had done; now she had spoiled it for him. They had been married for less than twenty-four hours and she had already done something to hurt him. How would that sound at marriage counselling?

Mind you, there had been brides who had done worse than that. She had recently read of the wife of one of the Happy Valley set in Kenya all those years ago. She was said to have had an affair with another man on her honeymoon, on the boat out to Mombasa. That took some doing; took some psychopathology.

She put her arms round Matthew. 'I'm sorry,' she said. 'I didn't mean to spoil it for you. I shouldn't have asked. It's just that . . .'

'What?'

'It's just that you should have asked me where I wanted to go, Matthew. What if I didn't want to go to Australia? What then?'

Matthew turned away. It was spoiled – already.

12. Of Love and Lies

But by the time they were in the taxi on the way to the airport, travelling through the well-set neatness of Corstorphine, past the Royal Zoological Society of Scotland's zoo, they had forgotten about their minor tiff over the secrecy of their destination. And the night had brought self-forgiveness, too, and reassurance that marriage would be an arrangement of delight and enhancement, not one of doubts and quibbles.

Matthew, who, like many young men, imagined that he could never be loved, not for himself, now at last thought: I have found the one person on this earth, the one, who loves me. And Elspeth did love him, and had proved it by drawing a heart in lipstick on his stomach, with their initials intertwined – that most simple, clichéd declaration that the love-struck have always resorted to: carved on tree trunks with penknives; traced in the dust on the back of unwashed cars; furtively scribbled on walls in pencil; and which, for all its simplicity and indeed its naiveté, is usually nothing but believed-in and sincere. It had been a strange thing to do, but Matthew had been touched, and when he looked out of the window the next morning – he was up early, to bring her a cup of tea in bed – India Street itself seemed transformed, as a lover's eyes will do to any landscape; will do to any company. The prosaic, the quotidian are infused with a new gentleness, a new loveliness, by the fact that one senses that there is love in the world and that one has glimpsed it; been given one's share.

The taxi driver, looking in his mirror, said, 'So, where are we off to today?'

'Australia,' said Matthew, and turned to smile at Elspeth.

'Oh yes,' said the driver. 'Honeymoon?'

Neither Matthew nor Elspeth replied immediately. They were passing a large computer shop, painted in garish purple, a building of great aesthetic ghastliness, and their eyes were drawn to that. The taxi driver glanced into the mirror again. 'Yes,' he said. 'People come in along this road – visitors – and they're thinking I've heard Edinburgh's one of the most beautiful cities in Europe and what do they see? That place.'

'Then, when they get to town they see the St James Centre,' said Matthew. 'Who inflicted that on us?'

'Oh well,' said the taxi driver. 'At least they're trying to disguise it now. So it's your honeymoon. We went to Florida, you know. Six years ago. That's when we got married.'

'Florida is very . . .' began Matthew, and then stopped. What could one say about Florida, particularly if one had never been there?

The driver waited for a moment, but when the sentence was not completed merely added, 'Yes, it is. It's a great place for golf. They have these highly manicured golf courses, the Americans. They go round them with nail scissors.'

'Well, at least you never lose the ball,' said Matthew. What did one say about golf when one has never played it? Did one ask somebody if he had ever got a hole in one?

'Did you ever . . .' he began.

'We went on British Airways,' continued the taxi driver, waving to another taxi coming in the opposite direction. 'We were in the back of the plane and the purser happened to ask us right at the beginning how we were doing. He was Scottish, and when we told him we were on our honeymoon, he indicated that we should get up out of the seats and follow him, bringing our hand baggage.'

'Upgraded?' asked Matthew.

'Yes,' said the driver. 'There was hardly a soul in business class and so we settled in there. Champagne. Feet up on those stools they have. It was a great start to our marriage. One Scotsman doing a good turn for another.'

'The so-called Scottish Mafia,' said Matthew.

'It exists,' said the driver. 'Thank goodness.'

They were now approaching the airport turn-off; close by, a plane climbed up into the air, as if from a mustard-yellow field.

'The following year,' the driver continued, 'when we went back to Florida, I thought that I might try the same thing. I told the attendant that we were on our honeymoon and she smiled. I'll see what I can do, she said. And then I looked further down the plane, and there was the same man, the one who had helped us.'

38

Matthew and Elspeth exchanged glances. An act of kindness had been repaid with an act of dishonesty. Suddenly, the whole story soured.

The taxi driver looked in his mirror and laughed. 'I'm only joking. I didn't. But I thought that's what would happen if you did something like that. That would be the result, wouldn't it?'

The tension dissipated. 'People don't think it wrong to lie any more,' said Elspeth. 'They don't see anything wrong.'

'Too right,' said the taxi driver.

They turned off the main road and started to negotiate the series of traffic roundabouts that preceded the terminal.

'I was only joking back there,' said the driver. 'That bit about doing the same thing twice. Only joking.'

'Of course,' said Matthew.

'I count the air strokes on my golf card,' the driver went on. 'Put them all down. Which is more than some do.'

'Naturally,' said Matthew.

They paid and got out of the taxi. 'I'm afraid that I don't believe him,' said Matthew, as they walked through the doors into the terminal.

Elspeth disagreed. 'Why?' she asked. 'Why disbelieve him?'

'I bet that he tried it twice.'

Elspeth shook her head. 'You have to believe people,' she said. 'You have to start off by trusting them.' She felt that, of course, but then she thought for some reason of Tofu, and Olive, and of the facility, the enthusiasm, with which they distorted the truth. Bertie was the only completely truthful child she had known, and perhaps Lakshmi. The rest . . .

They went to the check-in and handed in their suitcases. The woman behind the desk smiled at them. 'Honeymoon?' she asked.

Matthew showed his surprise. 'How did you know?'

'Because you have that look about you, and . . .' she paused for effect, 'you didn't say that you were on honeymoon. So many others do. Looking for special treatment. And then you look at the finger, and what do you see? No ring.'

Matthew glanced at his left hand. So strange; it was so strange, this public declaration of commitment, this announcement of love, made gold in this modest band.

'We're going to have such a marvellous time,' he whispered to Elspeth, who looked up at him and said, 'Yes.'

He was thinking of life; she of Australia.

13. A Poser for Bruce

Bruce Anderson, erstwhile surveyor and persistent narcissist, had not been invited to Matthew and Elspeth's wedding, although he had heard about the engagement and had congratulated Matthew – in an ostentatiously friendly way – when they had bumped into one another in the Cumberland Bar one evening.

Bruce himself was now engaged, to Julia Donald, the daughter of a wealthy hotel owner and businessman, a man who understood Bruce extremely well and had realised that money, and an expensive car, were just the inducements required to get him to marry his daughter. And for her part, Julia understood Bruce too and had realised that what was needed to trap him was not only her father's inducements but wiles of her own; female wiles involving her unexpected pregnancy – 'Such a surprise, Brucie, but there we are!'

For Bruce, the idea of marriage was not completely without appeal, but it was an appeal that depended on its being distant; imminent marriage, followed by fatherhood, was not what he had had in mind. But when Julia's father made clear the terms on which he would welcome Bruce into the family – generous ones by any standards – Bruce's misgivings had been allayed. Perhaps being married to Julia would not be so bad, he thought. He could switch off in the face of constant wittering. Most men did that, he thought, with their wives. And he would never have to worry again about buying a flat – Julia owned a perfectly good flat in Howe Street, worth, Bruce had calculated, at least six hundred thousand pounds at current market prices; and she had no mortgage. In fact, Bruce was not sure if she even knew what a mortgage was; whereas Bruce, like most people, knew very well what a mortgage was and understood the difference between those who had a large mortgage and those who had no mortgage at all. They walked differently, he thought.

He would also never have to worry about a job now that Julia's father had made him a director of his property company and given him sole charge of the wine bar he owned in George Street. If Julia came with all that, then the least he could do, he decided, was to be civil to her.

'We're going to have to decide about names, Brucie,' she said at the breakfast table that morning.

Bruce looked up from his bowl of muesli. Since he had taken to reading a magazine called *Men's Health*, he had become quite health-conscious and broke a series of nuts and antioxidants into his plate each morning. A body like mine, he thought, one takes care of it. And he could look at the bare-torsoed men pictured in *Men's Health* without feeling inadequate; he could look them in the pectorals.

'Names?'

'For . . . for you know who,' said Julia, looking down at her stomach.

'Oh.' Bruce stared down at the mixture of nuts and powdered flax seed on his plate.

'I thought that for a boy we might go for Jamie,' said Julia. 'It's such a nice name. Strong. Or Glen.'

'Jamie's all right,' said Bruce. 'But not Glen. I knew a Glen at Morrison's, and he was a real waste of space. Collected stamps.'

'Well, Gavin. There's Gavin Hastings.'

'It could be a girl,' said Bruce.

Julia shook her head. 'I've got a feeling it's a boy,' she said. 'Just like you, Brucie.'

Bruce said nothing. Thoughts of Julia's baby – and that is how he regarded it – had not been to the forefront of his mind. It was her baby, her idea, he told himself, and even if he had had a part in it, it was not something that he had intended or embraced. She wanted this baby – that was obvious – and so let her do the thinking about it.

The problem with babies, in Bruce's view, was that they spoiled everything. What was the point of living in this nice flat in Howe Street, with the money to do exactly what you wanted to do – to travel, to go out to all the best restaurants, to be seen – if you had a baby to think about? Babies tied you down; they demanded to be fed; they yelled their heads off; they smelled.

He finished his breakfast in silence. There was no further discussion about babies, and Julia was absorbed in a magazine that had dropped through the letter-box with the morning post; one of her vacuous fashion magazines, full of glossy pictures of models and bottles of perfume; pictures which Bruce took a guilty pleasure in looking at while affecting to despise them.

'This stuff,' he said, pointing at the box of flax seed, 'contains all the omega oils you need.'

'That's nice,' said Julia.

'I'm thinking of joining that gym up at the Sheraton Hotel,' Bruce went on. 'You know the one, with all those pools. That one.'

'I'll come too,' said Julia. 'I need to get in shape.'

Bruce said nothing. He was not sure if he wanted Julia tagging after him at the gym; and what would happen when her baby arrived? The gym was no place for a baby.

'I was reading their magazine,' Bruce continued. 'There's a trainer up there who takes groups of people to Thailand and detoxes them. They come back really toned up.'

'Maybe we should do that,' said Julia. 'Daddy always wanted to take me to Thailand. We could go with him. We could all get detoxed.'

Bruce ladled a spoon of muesli into his mouth and munched on it. He glanced across the table at Julia. There was something silly about her face, he decided. There was a quality of vacuousness; a quality that displayed no long-lasting emotion or thought, just flickering states. Talking to her, he thought, was like turning the dial on a radio; one heard a snatch from a station and then, in a second, it was gone. He sighed. I've done it. I've got myself hitched up with a really dim girl.

And yet, and yet . . . there was the Porsche, and the flat, and the money. Money. That was all it came down to, ultimately. Money. And we shouldn't deceive ourselves, Bruce thought; every single one of us makes compromises for money.

He stole a glance at himself in the glass panel of the microwave. I'm still to die for, he thought; that profile, that hair, those pecs. Everything. But I won't have that forever, in spite of the powdered flax seed, and then what sort of deal will I be able to negotiate for myself? Hold on to it, Brucie, he said to himself. And as he did so, he reached out to touch Julia's hand and he smiled at her. You may be dim, he thought, but I'm not.

14. From Arbroath with Love

If Bruce was largely made up of braggadocio and narcissism, the character of Big Lou, proprietrix of the Morning After Coffee Bar in Dundas Street, was composed of very different stuff. Big Lou had been brought up in Arbroath, a town noted for those typically Scottish virtues of caution, hard work and modesty. She had the additional advantage of having been raised on a farm – not a large or a prosperous one, but one that consisted of a few hundred tenanted acres, an appendage to an estate which had never been very well managed and which, as a result, had had little money available for investment in the fabric of the place. The fences, some of which were made of rusted barbed wire dating back to the First World War, were patched up as best Big Lou's father, Muckle Geordie, could manage; and the byres, rickety and oddly-angled, looked as if a good puff of wind off the North Sea, or even a flaff from the hinterland of Angus, would be all that was required to bring them tumbling down.

In a more justly ordered world, Big Lou's native intelligence would have been nurtured and would have flowered; as it was, instead of bettering herself she was obliged to spend years looking after an elderly uncle. Then, when her chance of freedom came, she went north rather than south; and north, in the shape of Aberdeen, brought only more drudgery, with a menial job in the Granite Nursing Home. When she eventually escaped from that, it was to Edinburgh, and to freedom at last, financed by the legacy left her by an inmate of the Granite. Now she had her own flat in Canonmills and her own coffee bar, the latter occupying the basement premises previously used as a bookshop. This had been frequented, for a time, by the late Christopher Murray Grieve, better known as the poet Hugh MacDiarmid, who had once fallen down the dangerous steps that led down to the basement. For Edinburgh was like that – every set of steps, every close, every corner had its memories, spoke with the voices of those who had been there once, a long time ago, but who were in a way still there.

As well as acquiring the shop, Big Lou took possession of all the stock that went with it, and over the years she had worked her way through many of the books that she had bought. Topography and philosophy had kept her busy for two years, and history for one. Now it was literary theory and psychology, leavened with fiction (Scott and Stevenson) and poetry (she had just read the complete oeuvre of Sydney Goodsir Smith and Norman MacCaig).

The judgement and control that Big Lou evinced in her reading was not mirrored in her romantic life. Like many good women, she attracted men whose weaknesses were the converse of her strengths. She had wasted years in her relationship with a chef who could not resist the attractions of much younger women. He had broken her heart again and again until enlightenment came and she saw him for what he was; and that was best expressed by those simple words: no good. His place had been taken by Robbie, a plasterer who specialised in the restoration of ceilings, and it was Robbie whom she was still seeing, in spite of Matthew's conviction – eventually articulated in an unguarded moment – that Robbie was half-mad.

'He's obsessed, Lou,' Matthew had said. 'I'm sorry to have to say it, but he really is. Who would be a Jacobite these days? Do you think any rational person would? And look at the people he runs around with – that bampot, Michael what's-his-name, and that callow youth who hangs on his every word. And that woman with the shouty voice, the one who says she can trace her ancestry back to Julius Caesar or whatever. These people are bonkers, Lou.'

'Robbie's interested in history, Matthew,' Lou had replied. 'The Stuarts are important for some people. There are plenty of people who find them interesting.'

'Yes,' conceded Matthew. 'But there's a difference between finding something interesting and believing in it. He actually believes in the Stuarts. How can he do that? Prince Charlie was an absolute disaster from every point of view. And as for his ancestors . . .'

Big Lou had changed the subject. At one level she knew that Matthew was right; Robbie was odd, but he was kind to her and he did not run off with other women. That, she felt, was all she was entitled to ask, and she was realistic too: there were not enough men to go round, not in Arbroath and certainly not in Edinburgh, and she knew that she was in no position to be picky.

Now, opening up the coffee bar for the morning, she polished the stainless steel bar before the first customers arrived. These tended to be office workers, often employees at the Royal Bank of Scotland offices down the road. They would not linger long, but sit engrossed in the newspapers before glancing at their watches and rushing out again. Then there would be a quiet spell before

45

her mid-morning regulars arrived, Matthew and Angus Lordie among them. Of course with Matthew away on honeymoon, she was not expecting him, which meant that Angus Lordie would sit closer to the bar and address all his comments to her.

She could tell his mood immediately he came in, and this would tell her how his work was going. A difficult painting, or one that was not turning out as expected, would give Angus a morose expression and make him stir his coffee rather more aggressively than necessary. His expression today, though, was thoughtful rather than morose, which suggested to Lou that he had something on his mind other than an uncooperative canvas.

'I've been thinking about your situation, Lou,' Angus began.

'My situation? Here?'

'Not so much just here,' said Angus, waving a hand around to encompass the general area. 'Everywhere. Your whole life.'

'There's nothing wrong with my life,' said Big Lou.

'But there is, Lou,' said Angus. 'You need a companion. That chap of yours, Robbie, is all very well, but . . .' He looked at her cautiously, sensing that he was on dangerous ground. 'What I thought, actually, is that you need a dog. A puppy. You need one, Lou. Maybe even a couple of puppies.'

'I'd love one,' said Lou. 'Even two. I really would.'

Angus beamed. 'Well, isn't that an amazing coincidence! As it happens . . .'

'But I can't,' interjected Lou. 'I'm mildly allergic to dogs, Angus. Even your bringing Cyril in here makes me slightly wheezy. So I couldn't have one in the flat. It's impossible.'

15. When even Puppy Love has its Limits

Angus, dispirited by the realisation that Big Lou could not reasonably be expected to accept one or more of his boisterous litter of puppies, looked down into his coffee cup. And a coffee cup, as we all know, is not something that it pays to look into if one is searching for meaning beyond meaning; coffee, in all its forms, looks murky, and gives little comfort to one who hopes to see something in it. Unlike tea, which allows one to glimpse something of what lies beneath the surface, usually more tea.

Although they had been in the flat for only a day and a half, the puppies were proving to be a waking nightmare for Angus. A flat without a garden is not the ideal place in which to raise a small dog, let alone six. To begin with, there was the problem of hygiene. A dog may be trained to restrain itself until taken outside, a fact which one would not have to be Ivan Petrovich Pavlov to discover, but this considerate view of the matter is not one which a puppy adopts until it has been conditioned to do so, something which involves a great deal of angst for the dog's owner. Angus realised that he simply could not face however many weeks, or indeed months, would be required before house-training might be accomplished. In Cyril's case, of course, the process had been remarkably quick, such was the dog's unusual intelligence and, indeed, empathy. Cyril understood the issue immediately when it had been pointed out to him by Angus; he had simply looked at his master and nodded, to indicate that he knew that in future he would wait until he was taken outside. Angus had been astonished at the rapidity of Cyril's understanding, and had mentioned this to one of his Scottish Arts Club friends, who happened to be a member of staff of the Royal (Dick) School of Veterinary Medicine. 'Impossible,' his friend had said, cutting off further discussion. 'Animals can't grasp these things. You have to condition the dog to associate conduct with bad consequences – pain or your displeasure, which amounts to the same thing to the besotted canine. That's all. They don't understand these things, you know. Your dog will be no different.'

But it had been true; it had happened, and Angus felt the same sense of frustration that must be felt by those who have witnessed a miracle and find that the person whom they wish to tell about it is a convinced Humean and believes that no human account of the miraculous can be true. It was no good his insisting that Cyril had understood immediately; he would simply not be believed. And of course the most powerful refutation of the likelihood of Cyril's having required no house-training now lay before his eyes, in the conduct of these six puppies.

And there was more. Not only was there the house-training issue; there were other forms of damage that the puppies were wreaking. One had chewed a roll of canvas that Angus had stacked at the side of his studio; another had worried away at a small Persian rug in his hallway, creating an untidy edge along one side and a small hole in the middle. And if this was not enough, another had succeeded in upsetting the small table on which Angus had carefully placed the items for his current still life, shattering the Glasgow jug that formed the centrepiece of this arrangement. The jug lay in fragments; the painting could not be completed now as Angus could not re-create the moment of juxtaposition that lies at the heart of a good still life; the painting, half-finished, was useless.

Big Lou looked at Angus with something that was close to pity. Of course he would have imagined that it would be a simple matter to palm off a puppy on her. Angus had no inkling that she could read his motives with no difficulty at all, and his motives here were nothing to do with his professed belief that she would be better off with a dog. But in spite of the self-serving nature of his remarks, she found herself feeling sorry for him now – seven dogs in one flat, and a man – what bedlam that must be!

As she looked at Angus, she reflected on what it must be like to be him. It required some imagination, of course; it was such a different life, a life of strange odours and textures: paint, turps; hours spent in the Cumberland Bar with all his fusty friends; being pushed about by that woman, Domenica Macdonald; those long conversations with Cyril; a diet that consisted, as far as she could make out, of kippers and oatcakes. It could not be much fun.

She imagined for a moment the advertisement that Angus might place in the *Scotsman* lonely hearts column: painter, with seven dogs, seeks understanding woman. That would attract no replies, surely, or deserved not to; the trouble was that desert did not come into it: there were just not enough men. Every man, even the most unpromising one, who placed an advertisement in that column received, on average, eighty-two replies, while even the most meritorious women who advertised there was lucky to get a single reply, and this single reply, at that, would often be from a man who would have replied to several other advertisements at the same time. Big Lou had once overheard, while walking down Dundas Street, two well-dressed women talking about the difficulty of balancing the seats at a dinner party. 'We know no single men for our single girlfriends,' one said, 'not one. They simply don't exist.'

'The world has changed,' said the other.

'No. It's always been thus. We women wait for men who never turn up.'

And Big Lou thought: is this the lot of women? Is this what we

really think? That we either reflect on our good fortune in having found a man, or bemoan his non-appearance? Surely not. Was it for this that the clay grew tall? The more she thought about this, the more she thought: the answer is probably yes. In which case, I shouldn't even think about giving up Robbie; for all his flaws, for all his Jacobite dreaming, I must keep him. And that means marriage. I can change him. I really can. Marriage changes men – always.

16. Paradise Found

Matthew certainly felt changed by marriage. Even now, after only three days of being married to Elspeth Harmony, and sitting in the Singapore Airlines aircraft as it curved an arc over the East Timor Sea, he felt a very different person from the person he had been before. I'm a married man, he whispered to himself; a whisper unheard over the background noise of the great engines, that half-hushed hissing that makes the white noise of a jet cabin. He glanced at Elspeth in the seat beside him, asleep under the thin airline lap-rug, a shaft of high altitude sunlight falling across her forearm, making the skin warm and gold. Such smooth skin, thought Matthew; like that of a nectarine. *Ma petite nectarine*, he thought; something that the French might say, with their taste for culinary endearments.

He had been in no doubt that he loved her. He had believed that from their first meeting, even though he knew that it was absurd that one might love another whom one did not really know. Or was it? Could one have a generalised love for humanity, something between *agape* and passionate love, a state awaiting transformation into full-blown love when the opportunity arose? This meant, of course, that at least part of the love one felt for one's beloved was of another origin, came from somewhere else, and merely settled opportunistically on the chosen person; but that, he thought, was inevitable.

Their time together, as husband and wife, an expression so much richer, so much dearer, than the anodyne, soulless 'partners', had convinced Matthew that in proposing to Elspeth he had done exactly the right thing. They were happy, entranced with the leisurely discovery of each other, fulfilled in a way that Matthew would never have thought possible. Eros himself had sent a vision in the hotel room in Singapore in which they had spent the night halfway through their long journey to Perth; he had appeared to them in Raffles Hotel, no less, under the swirling fan of their room overlooking the courtyard. And Matthew had lain awake and thought how pale an imitation of erotic delight was anything that he had experienced before. This was love with commitment, and that, he realised, made a profound and unmistakable difference. How shallow, by comparison, was mere physical dalliance; how empty!

The journey from Singapore to Perth took barely five hours. From the window of the plane, Matthew watched the coast of Western Australia reveal itself below; a long line of brown on the edge of the steely blue of the sea. A thin lacing of white on the edge of the brown marked the littoral divide, and then, behind that, a nothingness of both land and sea. From up there the world looked neatly laid-out, like a map, with well-behaved expanses of brown, blue, green, all in their place. Their height made the landscape look easy, though he knew it was tough, waterless, unforgiving of anyone who found himself cast upon it; a place where unfortunate sailors had died on the shores and cliffs or had wandered off into the interior and never been seen again. Australia swallowed people; sucked them into its great emptiness.

Elspeth woke up just before they dropped down towards Perth itself.

'Down there,' said Matthew, and pointed to the forests of eucalyptus coming into sight beneath them.

She looked. The tops of the trees were swaying gently in a breeze; they were like a silver-grey sea in motion. A road cut through, die-straight; the top of a white truck could be seen moving slowly along it. And then the outer works of the airport, the perimeter fence, here as much, surely, to keep this great extending wilderness and its creatures out as to exclude human malevolence. Matthew took Elspeth's hand. There was something significant about this landing, he felt; and yet we are here for only two weeks. Imagine arriving here knowing, as so many new arrivals had done before them, that one was going to stay, that this was where one would grow old and die.

They took a taxi to their hotel, a small private hotel in Cottesloe. It was morning, and they passed by people going to work, sitting in their cars listening to the morning news from the Australian Broadcasting Corporation, looking in their mirrors, scratching their heads, looking up at the sky to see what the weather had in mind. It was all so ordinary, but so different.

For the rest of that day they did very little, other than to take a walk along the beach, which was only two blocks away from their hotel. This beach stretched for miles, a broad sweep of sand, its surface broken here and there by outcrops of rock. Along the beach, atop the sand dunes that kept suburban Perth from toppling into the Indian Ocean, a long coastal path was the haunt of walkers, runners, exuberant dogs, the sea breeze in the hair and lungs of all.

And there was sun; everywhere there was that sun that painted everything with slabs of light, impasto thick.

'I had no idea,' said Elspeth.

He looked at her. 'No idea of what?'

'Of all this,' she said. 'It's like discovering a parallel universe.'

He pondered her words. He knew what she meant, he suspected, because he had been thinking much the same thing himself, but had not found the words to express it. Perth was a world away from Edinburgh, but was not, because in many ways it was so familiar, so redolent of some distant idea of what Britain once had been, but was no longer. The signs of this were sometimes subtle, like the echoes of a familiar tune that one heard a long time ago; at other times they were obvious and arresting. On the drive to the hotel, from the back of the taxi, they had passed a school, and he had seen ranks of boys outside what looked like a school hall beginning to march into assembly. The boys wore khaki shirts and shorts and swung their arms like soldiers on parade; the morning sun shone upon them, benignly. The sign outside the school proclaimed its name: Scotch College.

'It's very nice,' said Matthew. He felt a momentary guilt, embarrassment perhaps, that he should think such an old-fashioned thought, but it passed. There was nothing wrong, he reminded himself, in appreciating a bourgeois paradise when every other sort of paradise on offer had proved to be exactly the opposite of what paradise should be.

Why do people like Australia so much? he asked himself. And

an unexpected answer came to him: it's because everything that has been destroyed elsewhere, in an orgy of self-hatred, still survives here.

17. A Dream of Love

The proprietrix of Matthew and Elspeth's hotel in Perth, a woman in her late fifties who wore a faded pink housecoat, had recommended a restaurant overlooking Cottesloe Beach and had helpfully made a reservation for them.

'You have to reserve if you want a table in the front,' she said. 'If you get there for sunset you can have a drink while the sun goes down over the sea. That's a sight for the eyes, I can tell you.

'I went there for dinner,' she continued, 'a couple of weeks ago, with my sister. Her husband was an agricultural machinery representative in the wheat belt, you know, and then he died. Men do, don't they? They die.'

Elspeth laughed nervously, uncertain whether or not she should do so, but unable to stop herself. Men did die; this woman was right, and in taking on a husband you increased your chances of becoming a widow from nothing to . . . well, to whatever the chances were. It was a morbid thought, and not one that you should think on your honeymoon, although it was inevitable, she felt, that happiness should prompt thoughts of how that happiness might end. It was the same with anything that you might have or might acquire in life: physical possessions might give pleasure, but ownership led to the anxiety – did it not – that somebody would take away from you that which you had. Or you might lose your possessions in some other way. Or your looks; they would go too, as certainly as the sun rose; everything was built on sand, was sand.

She reached for Matthew's hand and squeezed it. She wondered if such thoughts crossed his mind. Men, of course, were said to be less emotional, more matter-of-fact than women. Did that mean that they did not worry in the way in which women worried? Ever since Matthew had proposed to her and she had accepted, she had worried that he would change his mind. He had shown no signs of doing this, and had seemed every bit as keen as she was to get married, but she had still thought about this, several times a day, and in her dreams too. She had awoken from nightmares in which Matthew had suddenly said things like 'What engagement?' or, in one particularly distressing dream, had turned out to be married already, to three women.

Elspeth could not imagine Matthew, nor any man perhaps, dreaming such things.

'What do you dream about?' she had asked him several weeks before the wedding.

He had thought for a moment before he answered. 'You, of course.'

'No, I'm serious. Do you have . . . strange dreams?'

This question had caused a shadow to pass over his face. He did have strange dreams, and some of them he could not relate to Elspeth because she would be shocked. Most people had shocking dreams, he thought; or rather, most men did. They did things that they would never normally do, or even imagine doing, and they never confessed to anybody about such matters; quite rightly, thought Matthew.

'I have strange dreams from time to time,' he said guardedly.

'Such as?'

He was nonchalant. 'Oh, I forget. You know how it is with dreams. You don't remember them for very long after you've had them. It's something to do with how we don't commit them to memory because we know that they're unimportant.'

'But they are important!' she protested. 'They tell us so much about what we really are. About what we really want to do.'

Matthew was privately appalled, but his expression showed it. 'Do they?' he asked. 'Do you really think so?'

Elspeth was studying him closely. She had seen him frown when she had suggested that dreams revealed suppressed wishes, and that worried her. He must be remembering something that he had

54

dreamed, some dark thing, and it was worrying him. It had not occurred to her that she might be marrying a man who had a dark thing in his life. 'But you shouldn't worry,' she said. 'All of us want to do things that we would never really do, not in a month of Sundays. I don't think it matters really, because we know that we'll never do it.'

She was trying to make him feel better, and she succeeded. 'Yes,' said Matthew. 'I agree. The important thing is what you're like when you're awake rather than what you're like when you're asleep.'

He was not sure about this, although he expressed the thought with some confidence and authority. And it was a comforting thought, an aphorism of which one might remind oneself after a dream in which one is revealed in perhaps not the best of lights.

'And I really have dreamed of you,' he said. 'I meant that when I said it.'

It was true. He had dreamed of Elspeth a few nights earlier. They had been walking along Princes Street together, arm in arm, on the unspoiled side, and he had looked down into the gardens, to the Ross Pavilion, where there were flags all around the open auditorium and a Scottish country dance band was striking up. He had felt so safe, so secure, and had looked up at the Castle on its rock and felt even more so.

It had been a dream of contentment, and would no doubt have been forgotten on waking up, had it not suddenly changed. He had looked down below again and the band had gone, danced away, and the flags hung limp and dispirited, no Saltires, just alien, puzzling symbols – put there without a referendum, without asking the people! And he had turned to Elspeth for reassurance, but she was no longer there. The woman on his arm was his mother.

He could not tell Elspeth this, of course, and he blushed even at the memory. Somebody had once remarked to him that men married their mothers, and girls married their fathers; or at least chose those who came as close as possible to these ideals. He did not think that true, though; it was just another piece of misleading folk psychology.

'Let's change the subject,' said Matthew. 'Let's not talk about dreams. Tell me, Elspeth, what was your father like?'

She thought for only the briefest moment before she answered. 'You,' she said.

18. The Blind Biker of Comrie

Matthew thought: perhaps it's true, perhaps I really am like Elspeth's father, and she, in turn, is like my mother. Perhaps we really have fulfilled the old saw that one marries one's parents. And what had Freud said? That at the conjunction of two there are four other people present? That was an observation invested with great unsettling power: that we are not ourselves, our own creation, reduces us rather more than we might wish to be reduced. And yet there was the social self, was there not, which was undoubtedly the creation of others, of tides of history, of great sweeps of human experience over which we had exercised no control; and ultimately the creature, too, of tiny strands of DNA bequeathed, wrapped, handed over to us as a present at birth – a little parcel bomb to carry with us on our journey.

What did he know about Elspeth's father, Jim Harmony, whom he had never met, and who existed for him merely as a photograph on Elspeth's table?

'My father, Jim,' she had said as they packed up the contents of her flat in preparation for her move to India Street.

He took the small, silver-framed portrait and examined it. The frame was worn, with the silver-plating rubbed away across the top and sides, but the photograph inside seemed fresh enough.

'That was taken in Bridge of Allan,' said Elspeth. 'Years ago. They lived there then, and I did too, of course, until I was eighteen.'

'Bridge of Allan,' muttered Matthew. It was the right place for her to come from; a reassuring small town of the sort that one found scattered throughout Scotland.

'He worked for an insurance company,' said Elspeth. 'He was a loss adjuster, and he used to cover Stirling, Linlithgow, Falkirk – places round there.'

'Loss adjusters have to be tough,' said Matthew. He looked at the picture. Jim Harmony's face was not a tough one. If one had to pick an adjective to describe it, then the best choice, he thought, would be kind.

Elspeth shook her head. 'He wasn't tough,' she said. 'He was the kindest man I ever met. A most trusting man too. I think that he approved just about every claim.'

'I'm sure that's right,' said Matthew, looking down at the picture again. 'He has that sort of face.'

'He had to retire early because he began to have problems with his eyes,' said Elspeth. 'So they went up to live in Comrie when I came to Edinburgh to do my teacher training. They sold the house in Bridge of Allan and bought a small house in Comrie. They were very happy there.

'My father had always been a keen amateur mechanic,' Elspeth went on. 'My grandfather had been a diesel mechanic with MacBraynes, the ferry people. And he passed on some of that to my father, who was always tinkering with old cars he bought. He did them up and then sold them, not at much of a profit, but enough to fund the next one.

'His favourite car was a Citroën. You know the sort of old Citroën, with a wide running board, that Inspector Maigret used to drive? That sort. The Citroën Traction. Well he had one of those, which he had made from two old Citroëns that had had an accident. He grafted the front of one onto the back of the other – so it was really two cars. It didn't drive quite straight as a result; it drove almost sideways.'

Matthew listened, fascinated. He had known none of this, and he found the story curiously poignant: Jim Harmony, the kind loss adjuster, going to live in Comrie with his wife and his crab-like double Citroën . . .

'He was a biker too,' Elspeth continued. 'He always had motorbikes. He had an old BSA 250 and a bike called an Aerial, or that's

57

what I thought it was called. It was painted grey and had a small badge featuring a pair of wings. I remember that badge from when I was a little girl.

'When he lived in Comrie he stopped driving the Citroën so much and he took to using his bike. He used to go to rallies for veteran bikers. I went to one or two of those with him, and I remember the talks that they had in the evening. One which I particularly remember was: what sort of bike were you riding when President Kennedy was shot? That sort of thing. They saw the whole world through their bikes, you see.'

She paused, gently took the photograph from Matthew, and slipped it into a packing case. 'It was very hard for him, losing his sight. I thought that this would stop him from riding his bike, especially when it got so bad that he had to get a guide dog. But you know what he did? He trained the guide dog to run alongside the motorbike. That's how he did it. That's how he became the only blind biker in Scotland.'

Matthew listened in astonishment. 'Do you mean . . .'

'Yes. The dog was called Rory and he used to run alongside the bike, with my father holding his lead in one hand and the other hand on the handlebars of the motorbike. Of course he couldn't go all that fast, as Rory used to get tired after a while, but he once went all the way from Comrie to Crieff and back again.'

'But surely it was illegal?' Matthew stuttered. 'Surely you can't use a guide dog to lead a motorbike . . .'

Elspeth shrugged. 'I didn't think it was very wise. My mother and I tried to persuade him to give it up, but he was very independent in his outlook and he loved biking. He really loved it.'

Matthew did not know what to say. 'Well . . .'

'And it worked all right for about a year,' said Elspeth. 'Then . . .'

She left the sentence unfinished. 'He was such a good man,' she said, her voice faltering.

Matthew reached out and took her hand. 'I'm sure he was,' he said. 'I would have liked your father very much. I'm sure I would.' Even if I would not have ridden pillion with him – the unexpressed rider: no rider. He thought he knew how she felt. He thought he knew how it was to lose a father, although he had not lost his, not entirely. And what, he might have asked himself, but did not, what is it like when a whole society, a whole culture, loses father?

19. Heavenly Thoughts

For Bertie, the departure of Elspeth Harmony from the Steiner School was the first real loss of his life, just as it was for many other members of the class. The child yearns for things to remain the same. He knows that this cannot be; that his little world contains within itself the seeds of its transformation into something else; but awareness of what is coming rarely softens the blow.

Of course there was a great deal in Bertie's life that he would have liked to change and, had he made a list of these things, his mother would have headed it. Not that he did not love his mother; he loved her deeply, as every small boy must do, but he wished that she could somehow be a different person. That is not to say that he wished that he had, for instance, Tofu's mother, or Olive's mother, as his own mother; he wanted to keep Irene in her external particulars, but nevertheless completely changed in attitudes, voice and register. He wished, then, that Irene would become a completely different person. And once that happened, this new person, this new mother, would not see the need for psychotherapy, would not converse in Italian, would not insist on yoga, and would rarely, if ever, mention the name of Melanie Klein.

Bertie wondered how this transformation might be achieved. He was a little boy of wide reading, and had come across several examples of complete change. There was St Augustine, for instance, who had, Bertie understood, been a bad man and had become a good one. But that entailed religion, and Irene had never shown any signs of religious belief; in fact quite the opposite. When Bertie had innocently asked her where she thought heaven was, Irene had replied that it was here and now, and that we could create it if only

we brought into existence the right social and political arrangements, as advocated, she indicated, by the leading articles in the
Guardian.

'Heaven, Bertie,' she explained, 'is not a place like . . . like
Edinburgh or even Glasgow. *Non c'è nessun paradiso esterno*. Heaven
is potentially within each of us. Don't look for heaven anywhere
else, Bertissimo.'

Bertie had been puzzled by this answer to what he had thought
was a simple question. He rather liked the idea of heaven being a
physical place that one was let into if one deserved it. He thought
that Miss Harmony would certainly get there, and Matthew, her
new husband, as God would surely not want Miss Harmony to be
lonely. And that nice lady who ran the coffee bar, Big Lou; she
would go there, and maybe Mr Lordie too, if you were allowed to
take dogs. Perhaps you could if the dog had been good, too, which
would mean that Cyril would definitely get in. Olive, of course,
would have to be turned away. It would be awful, he thought, to
get to heaven and find her there, bossing everybody about –
including God – for the rest of time.

No, his mother's transformation would never be achieved by any
religious experience; for her there would be no blinding light on
the road to Damascus, no sudden espousal of the Eightfold Way,
nothing of that sort. There were other ways, of course, of changing,
and Bertie had heard about these too. People sometimes changed,
he had read, if they had some sort of shocking experience – if they
saw something frightening, if they were kidnapped, if their hearts
stopped, or something of that sort. Such people realised that they
had wasted their time, or been wrong about things, and resolved
that in future they would lead a better life. Not that it always
happened that way: Tofu was a case in point. He had told Bertie
that he had once received a strong electric shock when he had put
a knife into an electric toaster, and that his hair had stood up straight
for half an hour after the experience. But there had been no other
changes, unfortunately, and he had remained very much the same.

Irene, Bertie reluctantly concluded, led far too sheltered a life
to encounter a transforming traumatic event. The daily round of

taking Bertie to school on the 23 bus, of going to psychotherapy, of spending hours in the Floatarium – all of these were unlikely to lead to the sort of experience that would make his mother a different person. And so he was stuck with her as she was, and had decided that the only thing to do was to endure the twelve years that lay between him and his eighteenth birthday.

When eventually he left home, on the morning of that birthday, he would be free and it would not matter any more what his mother was like. He would write to her, of course, every six months or so, but he would not have to see her, except when he wanted to. And there was no law, Bertie reminded himself, which stipulated that you had to invite your mother to your flat once you had moved out of the family home; Bertie, in fact, was not planning to give her his address once he had moved out.

But twelve years seemed an impossibly long time for a boy of six; indeed it was twice the length of his life so far, an unimaginable desert of time. In the meantime, he realised that he would have to negotiate such excitement for himself as he could, finding a place for it in the interstices of the psychotherapy and yoga and Italian lessons that his mother arranged for him.

Tofu, for all his manifold faults, was a potential source of diversion for Bertie. His friend's life was subject to constraints of its own – his father, the author of several books on the energy fields of nuts, followed a strictly vegan diet and insisted that his son do the same. This made Tofu extremely hungry, and explained his penchant for stealing other children's sandwiches. But apart from that, Tofu was left to his own devices, and boasted of having gone through to Glasgow on the train several times with neither an accompanying adult nor a ticket. He had also attended a football match when he was meant to be at a Saturday morning art club favoured by his father and had spent the art class money on a pepperoni pizza. This was a heady example to Bertie of just what freedom might mean, as was his suggestion to Bertie that together they should join a cub scout pack which had recently been established in the Episcopal Church Hall at the head of Colinton Road.

'They need people like us,' Tofu said.

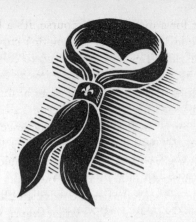

20. Be Prepared for a Little White Lie

'I can't, Tofu,' said Bertie. 'I can't join the cubs.'

Tofu was dismissive of Bertie's protestation. 'You can't? Why? Is it because you think you'll fail the medical examination? There isn't one. That's the army you're thinking of. The cubs will take anyone – even somebody like you.'

'It's not that,' Bertie said miserably. 'It's just that . . .'

'Well,' Tofu pressed. 'What is it? Are you scared or something? You can be a real wimp, you know, Bertie.'

Bertie glowered at Tofu. It was typical of the other boy that he should jump to conclusions – and, as was always the case with Tofu, he was wrong. 'No, it's my mother,' he said. 'She found me reading a book about Mr Baden-Powell and she said that I could never join the cubs or scouts. She doesn't like them.'

Tofu frowned. 'What a cow your mother is, Bertie,' he said sympathetically. 'But I suppose it's not your fault.'

Bertie said nothing. He did not like Tofu referring to his mother in those terms, but it was difficult to contradict him. The barricades in this life, his father had once observed, are often in the wrong place. Bertie had not been sure what this meant, but he felt that it might have some bearing on his dilemma in the face of anti-Irene comments from people such as Tofu.

Tofu thought for a moment. 'Of course, it's a bit awkward that your mother thinks like that, but it shouldn't stop you.'

Bertie was puzzled. 'But how could I go to cubs if she won't let me?' he asked. 'How could I? Don't they wear a uniform?'

He was not sure whether cubs still wore a uniform or not, but he very much hoped that they did. Bertie had always liked the thought of wearing a uniform, particularly since his mother had such strong views on them.

'Yes, there is a uniform,' said Tofu. 'But I could get hold of one for you. Your mother wouldn't have to buy it.'

'But she'd see it,' said Bertie. 'I'd have to change into it and then she'd see it. She'd say: "What's that you're wearing . . . ?"'

Tofu was shaking his head in disagreement. 'She needn't see it,' he said patiently, as if explaining a rudimentary matter to somebody who was rather slow. 'There's a place nearby, a place where they sell coffee. It's called Starbucks. We can go in there and change into our uniforms in the toilet. See?'

Bertie was still not convinced. He was a truthful boy, and he would not lie to his mother; he would not mislead her as to where he was going and it was inconceivable that he could just slip out of the house, as Tofu appeared able to do. He looked at Tofu with admiration and a certain amount of envy – what it must be like to have such freedom.

'I'm sorry, Tofu,' he said. 'I don't like telling fibs.'

'But I do,' said Tofu. 'I'll tell her that we're going to a special club. I'll get her to say yes.'

Bertie felt quite torn. One part of him wanted no part of Tofu's machinations; another was desperate to join the cubs, indeed was desperate to have any sort of life of his own. 'But what will you say?' he asked. 'What sort of club?'

Tofu shrugged his shoulders. He saw no particular challenge in this deception; the name of the club was a minor detail. 'I'll tell her that it's . . .' he paused. Bertie was listening carefully. 'I'll tell your mummy that it's the Young Liberal Democrats Club.'

Bertie's eyes opened wide. The Young Liberal Democrats sounded almost as good as the Junior Melanie Klein Society, if such a thing existed. 'She'll like that,' he said. 'It's the sort of thing . . .'

'Of course it is,' said Tofu nonchalantly. 'Now all you have to do is to invite me to play at your house some afternoon and then I'll talk to her. How about tomorrow?'

Bertie swallowed. There was a very good reason why tomorrow would not be suitable, but all his other afternoons were taken up with Italian lessons and saxophone practice and it was difficult to see how he could otherwise fit Tofu in. 'There might be somebody else there tomorrow,' said Bertie. 'But you can come too.'

'That's settled then,' said Tofu. And then, quite casually, he asked, 'Who is this other person, by the way?'

Bertie looked away. 'It's Olive,' he said shakily. 'My mother invites her to play at my house. It's not me, Tofu. I don't invite her. I really don't.'

Tofu wrinkled his nose in disgust. 'Olive! You actually let her into your house?'

'I can't stop her,' wailed Bertie. 'It's my mother, you see. She likes Olive.'

'You have big problems, Bertie,' said Tofu, shaking his head. 'But I suppose I'll have to come anyway. Olive!'

The conversation ended at that point and Bertie went away to think about what Tofu had said. His feelings were mixed. While he was excited at the prospect of joining the cubs – a uniform! – he felt anxious about the web of deceit that Tofu was so nonchalantly proposing to weave. The deception might work, but what if it did not, and his mother discovered that he had secretly enrolled in the cubs? There would be a most terrible row if that happened, and Bertie could just hear what his mother would say. When you tell a fib, Bertie, you're telling a fib to yourself. Did you know that? And why, Bertie, why ever do you feel the need to wear a uniform? Is there something missing in your life?

Bertie shuddered. The dressing-down would be bad enough, but what would be worse would be the practical consequences. More psychotherapy. More Melanie Klein. More everything. More mother.

But then suddenly his defeatism lifted. He remembered a few days ago he had bumped into Angus Lordie, who was walking Cyril – and some boisterous puppies – in the Drummond Place Gardens. It was shortly after Bertie had read the Baden-Powell book and he asked Angus Lordie if he had ever been a scout.

'I was both a cub and a scout,' answered Angus. 'And a great time I had too. I was kicked out of the scouts, of course, but I enjoyed it when I was in. Yes, you should join up, Bertie. Absolutely.'

He remembered now. It had been such a humiliation being kicked out of the scouts. It was like being excommunicated from the Catholic Church, where a candle was ceremoniously snuffed out to signify the exclusion. In Angus Lordie's case, the scout master had taken his woggle from him. Such humiliation. Dewoggled.

21. Lost Opportunities

Domenica Macdonald, anthropologist, native of Scotland Street, confidante of the portrait painter and dewoggled scout, Angus Lordie, was sitting somewhat morosely at her kitchen table. Before her on the table was an open copy of that day's *Scotsman* newspaper. She had just finished reading the letters column, a daily task she set herself in order to keep abreast with what people were thinking about. Today it had all been rather tame, and she found herself thinking back nostalgically to the days when the *Scotsman* letter column contained a greater number of letters from regular correspondents with a sense of mission. There had been Anthony J. C. Kerr of Jedburgh, for instance, who had written a letter to the paper virtually every week, and sometimes more often than that. His letters had been well informed and entertaining; perhaps just rather frequent. Then there was the late Major F. A. C. Boothby, an energetic writer of letters on the subject of Scottish nationalism – right up to the time of his unfortunate removal to prison for conspiring to blow up an electricity pylon. Such people certainly had things to say, but blowing up pylons had been no way to convince anybody, thought Domenica.

Fortunately those days of excitable Scottish nationalism were over. While it had been necessary, Domenica felt, to repatriate the Stone of Scone by direct action, that is, by stealing it back, it was no longer necessary to do things like that in an age when the Government actually sent it back voluntarily, in a blaze of absurd, Ruritanian ceremony. She herself had been there in Parliament Square, watching in bemused astonishment as the Stone of Scone was driven up the High Street on a cushion; such a stressful day for any stone. And then it had been taken to the Castle where it had been examined by a geologist! Really, she thought, was there no end to the comedy? Of course, Domenica rather approved of Ian Hamilton and his friends who stole the Stone of Scone back from underneath the coronation throne in Westminster Abbey; indeed, she took the view that the stone should have been repatriated a great deal earlier than it was. After all, it was stolen property, rather like the blue Spode teacup which her neighbour Antonia had removed from her flat, and both it – the stone – and the teacup should have been restored to their rightful owners a great deal earlier.

She glanced at the letter column in front of her and sighed. Those heady days were over. Now there were no more theological disputes, or historical debates, just letters about airport runways and European treaties and the like. And the *Times* letters column was much the same; the eccentrics, it seemed, no longer bothered to write letters about hearing cuckoos or, as in one famous letter, seeing a horse wear a pair of spectacles. It was all very bland.

She looked up at the ceiling. It was almost half past ten in the morning and she had not achieved a great deal that day. In fact, she had achieved nothing, unless one could count reading the paper as an achievement. And what about the rest of the day? What lay ahead of her? Domenica had never been one to be bored, but now, for the first time in years, she felt the emptiness of her future. Her social diary for the week was virginal, unsullied by any appointment; not one solitary invitation, not a single engagement of any sort. That, she knew, was the fate of those who made no effort to socialise, who never invited others and who received no invitations in return. But she had heard that it was also the fate of those who were very well known; famous people who received no invitations because everybody assumed that they would not be able to come. This point had been made to her very poignantly by Iris Murdoch, the novelist and philosopher, who had been in Edinburgh to deliver the Gifford Lectures and who had been seen by Domenica sitting alone in the University Staff Club in Chambers Street. Domenica had hesitated, and had then gone up to her and asked her, somewhat apologetically, whether she minded if she came and said hello.

'Of course not,' said Iris Murdoch. 'Nobody comes up to me and says hello. They feel that they cannot, and yet I wish they would. I'm sometimes terribly lonely, sitting by myself, with nobody daring to come up and say hello.'

That had surprised her, but then she had remembered that W. H. Auden experienced the same problem when he returned to Oxford and had taken up residence in a cottage in the gift of Christ Church. It had been hoped that Auden would sit in a coffee shop and undergraduates would come up and engage him in – for them – improving conversation. Auden was willing to sit in the coffee shop, and did so, but very few people plucked up the courage to go and sit at his table and talk to him. So mostly he sat alone. Mind you, Domenica thought, Auden, for all his brilliance and for all the timeless beauty of his poetry, was very dishevelled. His suits were dirty, stained with soup and as covered with ash as the higher slopes of Etna; both Auden and Etna smoked. Of course the great poet did not change his clothing as frequently as he might have done; that may have discouraged people from joining him at his table. How sad, and what opportunities lost! To have been able to sit down at Auden's table and ask what exactly he had meant when he wrote some of his more obscure poems – those puzzling words, for example, about looking through the lattice-work of a nomad's comb: Domenica had her theory about that and would have liked to try it out on the poet himself. Too late now. One could no more have coffee and a chat with Auden than one could pop into Milne's Bar and buy a whisky for more or less the entire Scottish Renaissance. We have lost so much, she thought, and here am I sitting in my kitchen thinking about loneliness and what one cannot do, when what I need to do is to go next door, immediately, and visit Antonia; not my first choice of company – especially after the incident of the blue Spode teacup – but better than nobody, and, of course, a source of amusement, with her extremely questionable taste in men.

22. Room for Misunderstanding

There were two flats off the top landing at 44 Scotland Street – that belonging to Domenica Macdonald and that belonging to Antonia Collie. Of the two, Domenica's flat was the better-placed: its front windows gave a view of a slightly larger slice of Scotland Street and allowed a glimpse, too, of the distinguished roofs of Drummond Place. Antonia's view, although pleasant enough, was mainly of the corner of Royal Crescent. And although the symmetry which inspired the architecture of Scotland Street and indeed of the entire New Town should have led to both flats having the same number of rooms, Domenica had one more room than her neighbour. This was strange, and could only have been explained by the carrying out in the mists of the past of a structural rearrangement within the building; a wall had been knocked through and a room had been taken from Antonia's flat and added to Domenica's. Such modifications were not without precedent in the area, and had occasionally been carried out when two adjoining flats had ended up in the ownership of the same landlord.

When Antonia had bought the flat from Bruce Anderson at the end of his first Edinburgh sojourn, he had said nothing about the clear outline of a doorway which could be made out on one of the walls adjacent to Domenica's kitchen. It was only when Antonia had been invited into Domenica's flat for drinks one evening shortly after her purchase of the flat that the subject had been brought up, and even then raised indirectly.

'You're most fortunate,' Antonia had said, 'to have an extra room. You really are.'

Domenica had affected surprise. 'But I don't have an extra room,' she said. 'I have the number of rooms that I have – and always have had.'

Antonia had looked into the glass of wine that Domenica had poured her; the wine came barely halfway up the side of the glass, but that, she thought, was another thing. 'What I meant,' she said, 'is that your flat, which one would have thought would be the mirror image of mine – being on the same landing – appears to have two more rooms than I do. That's rather surprising, would you not agree?'

Domenica would not. She knew exactly what Antonia meant – she was suggesting that the owners of Domenica's flat had at some point stolen a room from next door. What a ridiculous thought! 'No,' she said. 'Not really. Many flats in this part of town are of different sizes. Some flats were intended for people of greater means than other flats. Some flats had maids' bedrooms, for example.'

Antonia looked out of the window. She, or her predecessors in title to the flat, had lost a room, and she was in no doubt about where it had gone. It was, she thought, like one of those historic injustices that resonated down the centuries – a land grab of the sort that was imposed on the weak or the inattentive. This was exactly how Paraguay must feel about the loss of so much of its territory to its now larger neighbours. But, like Paraguay, there was not much she could do, and the conversation had turned to other matters.

Domenica remembered this conversation as she stood before Antonia's door and prepared to press the bell. The two women had known one another for a long time, even before Antonia had moved to Edinburgh from Fife on the break-up of her marriage, but their relationship had not developed into the friendship which both had initially wished for. Now they had settled into a reasonably amicable, if slightly strained, modus vivendi in which each kept largely to herself but responded readily and with good grace to the duties of neighbourhood. Social invitations were extended and reciprocated, but they were carefully judged so as not to be so frequent as to lead to any form of imposition.

When Domenica had been on field work in the Malacca Straits, her flat had been looked after by Antonia. This had been a convenient arrangement for both of them, but on Domenica's return she had made the shocking discovery that Antonia had removed a blue Spode teacup from her flat and was using it, quite openly, in her own. It was this teacup that now crossed her mind as she pressed Antonia's bell.

When Antonia appeared at the door she did not seem to be at all surprised that it was Domenica who stood on her doorstep.

'Oh, it's only you,' she said.

Domenica caught her breath. Only you . . . 'You were expecting somebody more exciting?'

Antonia treated this as a joke. 'Oh no! Well, maybe yes. But that's not to imply that you're not exciting . . . in your way.'

A short silence ensued. Declarations of war have come in more subtle forms than this, and Domenica would have been quite within her rights to interpret this as such, but then Antonia smiled and gestured for her to come inside, and Domenica decided that she would forgive the other woman's tactlessness. There was no point in being at odds with one's neighbour, whatever the provocation: selfishness in all its forms was what neighbours manifested and one simply had to accept it – unless one wanted distrust and downright enmity.

'Who were you expecting?' she asked. 'I don't want to get in the way, you know.'

This last remark was intended to imply that Antonia was the sort of woman to engage in trysts at ten-thirty in the morning, and that was exactly how it was interpreted.

Antonia smiled sweetly. 'It's a bit early for that,' she said. 'Even for me.'

Domenica watched her neighbour. What exactly did that mean? That even if she were the sort to entertain a lover at eleven in the morning, ten-thirty would be slightly early?

'But let's not stand in the hall forever,' Antonia continued, ushering Domenica into the living room. 'As it happens, I've brewed some coffee already.'

And will it be served, Domenica asked herself, in my cup?

Antonia left to go into the kitchen. And it was then that Domenica noticed the smell. It was not an unpleasant smell, sweetish perhaps, slightly cloying, but certainly sufficiently pronounced to linger in the nose and on the palate; an olfactory memory without a link to substance. It was not the smell of coffee, Domenica thought. Definitely not.

23. Omen Away

After their walk on the path that led along the top of Cottesloe Beach, Matthew and Elspeth had returned to the hotel and sunk into a deep jet-lagged sleep that lasted for over two hours. When they awoke, it was almost six in the evening, and the fiery Western Australian sun had been drained from the evening sky, leaving it a strange, washed-out colour, almost a soft mauve.

What awoke them was not the change in the light, but the sound of a flock of parrots returning to one of the trees that towered over the hotel's back garden. It was a sharp chattering, an excited flurry of sound that seemed to fill the air completely, echoing off the walls of the hotel courtyard in a profusion of high-pitched squeaks. 'Our little friends,' said Matthew, raising himself on an elbow to peer out of the window at the small green birds. 'Hundreds and hundreds of them.'

He shook his head and let it flop back onto the pillow. The air was still warm, and a light film of perspiration was making him feel sticky. He would shower, he thought, or have a swim.

'If you want a swim,' said Elspeth drowsily, 'then remember to shower before you get in. In this hot weather . . .'

'I know that,' said Matthew. Did she think that he would jump into the water all sticky with sweat? He felt slightly irritated by her remark; he was not one of those children of hers, and he did not need to be told what to do. But then he thought: she must be used to telling people to wash their hands, to do this and that; teachers couldn't help themselves, but it would pass now that she had stopped being a teacher.

And then he thought: what will that funny little boy be doing now? Bertie. With that dreadful mother of his and that ineffective father, Stuart. Why did Stuart not face up to that woman and tell her to leave Bertie alone? Of course, he would be scared of her, Matthew decided, as some men are terrified of their wives, and wives of their husbands.

He gazed at Elspeth, whose eyes were still closed in the appearance of sleep, but who had moved her arms and was awake behind the shut eyelids. Matthew had been told that in every marriage there was a dominant partner – Angus Lordie had said that to him – and that if you looked closely enough you could always work out who this was. It was a subtle matter, Angus had said, but it was always there. But what did Angus know of marriage? If ever there was a bachelor by temperament, then it was Angus. At least he – Matthew – had some experience of marriage now, wore the ring Elspeth had given him, could write married the next time an official form asked for his status.

They got up together and went outside for a swim in the hotel pool. Then, refreshed, they walked the short distance to the beach-side restaurant that had been recommended to them. The woman

72

in the hotel had been as good as her word and had insisted on a table near the window, and now they sat looking down over the beach and the sea, a glass each of chilled West Australian wine at their side.

Matthew raised his glass to Elspeth. 'The beginning,' he said.

She reached for her own glass. 'To the beginning.'

'Shall we swim tomorrow?' he asked. 'I don't mean in the hotel pool. Shall we swim down there, off the beach?'

They had seen people swimming when they went for their walk earlier that day and also one or two people surfing, catching the waves quite far out and riding in until the waves collapsed in a maelstrom of sand and water.

'I've hardly ever swum in the sea,' said Elspeth. 'I swam in Portugal once and then a couple of times when I went to Greece with a couple of girlfriends. We went to the islands. Corfu. Places like that.'

'But you'd like to swim here?'

'Of course I would. It looks very inviting.'

Matthew smiled, reaching out to take her hand on top of the table. 'Don't you think that we could just stay here? I could run a gallery. You could . . . well, you could do whatever you wanted to.'

She looked out of the window. 'You can't just go somewhere and not come back. Not these days.'

'Yes, you can,' said Matthew. 'What about those football fans who went off to watch Scotland play in Argentina and never came back? They married local girls and stayed.'

Elspeth sighed. 'That's different,' she said. 'People like that are very uncomplicated. They don't think things through. They see that alcohol is cheap and they decide to stay.'

She paused. 'It would be very nice to be that uncomplicated. To live for the day – not to think about what lies ahead.'

Matthew thought about this for a moment. 'Goethe deals with that in *Werther*,' he said. 'He was interested in the question of whether we could ever be happy if we worried about things.' He looked at her gently. 'But of course there's a world of difference between Goethe and the average Scottish football fan.'

It was an observation that nobody could deny. Now the waitress appeared. As she handed them the menu, she looked out of the window, out towards the beach. The waves, whipped up by a storm somewhere far out at sea, were pounding heavily on the beach, producing a low rumbling sound.

'Surf's up,' said the waitress.

'I can't wait to go swimming in that,' said Matthew.

'Be careful,' said the waitress. 'You can get rips when it's like this. Carry you right out.'

She opened her notebook, fiddling briefly with the tip of her pencil. 'And then there's the Great Whites.'

'Great White whats?' asked Elspeth.

The waitress looked at her pityingly; poor uninformed Pom. 'Great White sharks,' she said. 'They're out there, and sometimes they come in a bit too close for comfort. People get taken, you know. Right off the beach. Sometimes in water that's no deeper than this.' She held a hand at the level of her waist, watching the effect of her words. 'My brother's friend was taken a year or two ago. He was a surfer and the shark took a great bite out of his board. He almost made it back in on a wave, but the shark came for him again and that was it. It's their element, you see. We're the ones who shouldn't be there.'

Matthew gazed out over the water, over the darkness. The tumbling lines of surf were white, laced with phosphorescence against the inky sea beneath. Their element.

24. The Sea, the Sea

Outside the restaurant, when Matthew and Elspeth made their way out after their meal, the night had that smell of sea, of iodine and foam, of churned-up water, of air that was washed and washed again in salt.

Matthew breathed in deeply, drawing the heady mixture into his lungs. 'Let's take off our shoes and walk along the beach,' he said, nodding in the direction of the darkness. 'And then we can go up onto the path above the dunes, later on, and get back to the hotel that way.'

She took his hand. 'Yes.'

'I feel wide awake,' he said. 'It's ten, or whatever, but I feel wide awake.'

She had read about jet lag and printed out a chart which purported to prevent it. 'We shouldn't have slept this afternoon. They say that you should try to stay awake until night-time.'

Matthew was not listening. He had run a few steps ahead of Elspeth, relishing the yielding of the sand beneath his feet. Now he turned round to face her, and she was a shadow in the darkness. There were lights off to their left, above the dunes, where the houses faced out to the sea, and there were the lights of the restaurant behind them. But for the rest it was dark, and filled with the sound of the waves.

'The Southern Cross,' called out Matthew, and pointed. 'Look. Down there.'

She turned her head. The lights of Perth yellowed the sky immediately above them, but towards the horizon the sky became darker and more filled with stars. She saw where he was pointing and identified the tilting cross.

'That way,' said Matthew 'is nothing. Just the southern oceans and Antarctica. All that empty sea.'

She shivered. We were tiny creatures on small islands of land; suddenly she felt vulnerable.

Matthew had stopped walking and had dropped his shoes on the sand. Now he began to roll the bottom of his trouser legs up. 'I'm going to get my feet wet,' he said. 'The water's so warm. Have you tried it? It's gorgeous.'

She shook her head. She did not want to get her feet wet, not now; there would be plenty of time for swimming tomorrow, when the surf would be less boisterous perhaps. Matthew shrugged. 'You don't have to,' he said. 'Just see that my shoes aren't carried away by the tide.'

He took the few steps needed to bring him to the edge of the sea, where the waves, their energy spent, rolled in a final tiny wall of water up the beach. He felt the water sucking around his feet and the movement of the sand beneath his toes, as if the sea were trying to undermine him. They walked on, Elspeth in the moist sand above the water line, Matthew in the shallow rim of surf and spume, the water at its highest just below his knee.

They were alone, or almost alone. A man walked past with a dog, a large black creature that tugged impatiently at its leash; they came out of the dark and disappeared back into the dark. Up on the path above the dunes an occasional figure could be made out against the light from the houses beyond or caught in the beam of a passing car. There was a wind now, the ragged end of the storm out at sea, but unusually warm, like the breath of an animal.

Matthew saw a piece of driftwood floating a few feet out, tossed about by the waves. Deciding to retrieve it, he pulled his trousers further up – and took a step towards it. As he did so, a wave, considerably larger than the others, suddenly swept in. From being in no more than eighteen inches of water, he now found himself in several feet, the water rising quickly up to his waist. Then there was another wave, also larger than the others, and he felt the water at his chest. He tried to turn but lost his footing and felt himself go down in the water. He looked towards Elspeth and shouted. She was waving her arms about. He shouted again. 'I'm . . .' But now he seemed to have lost the sand beneath his feet; he was out of his depth and the sea seemed to be dragging him. He kicked out sharply, expecting the movement to get him safely back into the shallows, but the dragging was more pronounced now and there were more waves, so hard upon one another, tumbling over his head, buffeting him. They should be taking me back in, he thought, but they were not.

For Elspeth it happened very quickly. When she saw Matthew go in up to his waist, she laughed and called out to him not to ruin his clothes. 'Saltwater,' she cried out. 'Saltwater ruins things. Don't get any wetter, Matthew. Matthew . . .'

Then she saw the waves cover him and she became alarmed. Matthew could swim – she knew that – but why had he decided to swim at night? Suddenly she thought of what the waitress had said that evening. Their element. The Great Whites. She screamed and waved frantically, but Matthew seemed to be ignoring her. She saw his head, bobbing in the surf, but then it disappeared and when the surf cleared it was not in the spot she had seen him in; or was that him, that darker patch in the water?

Within the space of a couple of minutes, she could see no trace of him. She advanced to the edge of the water and took a few steps into the waves; but what point was there in her going in? She could not see him; she had no idea where he was. The rips. The waitress had said there were rips.

She turned round, half panicking. Down the beach, about ten minutes away, was the restaurant with its lights and people and telephones. She started to run, stumbling in the sand, which slowed her down. She began to sob, struggling for breath. Matthew was going to drown. Her husband. She was going to lose him.

When she arrived at the restaurant she burst through the first door she found. Several people were sitting round a table, one of them the waitress who had served them earlier on.

'Left something behind?'

'My husband . . .'

They laughed.

But then, in a moment, they understood.

Bertie had been dreading the afternoon on which both Tofu and Olive were to come to his house. In normal circumstances he would have been pleased – Tofu may not have been the best of friends, but he was the closest thing to a friend that Bertie had. And Bertie had a sneaking admiration for Tofu, in spite of all the fibs that his friend told, his tendency to spit at people, and all his outrageous exploits; at least Tofu did the things that he wanted to do. At least Tofu didn't have a mother breathing down his neck all the time.

There was some debate about Tofu's mother. Tofu himself never spoke about her, but waved his hand vaguely when the subject of mothers arose. This could be interpreted as insouciance – a gesture indicating that mothers might be a problem for some, but not for him. Or it could have been intended to convey that Tofu was not sure about the precise location of his mother – the sort of gesture one makes when giving directions to a place one is not entirely familiar with: it's somewhere over there.

Certainly Tofu's mother had never been seen by any of the other children at the Steiner School. When Tofu was picked up at school it was always by his father, the author of well-known books on plant energy fields. And sometimes, Tofu simply walked out of the school gate, announcing that he did not need to be picked up and that he was perfectly capable of catching a bus unaided. That always drew gasps of admiration from the others, except from Olive, of course, who simply narrowed her eyes in hatred and said nothing.

Olive had a variety of explanations for the apparent absence of Tofu's mother.

'She's in Saughton Prison,' she said. 'She's been there for years.'

Bertie doubted this. He had read about Saughton Prison in the newspapers and it had been described as a male prison. But when he pointed this out to Olive, she had been undismayed.

'That's what you think, Bertie,' she said. 'But you don't know anything about prisons, do you? So who do you think does the cooking in Saughton Prison? Men can't cook, can they, Mr Smarty

Pants! So they have a special room there for bad ladies and they do the cooking. So there!'

This struck the others as entirely feasible, but Bertie remained doubtful.

'I don't think that she's in prison,' he said. 'Why would she be there anyway?'

'Murder,' said Olive.

Bertie plucked up his courage. Olive was not an easy person to argue with. 'All right,' he said. 'Who did she murder, Olive? You tell us if you're so sure.'

Olive thought for a moment. She looked first at Bertie and then at the faces of the other children around them. 'You'll find out,' she said. 'Just you wait. You'll find out.' And with that she changed the subject.

The other theory about Tofu's mother was that she had starved to death. Olive herself, ignoring the inconsistency which this idea involved with her remarks about her being in prison, had put about the notion that Tofu's mother had starved because the whole family was vegan. 'She became very thin,' she announced. 'That's what happens to vegans. They don't last long.'

Bertie had eventually decided to ask Tofu whether he had a mother or not. He did not like the rumours that Olive was putting about and he thought that the best way of putting an end to these would be to find out the truth.

'Where's your mother, Tofu?' he asked one day in the playground.

'At home,' said Tofu, waving a hand vaguely.

'Are you sure?' asked Bertie.

'How do I know what my mother's doing?' Tofu snapped back. 'I can't look after her all the time.'

Bertie had dropped the topic, but it worried him. Tofu was so full of bluff and bravado, but was he really sad inside? A boy with no mother to look after him and a father who went on about nuts and broccoli? Bertie reflected on his own mother situation and wondered if he was not, in fact, fortunate in having the mother he did. What would it be like if his mother were suddenly not to be

79

there? He had so often wished for that, but now he remembered seeing something in that small antique store on the corner of Great King Street. One morning he had stopped and seen in the window an elaborately worked Victorian sampler mounted on a stand. 'Be careful what you wish for,' it had read, and Bertie, puzzled, had drawn the message to the attention of his father.

'What does that mean, Daddy?' he asked. 'Why should you be careful what you wish for?'

Stuart smiled. 'They were always coming up with things like that in those days,' he said. 'We used to have one of those at home. It was made by your great-grandmother, Bertie. It said, "Save your breath to cool your porridge."'

'That's very funny,' said Bertie. 'Did it mean that you shouldn't talk too much?'

'Exactly,' said Stuart, ruffling his son's hair and thinking he could name at least one woman who might consider that. But he immediately felt disloyal and put the thought out of his mind.

'So what do they mean about being careful what you wish for?' Bertie asked.

Stuart reached for Bertie's hand as they stood on the pavement in front of the shop. Behind them, a 23 bus lumbered up Dundas Street; above, a gull mewed and circled. He looked down at his son, at the eager face staring up at him. There were so many questions – and so many wishes. Wishes, he thought, are usually for the world to be quite different from the way it currently is, but do we really want that?

'The thing you wish for,' Stuart began, 'may not be what you really want. You may think it would be nice if something happened, but then, when it happens, you may find that it's not really what you wanted. Or you may find that things are worse.'

He looked at Bertie. What did this small boy wish for? What hopes were harboured in his brave little heart?

'What are your special wishes, Bertie?'

Bertie thought for a moment. 'I thought you shouldn't speak about wishes. I thought that if you spoke about them they wouldn't come true.'

'Maybe you're right,' said Stuart. 'Maybe.'

'But I'd really like to join the cub scouts, Daddy.' He hesitated. 'And wear a uniform.'

Stuart gave Bertie's hand a squeeze. 'Good idea, Bertie. Why not?'

Bertie looked away. He had uttered a wish.

26. Gender Agendas

The arrangement had been made between Tofu's father and Bertie's mother. 'Tofu can travel back with us on the bus,' said Irene. 'I've arranged that with his father. Olive will be coming a bit later.'

Bertie looked pleadingly at his mother. 'Do you really think there'll be time for Olive to come to my house, Mummy?' he asked. 'If she comes later, then everything will be finished.'

Irene laughed. 'Everything will be finished? You make it sound like a formal dinner party, Bertie! There'll be a bit of Dundee cake and tea. Plenty to go round.'

'I didn't mean the food, Mummy,' protested Bertie. 'I meant the . . . the playing. We'll have finished playing by the time that Olive comes. I wouldn't want her to be bored.'

Irene did not think that there was much prospect of Olive's being bored. She was a somewhat busy little girl, she reflected, with a great organisational talent, but she was still a good influence on Bertie, who needed to allow his feminine side to flourish. And she was certainly a good antidote to the somewhat unsavoury Tofu, with his unresolved masculinity; Tofu was certainly not a good companion for Bertie at all, but *faute de mieux* . . .

'You'll both have a lovely time with Olive,' said Irene. 'I've noticed that her head is full of ideas for games. Positively buzzing with ideas for creative play. What was that game you played when she was last at the house? She had her nurse's kit with her, didn't she?' She paused. 'On which subject, Bertie, one wonders why Olive chose to have a nurse's kit rather than a doctor's kit. One might reflect on that, might one not?'

Bertie thought for a moment. His mother did not know, of course, what Olive had housed in her junior nurse's kit – a real syringe with which she had forcibly taken a blood sample from Bertie. There had been enough fuss from Miss Harmony when she had heard of that – and of the subsequent test for leprosy that Olive claimed to have conducted on Bertie's blood sample. Bertie did not want that row to continue, and so he said nothing of that. But why did girls like to have junior nurse's kits? In his view, the answer to that was simple: some girls liked to play nurses, and some did not. He supposed that boys could play nurses if they wanted to, but Bertie had not met any who did. It was as simple as that.

'I suppose that they have nurse's kits, Mummy, because girls like to be nurses. They play with dollies and nurse them.'

Irene cast her eyes heavenwards. 'Wrong, Bertie! Wrong!'

Bertie said nothing, but looked at the floor. He had simply reported what he had seen, but his mother, for some reason, did not seem to approve. It was something to do with Melanie Klein, perhaps.

Irene sighed. It was a constant battle to explain the evils of gender stereotyping, really it was. 'Haven't you noticed, Bertie,' she began, 'how most of the doctors at the health centre are women? Haven't you noticed that? That doctor who looked at your foot when you hurt it the other day, she was a woman, wasn't she?'

Bertie thought back. The doctor had indeed been a woman, but then all the nurses at the health centre were also women.

'But all the nurses there, Mummy,' he pointed out, 'were ladies, weren't they? I didn't see any men.'

Irene thought quickly. 'There are male nurses, Bertie. And they are very good at what they do, even if they're just men.'

Bertie was silent.

'So you see,' went on Irene, 'the fact that the shops sell those silly nurse's kits to girls is just keeping alive these ridiculous preconceptions that girls like to be nurses. They don't. They're only nurses because they can't be doctors. They've been conditioned, Bertie, to accept that they must do what's second best.'

Bertie frowned. 'But is it second best to be a nurse, Mummy? I read in the paper that some nurses don't like people to say that.'

Irene smiled encouragingly. 'No, they don't, Bertie. You're right. Many nurses nowadays don't like doing the things that nurses used to have to do. Changing sheets and collecting bedpans – that sort of thing. Nursing has moved on, Bertie.'

Bertie was puzzled. 'But if they don't do that,' he said, 'then who does? Do people have to tuck themselves into bed when they're in hospital?'

Irene was amused by this and raised her eyes again. 'Dear Bertie, no, not at all. They have other people now to do that sort of thing. There are other wome . . . people who do that.'

'So they aren't nurses, Mummy?' asked Bertie.

Irene waved a hand vaguely. 'No. They call them care assistants, or something like that. It's very important work.'

'So what do the nurses do then, Mummy? If they have some-body else to take the bedpans to the patients, what's left for the nurses to do? Do they do the things that doctors do? Can nurses take your tonsils out?'

'I think they'd like to,' said Irene. 'And I'm sure that they'd be very good at it.'

She patted Bertie on the head. 'Enough of that, Bertie! If Tofu and Olive are coming this afternoon, then Mummy must check to see that she has all the ingredients for the Dundee cake. And I must go and see if Ulysses is awake.'

She left Bertie to his own devices. But he just stood there, staring down at the floor. Grown-ups did not understand, he thought. They did not understand how difficult it was being six and having to live with people like Olive and even Tofu. Grown-ups spoke as if the world were simple; as if people behaved nicely to one another. But Bertie knew that they did not. When you were a boy, as he was, and saw the world the way in which boys saw it, it all looked very different. Olive and Tofu would fight because that's what people like that did: they fought. And it would end up with Tofu spitting at Olive, and Olive screaming and perhaps even trying to stab Tofu with the syringe from her junior nurse's kit. Bertie could see it coming, but why was his mother so blinkered, so utterly unaware of the strikingly obvious? There was so much that she seemed just not to notice, thought Bertie – obvious things, like the way that Ulysses looked so like Dr Fairbairn. Little things like that.

27. Pink for Danger

'So this is your place,' said Tofu, looking round him, wrinkling his nose slightly, as if there were a faintly unpleasant odour. Bertie, standing in the hallway, watching Tofu guardedly, wondered if his house smelled. People said that if your house smelled you might never know it because you became so used to it. And it was the same with people themselves, he believed; Hiawatha presumably did not know that his socks smelled but just accepted that this was what socks were like – naturally. Of course Olive had told him, quite bluntly in fact, but he had just laughed and pretended not to understand what she was talking about. That was the best tactic with Olive, thought Bertie. One should just laugh and pretend not to hear what she was saying; it was difficult, though, as sound advice so often was.

'So who lives here with you, Bertie?' asked Tofu, still looking round.

'My mummy,' said Bertie. 'And my dad. And my little brother . . .'

'Is it true that your dad's a wimp?' interrupted Tofu. 'Not that I say that, of course. It's just that everyone else does. Just like everyone else says your mummy's a cow. Not me. Everyone else, though.' He looked at Bertie, waiting for the answer.

Bertie felt flustered. He admired his father and could not understand why anybody would consider him a wimp. He was not. 'That's not true,' he said hotly. 'My dad's—'

Tofu cut him short. 'Keep your hair on! I didn't say it, remember?'

'Well you shouldn't repeat fibs,' said Bertie. 'Especially about people's dads. What about your mummy then?'

Tofu became defensive. 'My mummy? What about her?'

Bertie felt the advantage switch to him. 'Olive says that your mummy's in Saughton Prison. She said that she's there for murder. I didn't say it. Olive did.'

Tofu's eyes narrowed. 'She's not,' he said. Then he looked down at the floor. 'She . . . she was eaten by a lion in the Serengeti Game Reserve. I was very small. I don't remember it. But my dad does, and that's why he became a vegan.'

Bertie was a naturally sympathetic boy and his heart went out to Tofu. He had seen a picture of the Serengeti Game Reserve and it had been full of lions. Although Tofu was a notorious liar, this, at least, had the ring of truth. 'I'm really sorry, Tofu,' said Bertie. 'Let's talk about something else.'

Tofu seemed relieved to be off the subject of mothers and now expressed an interest in seeing Bertie's younger brother. 'He's probably sleeping,' said Bertie. 'But we can take a look in his room if we don't make a noise.'

They walked along the corridor and Bertie pushed open the door into Ulysses' room. The baby, snuffling quietly, was lying in his cot.

'That's him,' said Bertie. 'He can't say anything yet. And I don't think he can think very much either. But he's quite happy, most of the time. He's called Ulysses.'

'Stupid name,' said Tofu. 'But I suppose that's not his fault.'

'Ulysses was a Greek,' said Bertie. 'He was a Greek hero. In a legend.'

'Still stupid,' said Tofu, peering at Ulysses over the edge of the cot. 'He looks really ugly, Bertie. Are you sure that he's the right way up? Is that his face – or is it his bottom?'

'He's not ugly,' said Bertie, defensively. 'Babies can't help looking like that. All babies look like that.'

'But some are uglier than others,' retorted Tofu. 'And that's a really ugly one you've got there, Bertie. Do you think that there's a competition for ugly babies? Because he could win a prize, you know. You should ask.'

This conversation was interrupted by the arrival of Irene, who had heard the boys going into the room and had come to find out what was going on. 'I know you've come to admire little Ulysses,' she whispered. 'But he needs his sleep, or he becomes a little bit crotchety. Why don't you go and play in Bertie's room?'

This is exactly what Bertie had hoped not to do. His room, which had been painted pink by his mother, was an embarrassment, and he had made a small sign for the door: Closed for Renovation. That, he hoped, would prevent Tofu from seeing the room at all.

'Good idea,' said Tofu. 'Let's go, Bertie.'

Bertie was trapped. Tofu would laugh at his room – he knew it, but it seemed to him that he now had no alternative.

'Closed for what?' asked Tofu as he peered at the sign. 'What does this say, Bertie?'

'Nothing,' muttered Bertie, as he took the sign down.

They went in. Tofu took a step or two into the room and then stopped. He looked around at the walls, and at the ceiling; then he turned to look at Bertie. 'Pink,' he said.

Bertie felt himself on the verge of tears, but checked himself. It was bad enough Tofu seeing his pink room; how much worse would it be if Tofu saw him crying.

'That's an undercoat,' he said miserably. 'The next coat of paint will be white.'

It was as if Tofu had not heard him. 'Pink walls!' he gloated. 'Boy, wait until the others hear this. Pink walls!'

Bertie said nothing.

Tofu, smirking, stared at his host. 'Do you know what pink means, Bertie? Do you know?'

Bertie shook his head. He had no idea what pink meant, other than that it was a girl's colour. That was all he knew.

'Pink is a colour for sissies,' said Tofu. 'You know that? Sissies.'

Bertie was not sure what a sissy was, but he did not think that he was one. He was just an ordinary boy, like any other boy, and it was so unfair that he had this pink room and those pink dungarees. And what sort of friend was Tofu, that he should rub it all in? It was so unfair.

'I'm not a sissy, Tofu,' stuttered Bertie. 'I'm not.'

'Then why do you have a pink room?' asked Tofu.

Bertie did not answer. He was wondering if he could somehow get rid of Tofu; if he could ask him to leave. He did not think so. Tofu had come to play and was to be there until five o'clock when his father came to collect him. There was no escape . . .

Then there were steps behind him and the door was opened. 'Look who's here,' said Irene brightly. 'Olive.'

Tofu spun round and glared at the new arrival. 'Hello, Bertie,' said Olive, ignoring Tofu. 'Are we going to play in your pink room?'

'It's not pink,' growled Tofu. 'It's . . . sort of red. Are you colour-blind, Olive?'

Bertie, defended in this way, the beneficiary of male solidarity, could have embraced Tofu with gratitude. But did not, of course, as that would have been sissy.

28. *Unmarried Bliss*

Bruce had not expected to find his new job difficult. And it was not. 'Anybody could manage a wine bar,' he said to Julia one morning over breakfast. 'Even you.'

Julia looked up from the catalogue she was reading. Mauve was in this year; look at all that mauve. Even that full-length cashmere coat. Mauve. It was the sort of thing that she had seen at Barney's in New York when her father had taken her over there for her birthday. It was expensive, of course, but Barney's was worth it. Everything there had edge. That was pre-Bruce, of course. Perhaps she should take Bruce over for a weekend and show him round.

'Me?' she said. 'Me what?'

'Nothing,' said Bruce, smiling. 'You, nothing. I was just talking about running the wine bar and what a doddle it is.'

Julia returned to her catalogue. 'That's nice,' she said.

Bruce reached for his acai juice. He had looked in the mirror a few days ago and had experienced a bit of a shock. There was a line, a wrinkle even, at the side of his mouth. At first he had thought it was a mark of some sort, a smudge, but after he had rubbed at it, it was still there. That had made him think. It was all very well being drop-dead gorgeous, as he admitted to himself he really was, but could you be drop-dead gorgeous with wrinkles?

Moisturiser, he thought. More moisturiser and more anti-oxidants, such as acai juice, which was also good for the . . . in that department. Now, drinking his acai juice, he looked over the rim of the glass at Julia, his fiancée, sitting on the other side of the table. There was no sign of her being pregnant – no visible sign yet – and she was still a bit drop-dead gorgeous herself. Both of us, he thought; both drop-dead gorgeous.

Bruce had to admit that he was happy. He was not one to sit down and count his blessings, but they were, he decided, manifold. Firstly, he had this marvellous flat in Howe Street – it was in Julia's name, actually, but a brief 'I do' in front of some minister wheeled out for the purpose and all that would be changed! God, it's easy, he said to himself. Marriage brings everything: a flat, a job. Get married, boys; that's the life!

And then there was the car, the Porsche – not quite the model he would have picked if he had been given a totally free rein, but a Porsche none the less. A Porsche was a statement. It said something about you, about how you felt about yourself. Of course there were always those wet blankets who said that you only drove a car like that if you were making up for something – some inadequacy, perhaps. But that was rubbish, Bruce thought. That was the sort of thing made up by people who would never get a Porsche and knew it. They had to come up with something to make themselves feel better about their Porsche-less state.

And of course there was money. Bruce had suggested to Julia that they have a shared current account.

'No need to double things up,' he said. 'You know how banks slap on the charges. Keep it straightforward. One account for both of us. Simple.'

Julia, who received a monthly allowance of three thousand pounds from her father, and who had only the vaguest idea about money, was happy enough to do this. Bruce's salary from the wine bar, once tax was deducted, also turned out to be three thousand pounds, and so together they had a disposable income of six thousand pounds a month. Bruce had discovered that Julia rarely used much more than a quarter of this, as she liked to try on clothes but not necessarily buy them. So he was in a position to spend more than his salary, if he wished, although that proved to be rather difficult. He could get more clothes, of course, and shoes and general accessories, but beyond that, what could one spend the money on? It was a bit of a challenge – a pleasant challenge, of course, but a challenge none the less.

Recently Bruce had bought himself five pairs of shoes and one pair of slippers from the Shipton & Heneage catalogue (he had acquired the habit of reading catalogues from Julia). He had bought two pairs of single-buckle monk shoes – one pair in brown and the other in black; a pair of burgundy loafers; a pair of patent leather evening pumps, with discreet fabric bows; and a pair of George boots in supple black leather. The slippers were monogrammed, BA, and had embroidered gold Prince of Wales feathers on the toes for good measure. They were made of black velvet and had firm leather soles.

But all this material comfort was topped by having Julia herself. In the earlier days of their relationship, Bruce had wondered how he would possibly be able to bear her vacuousness and her simpering.

He had gritted his teeth when she called him Brucie, and when she insisted on sharing the shower with him. Of course, she's mad about me, he told himself. That was understandable – women just were. But I wish she'd give me a bit more room. You can't have somebody stroking you all the time, as if you were a domestic cat.

Then, slowly and almost imperceptibly, his attitude towards Julia had changed. From mild irritation at her apparent obsession with him, he had come to appreciate it. He found himself looking forward to coming back from work – if his job could be described as work – and finding Julia waiting for him with her cooing and her physical endearments. I'm fond of her, he found himself thinking. I actually like this woman.

Miracle! thought Bruce, in French. I'm settling down at last. And what a way to settle: money, flat, Porsche, sexy-looking woman who thinks I'm the best thing ever – and who can blame her? All on a plate. All there before me for the taking. And I have taken it.

He drained his acai juice. 'Let's go out for dinner tonight,' he said. 'The St Honoré?'

Julia shrugged. 'Maybe.' Then, after a pause, 'Actually, I've been invited to a party. And I'm sure they won't mind if you come too. I meant to tell you. There's a party down in Clarence Street.'

'Clarence Street? Who do we know there?'

'I know them. I don't think you do. Watson Cooke? Do you know him?'

Bruce thought. Watson Cooke? Where had he heard that name before? Somewhere. But where?

29. An Unwelcome Message

Bruce felt vaguely irritated. He had not particularly wanted to go out to dinner and had proposed that they should do so more for Julia's sake than his own. What annoyed him was that she should not want to spend time with him in the intimate circumstances of a table for two at the St Honoré; this both angered and surprised him, in fact. Most girls – every girl he had ever met – would jump at the chance to go out to dinner with him, thought Bruce, and who did Julia think she was to come up with a counter-proposal? Watson Cooke? Bruce was at first inclined to say No, I don't want to go to a party in Clarence Street at Watson Cooke's place. But then, just when he had decided to say this, Julia arose from the table and said, 'I'll tell Watson that we can come. You'll like him.'

'Who . . .' Bruce began, but she had left the room and the rest of his question – which was who was Watson Cooke – would have been addressed to an empty kitchen.

Bruce's feeling of irritation lasted for much of the rest of the day. That morning he had to conduct interviews for new bar staff, a task he did not really enjoy as the applicants were, for the most part, unappointable. It was not that they lacked experience – some of them had served in bars for years – it was just that, well, he had to admit it privately, it's just that they were so unattractive. The women were such frumps and the young men so pale and . . . He could not find quite the right word to describe the young men, but unappointable would have to do.

In desperation he telephoned the agency which had sent the candidates over. 'Those people,' he said. 'Not much of a bunch.'

The woman at the other end of the line sounded puzzled. 'Not much of a bunch?'

'Useless,' said Bruce. 'Dross. Human dross.'

There was a silence at the other end of the line. Then, 'I'm sorry, I don't quite understand. Are you saying that they weren't suitable in some way? Not sufficiently qualified?'

'Unsuitable,' said Bruce. 'I wouldn't want any of them cluttering up my wine bar. We're a place, well, I suppose one would just have to say, we're a place with a certain coolness. Do you know what I mean?'

'So you're saying that all of those young people weren't cool enough? Do I understand you correctly?'

Bruce laughed. '*Exactement*,' he said. 'Haven't you got anything better? My customers like to have somebody halfway presentable serving them. They don't want to be served by somebody who looks as if she's on day release from Edinburgh Zoo.'

Again there was a silence at the other end. 'I'm not sure if I understand you.'

Bruce sighed. 'Well, let me explain. You sent four men and two women – right?'

'I believe so.'

'So,' said Bruce. 'Take the two women first. There was one called Shona, I think. Now, I don't like to be unkind, but, frankly, she was pretty gross. I don't know where she got her nose from, but . . . there are limits, you know.'

'Her nose? Shona's nose?'

'Yes. Helen of Troy's face may have launched a thousand ships, but Shona's nose must have sunk a few. More than a few, maybe.'

Bruce heard the woman breathing heavily. Asthma, perhaps. But then, 'I suppose she got her nose from me,' said the voice. 'I am her mother, after all.'

Bruce bit his lip. 'Ah,' he said. 'Her . . .' He stopped; the receiver at the other end had been put down.

He shrugged. Some people had no sense of humour and he had never liked that woman, anyway; not that he had met her, but one could tell. The call, however, had unsettled him and the rest of the day was spent in a state of discontent. By the time that five o'clock arrived, he was ready to go home and to tell Julia that he had decided that they would not go to the party in Clarence Street after all. Julia, however, was not in when he returned to Howe Street.

'It's me,' called Bruce, as he entered the flat, throwing a quick glance at the hall mirror. Nice profile. 'It's *moi*.'

There was no reply, and Bruce, frowning slightly, walked through to the bedroom. Julia sometimes had long afternoon naps, which could last into the early evening, and he half expected to find her on the bed, amidst scattered copies of *Tatler* or *Vogue*, fast asleep.

There was no sign of her in the bedroom. When he went into the kitchen he saw a note on the table. He picked it up and read it. Julia's writing was strangely childish, all loops and swirls. *Gone to have dinner with P. and B. at some Italian place they know. Don't know the name or where it is. See you at Watson Cooke's place later on. Nine o'clock. Maybe later. Don't arrive before nine as Watson's coming with us for a bite to eat and we won't be back until then, he said. Love and xxx's Julia.*

Bruce reread the note and then, crumpling it up in a ball, he threw it into the bin. So Watson Cooke was going for dinner at . . . wherever it was, with . . . P. and B., whoever they were. How dare she?

He went through to the bathroom, turned on the shower and stepped out of his clothes, throwing his shirt angrily onto a pile of unwashed laundry. She couldn't even wash their clothes when she had nothing to do all day but sit about in the flat and read those stupid magazines of hers.

He stood under the shower, feeling the embrace of the hot water, shaking his hair as the stream of the shower warmed his scalp. I don't have to put up with this, he thought. Julia is going to have to have one or two things explained to her, and he would do so that very night, after they came back from Clarence Street. She would probably cry – women tended to when you spelled it out for them – but he would be gentle afterwards, and she would be grateful to him, and it would all be back to normal. And tomorrow he would approach another agency to get the bar staff – attractive ones this time. He would tell them: don't send anybody who looks like the back of a bus. No uglies. Just cool, *s'il vous plaît*.

30. Edinburgh Noses through the Ages

That evening, while Bruce fumed and Julia dined, Angus Lordie painted. He did not normally paint at night, but it was the high summer and the light would be good enough until nine and even beyond. He was working on a portrait, that of a prominent Edinburgh commercial figure, and he was trying to get the nose right. Everything else had worked out very well – the eyes were, he thought, exactly right and the mouth, often a difficult feature to capture, was, he thought, very accurate. But the nose, which in this case was large and bulbous, was proving more difficult. Angus had several photographs of it, taken discreetly from various angles, and was now attempting to capture it in paint; it was not working.

One should not underestimate, he thought, the significance of the nose. Angus believed that this organ, so aplastic compared with those expressive, mobile features, the lips and the eyes, was often the focal point of a painting. He had learned this lesson at the Edinburgh College of Art when a visiting lecturer had spent an entire hour enlightening the students about the importance of the nose in Rembrandt's paintings and engravings. It had been a memorable lecture, illustrated with slides of any number of Rembrandt's self-portraits and his studies of derelict vagabonds, all possessed of noses weighed down with significance.

Now, looking at the nose that he had been painting on the canvas in front of him, Angus remembered what it was that made Rembrandt's noses so memorable. 'Look at the nose,' the lecturer had said, pointing to the slide behind him. 'See how it sits. It is not pointing towards us, you will observe, as we stand before the painting; it goes off at an angle, thus. That gives life to the face, because the nose has energy and direction. Whatever the subject's eyes may be doing – and in this painting they are looking directly at us – the nose has business of its own, off towards the right of the painting. And our eye, you will notice, goes straight to that nose, somewhat bulbous and over-prominent. The nose says it all, doesn't it?'

Yes, thought Angus; the nose says it all, and yet what could one do with one's nose to mediate the message, whatever it was? One might wrinkle it, to convey distaste; one could certainly not turn it up, as the metaphor suggested one might. Some of Rembrandt's noses were wrinkled, but that conveyed, in the etchings in question, not so much distaste as madness and terror. One might, he supposed, look down the nose, and convey haughtiness. But could the static nose say anything? Could the nose in repose, the sleeping nose, be made to convey a message of human vulnerability? Or the vanity of human dreams: one might have ambitions, one might wish to assert the essential dignity of the human creature, but the nose would act as a constant reminder of simple humanity. The sleeping nose: it made him think. Auden's beautiful lullaby enjoined him to whom the lines were addressed: 'Lay your sleeping head, my love . . .' Would those lines have had the same grave beauty if written, 'Lay your sleeping nose, my love . . .'? Angus smiled to himself, and then laughed. The nose was simply too ridiculous to be the subject of lyricism.

And yet one could not ignore the nose; certainly if one was a painter. There were fine noses in Edinburgh – noses which would have given Rembrandt much to think about; and which had certainly provided inspiration and amusement for John Kay, the late eighteenth-century barber and engraver who had been such a sharp-eyed observer of the Edinburgh of his day. Kay's subjects came from every sector of society: Highland grandees, Writers to the Signet, the wives of the common soldiery, the keelies of the toon. All were there, captured by his engraving pen, etched onto his plates with such delicacy and humour. And Kay, like Rembrandt, understood the importance of the nose, and what it could tell us about the soul within. In some of his drawing it is the nose itself that is the subject's burden in life – a large protuberance attached to a small body; so prominent, in fact, that one might imagine the nose catching the wind on the North Bridge and spinning the person off course, turning him towards Holyrood rather than Leith, requiring that he tack his way rather than walk directly.

'Spirit of Kay,' thought Angus, 'light up this city now . . .' Who had said that? Nobody, he thought; just Angus Lordie, painter and occasional poet. What had come to mind was that line of MacDiarmid: 'Spirit of Lenin, light up this city now . . .' MacDiarmid was talking about Glasgow, of course, although he had no doubt thought that Edinburgh could have done with a dose of Lenin too, even more so than Glasgow. But what nonsense MacDiarmid wrote when he became overtly political, thought Angus; and he offended everybody in the process. Any extreme political creed brought only darkness in the long run; it lit up nothing. The best politics were those of caution, tolerance and moderation, Angus maintained, but such politics were, alas, also very dull, and certainly moved nobody to poetry.

He looked at his painting. His subject, he believed, had led a largely blameless life, had loved his wife, had served on committees, had helped the requisite number of good causes. There had been, he suspected, little passion in his life, and relatively few disappointments. He had lived in Barnton, a comfortable suburb in which nothing of note happened, and he had loved the Forth Bridge, golf, Speyside whiskies, money, and going on the occasional summer cruise in northern waters – to Orkney and Shetland, to the Faroe Islands, and once, more adventurously, to Iceland. That was his life. And now here am I trying to capture this with a few strokes of my brush, to fix all this in oil paint on canvas; recording nothing very much with next to nothing.

This line of thought, connected with what Angus was doing, but only vaguely so, was now suddenly broken. The puppies, sequestered in a neighbouring room, had begun to yap again. Angus sighed. He would have to take them out again into Drummond Place; six frolicking, excited centres of canine consciousness, eager to get on with their own small lives. I am the owner of seven dogs, he reminded himself, utterly appalled.

NORTH BRIDGE
1807

NORTH BRIDGE
2007

after John Kay

31. Selling a Pup (or Six)

It took some time to get a leash on six puppies. As he busied himself with one, another would bite playfully at his fingers, covering them with canine saliva, while another would worry away at his shoe-laces. Then, when the biter and its sibling were safely clipped onto the ends of their leashes, the worrier would roll over on his stomach in an attempt to elude capture, and so on until, after ten minutes of effort, there would be six small bundles of leashed fur, all tugging in different directions, all barking or growling in anticipation of their walk in the Drummond Place Gardens.

There was still a good deal of light in the sky when Angus emerged from his stairway door and crossed the street to the gardens. The puppies, sensing adventure, yelped with excitement, one of them executing a complete somersault, such was his enthusiasm. Angus had to smile; Cyril's offspring were lively dogs, which was not surprising, as their father was a dog of noted character and had many friends in the human world.

He closed the gate behind him and bent down to release the puppies. They dashed off, falling over themselves in their eagerness. 'Don't go far, boys,' said Angus, but he was largely ignored: they had layer upon layer of smells to investigate and were setting to the task with relish, filing away the odours which make a dog's world a riot of impressionist olfactory exuberance.

Angus stood on the pathway and watched them, with mixed feelings. In the past, surplus dogs – and surely these puppies were surplus – would be bundled into a sack and tossed into the canal. There was little sentiment for animal suffering in those days, and the few moments of spluttering terror under the water would not be thought about. Such things simply were, they happened. Now, of course, the circle of our moral concern had widened – and happily so. Animal suffering was not tolerated, even if we still had abattoirs where bovine – and other – lives were brought to a sudden end. There was terror there, of course, in those last moments, and surely that meant suffering, but people did not think about that very much. We did not stroke cattle and sheep, or give them names

97

and hug them; we did not encourage them to sleep at the foot of our bed; that was what seemed to count.

He looked up at the evening sky, a sky which, in this final hour before darkness, was drained of colour. A vapour trail, bisecting it, had begun to transform itself into a wispy sweep of cloud, the tracks, he thought, of a group of people heading westward, each with business of his own, unaware that five miles below them all these little dramas were being enacted. 'I, a man with seven dogs,' he muttered, 'stand here / Looking up at the line of your journey / Indifferent each to each other / But recognisably in the same metaphorical boat / Even with five miles of air between us . . .'

He stopped himself. Fragments of poetry came to him with some regularity but were not always written down or remembered. And now, turning his head slightly, he became aware that a man had come up behind him, and was standing watching the puppies at play.

'How many?' asked the man.

'Six, I'm afraid,' said Angus, sighing. 'Six spirited, enthusiastic, hungry, incontinent, hybrid and utterly lovable dogs.'

The man laughed. 'They are very beautiful, aren't they?'

Angus raised an eyebrow. 'They are hardly likely to win at Cruft's,' he said. 'Their mother was an extremely odd-looking dog. Very common. My own dog, their father, is by contrast a fairly handsome fellow. He's got a gold tooth, you see, and a rather raffish grin. Great dog.'

'Tasty little things, though,' said the man. And then, after a few moments of hesitation, went on to ask, 'Have you got a home for them yet?'

Again Angus sighed. 'That's proving somewhat difficult,' he said. 'I've been asking around my friends, but nobody seems interested. Precious little support in that quarter when the chips are down.'

The man shook his head in sympathy. 'That must be very worrying for you. One or two puppies would be bad enough, but having six must be something of a nightmare!'

'You can say that again,' said Angus. 'In fact, I have already had several bad dreams about these little chaps. I dreamed a few nights ago that I was in the Scottish Arts Club with them and they were all over the other members. It was extremely embarrassing.'

The man looked at Angus, who noticed now his eyes, which were bright with enthusiasm.

'I like dogs,' said the man. 'I might be able to help you out.'

Angus caught his breath. 'You mean you'd take one off my hands?'

'I'll take all six,' said the man. 'If you're happy to part with them.'

Angus felt a sudden, overwhelming euphoria wash over him. 'Well, that's very generous of you,' he began. 'All six . . .'

'Certainly,' said the man. 'I can take care of them for you. Willingly.'

Angus paused. The prospect was thrilling, of course, but he was a responsible dog-owner and one could hardly just hand six puppies over to a complete stranger. 'I'm sorry to raise this,' he said, 'but I've only just met you. I don't really know anything about you.'

'Of course,' said the man, stretching out to shake Angus's hand. 'Of course. Well let me introduce myself.'

They shook hands, and Angus felt, quite unmistakably, the pressure on his knuckle. A Mason! Well that was all right. If one could not entrust a puppy – or even six puppies – to a member of a Masonic lodge, then to whom could one entrust him, or indeed them?

'Here's my card,' said the man. 'It has all my details on it.'

Angus took the card and slipped it into his pocket. For the first time since the puppies had arrived in his flat he felt a free man again. I am no longer the owner of seven dogs, he said to himself; I am the owner of one, which is just about right.

'Would you like to take them now?' he asked. 'Or perhaps tomorrow morning?'

'Well, no time like the present,' said the man. 'If you help me get them on the leash, I'll take them off your hands.'

He began to marshal the puppies together. As they did so, Angus noticed that the man seemed to lift each one up as he put the leash on, as if to weigh it. How caring, thought Angus; a concern with birth weight and development.

99

32. Last Thoughts

When Matthew felt the first tug of the water – the one that led to his overbalancing – he thought nothing of it. His mind at the time was on something quite different: on the meal he had enjoyed in the restaurant overlooking the beach; and on the name of the West Australian wine they had so enjoyed. Cape something or other. Menthol? No, that was not it. Menotti? No, he was a composer. And hadn't he lived out near Gifford somewhere? Yesterday House? No, that was not it. Yester . . . Yes, that was it. And he wrote that opera that . . .

So might our thoughts drift from one thing to another, by the loosest of associations, at precisely the time that imminent disaster threatens to engulf us. Before he fell into the water, the last thing in Matthew's mind was the word 'Amahl', and then 'Night Visitors'. Then the sudden, overwhelming embrace of the warm water, swiftly rising to his chest, lifted him off his feet, covering him entirely so that he spluttered and struggled for breath.

Now he felt the real tug, as the rip tide seized him and moved him swiftly from the shore. Within a few seconds the distance between him and Elspeth, whom he could still make out in the darkness, on the beach, had increased to twenty yards. Then again the tug and the sense of travelling really quite quickly, away from the beach, out into the deeper water. There were waves, of course, which gave him an up-and-down movement, a bobbing, but which seemed to take him nowhere nearer the beach. As the initial shock subsided, he thought, I can swim with the waves, into the beach, but the movement of his arms seemed to make no difference at all to the direction in which he was travelling. His clothes seemed to be dragging him down. He kicked hard and remembered his shoes, abandoned on the sand, which made him think: how will I find them now? Curiously, for one in such a plight, he wondered about the spare pair in his suitcase. Or had he forgotten to pack them? And then he thought: I should not be thinking of these things at the moment.

Putting reflections on spare shoes out of his mind, he tried to remember what he had heard about rip tides. They took you out to sea, of course – he knew that; but there was something else, some bit of ancient knowledge that now he tried to bring to mind. Swim diagonally – across the tide – not against it. That was it. Then, when the power of the current was reduced, one could go in again. But now, far away from the beach, he found that the waves were confusing him. Where was the beach? In the direction of the lights, of course, but the lights seemed to come round again on both right and left. Perhaps the beach curved.

It was while he was puzzling over this that Matthew suddenly remembered the sharks. Coming from Scotland, where nature was, on the whole, benevolent, and where the most dangerous of creatures was the reclusive adder, or perhaps an aggressive Highland cow protecting her calf, he did not think of what might reasonably be expected to have an interest in stinging, biting or even eating him. And yet Australia was full of such creatures. The western taipan was the most dangerous of land-based snakes – and Australia had it. Then there were all those spiders, and the box jellyfish up in Queensland. Even the duck-billed platypus, so ostensibly lovable, had a poisonous spike concealed on its back legs and could cause a lot of damage. And then there were the Great White sharks, and this very beach was one on which attacks had occurred.

Matthew now remembered that one should never swim at night. Even the locals, braver than most, would never enter the water at night. And here he was, in the sharks' element, utterly at their mercy – although mercy was not a concept one associated with sharks. I am simply prey, he thought; a floating meal. Involuntarily, he drew his legs up to his chest in an attempt to make himself less of a target, but this served only to make him less buoyant and he had to kick downwards again to stay afloat. And with each kick, he thought, I'm sending a signal down through the water into the depths: here I am; this way.

Terror was now replaced – even if only for a short time – by relative calm. Matthew realised that he was going to die, and the thought, curiously, made him worry less about what he imagined to be in the water below him. He wondered now how quickly the end would come; would it be, as he imagined, like being hit by an express train, pushed through the water; or would it be painless, almost analgesic, as the system shut down after the first large bite? Perhaps it would not be analgesic so much as analeptic: perhaps consciousness of what was happening would be heightened. Time, they said, slowed down when one fell a great distance. Perhaps that happened too in the course of a shark attack.

He stopped struggling against the current and began to allow it to move him where it would. He was feeling a little bit colder now, although the water was still comfortably warm. At least I didn't fall into the North Sea, he thought. Had that happened, I would have had very little time before succumbing to the cold – about four minutes, was it not?

He looked up at the sky. Against the deep velvet blue, halfway to the horizon, was the Southern Cross, as if suspended in the sky like a decoration; a symbol of this country that he had hardly yet got to know; which had welcomed him so warmly and was now dispatching him. At least I've seen the Southern Cross before I die, thought Matthew. At least there's that.

And then he felt something brush against him, against his shoulder. He let out a groan, a sound of anguish that was quickly swallowed by the waves and the empty air. Phosphorescence glistened on the surface, and then disappeared. A black shape. A fin.

33. The Longest Hour

Provided that they survive the experience – which unfortunately many do not – those attacked by sharks present us with a rather surprising account of what it is to face imminent annihilation in the jaws of a predator. Some describe feeling anger at the creature attacking them – understandable, perhaps, in the circumstances; others describe a feeling of calm verging on acceptance; yet others speak of an overwhelming determination to survive at all costs. This last reaction is perhaps the best response, as it can spur people on to heroic efforts to repel the shark with blows and kicks. And if these are directed at the sensitive part of the shark – the nose, which contains the shark's navigation and sensory organs – then such blows can be successful in persuading the shark to desist. After all, it is thought that we do not taste all that agreeable to sharks, and while they might go to more effort with a succulent seal, a surfer in a wet suit may be a less attractive proposition.

Not that Matthew was wearing a wet suit. He was clad only in the clothes in which he had gone for dinner at the restaurant on Cottesloe Beach, minus his shoes, of course, which he had dropped on the sand before he started to paddle. When he felt the shark brush against him, though, he felt the sleeve of his shirt rip, exposing more flesh to the sea. He was calm enough to know that this was not a good development: an exposed arm was a more tempting target than one that was clothed.

He thought that, at least. Beyond that, his reaction was neither to fight off his attacker nor to spend his remaining seconds on this earth in the contemplation of the life that he had led; in thoughts of his new bride, his gallery, his family, Edinburgh, his flat in India Street, and so on. He thought of none of these, because he lost consciousness. The human mind, faced with its end, can simply blot out the unacceptable; refuse to believe what seems to be the inevitable. Matthew's mind did that. But just before that happened, he opened his eyes wide to the sight of the creature approaching him in the water; to its fin, which was rather floppy, he noticed, and to its curious beak-like nose. Beak. Dolphins have beaks.

He became briefly unconscious, possibly through relief, possibly through shock, possibly through a combination of both. But his unconsciousness did not last long, as he was partly aware of being in the water and being propelled by this creature. He felt waves break over him; he felt the tug of water; and then he felt sand beneath his feet, just under his toes. And with one final tumble, he felt himself pushed into the line of surf right at the edge of the beach. There was foam; there was water in his mouth; there was sand in his nostrils. He spluttered; he dragged himself up onto the dry sand, which stuck to his wet skin like a layer of icing on a cake. Never had the feel of the earth, of its sand, been more welcome.

He lay down on the beach, gasping. Then he rolled over, and with his head cushioned by the sand he stared up at the sky, the star-studded sky that he had looked at from the water and which he had decided, then and there, he loved so much. It was so precious, as was this smell of seaweed, this sand all over him, this sound of surf. Everything, everything was precious beyond price.

He remained there for several minutes, gradually taking in what had happened to him. I almost drowned, he thought. I was almost attacked by a shark that was not there. It was a dolphin, and it pushed me . . . He paused. It could not have happened. He simply could not have been saved by a dolphin. It was ridiculous; the sort of thing that happened in Greek myths, not in real life, here on this beach in Western Australia, in a world of aeroplanes and electricity. This was a miracle – a sheer miracle – and miracles simply did not happen.

Rising to his feet he brushed the sand off his face and hands. Relief at still being alive had obscured any thought of Elspeth. She would think him drowned; he would have to get back to her as soon as possible. He glanced at his watch; the manufacturer's claim of waterproofing had proved to be well founded, and it had survived the ocean. He remembered that they had left the restaurant at nine-thirty, and they could only have walked for about ten minutes or so before he had started his ill-fated paddle. That meant that he had been caught in the rip tide at about twenty to ten; it was now ten-thirty. He had been in the water for almost an hour.

He looked about him. The beach was shrouded in darkness, but a hundred yards or so behind him were the dunes, and beyond that, blazing with light, the long ribbon of houses that lined the coastal road. He would go up there and get somebody to telephone the police, or the coastguard, or whoever it was who would now be searching for him.

Then an unsettling thought struck him. What if Elspeth had tried to save him? What if, unbeknown to him, she had gone in the water after him and had herself been swept away by the same rip tide? What if she had met, instead of a friendly dolphin, an unfriendly Great White shark? What if he was the widower rather than she the widow?

Matthew began to run across the beach in the direction of the dunes. Clambering his way up to the top, he grasped at the tufts of grass planted across the slopes for coastal protection. The grass was sharp and cut his hands, but he did not care; he had to get to a telephone at all costs.

He reached the top of the dune, still holding on to some of the grass he had torn off during his climb. There was tarmac under his feet, there were houses before him, there was a car cruising up the road towards him, its lights casting a pool of liquid yellow before it. The car stopped and a policeman emerged.

There was a shout. 'Can't you see the signs? Keep off the dune defences. Can't you read, mate?'

Matthew smiled. 'Sorry. I've just been rescued by a dolphin. Sorry.'

The policeman took a step back and muttered into the radio. 'Picking up a confused male, late twenties, sleeping rough. Possible drug-related hallucinations. Query psychiatric case.'

The irritation Bruce had felt in the shower abated slightly as he dressed for the party at Watson Cooke's flat in Clarence Street. It was always mollifying to stand in front of a mirror, as he liked to do, and observe oneself dressing; a calming activity, rather like meditation, he thought, but with a bit more point to it. Bruce towelled himself dry, then applied a new body butter for men that he had recently seen recommended in *Men's Health*. He had been intrigued by the contents of this preparation, which contained not only vitamins A and E, but sodium hyaluronate and arnica extract; and he had been taken with the smell, which was of lemon and sage, with a hint of sandalwood. This body butter, Bruce had read, would 'make dry skin history', and although he did not think that he yet suffered from dry skin, it was a good policy to nip history in the bud before it had the chance to occur.

Bruce stood before the mirror and rubbed the greasy aromatic substance over his skin. Once he had applied enough, he took a quick final glance at the sheer sculpted perfection of the image in the glass, and then donned the new pair of boxer shorts he had bought through a *Country Life* catalogue, *Gifts for Men*. These had salmon fishing scenes printed on them – not for everyone, of course, but Bruce thought they were rather becoming, and indeed on him, reflected in the mirror, he thought them almost perfect. Next, his shirt – an Oxford cut-away collar in blue – his blue Levis and a pair of brown topsiders. Then, after a quick application of the clove-scented hair gel he liked to use, he was ready for anything that Clarence Street could throw at him.

Clarence Street was further down the hill, and although it was clearly one up on St Stephen Street, it was several rungs below Howe Street, where Julia had her flat. Howe Street had that classical quality that the central New Town enjoyed and which faded into less confident proportions on its fringes. Bruce, as a surveyor, understood this well, as classical dignity was directly translatable into higher prices. Clarence Street was all right, he thought, but it was not Saxe-Coburg Place, which lay a block or two away to the north; perfectly respectable, but hardly stylish. A good place, thought Bruce, to begin; although he himself had begun in Dundonald Street and had now, effortlessly it seemed, climbed to the heights of Howe Street.

Watson Cooke! Bruce muttered the name to himself as he left the flat and began the short walk down to Clarence Street. Well, Mr Watson Cooke, we shall see. I shall have to remind you that Julia and I are an established couple, engaged (even if the announcement had not yet appeared in *The Scotsman*), and therefore any invitation to attend a party in Clarence Street, or anywhere else, should be addressed to both of us. It was like inviting the Queen to dinner and forgetting to invite the Duke of Edinburgh, a breach of protocol which no doubt Watson Cooke in his ignorance might make, but which nobody with any style or savoir faire would ever commit. That is what Bruce thought, and as he rounded the corner of Howe Street where, at basement level, the late Madame Doubtfire once had her second-hand clothing emporium – she who claimed to have danced before the Tsar – he muttered to himself: Watson Cookie, Cookie Watson, Watson the Cook, Watty Cook, Kooky Watty (what's his bag, *je me demande*), Cocky Watson. He smiled. Poor Watson Cooke, what a minger of a name. Typical.

He decided to follow the slightly longer route to Clarence Street, which involved walking through the bisecting radial of Circus Place and then along North West Circus Place to the corner of St Stephen Street. It was a fine evening, and Bruce noticed, with satisfaction, that he attracted one or two admiring looks as he made his way. Entirely understandable, he thought; indeed *he* rather admired the self-control of those who wanted to look and admire, but who allowed themselves only the most surreptitious of glances. He felt generous, and wanted to say to people, 'Go on, admire. Just admire. You may not be able to touch, but you can certainly look.' They could feast their eyes on him, whichever sex they were; they could even give him the look; he did not mind in the slightest. He was not selfish. In fact, he felt like something in the National Gallery of Scotland: an artefact of public beauty.

At the entrance to The Bailie, at the corner of St Stephen Street, Bruce hesitated for a moment. It was now about ten past nine and this meant that he had twenty minutes or so in hand before he should present himself in Clarence Street; he certainly did not want to arrive early and be thought to be too keen. Bruce was, in general, keen not to appear keen.

He went down the steps into the bar. There was a fairly large crowd inside, seated on red leather benches or standing about the circular bar of polished mahogany that dominated the room. It was, Bruce observed, the normal crowd for this part of town at this time in the evening, and as he ran his eye over the customers he recognised one or two people. These were casual acquaintances, though, and Bruce had no particular desire to speak to them. One of them, in particular, he wanted to avoid, as he was always going on about his golf handicap. Each time that Bruce had met him – in no matter what circumstances – he had talked about getting his golf handicap down. Bruce tried to remember what it was. Seven?

He paid for his drink and slipped the change into his pocket. It was then that he saw the man standing beside him looking at him, frankly, appraisingly. Hello! thought Bruce.

35. The Seriously Sexy Face of Scotland

Under the appreciative gaze of the urbane stranger at the bar, Bruce thought: these chaps find me attractive, which is quite understandable; who wouldn't? But sorry, I don't play for your team! The difficulty, he felt, was conveying this delicate social message without appearing to be hostile. And sometimes the message was just not received, as it seemed that some people took the view that one never knew one's luck. That could be awkward, and occasionally one just had to be blunt.

He took a sip of his beer and, as he did so, cast an eye around the room, studiously avoiding looking in the stranger's direction.

Suddenly the stranger addressed him. 'Bruce Anderson?'

Bruce gave a start. He had not expected this. 'Yes. That's me.'

The stranger put his glass down on the surface of the bar and extended a hand. 'Nick McNair. Remember? Morrison's. I was two years above you. We were in the photography club together. You came with me to take a photograph of that eagle up in Glen Lyon. Remember? The geography teacher drove us up there in his clapped-out Land Rover. Remember?'

Bruce looked at the other man and it came back, not vividly, or clearly, but in patches. Crouching in the rain holding a tripod for the older boy. Feeling the rain trickle down the back of one's neck. Brushing away the midges.

'Of course. That's some time ago, isn't it? Sorry that I didn't recognise you. You know how . . .'

'How it is. Of course I do. I doubt if I'd recognise half the people in my year if I saw them again.'

Bruce smiled. 'There are some you'd want to forget. Some you'd like to remember.'

'People remember you, though, Bruce. They wouldn't forget.'

Bruce looked away in modesty. Why would they remember him?

'You were a real looker then.'

Bruce blushed. It was true, he thought, but did one want it spelled out, particularly by Nick McNair?

'Thanks.'

'Not at all,' Nick said. 'In fact, that's the business I'm in these days. Photography. I do adverts.'

Bruce looked up. 'Magazines? That sort of thing?'

Nick nodded. 'Yes, for my sins. Fashion photography, it's called. I went down south, you see, to London and did a course at St Martins. Had a few lean years taking wedding snaps, that sort of thing. Then I got lucky with a series of shots in *Tatler* and *Vogue*. After that, no problem.'

Bruce listened with interest. Who would have thought it: from taking photographs of eagles in Perthshire to international fashion photography? He looked at Nick McNair. There was nothing special about him, and it seemed to Bruce fundamentally unfair that he should lead such a life while he, Bruce, was stuck behind in Edinburgh.

'Where are you based?' Bruce asked.

'Right here,' said Nick. 'I have a flat in Edinburgh. Down in Leith, in one of those new places, you know. Infinity pool on the eighth floor.'

Bruce raised an eyebrow. 'Infinity pool?'

'Yup. Not that I use it all that much. But it's great when you do.'

Bruce swallowed. 'It's your own? Just for your . . . your flat?'

'Yup.'

There followed a short period of silence. Then Nick reached for something in his pocket and handed it over to Bruce. A card. Nick McNair, Photographer. Fashion. Cars. Places.

Nick was studying Bruce, who found it rather disconcerting. Is he? Bruce asked himself. He had an infinity pool, after all. And St Martins. 'It's fortuitous our meeting,' Nick said. 'I've been given a big job by the Scottish Government. A bit of a change from women draping themselves over cars and such like. It's a big project on developing the Scottish image abroad.'

Bruce nodded knowingly. 'Promotion?' he asked. 'Scotland the brand?'

Nick warmed to the theme. 'Dead right. They want to get the idea over that Scotland is somehow . . . well, not to put too fine a point on it, sexy.'

Bruce smiled. That's where I come in, he thought.

'And it just occurred to me,' Nick continued, 'that this is where you might come in.'

'Could be,' said Bruce. 'What's your angle?'

'Well, we need a face, a body, the whole deal. We need somebody who would look good in posters. Somebody who can wear a kilt and not look like Harry Lauder. We need to have somebody who says: Scotland.'

'Scotland,' said Bruce, and smiled.

Nick raised his glass. 'I can't guarantee anything at this stage,' he said. 'I have to go back to the clients and show them the images. But you might just be the answer to my prayers. I've been hanging about for weeks looking for somebody who looks just right. Trying different bars, looking for a face. I've had some funny looks in the process, but it's work.'

'You could be misunderstood,' said Bruce.

Nick shrugged. 'Photographers have thick skins. We get used to going about sticking our lenses into people's faces. You get used to it.'

'When . . .' Bruce began.

'When can we get started? Well, I need to do an exploratory shoot – we could do that any time. Tomorrow? And then I have a conference with the agency people and they see whether you're right. I'm sure there'll be no problem there.

'They want an open face, good looks, a hint of West Coast and *Braveheart*. In other words, the sort of face that projects a dynamic, good-looking country that's . . . well, also a bit sexy. In other words, you.'

Bruce looked at his watch. 'All right. I do dynamic. I also do sexy. I'll get in touch with you tomorrow.' He took the card out of his pocket. 'This is the studio address?'

'That's it. I want morning light, so ten o'clock?'

'Perfect,' said Bruce. 'But listen, I have to go. I'm going to a party with my fiancée.' He thought that he might just mention Julia, before the photo shoot. 'Round the corner. Clarence Street.'

'I used to live on Clarence Street,' said Nick. 'Before I emigrated to Leith. Whose place are you going to?'

'Watson Cooke,' said Bruce.

'Oh,' said Nick. 'A rugby player. I thought about him for a beer advertisement I was doing once, but decided against.'

That was all the information Nick offered on Watson Cooke. Bruce took his leave and walked down St Stephen Street. As he walked past the window of a small shop, he glanced at his reflection in the pane of glass.

He saw the face of Scotland looking back at him.

36. Watson the Watsonian

Watson Cooke occupied a first-floor flat in Clarence Street. His front door, recently painted with a thick black gloss paint, had a small brass plate on it on which 'Watson Cooke' had been engraved. To the right of the door, a folded piece of paper had been stuck, which, when unfolded and read by Bruce, bore the message: Watson, Please don't forget to put Nancy's rubbish out on Wednesday, bearing in mind that she won't be back from Brussels until Friday. You're a trouper. Thanks, Kirsty.

Bruce refolded and replaced the scrap of paper. So Watson Cooke was a trouper. And where exactly does he troupe? He reached for the old-fashioned bell and gave it a firm tug; too firm in fact, as he heard the bell chime loudly at the same time as he felt the wire within give way. This released the brass bell-pull lever, which flopped uselessly out of its housing. Quickly he pushed the end of the wire back in and tried to stuff the lever back; to no avail. Then the door opened.

A tall well-built young man, somewhere in his late twenties, stood in the doorway in front of Bruce.

'Watson?' asked Bruce, stretching out a hand. 'I'm Bruce Anderson.'

Watson looked at Bruce and frowned. He seemed puzzled. 'Oh, Bruce . . . Yes.' He glanced at the protruding bell-pull. 'No, don't touch that again. I'll get it fixed.'

Bruce realised that further explanation was necessary. 'I'm Julia's . . .'

Watson's frown deepened. 'Did Julia . . . ?' He turned to face the hall, where several people were standing, drinks in hand.

'You are expecting me, aren't you?' Bruce asked. 'Julia said that there was a party.'

Watson now smiled. 'Yes, there is. Of course. Come in . . . Sorry, what was your name again?'

'Bruce.'

'Oh. Right. Well, come in. No, just leave the bell, I can get it fixed. The party's just started. Julia's through in the kitchen, I think.' He gestured towards the back of the hall and then, as Bruce entered, closed the door behind him.

'Nice place . . .' Bruce began, but Watson had walked away and begun to talk to a group near the door to what looked like a sitting room. Nice welcome, thought Bruce, mentally rehearsing what he would say to Julia. Your friend, Watson, made me feel seriously *bienvenu, n'est-ce pas* . . . He moved in the direction indicated by his host and looked through the kitchen door. Julia was there, alone, arranging savoury crackers on a plate. She looked up as Bruce appeared in the doorway.

'Oh, there you are, Brucie.' She flicked a strand of hair from her forehead. 'Great party, isn't it?'

Bruce moved over to stand beside her. He looked down at the crackers. Was this the best that Watson Cooke could do when it came to snacks? 'I wouldn't know about that,' he said. 'I've just arrived.'

'Well it is,' said Julia, returning to her task. 'It's really great. Watson has some very interesting friends.'

Bruce's lips twisted down at the edges. 'Yes, sure. And the dinner?'

'A really nice restaurant. Watson knew the chap who owned it.'

'Oh, did he?' Bruce sneered.

'Yes. He did.'

'And who was there?' Bruce asked.

Julia hesitated, only for the briefest moment, but Bruce noticed. 'A friend of Watson's. And me. That's all.'

Bruce knew immediately that she was lying. He reached for a can of beer that was on the table and opened it. He looked out of the window behind her. It was still light, and he could see the roofs of the street behind; a man standing at a window, the sky above, the last of the evening sun on the clouds. She was lying to him, and he knew at that moment that there was something between her and Watson Cooke. It had never occurred to him that she would even contemplate looking at another man when she had him, but she had. And she had looked at Watson Cooke.

He turned away. 'Good,' he said. 'I'm glad you enjoyed yourself.' Then he left the kitchen and went back into the hall. He did not see how Julia reacted; he did not want to look at her.

Watson Cooke was not in the hall, and so Bruce went through to the sitting room. There were about twenty people in the room, some sitting, some standing. The room was a large one and so there was no sense of its being overcrowded. One or two people looked at Bruce as he entered and one young woman, standing near the door, smiled at him. Bruce ignored her.

'Watson?'

Watson Cooke looked round. 'Oh. Yes. Hi.' He turned to the man he had been talking to and introduced Bruce. 'Sorry, what was your name again?'

Bruce grinned. 'Bruce. I told you.'

Watson laughed. 'Yes, sorry about that.' He gestured to his head. 'One game of rugby too many. Memory gets a bit mixed up in the rucks.'

Bruce raised an eyebrow. 'Rugby? Do you play these days?'

The man to whom Watson Cooke had been talking now smiled. 'Watson has a Scottish cap.'

Bruce swallowed. 'Oh . . .'

'Only the Scottish schoolboy squad,' said Watson modestly. 'I played against Ireland at Lansdowne Park. We won, actually.'

'But you almost got into the Scottish squad a couple of years later,' said the other man. 'Come on, Wattie. No false modesty.' He turned to Bruce. 'He captained Watson's when he was at school. Then he played for Watsonians.'

Bruce took a sip from his can of beer. 'You were a Watsonian, Watson?'

Watson had not been listening. 'What?'

'You played for Watsonians?'

'Yes. Watson's. Then Watsonians.'

There followed a silence. Then Watson asked, 'Do you play, Bruce?'

Bruce felt the moist cold of the beer can against his hand. 'Used to,' he said. 'But these days, you know how it is.'

'Injured?' asked Watson.

'Engaged,' said Bruce.

Nobody said anything. Bruce had been avoiding Watson's eyes; now he looked up and saw that his host was staring at him. 'Is she here?' Watson asked.

Bruce felt his heart beating wildly within him. Watson Cooke was taller than he was. 'In the kitchen, actually. Julia. You know her, don't you? You had dinner with her tonight.' He held Watson Cooke's gaze. I'm in the right here, thought Bruce. He's the one who should be feeling it.

The other man present, sensing the undercurrent of feeling, shifted awkwardly on his feet. 'I must get myself another drink,' he said, and turned away.

Watson continued to stare at Bruce. 'What position did you play?' he asked.

'I said that I was engaged. Engaged to Julia.'

Watson laughed. 'Yes, sure. I heard you. But you said that you played rugby. Who did you play for?'

'Morrison's,' muttered Bruce.

'We beat them,' said Watson Cooke. 'Watson's beat Morrison's. Always.'

37. Life Lines

Olive had come to play house. From her point of view, the presence of Tofu did not enhance the afternoon, as she enjoyed a very uncomfortable relationship with Bertie's friend. In fact, as she told her friends in the class, she hated Tofu like poison itself, to use her carefully chosen expression, and let pass no opportunity to undermine him. Sometimes her goading seemed to pass over him unnoticed; on other occasions, a carefully prepared dart might just hit home, as on the occasion that Olive, having just read a manual on palmistry, offered to read everyone's palms.

There was no shortage of takers, and Olive had started with Merlin, a boy whom she found less offensive than Tofu but considerably less attractive than Bertie (whom she had decided she would eventually marry in fifteen years' time, when they both reached the age of twenty-one). Merlin's hand was stretched out and Olive took it, peering carefully at the lines on his palm.

'You will be very rich and you will live in New York,' said Olive, pointing to several converging lines. 'That's a really good palm, Merlin. You're lucky.'

Hiawatha was, somewhat reluctantly, given a reading. 'You will eventually stop smelling,' said Olive. 'You will be given a big present of soap. That's what your palm says.'

Hiawatha seemed reasonably pleased with this and went off smiling. Now it was Bertie's turn.

'You've got some very good lines here, Bertie,' said Olive. 'You have a very good life ahead of you. You will meet a nice girl – you have probably already met her. That's what this line says. And then you will marry her and have lots of children. That will be when you're twenty-one. And this line here says that her name will probably begin with an O. That's all it says, so we can't be sure.'

Bertie said nothing, but withdrew his hand. Now it was Tofu who came up.

'If you're so clever, read my palm,' he said, stretching out his hand.

'I will,' said Olive. 'Hold it still, Tofu.'

There was a sharp intake of breath from Olive.

'What do you see?' asked Tofu. 'Am I going to be rich too? Like Merlin?'

Olive looked at him with pity. 'I don't know if I should tell you this,' she said. 'Maybe I shouldn't. It's best not to know some things, you know. I'm really sorry, Tofu. I'm sorry that I've been so unkind to you. This is not a time for being nasty to one another.'

'What do you mean?' snapped Tofu. 'Is there something wrong with my palm?'

The others, clustered around in a small knot, were silent. 'Everything,' said Olive. 'It's the saddest palm I've ever seen in all my experience.'

'One day,' snorted Tofu. 'This is the first time you've done this.'

'You may say that,' said Olive. 'And I won't hold it against you. Not since you're not going to be here much longer.'

'Bad luck, Tofu,' said Merlin.

'What do you mean?' asked Tofu. He was less confident now, and his voice wavered.

'Well, since you really want me to tell you,' said Olive, 'I shall.' She reached again for Tofu's hand and pointed to lines in the middle. 'You see this line here? That's your life line, Tofu, and you'll see that it's really short. So that means you're not going to last long. Maybe another couple of weeks. No more than that.'

'Rubbish,' said Tofu. But he did not sound very convinced.

'You can call it rubbish if you like,' said Olive. 'But that won't make it any less true. And there's another thing. You're going to die painfully, Tofu. See that line there – that means you're going to die painfully.'

If Olive had not embellished her reading with this last qualification, Tofu would probably have believed her. But this was one prediction too far, and Tofu had seized her own hand, turned it over, and pointed to a line on her palm. 'And what about you,

Olive?' he had shouted. 'Look. See this line here? You know what that means? It means that somebody's going to spit at you. There, and it's come true!'

Bertie wished that Tofu and Olive would not fight so much, and in particular that Tofu would stop spitting at her. But try as he might to make conciliatory remarks, they ignored his peace-making efforts and remained as bitter enemies as they ever had been. So having the two of them in his flat was not Bertie's idea of a promising social mix.

'We're going to play house,' announced Olive, looking defiantly at Tofu. 'I'm going to be the mummy. Bertie's going to be the daddy. And Tofu can be the marriage counsellor.'

'What's that?' asked Tofu.

'You don't know what a marriage counsellor is?' asked Olive.

'Neither do I,' said Bertie.

Olive sighed. 'It would take too long to explain to you, Tofu. You'll just have to make up your mind: do you want to play house or not?'

'No,' said Tofu. 'I don't.'

Olive turned to Bertie. 'And you, Bertie? You want to play, don't you?'

Bertie swallowed. 'Well . . .'

'That's fine then,' said Olive. 'Bertie and I will play house. You can do what you like, Tofu. We don't care.'

'I don't know, Olive,' Bertie began. 'Tofu is here to play too . . .'

Olive was not to be distracted. 'Don't worry about him, Bertie. Now let's pretend it's dinner time and you've come back from the office. I'll ask you how your day was and then I'll make you some tea. There, I've put the kettle on, and there, listen, it's already boiled. How many spoons of sugar do you take, Bertie?'

Tofu had been watching attentively. Now he interrupted with a sneer. 'If you were married to him, Olive, you would know. You don't get mummies asking daddies how much sugar they take. They know that already.'

Olive ignored this. 'There, Bertie dear. Two spoons of sugar. And now I'll cook your mince and tatties. Look, there it is. That's your plate and that's mine. What shall we talk about while we're having dinner? Or should we just sit there, like real married people?'

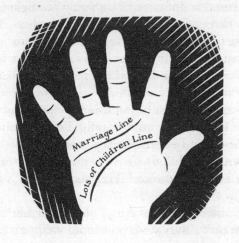

Marriage Line

Lots of Children Line

38. Stuart is Stupefied

'How did all that go?' asked Stuart when he came home that evening. Irene, who was standing in the kitchen looking pensively out of the window, rolled her eyes heavenwards. 'Not a conspicuous success,' she said. 'As you know, Bertie had two guests this afternoon.'

'That's nice for him,' said Stuart. 'I've always thought that he needed a few more friends.'

Irene looked at her husband disapprovingly. The trouble with Stuart, she thought, was that he had an outdated, possibly even reactionary vision of childhood. Childhood was no longer simply play and picnics; childhood was a vital time for potential self-enhancement, a time when one could develop those talents that would stand one in good stead in adult life. She had explained this to Stuart many times before, but he seemed incapable of grasping it. 'Friends are not the issue,' she said. 'Bertie gets plenty of opportunities for social interaction, both in the home, with you and me, and in the classroom, with his classmates. The issue with friends is not how many, but who.'

'Well, he seems happy enough with Tofu's company,' said Stuart. 'He seems a pleasant enough boy – in his way.'

Irene sighed. Stuart did not get it; he did not get this, and there were many other things that he did not get. Now she adopted the tone of voice that she used when explaining the obvious either to Bertie or to her husband, an *ex cathedra* tone redolent of the more condescending type of politician trying to avoid responsibility for some failure or other. 'Tofu is completely unsuitable,' she intoned. 'There is simply too much unresolved psychopathology there. He has a passive-aggressive personality, as you may, or may not, have noticed. He's the worst possible influence on Bertie.'

'I was just making an observation,' Stuart said meekly. 'That's all.'

'Well, it wasn't a very perceptive one,' snapped Irene. 'I don't know, I really don't. Bertie seems to be doing so well with Dr Fairbairn and now . . .'

Stuart raised an eyebrow. 'Problems?'

Irene spoke carefully. She sounded insouciant – perhaps excessively so. 'I meant to tell you. Hugo is going to Aberdeen. Very soon. Bertie has one more session and then that will be that.'

Stuart seemed relieved to hear the news. 'Well, he's had a long time with the good doctor. And I think he's a bit fed up with going along there. He'll be pretty pleased to hear the news.'

Irene's eyes narrowed. 'That,' she said, 'is the very last thing I had in mind. Interruptions in therapy are extremely counterproductive. We must try and arrange as smooth a transition as possible.'

'You mean . . .'

'Yes. Hugo is handing his practice on to a new therapist. A highly-thought-of Australian, I gather. He'll be fully briefed by Hugo. Bertie will be in safe hands.'

Stuart stood in silence, looking out of the window. He was remembering his conversation with Bertie in Dundas Street, the conversation in which the issue of joining the cub scouts had been raised. Did Irene know about this, he wondered; and, if not, should he raise it with her?

He turned away from the window to face Irene. 'Perhaps we should ask Bertie what he wants,' he said. 'He's old enough now to have views.'

'I know very well what Bertie wants,' said Irene coldly. 'I spend a lot of time with him, you know.'

Stuart was not sure if there was an element of censure in this last remark. Perhaps I am a failure as a father, he thought. But I don't seem to get a look-in. She decides, all the time. I try, but she decides.

He took a deep breath. 'So what does he want then?' he asked. She had not heard him. 'What?'

He repeated the question, louder now. 'What does Bertie want? You said that you knew what his views were. Well, what does he want?'

Irene opened her hands; a gesture to be made when answering the obvious. 'He wants to . . . He wants to learn Italian. He wants to go to yoga. And I suspect that underneath it all he enjoys his psychotherapy sessions. And, oh, he wants to have a train set. Which he'll get one of these days.'

'No,' said Stuart. 'He does not like learning Italian. He hates yoga. And he endures psychotherapy because he has no alternative.'

Irene looked down at the floor. This would pass. But Stuart was warming to his theme now. 'And as for what he actually wants to do,' he went on, 'Bertie confided in me that he wants to join the cub scouts.'

Irene gave a cry of triumph. 'Oh, I know all about that,' she said. 'That came up this afternoon. Our little friend Tofu announced over tea that he wanted Bertie to join a club with him. So I asked what it was and was told that it was the Young Liberal Democrats! Can you believe it? So a bit of probing and the whole thing collapsed and it emerged it was some cub scout pack in Morningside and that the Young Liberal Democrats was Tofu's idea of what I might approve of. Isn't that rich?'

As Stuart listened, he felt his sorrow grow. Sorrow. Sorrow that the boys had felt that they had to come up with such a ridiculous invention. Sorrow that Irene could not see what was so obvious.

'But he must join,' he said. 'It's a wonderful organisation. It's exactly what he needs.'

Irene raised an eyebrow. 'The matter's closed,' she said. 'I'm not having Bertie joining any paramilitary organisations. And I've told him that.'

Stuart let out an involuntary gasp. 'Paramilitary organisation? Are you aware . . . even vaguely aware of what scouting is all about?'

'Self-confessed male bonding,' Irene snapped. 'Reinforcement of primitive male rituals. It starts with the cub scouts and ends with . . . ends with Muirfield Golf Club. Is that what you want for our son, Stuart? Is it?'

Stuart said nothing. For a moment he looked at Irene in blank amazement, and then he walked smartly to the kitchen door and called down the hall. 'Bertie! Come along here, my boy. I want to talk to you about the cub scouts and when we can get you started.'

'Stuart!'

'Shut your face.'

39. The Teacup Storm Revisited

Domenica Macdonald had always been a believer in good-neighbourliness. Having spent her early years in the same Scotland Street flat in which she now lived, she understood the ethos which underlay the communal life of a Scottish tenement: you did your duty by those who lived on the same stair – you washed the steps according to the rota, you cut the green when it needed cutting (and you took on the turn of anybody who was ill or infirm), and you avoided arguments with your fellow residents. It was, she reflected, very much the same code of communal living that applied in any society in any country, and perhaps the most universal and the most important part of it was this: don't pick fights.

44 Scotland Street had always been at the equable end of the spectrum when it came to neighbourly relations. Domenica had her views on the Pollock family downstairs – she found Irene almost too ridiculous to be true – but there had never been any open hostility between them. With the two young men on the ground floor she got on perfectly well, although they kept very much to themselves; and as for the flat in the basement – that was something of a mystery: it belonged to an accountant in Dundee who used it occasionally when he came to Edinburgh on business, but he was never seen by anybody.

It was natural that Domenica should have more contact with the other flat on her landing, the flat currently owned by Antonia Collie. When Bruce had owned that flat, Domenica had enjoyed cordial relations with him, even though she had immediately and correctly identified him as, in her words, an eighty-four horse-power narcissist. She had liked Pat, Bruce's flatmate, and had sympathised with her when the young student found herself falling for her well-coiffed landlord. Indeed, Pat had become a good friend, in spite of the forty years that separated them in age, and she missed her now that she had gone back to live with her parents in the Grange. It was only the other side of town, not much more than forty minutes' walk away, and yet it was not a friendship that would survive geographical separation. And naturally so; Pat had a circle of her own age – and now that Matthew was married she would be less in evidence in Dundas Street, where she had worked closely with Matthew at his gallery.

When Antonia had moved in, Domenica had imagined that they would see a great deal of one another, but it had not worked out. Antonia had changed since the days when they were close; she seemed preoccupied with her novel about the early Scottish saints and her conversation often turned on the subject of men, the very topic where Domenica felt Antonia's judgement was weakest.

But what had caused the biggest rift in the relationship – at least from Domenica's point of view – was the matter of the blue Spode teacup that Antonia had stolen – there was no other word to describe it – from Domenica when she had flat-sat for her and that was now somewhere in Antonia's kitchen, along with heaven knows how much other stolen crockery. After all, one who stole a teacup from a neighbour would surely not be above stealing crockery from all sorts of places – including Jenners tea room and the North British Hotel (currently demotically known as the Balmoral Hotel).

Now, however, a heaven-sent opportunity had arisen to set right this gross wrong. It had arisen because Antonia had asked Domenica if she would be in to receive a delivery that she was expecting the following morning.

'These people are hopeless,' said Antonia. She used the expression 'these people' to refer to anybody of whom she disapproved. 'These people are bad losers,' she had said of some politicians after they had been defeated in the Scottish parliamentary elections. And then she had said, 'These people certainly like their whisky,' pointing to a picture of a political party conference in Aviemore. It was a useful expression, which she was now using in relation to a firm of deliverers who refused to disclose when they would deliver a new armchair that she had ordered from a furniture catalogue.

'I shall be out all morning,' Antonia said to Domenica. 'And so I wondered if I could leave a note on my door asking them to deliver to you if they arrive in the morning. That is if you're going to be in.'

'I shall be in,' said Domenica helpfully.

Antonia smiled, and handed her the key to the flat. 'I thought as much.'

Domenica wondered how she should take that. Did Antonia mean to suggest that she, Domenica, was bound to be in because she never received any invitations to go out? Or had nowhere to go, even uninvited? How often did Antonia herself go out?

'I'm out quite a lot, of course,' Domenica found herself saying. 'You know how it is. But, as it happens, I shall be in tomorrow morning. Until about twelve. Then I shall be going out for lunch with friends.'

There was no such meeting yet arranged, and Domenica felt a bit petty inventing it on the spot. But she would be going out, she decided; she would telephone her friend Dilly Emslie and meet her for lunch in the Scottish National Portrait Gallery. So she had not exactly told a lie. And anyway, it was Antonia's fault, with that silly implication that Domenica had a thin time of it socially. If you make that sort of comment, then people will feel it necessary to retaliate.

'Thank you,' said Antonia, adding, 'I know how busy you are.'

Domenica pursed her lips. 'Yes.'

'So if you wouldn't mind getting them to put it in the sitting room, next to that green chair of mine. I've put four of those round castors out on the floor – ask them to rest the legs on those – you know how these people are. They don't care a jot about your floors.'

Domenica took the key and nodded. 'I'll do my best,' she said. Then she paused. 'Going anywhere interesting?'

Antonia looked away. 'National Library,' she said. 'It's my novel. I'm on to something.'

Domenica waited for more, but nothing came. The Scottish saints, in Antonia's hands, were a strange and secretive quantity, quite unlike other saints, with their bland and worthy lives. The early Scottish saints were, Antonia had hinted, ever so slightly bitchy, but in the nicest possible way, of course. Had anything changed?

40. A Delivery that Leads to Temptation

Temptation comes in many forms: the bottle, the beguiling face, the tray of chocolates – these can all lure any of us off the path of rectitude which often seems, if not steep, then at least rather dull. For Domenica, on whom any of the above forms of temptation would have little effect – even if the bottle, in the shape of a slightly larger helping of Crabbie's Green Ginger Wine, would occasionally beckon

– temptation now presented itself in the shape of the key to Antonia's flat. Antonia had pressed this into her hand with the request to supervise the delivery of a new green armchair, and Domenica, quite naturally, had agreed. But when, as she sat drinking her morning coffee, she saw the key lying innocently on the kitchen table it occurred to her that she now had unfettered access to Antonia's flat, at least for that morning, and that this meant that she could retrieve the blue Spode teacup that Antonia had stolen from her and which she knew was in use next door.

That was her initial thought and, at first blush, it seemed a perfectly reasonable thing to do. The teacup remained her property and surely an owner of property was fully entitled to vindicate her right to it wherever and whenever the opportunity to do so arose. To enter the flat, then, with the sole purpose of claiming what was hers, was not house-breaking or anything remotely similar – it was merely recovering unlawfully purloined property. The act of going into the flat was akin, she thought, to the technical violation of national sovereignty which occurs when one country crosses the border of another in order to deal with a previous unlawful incursion. That was clear. And if the United Nations and the whole corpus of international law allowed that, then surely she would be entitled to go in pursuit of her teacup. And yet, and yet . . .

The problem with entering the flat for the purpose of retrieving the cup was that it would be a breach of trust. Antonia had given her the key for the express and limited purpose of helping with the delivery of an armchair. If she were to use the key for any other purpose – even for that of retrieving what was hers – then that would amount to an abuse of the original trust. So she simply could not do it.

That is what she had decided when Angus Lordie knocked on her door. He occasionally called unannounced – usually when he felt like a cup of coffee and some conversation – and Domenica normally welcomed these visits.

'I smelled the coffee,' Angus said from the doorstep. 'Or rather, Cyril did. He has a particular nose for Jamaica Blue Mountain blend, which I take it is what is producing that singularly agreeable odour wafting about.'

'Blue Mountain it is,' said Domenica. 'And a rather expensive brand, if you don't mind my pointing out, Angus. But do come in. Perhaps dear Cyril would find it more comfortable out on the landing. How are his puppies, by the way?'

Angus waved a hand in the air. 'Perfectly all right,' he said. And they were – as far as he knew. That agreeable stranger he had met in Drummond Place had seemed most solicitous as to the puppies' welfare; of course they would be all right.

They went through to the kitchen, where Domenica poured Angus a cup of coffee and invited him to sit down at the table. The newspaper, open on the table in front of her, had much that she wished to discuss with him. Duncan Macmillan had written another witty denunciation of the Turner Prize for Modern Art, which had just been awarded to a loop of washing line draped around an old suitcase. This installation had been very well received in London, but not in Edinburgh, where such pretentious posturing was fortunately seen for what it was. Duncan Macmillan pointed this out in no uncertain terms and Domenica was keen to see if Angus agreed. He did.

'I agree with everything he writes,' he said. 'Everything.'

So that settled that. Then, just when Domenica was about to proceed to the next item on her agenda, they were disturbed by barking from the landing outside.

'Strange footfall,' said Angus. 'How fortunate that Cyril is there to warn us.'

Domenica rose to her feet. 'That will be Antonia's delivery,' she said. 'She has entrusted me with her key to let the delivery men in. Will you please come and move Cerberus from his position at the edge of Lethe.'

'Leith.'

'That's what I said.'

They went out onto the landing. Down below, muttered voices told them of the approach of two delivery men who were manhandling a substantial armchair up the stairs. Angus silenced Cyril and led him back into the flat while Domenica opened Antonia's front door. Angus then returned to the landing and waited with Domenica.

The burly delivery men, puffing and panting from their exertion on the stairs, carried the armchair into Antonia's hall, followed by Domenica and Angus.

'I shall show you exactly where she wants it,' said Domenica, gesturing to the sitting room. 'And if you wouldn't mind, please put it on those castors. Yes, that's right. Thank you.'

The two men manoeuvred the chair into position; one made a remark about the weather; and then they left.

Domenica and Angus stood next to the armchair. Neither said anything at first, but glances were exchanged. 'Ghastly shade of green,' said Domenica.

'But *à chacun son fauteuil*,' added Angus.

A further short silence followed. Then Domenica spoke again. 'Do you remember that blue Spode teacup of mine?' she asked. 'The one I was particularly fond of? You had numerous unreciprocated cups of coffee out of it. Numerous.'

'How could I forget it?' replied Angus. 'The one you said she stole?'

Domenica nodded. 'The very one.'

'And to think that it is in this flat, even as we speak,' said Angus. 'Probably sitting through there in the kitchen. Ready for illegal use.' He paused. 'Should we take a look?'

For a few moments Domenica wrestled with her conscience. The situation would be quite different, she thought, were Angus to go into the kitchen and find the cup. Antonia had burdened him with no obligation of trust and so if he went in and found the cup it would be nothing to do with her.

She chose her words carefully. 'As you wish.' So had Pontius Pilate spoken all those years ago. It would be up to others.

'Right you are,' said Angus. 'I'll go and have a shufty.'

A shufty. What an appropriate word for a shifty action. Perfect.

41. Police Questioning

Because he was still damp, with that particular, uncomfortable dampness that comes from immersion in salt water, Matthew found that he was sticking to the seat of the police car into which he had been bundled. It was a double discomfort: that of being arrested, or at least detained, coupled with that of being soaking and sticky.

'I wonder if you would mind taking me back to my hotel,' he said politely. 'It's not far from here.'

There were two policemen in the front – one at the wheel and one in the passenger's seat. The one in the passenger's seat turned round and glanced at Matthew through the grille that separated back from front.

'Your hotel?' he said, not unkindly. 'You think you've got a hotel?'

'Yes,' said Matthew. 'It's somewhere over there. You see, I was washed out to sea and my wife will be wondering where I am. It was a dolphin, you see . . .'

The policemen glanced at one another. 'There, there,' said the one behind the steering wheel. 'You'll be all right, mate. Don't get too excited. No worries.'

'But I am worried,' protested Matthew. 'My wife will be frantic with worry, too.'

One of the policemen smiled. 'Yes, well, you may be right there, mate. It might be a bit worrying being married to you. Know what I mean?'

Matthew leaned forward. As he did so, there was an uncomfortable sucking noise as his clothes detached themselves from the seat. 'May I ask where you're taking me?'

'You can ask, mate,' said one of the policemen. 'No harm in asking.'

'Well, where are we going? I've done nothing illegal. You can't just . . .'

'Oh we can,' said the other policeman. 'We can pick up people who are a danger to themselves or others. Not that it's your fault, mate. We know that.' He paused, and looked at Matthew through the grille. 'Were you in hospital before . . . before you met the dolphin?'

Matthew stared at the policeman in astonishment. He now realised what they were assuming: they thought that he was mad. They did not believe his story about the dolphin – and who could blame them?

He knew what he would have to do. 'I'm sorry,' he said. 'I really am. I think that there's been a misunderstanding. There was no dolphin.'

The policeman nodded. 'No dolphin now? Well, you did tell us. And of course we believed you. Why would we not believe that you met a dolphin? So what was it? A whale, maybe?'

Matthew laughed. 'Certainly not! Listen, I know that you think that I'm round the bend. I know you think that I am one of these people who imagine all sorts of things. Well, I'm not. There really wasn't a dolphin and I was just making it up. Just to . . . Just to amuse myself. So, if you wouldn't mind, just let me get out and get back to my hotel.'

The policemen stared fixedly ahead.

'Did you hear me?' asked Matthew after a while.

'Oh we heard you all right, mate,' said one of the policemen. 'But you just sit back and keep calm. We don't want to have to use handcuffs, do we? Everything is going to be all right. They'll fix you up nicely at the hospital.'

Matthew looked through the window of the police car. This could not be happening; it simply could not be happening. He could not be in a police car, here in Perth, being treated by two policemen as a raving lunatic. It simply could not be happening.

And it was while he was thinking of the complete impossibility of his situation, that the radio in the police car crackled into life. There was an incident on Cottesloe Beach, the voice reported. Further help was required to co-ordinate the search for a missing swimmer and could cars report back in if in the area. The policeman in front of Matthew turned round and looked at him. When he spoke, his tone had changed.

'What's your name, mate?'

Matthew told him, and the policeman reached forward for the radio handset and muttered a question into it. There was a short pause before a voice came back over the speaker. Matthew recognised his name.

'That's me,' he said. 'That's me. I was the one washed out to sea.'

The policeman frowned. 'You should have told us that, mate! Jeez. You should have told us that. We thought that you were mad as a cut snake. That dolphin business . . .'

'Please just get me back there,' interrupted Matthew. 'My wife will be worried sick.'

The car slowed down and then made a swift U-turn. The policeman at the wheel now concentrated on his driving while the other one spoke briefly and urgently into the radio. In the back seat, Matthew was no longer concerned about the feeling of stickiness; his clothes had now started to dry and were clinging less to his skin. And he felt, too, the relief that comes with waking up from a nightmare.

Within ten minutes they were back at the restaurant. A small knot of people was standing at the top of the path that led down to the beach, several of them holding torches; there was a man in a swimming costume with a curious belt-like apparatus around his waist – a lifeguard prepared for rough seas; and there was Elspeth, standing a little bit apart.

Matthew tried to open the door of the car before it came to a complete halt, but the door would not budge.

'Kiddie-locked, mate,' said the policeman in front. 'Just calm down. You've had enough accidents for one night.'

'I have to see my wife,' said Matthew. 'I have to see her.'

'Strewth,' said the policeman. 'I know a lot of blokes who'd willingly be washed out to sea just to get away from their old ladies.'

Matthew said nothing. This was not a time for such comments. He was going off Australia quite quickly; how odd, he thought, that one can rather like a country and then not like it quite so much, all within the space of a couple of hours. Mind you, how would an Australian visitor feel if he were to be washed into the sea off Gullane beach? Cold, thought Matthew. And would one be carted off to a psychiatric hospital quite so quickly, just for claiming to have been rescued by a dolphin? Probably not, Matthew thought. There would be waiting lists for that.

42. Beach Bureaucracy

Matthew's return had a strange effect on Elspeth. When he ran up to her, she barely registered his presence. 'Is there any news?' she asked, barely looking at him. 'Is he . . .' And then she realised that it was Matthew standing in front of her, bedraggled, still damp, but undeniably her husband. She screamed, and flung her arms about him. He held her, supporting her weight, calming her as best he could.

Witnessing the reunion, the small crowd of onlookers – the restaurant staff, a couple of lifeguards, the police – looked away or turned to talk to one another, though some sneaked a glance. They knew, though, that they were seeing somebody find another believed to be dead, a human reunion surely more moving than any other.

Elspeth could not talk at first, but soon recovered. 'What happened?'

'I was washed out to sea,' Matthew said. 'It was a rip tide. I didn't stand a chance. I tried to swim back, but I couldn't even see you.'

'It was so quick,' Elspeth whispered. 'One moment you were there and then . . .' She shuddered; he had disappeared so quickly. 'There was one wave in particular. It came right up the beach.'

'They call them rogue waves,' said Matthew. 'And yes, that was the one.'

One of the policemen stepped forward. 'Well, it looks as if you're all right,' he said. 'Sorry about that misunderstanding, mate. But all's well that ends well, as they say.'

Matthew turned round and shook hands with the policeman; he had only been doing his duty. 'Thanks very much for . . .' For what? he wondered. For arresting him? 'For bringing me back here.'

'No worries, mate. But take care in future. The sea here is not like your sea over in England.'

'Scotland, actually,' said Matthew. And our sea, he thought, was every bit as dangerous, if not more. But this was not the time to argue about that.

'Yes, whatever. But just remember, Australia's a big place. You've got to be careful.'

Matthew smiled. 'I will.'

One of the lifeguards now produced a form that he handed over to Matthew. 'Do you mind signing this just here?' he said, pointing to a dotted line. 'It's just the paperwork.'

Matthew glanced at the form. 'What's it about?'

'Oh, it just says that it was your fault,' the lifeguard said cheerily. 'And that you went into the water at a time when the no-bathing flag was up. Otherwise people blame us, you see.'

'But it wasn't my fault,' said Matthew. 'I didn't go swimming.'

The lifeguard exchanged glances with his colleague. 'But you must have, mate,' he said. 'Otherwise how could you have been swept out?'

Matthew shook his head. 'No, that's not the way it happened.'

Elspeth agreed with him. 'No. He's right. I was there. He didn't go swimming.'

Matthew returned the piece of paper to the lifeguard. 'Thank you anyway,' he said. 'I'm very grateful to you for your attempts to rescue me. But I can't sign something that says it's my fault. It wasn't. It wasn't anybody's fault.'

The lifeguard took the form reluctantly. 'So you're not going to sign?'

'No.'

'Even though you entered the water voluntarily?'

Matthew sighed. He was beginning to feel cold, although the air was still warm. Being in the water for some time, he remembered, can lower one's core temperature, which can take some time to recover. 'I didn't enter the water voluntarily,' he said. 'I was swept out. I've told you that already.'

But how did you get swept out?' the lifeguard said truculently. 'You don't get swept out unless you're in the water in the first place. Not in my experience, at least.'

Matthew rolled his eyes upwards. 'I didn't go swimming,' he said, his voice edgy with irritation. 'I went in, just a few inches, to pick up a piece of wood. Then . . .'

'Hah!' said the lifeguard. 'You went in voluntarily to get something out of the sea. Voluntarily.'

'A couple of inches,' snapped Matthew. 'Up to my ankles – no more.'

'That's enough. I've seen people just getting their toes wet, mate. Then, bang, they're in up to their knees and then they lose their footing and that's them in deep trouble.'

'Yeah,' said the other lifeguard, who had been silent up to that point. 'We seen that. A bloke the other day. Remember him, Merv? That fat guy.'

'Yup. Almost a goner. Took a lot of resuscitation.' There was a pause. 'He signed the form.'

'Well, I'm not going to,' said Matthew.

The lifeguard folded the form up and tucked it into a small kitbag at his feet. 'Well, in that case, we'll have to report you for prosecution.'

Matthew gasped. 'What for? For getting swept out to sea?'

'For endangering life by entering the sea voluntarily,' intoned the lifeguard, 'in circumstances where a rescue could have been anticipated.'

'That means for endangering our lives, mate,' interjected the other lifeguard. 'For endangering Merv and me's life.'

'Oh really!' exploded Matthew.

'Why do you become lifeguards if you don't want to rescue people?' asked Elspeth.

The lifeguards both turned to stare at her. 'Who says we don't want to rescue people?'

One of the waitresses from the restaurant now decided to enter the conversation. 'They like to stand on the beach and chat up girls,' she said. 'Yes, you do, Merv Andrews! Don't deny it. I've seen you.'

Matthew decided that it was time to act. 'Look,' he said. 'I'll sign if it makes you feel any better. Give me the paper.'

Merv reached down to extract the paper. 'Good on you, mate,' he said. 'You sign this – it keeps the paperwork regular and we forget about the whole thing.'

'So I won't be prosecuted?'

'No, of course not. It's just these forms. We have to get them signed or we get into trouble. Nobody ever looks at them. All they want to know is that the form's been signed.'

Matthew took the piece of paper and scribbled his signature along the line. 'There,' he said, handing it back to the lifeguard.

'That's beaut,' said the guard. 'Now we can forget about the whole thing.' He paused. 'But tell me one thing – how did you get out of that rip?'

Matthew hesitated. He could not tell the truth – that was obvious. Telling the truth was an option, but only if one's version of the truth was consistent with that which other people were prepared to accept as the truth.

'Washed back,' he said.

'A miracle!' said the lifeguard.

'Yes,' said Matthew. 'It was.'

43. Marching Orders

Bruce left the party at Watson Cooke's flat without saying goodbye to Julia. From his point of view, the whole thing had been an unmitigated disaster.

For a short while Bruce had toyed with the idea of talking to the woman who had looked at him invitingly, but he found that he simply could not face it. It would have been a way of reminding Julia that she was not the only one and that he could get anybody

– anybody – at the flick of his little finger. But somehow that was not what he really wanted. He wanted Julia herself, that infuriatingly stupid, gormless girl; he wanted her. He wanted the woman who was bearing his baby.

So he prepared to slip out of the flat while Julia was still in the kitchen, where he now glimpsed her talking to a dark-haired woman and the tall, rather thin man whom he had earlier on seen with Watson Cooke in the sitting room.

Watson came across him just as he was about to open the front door. 'Leaving already, Duncan?' asked Watson.

'Bruce. It's Bruce. I told you three times. Bruce.'

'Yes, sure. Leaving?'

'What does it look like?'

Watson smiled. 'Looks like you're leaving.' He paused. 'Do you want me to tell Julia?'

Again Bruce felt his heart beating hard within him. He wanted to punch this man, with his supercilious, superior manner. He wanted to reach out and punch him on his . . . on his Watsonian chin. It would be so easy. Then he could slip out of the door and run downstairs before his host had the chance to react.

Bruce took a deep breath. 'Oh, Julia. Yes, well I'm sure that she'll come home in her own good time. She's obviously enjoying herself. What with the dinner you had. Now the party. It's been a great evening for my fiancée.'

He stressed the word fiancée and watched the effect on Watson Cooke. It registered. Watson's mouth twitched slightly at the edges.

'Oh yes,' said Watson Cooke. 'You should take her out a bit more yourself, you know. Women like to be fussed over. Did you know that?'

Bruce's eyes narrowed. Does he think that I don't know about women? Does he really think that? How many girlfriends has this stupid . . . stupid hunk had? Two?

'I have to go,' said Bruce suddenly. 'Thank you very much for the party.'

He opened the door and went out onto the landing, slamming the door behind him. On impulse, he stopped for a moment and detached the note from the neighbour that he had found stuck to the door. To the message which the neighbour had written, he added two brief, scrawled scatological words, addressed to Watson. Then he pinned the note back on the door and went downstairs, out into the night.

He walked straight home, mentally rehearsing exactly what he would say to Julia when she came back that night. He thought that for a few minutes at the outset he would refuse to talk to her at all; the cold shoulder always registered with women. She would approach him, of course, and come up with something about not knowing why he was being so cold, and that would be his signal.

'Cold?' he would say. 'So I'm cold, am I? Well, that's not something that you suffer from, is it? Particularly when it comes to other men. Nobody would describe you as cold.'

Her jaw would drop. 'I don't know what you mean.'

'Oh don't you? Little Miss Innocent? Well, I refer to your habit of dining tête-à-tête with other men when you're meant to be engaged. That's what I mean. Dining with that Watsonian gorilla and lying about it. Yes, lying. Oh, I can tell all right. Don't think for one moment that I couldn't tell that you were lying.'

Her face would crumple. 'Oh, Bruce, don't! I beg you! I love you so much. I worship the ground you tread on, I really do. I'd do anything for you, Brucie, anything. Oh Brucie, please forgive me. It was madness, pure madness. And he's such a creep, Watson Cooke. I hate him. I really hate him. He's useless. And he's impotent. Did you know that? Something happened in a rugby scrum and he's impotent. You should feel sorry for him, Brucie. You should. You're so . . . so . . . and he's so . . . so . . . Really, Brucie, it's true. Please forgive me. I feel wretched.'

He would be magnanimous. 'All right. And are you going to be a good girl from now on? Promise.'

'Oh, Brucie! You know I'll be good.'

He reached the flat with this satisfying dialogue still in his head. It made him feel considerably better, and by the time he had had another shower and slipped into his purple dressing gown he had almost forgotten his distress of the earlier part of the evening. Now he went through to the kitchen, prepared himself a bowl of muesli and began to watch a television replay of a Scottish football defeat.

He was still watching that when Julia came in.

'Why did you leave without me?' she asked, flinging her coat down on the kitchen floor.

'Leave?' asked Bruce. 'Oh, the party. Well, it was pretty dull. I got bored, I suppose.'

'And how do you think I felt?'

Bruce looked up from his muesli. 'You had your friend there. Watson Cooke. You could talk to him.'

Julia picked up a copy of *Vogue* from the table and then, quite suddenly, but accurately, threw it across the table at Bruce.

'Temper!' said Bruce. 'Temper! Temper!'

'You can get out,' said Julia quietly. 'Tomorrow morning. Get out.'

Bruce stared at her. 'You . . . You're my fiancée,' he said. 'And that, that's my baby. You can't . . .'

'Oh yes I can,' she said. 'Engagement over. And the baby . . . well, sorry, Bruce, it was Watson Cooke's all along. I meant to tell you, but you know how it is. Anyway, please move out tomorrow morning. I'll phone Daddy and ask him to get a couple of his men to help you. You know those bouncers from that place he owns? They'll help you move.'

44. Moving Stories

'Is there anything wrong?' asked Nick McNair as he ushered Bruce into his studio the following morning. 'Or shouldn't I ask? A hangover from the party last night?'

Bruce shook his head. 'No. It's not that. And I'll be all right.'

Nick looked sideways at Bruce. 'You look a bit washed out, if I may say so. Not quite yourself.'

Bruce rubbed his face in his hands. 'Maybe. It's just that . . . Well, the truth is that I broke up with my fiancée last night. It was a bit heavy.'

Nick put on an expression of sympathy. 'Oh, poor girl! Was it hard for her?'

Bruce nodded. 'Yes, it was. Still, it's probably better to do it at this stage than to do it after the wedding.' He smiled weakly. 'Cheaper this way.'

'That's true,' said Nick. 'I split up with Colleen – she's my ex – about two years ago and, oh my goodness, did we ever fight! This is mine. No, it's mine. And this is mine too. And so on. We even fought about forwarding mail. She chucked my mail in the bin – wouldn't even drop it in the post for me.'

'They hate us,' said Bruce. 'I don't know what we do to deserve it, but they hate us.'

Bruce closed his eyes for a moment. He would have to try to forget that morning's scene, but he felt that it would be difficult. When he had woken up – after a night spent on the less-than-comfortable couch – it was to the sound of knocking on the door. Julia, he learned, had already made a telephone call to her father and he had arrived on the doorstep with the two bouncers Julia had talked about. They were dressed in the ill-fitting black suits of their calling, with thin, dark-coloured ties. One of them, Tommy, had HATE tattooed on the knuckles of one hand . . . and HATE on the knuckles of the other. The other, Billy, had a line tattooed across his forehead. Bruce could not help but peer forward to read it: BRAINBOX.

Julia appeared in the doorway of the bedroom and conferred briefly with her father, who then walked over to Bruce. 'I'm sorry that it's come to this, Bruce,' he said. 'But I always think that it's best for incompatibility to be discovered at an early stage. I would have appreciated you as a son-in-law, but it's not to be. I hope that there's no ill-feeling.'

'It's her,' said Bruce. 'She's chucking me out.

'Well, it must have been something you did. I don't think I should go into that.'

'Something she did,' snapped Bruce. 'She was seeing another man.'

Julia's father frowned. 'I don't think my daughter would do that,' he said. 'We're not that sort.'

'Well, she did,' Bruce retorted. 'Watson Cooke. You know him? Watson Cooke.'

There was a flicker of recognition, and Bruce suddenly realised that Julia's father looked pleased. 'Well, I don't think we should go into all that,' said the older man. 'Julia has asked me to help you move your stuff out. I've brought the men. They can pack things up and store it somewhere for you. And if you wouldn't mind giving me the keys of the Porsche, I'll take care of that. And as far as the job is concerned, I'll arrange for the accounts department to send you a couple of months' salary in lieu.'

Bruce had been sitting on the couch during this conversation. Now he stood up. 'Now hold on! Just hold on. You gave me that car.'

Julia's father looked down at his feet. 'Not gave, Bruce. Provided. And the registration documents, I'm afraid, are in the company's name. So if you wouldn't mind giving me the key?'

'Actually, I would mind,' said Bruce. 'I'd mind a lot.'

Billy now stepped forward. Bruce saw the legend BRAINBOX in close proximity. It was tattooed in Times New Roman, he thought. Or maybe Palatino.

'Youse just gie us the key of the motor,' said Billy. 'Right?'

Bruce hesitated, but only briefly. The key for the Porsche was in his jacket pocket and he retrieved it.

'Thank you,' said Julia's father. 'There really need be no unpleasantness. So, if you wouldn't mind showing the boys what they need to pack, they'll get it into a couple of suitcases and we can all get on with our lives. So sorry.'

Bruce opened his eyes. The scene was far from expunged, but there was no point in thinking about it now.

'You don't have any coffee, do you?' he asked Nick.

'Natch. I keep coffee on the go all the time. But I always limit myself to three cups a day. More than that and . . . zoom!'

Nick went off to a coffee machine at the side of the room and Bruce looked about him. The studio, which occupied a small mews flat behind North West Circus Place, consisted of a largeish room, in which they were now standing, with smaller rooms off it. One of these smaller rooms looked like a darkroom, and another had an array of computer equipment. In the large room there were several open shelves on which various cameras and lenses had been stored, along with tripods and folded reflectors.

'I'm mostly digital these days,' said Nick, returning to Bruce. 'But I still like actual film. I love the hands-on feel of it.' He handed him a cup of coffee and Bruce raised the mug to his lips. Even the smell alone was enough to revive his spirits. The face of Scotland! What did it matter if he had been thrown out by that dim blonde; he was going to be the new face of Scotland. That was infinitely more important. Watson Cooke was welcome to her.

'So is she moving out then?' asked Nick.

'Who?'

'Your ex.'

Bruce shrugged. 'I think I'll let her stay,' he said. 'I don't want to be unkind.'

'That's good of you,' said Nick. 'So where will you go? Have you got another place lined up?'

Bruce took another sip of his coffee. 'Actually, I haven't. And I was wondering, you wouldn't possibly . . .'

'Of course,' said Nick. 'You can stay at my place down in Leith. I've got a couple of spare rooms and I was going to get somebody for one of them anyway. So that will be fine.'

'That's very kind of you,' said Bruce. And he thought of himself in the infinity pool, looking out over the North Sea. The face of Scotland looking out over Scottish waters.

Oh, Julia Donald, he thought, you don't know what you're missing, do you?

45. *Apposite Posers for a Poseur*

Nick looked at his watch. '*Tempus fugit*,' he said. 'Remember old Rait, the classics teacher at Morrison's? The one with the nose. Remember him? That's all the Latin I remember. *Tempus fugit*. Time flies.'

'Yes,' said Bruce. '*Et cetera*.'

Nick was busy erecting a small umbrella reflector at the side of the room. '*Et* what?'

'*Et cetera*,' repeated Bruce. 'It's the Latin for whatever.'

'Useful,' said Nick. 'I must remember that. Now, Bruce, I think that we'll start with a few face shots. Full on.' He indicated a place in the middle of the floor. 'You stand just there and look over here where my hand is. That's right. Great.'

Bruce, positioned in front of the reflector, looked at the space previously occupied by Nick's outstretched hand. He sucked his cheeks in slightly, but only slightly; years of practice in front of the mirror had taught him that the key to cheek control was very gentle inward pressure. If you sucked in too much you ended up looking like those boy band members who all tried to look so intense when there was nothing, or almost nothing, in their heads. Young pop musicians trying to look all intense and serious – it was laughable.

There was, by contrast, a lot in Bruce's head. He was thinking of life, and of how it has a funny way – an uncanny way, at times – of working out. Every time things had gone wrong for him – through no fault of his own of course – they had righted themselves in no time at all, just like the Campbeltown lifeboat. If there was a Campbeltown lifeboat, which Bruce thought there was. When he was a boy he used to be sent up to the Mull of Kintyre to stay with Doreen and Victor Douglas, distant relatives of his father. They had taken him into Campbeltown and there had been a pipe band playing in aid of the lifeboat; he remembered that. And people had come up to him in the street and tousled his hair and said what a 'bonnie wee boy' he was. He smiled at the memory. There were lots of people who would still like to do that, although now there was hair gel to consider.

Yes, his life was like the Campbeltown lifeboat. A wave, or misfortune, would come along and turn him over and within moments he would be back on an even keel, getting on with life at full steam. That had happened when he lost that job at Todd's ridiculous firm; when that neurotic woman had invited him to lunch at the Café St Honoré and had more or less seized his hand – for emphasis, she said – what an explanation, he thought; I must remember that – and her terminally boring husband had come in and created such a big fuss. Over nothing! I would no more have touched her than have flown to the moon. Mind you, I must be honest. Would I? Is there any woman in need whom I would turn away? Probably not . . . St Bruce, patron saint of needy women. *C'est moi*. No, there are some. There are some I would have to say, 'Sorry, appointments only!' Some of those political women, those bossy Labour types always thinking of new ways of restricting men. I would have to draw the line at them; I really would.

And then there was the wine business. That chap Will Lyons thought I knew nothing about wine. *Rien*. I showed him. Château Pétrus – no problem! And I made a tidy profit there; enough to set me up in London, not that I should have even bothered to go down there. London. What a waste of space. And when things had gone wrong there, had it worried me for more than three seconds? *Non*. It was straight back up to Edinburgh and kapowski into a new job – looking after Julia – that was the job. Running the wine bar was simple by comparison. What a stupid, stupid woman! Talk about wastes of space; she was a positive environmental disaster. And as for Watson Cooke, with his Scottish schoolboy rugby cap. Well, if the cap fits, wear it, Watson Cooke! You're welcome to Julia and her stupid, stupid baby. If it looks like you, W. Cooke, it's going to look like a rugby ball. That would be a great birth announcement in *The Scotsman*: To Watson and Julia, a rugby ball, at Murrayfield Stadium. Thanks to referee and linesmen.

'Something amusing you, Bruce?'

Bruce looked at Nick, who was pointing his camera at him from a couple of feet away, crouching for the right angle.

'Nope. Just thinking.'

'The smile's great. Try and think about something else amusing. Great smile. It'll wow them down at the agency. Most people these days have forgotten how to smile naturally. It's all teeth.'

Bruce applied his mind to the thinking of something amusing. It was quite difficult when one was asked to do that, as amusing things tended just to crop up of their own accord. What was there to laugh about? Watson Cooke? Watson Cooke, the Watsonian?

'Knock, knock,' he said.

From behind the camera Nick muttered: 'Who's there?'

'Emma.'

'Emma who?' asked Nick.

'Emma Watsonian.'

There was a brief silence. Then the camera was lowered and Nick beamed back at Bruce. 'Emma Watsonian? That's really funny, Bruce. Oh, I can hear it. I'm a Watsonian. Emma Watsonian. Oh, that's really great, Bruce.' He paused. 'The old jokes are always the best, aren't they?'

Bruce frowned.

'Hold it!' shouted Nick. 'Hold that expression. Great. Just great. That's the face of Scotland being serious. Thinking about the environment, maybe. Or wave power. Stick the chin out a bit more – great – that's the face of Scotland thinking about those new power generating thingies you stick at the bottom of the sea so that the currents move the doodahs and the power comes surging out to charge all our Scottish iPods. That's it. Great.'

The shutter clicked a few more times and then Nick straightened up and lowered the camera. 'Have a break now, Bruce,' he said. 'This is going really well.'

'You're pleased?'

'Ecstatic,' said Nick. 'I'll show them these tomorrow, just to whet their appetites, and they'll go wow, totally wow! Give us more of that face! Give us more! More!'

46. Rank Insiders in the Pecking Order

'So where have you been?' asked Big Lou. 'Everyone seems to have been away. Matthew. You. The place has been deserted.'

'Matthew is on his honeymoon,' said Angus, directing Cyril to his accustomed place under the table. 'And I have been painting. However, here I am now and ready to bring you up to date. So, fire away.'

'How are your dug's puppies?'

Angus waved airily, for the second time that morning. 'They've found a home. I'm sure that they are in very good spirits.' He did not want to prolong this conversation and so changed the subject. 'You may recall that Domenica lost a teacup, a blue Spode teacup . . . ?'

But Big Lou was not to be diverted. 'A home? Where? All together?'

'I believe so,' said Angus. 'Now this blue Spode teacup . . .'

'Who in their right mind would take six puppies?' asked Big Lou. Then she laughed. 'You didn't sell them to a restaurant, did you, Angus?'

Angus looked down at the floor. Then he looked at Cyril, who was looking into the space immediately before his nose. That was the place where, on normal days, Matthew's ankles were to be found, and Cyril was wondering where they were. There was something missing.

'What are you reading, Big Lou?' he asked, gesturing to a book lying open on the coffee bar.

Big Lou tipped coffee beans into the grinder. 'Excuse the noise, Angus. There we go. That book? It's about how to behave. How to write a letter to the Moderator or the Lord Provost. That sort of thing.'

Angus laughed. 'Do you really need to know that sort of thing, Lou? Why would you need to write to the Moderator?'

'You never know,' said Lou.

'I suppose not.' Angus reached across for the book and began to page through it. His attention was caught, and when Lou turned round he was studying a double-page spread with considerable interest.

'See,' said Lou. 'You're finding it interesting too.'

Angus tapped the open page with a forefinger. 'This is the table of precedence in Scotland. Have you looked at it yet?'

Big Lou shook her hand. 'I'm working my way through from the beginning. And I'm only as far as how to write letters.'

'Well, this is wonderful stuff,' said Angus. 'It goes all the way down to 122. From number 1 – the monarch, of course – down to 122. Gentlemen. That's me, I suppose. I'm at the bottom, Lou, and so are you, in the ladies' table – you have a separate one, Lou, like a separate changing room. Mind you, Cyril's probably even lower. 123 should be for dogs.'

'They could have a table of precedence just for dogs,' suggested Lou. 'Useful dogs at the top and then dogs like Cyril at the bottom.'

Angus ignored the taunt. 'This is fascinating stuff,' he said. 'Did you realise that a Sheriff Principal ranks just below the Lord Lieutenant of a county, but only when he's in his sheriffdom? When he's not in his sheriffdom he ranks much lower. And the First Minister – do you know where he ranks? Number 20. Which is just above the Lord High Constable of Scotland, who ranks twenty-third. That's the Earl of Erroll. Still going strong, I see, at number twenty-three. Erroll was at Flodden, but I suppose that would have been another one, his father, perhaps. And look, Lou, the Lord Justice General is only thirty-sixth! And they put him below – below, Lou! – below the younger sons of dukes. Don't you think that's ridiculous! And what about this, Lou. The Lord Lyon, King of Arms, is seventy-first, which is not much better than the position of Commanders of the Order of the British Empire, who are eighty-first. Now they should be much, much higher, Lou. There's no doubt about that. And the same goes for the Lord Lyon. He should be right up there near the top. Surprising that he isn't, of course, given that he probably draws this list up. But there you have the difference, Lou. The Lord Lyon is not like your pushy younger sons of dukes, who look after themselves. He stands back and says, "I think I'll be seventy-first." How's that for gentlemanliness, Lou?'

Angus suddenly gave a whoop of delight. 'But look at this, Lou! I bet you never knew this. Guess who's at number 120? Queen's Counsel. That's not so good, Lou, is it? That's just one above so-called esquires (lairds, I suppose) and only three above dogs! Not such good news for all those chaps up at Parliament House with their strippit breeks. By the time they get to the sandwiches at the Garden Party all the best ones will be gone, Lou. Only a few bits of soggy cucumber for them! Lord Erroll will get pretty good sandwiches at number 23, of course, and the Duke of Argyll will be all right at number 24. He'll be able to help himself to as many sandwiches as he likes. Which is reassuring. Except for people called Macdonald; you know how they refuse to forget the past.'

Big Lou finished with her coffee beans. 'Did you say something, Angus?'

Angus looked up. 'No, not really, Lou. Just talking to myself.'

'Well, you know what they say about that,' said Lou, sliding Angus's cup of coffee over the bar towards him.

'Oh, I know,' said Angus wearily. 'But who do I have to talk to otherwise, Lou? I talk to Cyril, of course, but he's heard it all before. I suppose there's Domenica, but she sits there while I'm talking and looks at me as if I'm of purely anthropological interest. And you, Lou; you're a good listener. You let me talk.'

'Haud yer wheesht,' said Lou.

'No, you do, Lou. You're very good.'

148

'Wheeksht,' repeated Lou. 'Drink your coffee, or it'll get cold.'

Angus sipped at his coffee, and smiled at Big Lou. 'How's that man of yours, Lou. Robbie? Is he still doing away?'

Big Lou was wiping the surface of the bar with a cloth. At the mention of Robbie's name, she began to wipe more vigorously. Angus noticed this.

'Is everything all right, Lou?' he asked. 'You would tell me if anything . . .'

'Oh, Robbie's fine,' said Big Lou. But then, almost immediately, 'No, he's not. I'm worried, Angus. I'm worried sick.'

'You tell me,' said Angus. 'You've always been there for all of us, Lou. Now we must be there for you. Sorry to use a cliché, but there are times when clichés are just right, and this, I suspect, is one of them.'

PRECEDENCE IN SCOTLAND

47. *The New Pretender*

Angus knew just what Big Lou had been obliged to put up with: of her trials with those various unsuitable men; of her struggle to make something of her life; of everything she had endured. She never, or rarely, complained, and so to see her now in this state of distress was a real cause for concern. Of course he had known from the beginning that Robbie was, as Matthew had so succinctly put it, 'bad news'. It was not as if Robbie were violent or drunken, or suffered from any of the other obvious defects to which the male was heir; it was not that. It was more a question of his being a man with a cause, and the cause in question being so . . . well, one would really have to say odd.

'Oh, Lou,' said Angus. 'Tell me. Tell me what's wrong.'

He reached out over the bar and laid his hand over hers. It was a gentle gesture; a gesture of fellow-feeling that was immediately appreciated. She looked at him.

'Robbie?' he asked. 'He's making you unhappy? Is that it?' Of course he was; what else could it be?

Big Lou bit her lip. 'I'm very fond of him, Angus. You ken that. Very fond.'

'Of course you are, Lou. And I'm sure he's fond of you.' But not as fond of you, he thought, as he is of Charles Edward Stuart and James VII and all that crowd.

Big Lou nodded. 'I think he is. He tells me he is. But . . .'

'But what, Lou?' He hesitated. 'Is it something to do with his Jacobitism? Is that the problem?' He knew that it was; of course it was. Robbie had a screw missing, as Matthew again had put it.

Big Lou confirmed that it was. 'I understand what it means to him,' she said. 'And I've tried to enter into the spirit of it. But now I think that they're taking it too far. It's all very well having an interest in history, but when you can't seem to tell the difference between reality and fantasy . . .' She paused. 'You know that they've been planning a visit from their pretender? Some Belgian who claims to be the successor of Bonnie Prince Charlie. They're tremendously excited. And I think that they're going to do something stupid. I really do.'

Angus's first reaction was to laugh, but, with effort, he controlled himself.

'And when does the Pretender arrive?'

Big Lou looked towards the door, as if to check that the Pretender was not already there, waiting outside. Did pretenders knock, Angus wondered, irreverently, or did they merely barge in?

Speaking in a whisper, Big Lou answered Angus's question. 'He's already here.'

Angus's eyes widened. 'Here in Edinburgh? Or . . . or out in the heather?'

'Here in Edinburgh.'

There was a silence. The Pretender had been a joke when he had merely been a possibility. Now that he was real, and was in Edinburgh, it seemed different. Angus found himself clasping Big Lou's hand more tightly when he eventually spoke. 'Where, Lou? Where?' His voice was lowered; so might one covert Jacobite speak to another as Whig agents passed by.

'In my flat,' replied Lou. 'Down in Canonmills.'

'Lou!' exclaimed Angus. 'What on earth are you doing – sheltering a . . . a pretender?'

Lou sighed. 'I didn't invite him,' she said. 'Credit me with more intelligence than that. Robbie did. Robbie brought him along after he had arrived. They came straight to my place. I couldn't very well turn him away.'

Angus wondered how the Pretender had arrived. By boat from France? Perhaps he had come from the Zeebrugge ferry, if he was Belgian. That would have brought him in to Rosyth, and then there was a bus that crossed the Forth Road Bridge and would have dropped him off at St Andrew Square bus station. But that was hardly a very romantic way for a pretender to arrive in his kingdom.

Big Lou confirmed this was, indeed, the way in which the Pretender had arrived. 'Robbie met him at the bus station,' she said. 'Along with others. They had a piper who played "Will Ye No Come Back Again" and "Roses of Prince Charlie".'

Angus smiled. 'And then?'

'And then they walked with him down onto Queen Street and hailed a taxi. There was a bit of an incident, though, before they left.'

'With the authorities? The authorities got to hear of it?'

'No,' said Lou. 'It was nothing to do with that. It's just that Michael – you know, the one who's in charge of . . . of the cause . . . he dropped the Pretender's duty-free whisky on the pavement and the bottles broke. Apparently the Pretender was furious and said that Michael would have to buy him some new bottles. He started to shout in Flemish, Robbie said, and only stopped shouting once Michael had agreed to buy the whisky on the way to my flat.'

Angus listened to this story in complete amazement. 'And so now he's staying with you, Lou?'

Lou nodded. 'Yes. Robbie said that they looked into the possibility of a hotel, but the Pretender said that it would be more secure for him to stay with one of the supporters. I think he believes that there are more supporters than there really are. In fact, there are only eight or nine of them, as far as I can see.'

'But why can't one of them put him up?' asked Angus. 'It seems a bit unfair to land him on you when you're not a real supporter.'

'Robbie said that it was best for him to stay with somebody who wouldn't be known as a Jacobite. He said it would be safer that way.'

'And now what?'

Big Lou shrugged. 'I have no idea. He's sleeping in my kitchen, on a camp bed. And this morning he used all the hot water – every drop of it. And there were only two eggs in the fridge, but he ate both of them. Robbie says that we must cater to his every need. Those were his exact words. And the Pretender seems to think so himself. He never says thank you. He just looks at you as if it's your job to wait on him hand and foot. He takes everything for granted.'

Angus frowned. Everybody took advantage of Big Lou's kindness: customers at the coffee bar, demanding relatives, boyfriends, pretenders . . . 'You'll have to put your foot down, Lou,' he said. 'Tell Robbie that he'll have to find somewhere else for the Pretender to stay. Send him up to the Highlands. To the Outer Hebrides. Anywhere.'

Big Lou began to polish the bar once again. 'That's what they're planning,' she said. 'He's going up north. Robbie says they have a plan. But I have a bad feeling, Angus. A gey bad feeling.'

48. Loyalties Tested

When Angus Lordie emerged from Big Lou's coffee bar he had a great deal to think about. It had been an eventful morning, what with Lou's surprise announcement, and the retrieval of Domenica's blue Spode teacup. His artist's eye detected a certain symmetry in these events – the welcoming of the Pretender represented an absurd, misguided attempt to rectify what was seen by some as a historical injustice; the restoration of the teacup was also an attempt – and a successful one at that – to set right a wrong.

Now Angus knew that there were those who would regard the whole matter of the teacup as a small thing, a minor issue between neighbours that should hardly merit our notice. In the scale of wrongs which plagued the world, the theft of a teacup, even one which was of sentimental value to its owner, might seem to count for very little. Certainly it was dwarfed by the crying injustices with which humanity had to contend; but that was not really the point, at least in Angus's view. Every small wrong, every minor act of cruelty, every act of petty bullying was symbolic of a greater wrong. And if we ignored these small things, then did it not blunt our outrage over the larger wrongs?

It was, thought Angus, a question of zero tolerance. When Mayor Giuliani decided to tackle petty street crime in New York, he realised this fundamental truth: the small things stand for the big things. And by stopping minor street crimes – littering, riding bicycles on the pavement, pushing people out of the way and so on – he signalled that anti-social behaviour of any sort would not be tolerated. And the result? One of the safest large cities in the world.

Mayor Giuliani, thought Angus, would not have tolerated Antonia's removal of Domenica's blue Spode teacup. And nor had he, Angus Lordie. He had gone into Antonia's kitchen, quickly located the cup in question, and returned it to Domenica. Then they had both left the flat, locking the door behind them. Domenica had been effusively grateful and had invited Angus in for a further cup of coffee, but he had declined, as Cyril was restless now and wanted some exercise. They would walk together up to Big Lou's and have the second cup of coffee there.

'I'm immensely grateful to you for getting my cup back for me,' said Domenica. 'It had been rankling.'

'As well it might,' said Angus. 'It's never comfortable seeing evil flourish unchecked.'

'I don't know if I'd quite call it evil,' said Domenica. 'But it was certainly an act of dishonesty on Antonia's part.'

'And what do you think she'll do when she discovers that it's not there?' asked Angus. 'Will she suspect us?'

'She might,' Domenica replied. 'But even if she does, she can hardly complain. After all, we merely took back what was rightfully mine. She has no leg to stand on. She is quite without visible means of support.'

'White-collar crime,' mused Angus. 'Stealing somebody's blue Spode teacup is, I suppose, an example of white-collar crime. Which makes Antonia a white-collar criminal.'

'Well, there you are,' said Domenica. 'It just goes to show how frayed are the bonds that bind us one to another in this society. It used to be that you could trust your neighbour . . .'

Angus shook his head. 'That was when we had a society,' he said. 'That was before they dismantled the idea of community; the idea of being a nation.'

Domenica looked doubtful. 'But there's still a lot of talk about community. Don't we even have a Minister for Communities or some such thing?'

Angus shrugged. 'Possibly. But so much of that is just pious talk. The things that really bind people to one another are a shared sense of who you are – a shared identity. Common practices. Common loyalties. Those are the things that bind us together. But what is being done to those things now? They are being dismantled. Deliberately and with specific intent they are being dismantled. Look at Christmas. Look at those think-tank people who advocated diminishing Christmas so that those who adhered to other faiths would not feel excluded. The truth of the matter, though, is that the celebration of Christmas has been going on for an awful long time in this country and is exactly one of those customs that make us a community rather than just a random collection of people who happen to live in the same place. And you can say the same thing about a hundred other manifestations of our national culture. We have a national culture, just as other countries have. We have one, and we are entitled to say that we want to preserve it. It's a great mish-mash of social customs and observances; of ways of greeting one another; of memories of nursery rhymes and poems and people. All of that. And these wretched, arrogant relativists and pluralists are setting out – on what authority, one asks? – to dismantle it, bit by bit, so that there is nothing, absolutely nothing left. They prevent people from being who they are; they forbid them to express themselves in the name of preventing offence. Cyril's offensive to cats, but is he to stop being a dog? They pour scorn on those who have a sense of themselves. One might weep. One might weep for everything that is being taken from us, our fundamental, basic identity as Scots, as Britons too – all of that.'

He paused – and drew breath. 'And don't think for a moment that this sense of having something taken away is restricted to bourgeois dreamers, to middle-class romantics, to hopeless irre-dentists; don't think that. Look at what very ordinary people have lost, and think about that for a moment. What has happened to working-class communities in Scotland? To miners, for example.

155

To fishermen? Who? You might well ask. To men and women who work with their hands? Who again? These people are being swept away by globalisation. Swept away. Now they're all so demoralised that they're caught in the culture of permanent sick notes. And who speaks for the young Scottish male, as a matter of interest? Nobody. Where's he going to live? What's he going to do? Nobody cares. He's finished. Abandoned. And he knows it. And all the solace he can get he will have to get from football and drinking. That's the only meaning he can find for his life. Football! And an ersatz electronic culture of mindless cinematic violence from the cynical pyrotechnicians of Hollywood. But don't get me started, Domenica.'

'I won't,' said Domenica.

49. A Subtle Knife Question

The contretemps between Irene and Stuart over the question of whether Bertie would be allowed to join the cub scouts had been resolved in favour of Stuart. It was impossible for Irene to do very much now; certainly there was little that she could do in the presence of Bertie himself, as for all her faults she did not believe in presenting a child with mixed parental messages. But that did not prevent her from confronting Stuart once Bertie had been dispatched to bed.

That dispatching had been carried out by Stuart, who had supervised the cleaning of teeth and the various other small rituals that Bertie performed before settling down for the night. That evening, though, Stuart was aware of what awaited him in the kitchen, and prolonged his time with his son, sitting on the edge of the bed in the artificial gloaming provided by Bertie's small plug-in night-light.

'So you've had a good day, Bertie,' he said, taking the small hand that was resting on the top of the counterpane and giving it a brief, friendly squeeze.

Bertie hesitated before he replied. 'A bit,' he said. 'Some of it was good and some was bad. But thank you for asking, Daddy.'

'Oh, some of it was bad, was it?' asked Stuart. 'Why was that, Bertie? I thought you had fun having your friends round to play.'

'Olive's not really my friend, Daddy,' confided Bertie. 'She thinks she is, but isn't really. I never invited her here and once she comes all she wants to do is to play house. I hate playing house. We're incompatible.'

Stuart gave a start at the sophisticated word; his son had a great capacity for astonishing him, never less than in his vocabulary. He was sympathetic to Bertie's point. He had a vague memory of being forced to play house when he was a small boy and hating it too. And now that he came to think of it, his life with Irene was a bit like being obliged to play house on a prolonged scale. In fact, there were many men who were forced to play house when they really did not want to . . .

'Girls can be a bit different, Bertie,' he said.

'Mummy says they aren't,' chipped in Bertie. 'Mummy says that it's society that imposes different roles on boys and girls.'

Stuart looked at his son. He was probably right. That was exactly what Irene would have said.

'I'm sure that Mummy had a point,' he said loyally. 'But let's not worry too much about that. Tell me, did Tofu enjoy himself?'

'No,' said Bertie. 'Tofu and Olive fight every time they see one another. Tofu always spits at her and she scratches him. She tried to scratch his face this afternoon but only managed to scratch his neck. That made Tofu pull her hair and quite a bit came out.'

'That's not so good,' said Stuart. 'One does not expect such things to happen among one's guests. But at least you've got the cub scouts to look forward to.'

'Yes,' said Bertie. 'I can't wait.'

'We'll go and get your uniform tomorrow,' said Stuart.

'Can I carry a knife?' asked Bertie. 'That book I was reading, about Baden-Powell and *Scouting for Boys*, says that every scout should have a knife. Did you have a knife, Daddy?'

Stuart was silent. He had not thought about it for many years – and it seemed such a long time ago. But yes, he did have a knife, although he very much doubted that cubs had knives these days.

'I did have a knife, Bertie,' Stuart said. 'I had a lovely red Swiss Army knife with twelve blades, as I recall. Well, they weren't all blades – they did various things. One was a hook to take stones out of the feet of horses. And another was a corkscrew, I think. It was a lovely knife. I was very proud of it.'

Bertie was listening with rapt attention. It thrilled him to learn that his father had had a knife, and a Swiss Army one at that. He had seen a picture of a Swiss Army knife once, in a magazine – it was *Scottish Field*, he thought, which he read in Dr Fairbairn's waiting-room. It had never occurred to him that he might one day have such a knife, but now that his father had said that he had owned such a thing, then there was a chance, he supposed, a remote chance that he might get one.

He looked at his father. The warm intimacy of the half-light made him wonder whether now might not be the time to make the request.

'Do you think I could have a Swiss Army knife?' he asked, his voice small in the darkness. 'Do you think I could, Daddy?'

Stuart said nothing for a moment. He remembered that he had been given his Swiss Army knife at the age of eight, and Bertie, of course, was only six. But children grew up faster these days and six, perhaps, was the new eight . . . And how could he say no to this little boy who had been said no to so many times – by his mother – and all those nos had been left unchallenged by him? Well that was going to change, and it would change dramatically, whatever Irene said.

'Of course you can have a Swiss Army knife, Bertie,' said Stuart. 'We can get it tomorrow when we go to buy your uniform. You just remind me.'

'Oh, thank you, Daddy,' said Bertie, beaming with pleasure. 'Can we go in the car to get the uniform?'

'Of course,' said Stuart.

'Where is it, Daddy?' asked Bertie. 'I haven't seen our car for ages.'

Stuart smiled. 'Where is our car? Oh, in the usual place, Bertie. Parked.'

'But where?' pressed Bertie.

Stuart stroked his chin. Had he been the last to use the car? Suddenly his prospects seemed to be considerably less attractive. It was one thing to insist on the cub scouts, but it was quite another thing to promise Bertie a knife and to forget – again, it seemed – where the car was parked.

He looked down at his son. If there was one thing that he could wish for his son – one thing that he himself, as a father, did not possess, what would that be? Courage, he thought.

And Bertie looked up at his father and thought: how dare Tofu call my father a wimp? Tofu's father would never have owned a Swiss Army knife. Tofu's father . . . he drifted off to sleep.

50. Portrait of the Artist as a Surprised Man

Angus knew that after leaving Big Lou's coffee bar he should return to his studio, to work. His easel awaited him there, a half-finished subject staring out at him disconsolately from the canvas. He knew in which direction duty was pointing, but chose to ignore it; it had been a most unsettling morning and so, looking at his watch and realising that it was now shortly after twelve, he decided that it was lunchtime and that work could wait until the afternoon, or very possibly the evening. Some days were like that, he thought; they had 'liable to be cancelled at short notice' written all over them, and this was one. Better then, to walk up the road, cross at the junction of Dundas Street and Heriot Row, and slip into Glass and Thompson for lunch.

He looked down at Cyril. 'Not the most productive of mornings, Cyril,' he said. 'But then every day is like that for you. Apart from the day that you produced six puppies, that is. That's the cost of having an affair, Cyril, old chap: minor pleasure and major consequences.'

Cyril looked up at his master. He tried to make sense of what Angus said, but it was mostly meaningless sound to him. Some words were recognisable, and bore meaning: walk, bad, dinner, bone, fetch – but that was about all. If a universe is formed by language, then this was a small one indeed; a small circle of understanding described in a morass of confusion and puzzlement. The key, Cyril knew, was to ascertain the mood of these unintelligible sounds. If Angus sounded cross then he, Cyril, should look contrite. And that, he thought, was how he should look now.

But Angus did not dwell on reproductive irresponsibility, and the moment passed. They had now come up to the traffic lights at the Open Eye Gallery, and this was the signal for Angus to invoke one of Cyril's more unusual tricks. Knowing that Cyril might need to lift his leg at some point before lunch, he stopped aside the railings that ran along the gallery and gave the instruction for this to happen. 'Turner Prize,' Angus commanded, and immediately Cyril moved to a suitable position against a railing and lifted his leg.

'You have such sound judgement, my boy,' Angus observed as he waited for the dog to finish. Then, both nature and artistic opinion satisfied, they crossed to the welcoming doorway of Glass and Thompson, where Cyril took up his position under Angus's table while his master ordered lunch.

Glass and Thompson was relatively quiet; the lunchtime rush would not begin for another forty minutes or so, and there were only a few customers at the various tables, the last of the morning coffee crowd. Angus found a newspaper abandoned on a neighbouring seat and opened it at the bridge column, running his eye down the account of tricks made and lost. He was a weak player, but he loved the language of ruffs and ducking, broken honours and deception manoeuvres. Then he looked up, aware that there was a shadow obscuring the glass front door of the café just behind him; or so it seemed. In reality the shadow was an eclipse of the light caused by the massive form of an extremely overweight man, half-carrying, half-dragging a large wrapped item behind him.

Angus stared at the man, astonished by his vast bulk, and by the dingy beige jersey he was wearing under an outsize black donkey jacket. He had seen him somewhere before; but where was it? and then he remembered. This was the man who had come into Big Lou's café months ago, maybe even last year, and had dealt with that unpleasant boyfriend of hers, the one who had virtually cleaned out her bank account – and would have got away with it, had it not been for this man whose name was . . . was . . . Lard O'Connor. That was it. Lard O'Connor! And here he was in Glass and Thompson, of all places; not their usual sort of customer.

Angus rose to his feet, while Cyril cowered under the vast bulk of the new arrival. 'Mr O'Connor?'

Lard swung round in surprise. 'Aye, that's mysel. And you're . . .'

'Angus Lordie, sir. We met in Big Lou's last year, I think.'

Lard scratched his head. 'Big Lou? Oh, aye, that nice wumman. So youse were there, were youse? So you were. I canna remember everything these days. But mebbe . . .'

Angus gestured to the other chair at his table. 'Will you join me?'

Lard leaned his parcel against the wall and lowered himself into the chair. 'Do they do pie and chips?' he asked. 'I could dae wi' a wee pie and chips, so I could.'

Angus smiled. 'Well, it's quiche, actually, this being Edinburgh. And I fear they don't do chips.'

'Quiche? Ach well, make it a double for me. Double quiche. And lots of tomato sauce.'

Angus rose to his feet and passed the order to one of the young men behind the counter, who glanced at Lard and raised an eyebrow.

'I came over frae Glasgow,' said Lard, when Angus returned to the table. 'I wanted to see my wee pal, Matthew, at his picture shop. But there's a closed sign and it says he's away for another week. All the way frae Glasgow fur nuthin. Jings. What a waste of time.'

Angus glanced at the parcel – it was painting-sized. So Lard had acquired a painting, and how would he have done that? Fallen off something, no doubt.

'You have a painting to show him?'

'Aye. It's a picture of a man. A bonny picture. Old. Fifty years at least.'

Angus glanced at the parcel again. 'Perhaps you'd like to leave it with me,' he said. 'Matthew is on his honeymoon – in Australia. I can keep it for him until he comes back.'

Lard seemed to weigh this proposal for a while before he nodded his assent. 'It would be easier, right enough. I dinnae fancy carting that back tae Glasgow.'

'May I ask what the painting is?' asked Angus.

'Take a look if you like,' said Lard. 'Up at the top there. Take the paper aff.'

Angus reached over and peeled the paper away at the top of the parcel. The frame, he noted immediately, was of good quality, gilt, with a patina of age. He looked up at Lard. 'Nice,' he said. 'Very nice.'

He pushed the paper further down, and as he did so he caught his breath, loudly, so loudly that Cyril looked up. Raeburn. It was unmistakable. Sir Henry Raeburn, the greatest of the Scottish portrait painters of the late eighteenth and early nineteenth centuries, heir to the genius of Allan Ramsay, the man who captured the spirit of Edinburgh in subtle reds and blacks, in shadows and folds of cloth, and in cautious, astute eyes.

But when he looked further down, and saw the face, he could hardly contain himself. It was believed that Raeburn had painted Robert Burns, but the portrait had been lost. This was it. This was the Bard, caught on a visit to the capital; the comet of his genius passing quickly over the Edinburgh firmament, but slowly enough for Raeburn to preserve for posterity. And here was the result, in the parcel of a Glasgow heavy, in every sense of the word.

Lard studied Angus's expression. 'Will you look after it, then? Just for a week?'

Angus looked up from the painting. 'I'd look after it till all the seas gang dry,' he said. 'And the rocks melt wi' the sun.'

'Does that mean yes?' asked Lard.

Angus nodded. 'Yes, it does.'

'You've got an awfie odd way of expressing yoursels here in Edinburgh,' said Lard. 'You sez wan thing and mean anither.'

51. Prodigious Fibs

The day on which Bertie was due to go to his first meeting of the 1st Morningside Cub Scout Pack was, for him, a day of extraordinary excitement. He knew that the issue of his membership had divided his parents; he had heard the arguments between them – often intense – and he had picked up from his mother's manner that she had, on this question at least, been defeated. It was unlike his father to stand up to his mother – he knew that from long experience – but on this point at least he had done so. This new determination, however, had not carried through on the question of the Swiss Army knife, which had somehow been shelved. But Bertie had decided that one victory was enough, especially in a campaign in which one side had, until now, been consistently defeated. So nothing more was said of the knife lest it disturb the apparently settled matter of cub scout membership.

Of course there was another respect in which the member-ship of the cub scouts seemed an uncertain matter, and not one to be counted upon. This was the issue of age. In the literature on the matter that Bertie had perused, it stated quite clearly that the age at which one might join the cub scout movement was eight. Before that, it appeared that there was another organisa-tion, the Beavers, which one might join at the age of six before progressing, in the fullness of time, to the dizzy heights of the cub scout section itself. Bertie was six, and had been six for some time, and although there were occasions on which he had used the fact of being six as a defence, this was not one. When Irene had insisted, for instance, that he join the Edinburgh Teenage Orchestra, Bertie had pleaded that he was seven years too young for that; to no avail. Chronological age had never put Irene off – she had once talked about the possibility of Bertie's being admitted to university on the grounds that he was sufficiently advanced intellectually to hold his own there, and this had led to an acrimonious exchange with an admissions tutor at the University of Edinburgh who had, for some strange reason, taken a contrary view.

'And at what age did David Hume start at the University of Edinburgh?' Irene had shouted down the telephone. 'Would you care to inform me of that?'

'I have no idea,' said the tutor. 'But that is not the point, I'm afraid. There are now rules . . .'

'Eleven,' interjected Irene. 'Hume was eleven when he enrolled at your university.'

The tutor sighed. 'Things were very different in the eighteenth century. One can hardly . . .'

'And Mozart?' interrupted Irene again. 'Perhaps you could refresh

University of Edinburgh
RUDIMENTS of EMPIRICISM
aet. XI

DAVID HUME

my memory as to Mozart's age when he composed his first symphony?'

'Mozart was a prodigy. Yes. But these days . . . Health and Safety . . .'

'Mozart was eight,' said Irene. 'Eight.'

'And what age is your son, again?'

'He's six, in strict chronological terms. But the whole point that I'm making is that what counts is intellectual maturity. But let us not prolong this argument. I can see that you're unwilling to budge. There are other universities, you know. There's St Andrews.'

'You're welcome to phone them. Please don't let me inhibit you,' said the tutor. 'But if he went off to St Andrews, who would supervise bedtime? And make sure he brushed his teeth?'

That had been the last that had been said of university – to Bertie's relief – but the experience had taught Bertie that chronological age counted for his mother only if it would prevent his doing something that she was unwilling for him to do, whereas it did not count if it prevented his doing something that she wanted him to do. It was simple really. As far as the cub issue was concerned, he thought that she was probably unaware of the potential age bar, and so he decided to say nothing about it.

He had discussed it, though, with Tofu.

'Don't you have to be at least eight?' Bertie asked. 'Look. It says so here in this leaflet I found. It says that if you're under eight you have to join the Beavers. Then you can go to cub scouts when you're eight.'

Tofu had grabbed Bertie's leaflet. 'Give it here,' he snapped. 'Where does it say that?'

Bertie had shown him, and Tofu had frowned. 'So what?' he said. 'We just tell them that we're eight. I look big enough to be eight, and if you stand behind me they won't even see you when we join up.'

Bertie was shocked. 'But that's fibbing,' he said. 'And you mustn't tell fibs. It says that here too. Look, it says that cub scouts must be truthful. That means no fibs.'

Tofu laughed. 'They always say that,' he said. 'They say that you shouldn't tell fibs, but they don't really mean it.'

'Then why do they say it?' asked Bertie.

Tofu shrugged. 'Because it sounds good,' he said.

Bertie was unconvinced. He was worried about lying about his age, and he hoped that he simply would not be asked how old he was. If he was, then his only chance of avoiding a direct lie would be to reply 'Eight' in a loud voice and then, in the quietest voice he could manage, he would add, 'next birthday, after the one that's coming up'.

But now was not the time to have doubts. Arrangements had already been made that Tofu would come home with Bertie after school and that Stuart, who would leave the office early, would then take them both up to the church hall. They would drive up in the car, Stuart had promised – if he could remember where it was parked. Bertie thought this unlikely; he thought that he had seen their car in Dundonald Street but it had proved only to be one that looked like it. So unless it turned up, they would be likely to travel up in the 23 bus. And that would be fun: just the three of them – Tofu, Stuart and Bertie. Two boys and the father of one of them, going off together, leaving Irene and Ulysses back in Scotland Street. Poor Mummy, thought Bertie;

she could be so much happier if she just stopped worrying about things. Why couldn't she just relax and go off to tea or a film with her friend Dr Fairbairn? They got on so well, talking about Melanie Klein and things like that. Perhaps he would suggest that to his father, and together they could persuade her to do just that.

52. Scouting for Girls

Bertie was inordinately proud of the cub uniform that he had purchased with his father. When they returned from the shop, he had immediately changed into the new outfit and presented himself in the kitchen for inspection by his parents. The atmosphere there appeared tense – he could sense that – but they both smiled when he entered the room.

'Very smart, Bertie!' said Stuart. 'You look ready for anything.'

'The cub motto is Be Prepared,' said Bertie. 'B.P. It's the same as Mr Baden-Powell's initials.'

'Baden-Powell . . .' muttered Irene. 'I'm not sure if . . .'

'A very great man,' said Stuart.

Silence ensued. Bertie fiddled nervously with the woggle securing his scarf. He knew that his parents disagreed with one another over certain matters, and it seemed to him that it was always his mother's fault. What was wrong with Mr Baden-Powell? he wondered. And what was wrong with being prepared?

'And the green will mean that you'll be well camouflaged when you're out in the country,' said Stuart. 'That nice green sweat shirt. Nobody will see you, Bertie!'

'Which I think would be quite a disadvantage at times,' said Irene. 'One doesn't want the boys and girls to get lost. But still, you know best, Stuart.'

Bertie looked up. Boys and girls.

'Will there really be girls?' he asked.

'Of course,' said Irene. 'And I should hope so, Bertie. Why shouldn't there be girls?'

For a moment Bertie said nothing. He had originally hoped that cubs would be an organisation just for boys, but he had since learned that that was no longer the case. Of course he had nothing against girls – except for Olive – but he had never understood why boys should not be allowed to play with other boys – if they wanted to – and girls should be allowed to play with other girls. From his own observation of the girls at school, that is exactly what they did. They were always huddling together in the playground and when a boy approached they either screamed and ran away or glared silently at the boy until he moved off again. Everybody knew that that is how girls behaved, and Bertie had not thought much more about it. But he had hoped that cubs would be different; a vain hope, it seemed.

Stuart, who had been staring out of the window, now turned round. 'In my day, cubs and scouts were for boys,' he said. 'Girls had brownies and guides.'

'Yes,' said Bertie eagerly. 'Girls can join brownies and guides. I read about that in the book. It said that brownies and guides were for girls. That's where girls should go.'

'I believe that brownies and guides still exist,' said Irene. 'But girls can join the cubs and scouts if they wish. And quite right too.'

Bertie thought about this. 'And can boys join the brownies?' he asked. He could not imagine that any boy would wish to do that, but he was interested to find out.

Both Bertie and Stuart were now looking at Irene, waiting for her answer. 'An interesting question,' said Stuart. 'Very interesting.'

Irene shrugged. 'I believe that they cannot,' she said. 'I think that brownies are just for girls.'

Bertie frowned. 'But, Mummy, if girls can join the cubs, then why can't boys join the brownies? Surely that's not fair.'

Irene smiled; a tolerant, patient smile of the sort needed when one was explaining things to men and boys. 'There has been a lot of research,' she said, 'which reveals that girls wish to associate with one another. I think that they're happier at that age when they just mix among themselves.'

'Oh yes?' said Stuart. 'And boys? Might they not be happier mixing just by themselves?'

Irene cast a withering look in Stuart's direction. 'That's not the point, Stuart, as well you know. Girls and women have been historically disadvantaged. That must be corrected. That's exactly why male-only institutions need to reform. If you exclude girls from the things like the cubs, then these exclusive, patriarchal tendencies will persist.'

Bertie listened intently. 'But why should there be one rule for girls and another for boys?' he asked.

Stuart smirked. 'Good question,' he said. 'It seems to me that Bertie might just be right there. Why should women be allowed to have single-sex set-ups while men are not? Look at all those women's clubs – book groups and so on. And yet if men try to have such things they're frowned upon, to say the least. Or made illegal, courtesy of Brussels.'

Irene looked at her watch. 'There isn't time to go into all that,' she said. 'And besides, you're wrong, Stuart. Women-only organisations are purely defensive. They're a refuge from the oppression of men.'

Bertie watched closely. If anybody was oppressed, he thought, it was his father. And for a few moments, he experienced a feeling of utter bleakness. He had been looking forward to the cubs, to the excitement that it promised, and now it seemed to him that the cubs would be just like everything else; there would be no freedom there, particularly if Olive were to be there, as she had threatened.

'I know that you and Tofu have got something planned,' she had said a few days previously. 'I saw you two talking to your mummy at the tea party. You're planning something. And you think I don't know what it is!'

'We're not,' said Bertie.

'Oh yes you are!' Olive had said, wagging her finger under Bertie's nose. 'You should tell me, Bertie! You mustn't keep secrets from your girlfriend.'

Bertie had looked about him, anxious lest anybody should have overheard. 'I'm not your boyfriend, Olive,' he said. 'Thank you very much, anyway. But I haven't got a girlfriend.'

'Yes, you have,' said Olive. 'Me. I'm your girlfriend. Everybody knows that.'

Bertie took a deep breath. 'But what if I don't want you to be?' he asked. 'Surely you have to ask somebody to be your girlfriend.'

Olive's response was quick. 'Not any more,' she said. 'You're living in the past, Bertie Pollock. It's nothing to do with boys these days – whether or not they have a girlfriend is nothing to do with them.' She paused. 'Now, let me see. What are you and Tofu planning, I wonder? Is it something to do with . . . Yes, that's it, I think. Is it something to do with . . . cubs?'

Bertie struggled to keep his composure, but failed.

'Ah-hah!' crowed Olive. 'So I'm right! Well, that's very interesting, Bertie! Because I've been thinking of joining too. Isn't that nice, Bertie? We can all be cubs together.'

53. Be Prepared, Be Very Prepared

It was indeed the 23 bus that eventually took Stuart and the two boys up the Mound and in the direction of Holy Corner. Stuart had tried to locate the car, but had failed, and had been unwilling to seek Irene's help just yet. It was possible that she had been the last to use it, and knew where it was parked, but it was more likely, he admitted to himself, that he had been its most recent driver.

'I'm sorry, Bertie,' he said. 'I have no idea where the car is. We shall have to use the 23 bus after all.'

Bertie had accepted the situation gracefully. 'That's all right, Daddy. I know the 23 bus. The important thing is to get there. It doesn't matter how you do it.'

He felt disappointed, though. Tofu, who had come back with him from school in order that they might go off to cubs together, was usually rather disparaging about everything that Bertie possessed, but their car, Bertie knew, although somewhat old, was considerably more impressive than Tofu's own family car. Tofu's father had converted his car to run on olive oil, and this meant that it was considerably slower than the Pollocks' Volvo, which still ran on petrol. But Bertie's pride was saved – to an extent – when Tofu revealed that he had only a few scraps of uniform. In that respect, at least, Bertie was in a much stronger position.

'You don't really need a uniform,' Tofu said carelessly, eyeing Bertie's attire. 'Uniforms are silly.'

'Then why are you wearing that cap?' Bertie asked. 'It says cubs across the front, doesn't it? That's a uniform.'

'Who cares?' said Tofu. 'And what's that thing round your neck?'

'That's the scarf,' said Bertie. 'And this thing here is a woggle.'

'Woggles are stupid,' said Tofu, peering at the small leather ring through which Bertie's cub scarf had been threaded.

'I don't think so,' said Bertie, adding, 'I've got another one, you know. My dad bought me two, just in case I should lose one.' He paused. 'Would you like to borrow the other one, Tofu? Then we can make you a scarf out of a handkerchief.'

'Yes,' said Tofu immediately. 'Go and get it, Bertie.'

Shortly afterwards, Stuart shepherded the two boys along Scotland Street to catch the 23 bus as it lumbered up Dundas Street. The boys' pride in their uniform was very evident, even if in Tofu's case the uniform was eccentric and incomplete. And Stuart himself felt a certain flush of pride to be taking two boys off on such an expedition. When you are six, he thought, the world must be a grand place; and when you are thirty-six, as he was, it has shrunk so much; has become a place of worries and limitations and dismaying statistics. What was the point? What was the point of serving out the years, going to the office every morning and returning in the evening, and then going back into the office in the morning? Where was the enjoyment, the excitement in that?

These thoughts passed through his mind as they waited for the bus to stop, and continued as it began to make its way up Dundas

Street. By the time they reached Princes Street, though, Stuart's chain of thought had moved on to broader topics: it was all very well to wonder where one was going personally, but where was the whole country going? He looked up at the Castle as the bus began its journey up the Mound. The Castle was a work of man, but it seemed to grow out of the very rock, to be an extension of this exposed part of Scotland's spine. Above it the Union flag fluttered in the breeze; there were those who would change that, would hoist a different flag in its place, just as there were those who would defend the place of the current flag. How strange, thought Stuart, that we invest these symbols with such potency; how strange that people should be prepared to die for their flags, for territory that they might sometimes never even see. What really counts, he thought, is how we live – and yet that, perhaps, is why we care about flags.

Stuart looked at Bertie, who sat, nose pressed to the window of the bus, pointing some sight out to Tofu. He assumed that this evening the boys would be inducted and make their promise. He had spoken to Bertie about that, and his son had listened carefully as he explained the elements of the promise.

'You have to say, "I promise to do my best; to do my duty to God and the Queen,"' said Stuart.

'I know,' said Bertie. 'I've read about that, and I will do my best, Daddy. To God and the Queen. To both of them.'

'That's good, Bertie,' said Stuart. 'And then there's the cub scout law. That says that you must think of others first and do a good turn for somebody every day.'

'I'll try,' said Bertie. He was not sure what good deeds would be expected of him, but he supposed that they would be something to do with Ulysses. Ulysses seemed to require a great deal of attention, and there were always tasks that had to be performed to keep him happy.

And now, as they reached Holy Corner and the bus stop at which they were to alight, Bertie felt a great wave of anxiety come over him. He would shortly have to make the first public promise of his life, the very first, and it would be based on a lie. The cub scouts were for those of eight and above and he was only six. He was about to enlist under false pretences and take an oath that he was not even entitled to take.

As they approached the Episcopal church hall, Bertie tugged at his father's sleeve.

'What is it, Bertie?' enquired Stuart.

'I don't think I want to join after all,' Bertie whispered. 'I don't think it's such a good idea any more.'

Stuart bent down and put his arm about his son. 'Come on, Bertie,' he said. 'You'll have tremendous fun.'

'Yes, don't be such a wimp,' said Tofu.

Stuart scowled at Tofu. 'Bertie is not a wimp, Tofu, if you don't mind. And I won't have such language.'

Tofu was defensive. 'I was only saying what other people say,' he protested.

'And why should people call Bertie a wimp?' asked Stuart.

'It's not him, Mr Pollock,' said Tofu politely. 'It's not him they call a wimp. It's you.'

54. Badge of Honour

Bertie and Tofu arrived at the cubs at six o'clock. Rosemary Gold, the cub leader, the Akela, as she was known, introduced herself to Stuart and greeted the two boys warmly. Stuart withdrew, after saying goodbye to Bertie and promising to be back in an hour's time.

'And you are?' Akela said to Bertie once Stuart had gone.

'Bertie Pollock.'

Akela smiled encouragingly. 'And how old are you, Bertie?'

Bertie looked up at the ceiling. His heart was hammering within him and his mouth felt quite dry. He took a deep breath. 'Well, at the moment I'm ...' He was going to say eight, qualified by the formula he had prepared, but he did not have time to speak.

'I'm eight,' said Tofu. 'And Bertie's in my class. He's eight too. We're both eight. Eight.'

Akela smiled again. 'Very well, I think I get the message. And you are . . .'

'Tofu,' said Tofu. 'T, O, F, U. It's an Irish name.'

Bertie looked at his friend. This was the first he had heard of this.

'Irish? How interesting,' said Akela. 'It's not a name I'm familiar with. Are your parents Irish then?'

Tofu nodded.

Bertie was still staring at his friend. 'You never said your dad . . .'

'I don't have to tell you everything,' Tofu whispered.

'But your name isn't Irish,' persisted Bertie. 'You're named after that stuff that vegetarians eat. That white stuff. You've got the same name as that white stuff.'

'I'm not,' said Tofu. 'It's Irish. It means . . . it means chieftain in Irish.'

'Well, boys,' said Akela. 'If you go and sit over there, we'll start once everyone has arrived. And there are still a few to turn up. Here's somebody now. Another new member.'

The two boys looked in the direction of the door.

'It's her,' hissed Tofu.

Bertie groaned. 'I didn't tell her,' he whispered. 'I promise you, Tofu. I didn't tell her.'

Olive came skipping across the room to where Akela was standing, followed by her mother, who, seeing Bertie, waved in friendly recognition. While Olive's mother talked to Akela, Tofu and Bertie stared steadfastly at the floor.

'She's going to spoil it,' said Bertie miserably.

'Why doesn't she join the brownies?' Tofu asked. 'She just wants to spoil our fun.' He paused. 'I hate her. I really hope that she gets struck by lightning sometime. I really do.'

Bertie's eyes widened. He did not think that this sort of talk was compatible with the cub promise. 'I don't think that's very kind, Tofu,' he said.

'Not to kill her altogether,' relented Tofu. 'But maybe enough just to fuse her to the ground.'

Olive's mother now left, and Akela summoned the two boys over to her side. 'Olive tells me that you already know her,' she said. 'It's always better when people are friends at the beginning.'

'She's not my friend,' mumbled Tofu. 'And why doesn't she join the brownies?'

'What was that, Tofu?' asked Akela.

'Nothing,' said Tofu.

'And Olive says that she's been in the cubs before,' Akela went on. 'Which is a good thing, as we shall need to appoint some leaders. In the cubs we have somebody called a sixer. That person is the head cub of a six. You'll all be in the red six, and Olive will be in charge.'

This news was greeted with horrified silence by the two boys.

'Well, that's settled that,' said Akela. 'Now I'll administer the cub promise. This is a very solemn moment, boys and girls. So all stand in a line and put up your right hands like this. This is the special scout salute that Baden-Powell invented. No, Tofu, the fingers face inwards rather than the way you're doing it. That's right. Now I'll say the words of the promise and you say them after me.'

There was no heart in it, no conviction; not now that Olive

was there and had, in the space of a few minutes, been promoted above their heads. Bertie had a strong sense of justice, and this was now mortally offended. Olive did not deserve to be a sixer; the experience she claimed was completely imaginary – he was sure that she had never been a cub before. And how could Akela be fooled by Olive's false claims? Why did she not ask Olive exactly what her experience had been and get her to show some proof of it?

Now, with the promise administered and everybody duly enrolled, Akela began to tell the cubs about badges. There were many badges they could get, she explained: collecting, swimming, history, model-making, cooking, music; whole vistas of achievement opened up.

'I'd like to get my cooking badge, Akela,' said Olive. 'And music too. And map-reading – I always read the maps in the car. I read the map all the way to Glasgow once, and back again.'

'That's not hard,' said Tofu. 'There's only one road to Glasgow and it has signs all the way along. It says Glasgow this way. You can't go wrong.'

'Well, I'm sure Olive read the map very nicely anyway,' said Akela. 'And what badge do you boys want to get? Bertie, what about you?'

Bertie looked up. 'Mozart,' he said. 'If you've got a Mozart badge, I could do that, Akela.'

Olive laughed. 'Oh, Bertie, they don't have that sort of thing in the cubs. Why don't you do a cooking badge with me? I could teach him how to cook, Akela. Then we both could do the badge together.'

'That would be nice,' said Akela. 'Would you like that, Bertie?'

Bertie stared down at the floor. His hopes of the cubs were dashed beyond redemption now. He had wanted to learn how to do tracking and how to make a fire by rubbing two sticks together. He wanted to learn how to use a penknife and how to use a wrist watch and the sun to find south. He wanted to learn all that, but instead he was going to be cooking with Olive. Is this really why

Mr Baden-Powell had invented scouting – so that boys could learn how to cook?

'Well,' pressed Akela. 'Olive has made you a very kind offer there, Bertie? Would you like to take her up on it?'

Bertie stared at the floor. He felt the tears burning in his eyes, hot tears of regret over the ending of his hopes. Tofu, noticing his friend's distress, turned to Olive. 'You see what you've done,' he said. 'You see!'

Olive reacted with indignation. 'It's not my fault that Bertie's homesick,' she said. 'He's only six, after all.'

55. Profile of a Talented Talent-Spotter

Bruce's first photographic session with Nick McNair had been a resounding success. When the photograper had got the shots he wanted, he immediately downloaded them onto his studio computer and invited Bruce to look at the results.

'You know what I'd say, Bruce,' he remarked, tapping at an image on the screen. 'I'd say you've got it. There's no other way of putting it. You've just got it.'

Bruce leaned forward and stared at the image on the computer. This was one of the serious-looking poses, in which he was staring into the distance with a look of . . . well, how exactly would one describe his expression? One of determination? Confidence?

'Well, I suppose it looks all right to me,' he said. 'I hope that the people in the agency . . .'

'The people in the agency are going to love you, Bruce,' interrupted Nick. 'They can tell it when they see it.'

Bruce shrugged. 'Well, there's plenty more where that came from.'

'I know,' exclaimed Nick. 'Oh boy, is your profile going to be raised! You'll be on that poster in the airport. You know the one that greets you as you come down the steps at Edinburgh Airport?

The one that says Welcome to Scotland? Well, it's going to be you on that poster, Bruce. You – and underneath it's going to say: The Face of Scotland. That's the slogan. They've already approved that. Cost them two hundred thousand pounds.'

Bruce whistled. 'The poster? Two hundred thousand?'

'No, not the poster,' said Nick. 'The slogan. The poster cost . . .' He shrugged. 'I don't know what the poster cost. It's the words that cost two hundred thousand. Some guy in one of the agencies invented them. That's what a slogan costs these days. These things aren't cheap.'

'But two hundred thousand . . .'

'Yeah, well that's what quality costs, Bruce.'

Bruce was thinking. 'And my face? The image?'

There was a change in Nick's manner. Turning away from the screen he faced Bruce. 'We've got to talk about it,' he said. 'I was going to raise the issue with you tomorrow. But we may as well talk about it right now.'

'No time like the present,' said Bruce, suddenly wondering what was going to happen to the joint bank account he had set up with Julia. Would he have time tomorrow to draw something out of that – just his own money, of course – before she closed it down? She might be dim, he thought, but she had shown herself to be fairly astute when it suited her.

Nick rose to his feet. 'The thing is,' he said, 'we're in this together. I take the snaps, and you jut the chin. I have a lot of overheads, you know. This place. Getting the shots out to the agency. Lunch with creative directors, and so on. That mounts up.'

And my overheads? Bruce felt like saying. Personal grooming. The gym. That mounts up too.

'Some of the talent get an agent,' said Nick. 'Personally, I don't like working with agents, and I'm not sure how useful they are to the talent themselves. Twenty per cent for the local market; thirty per cent for overseas. So on, so forth. It all mounts up. And what does the talent get in the end? Far less than he would have got if he'd negotiated the deal directly.'

'So you think I don't need an agent?' asked Bruce.

'I'm not saying that. I'm not saying that agents are totally useless. It's just that I think that you have to be careful – especially at the beginning.'

Bruce nodded. It seemed to him that he was getting objective advice from Nick, and they had been at school together, after all. If there was anybody one could trust, then surely it would be somebody with whom one had been at school.

'So what I suggest is this,' Nick went on. 'I have a standard form agreement here in the studio. You could sign that right now. It's a sort of release form and working agreement rolled into one. Pretty standard terms. Sign that now, so that when we get down to brass tacks with the agency tomorrow, everything will be in position.' He paused. 'That's what I'd do if I were you, Bruce.'

Bruce stared at Nick. It was hard not to smile, but he managed to control himself. You must think I was born yesterday, he thought. You really must. 'I don't think so,' he said evenly. 'I think maybe I should get an agent after all.' Then he added. 'It's not that I don't trust you, Nick. It's not that at all.'

Nick waved a hand in the air. 'No, that's fine. That's absolutely fine. We can get you an agent tomorrow. No problem there. I know a good one.'

'Great,' said Bruce. 'What's his name?'

'David.'

'David what?'

Nick walked across the studio to pick up a lens hood that he had laid down on the floor. 'McNair, actually. Same as me. He's my brother, actually. He's really good.'

Bruce's eyes widened. 'Your brother?'

Nick shrugged. 'Yup. You'll like him.' He looked at his watch. 'I'm going to have to scoot. When do you need to move into the flat?'

Bruce explained that it would be most convenient if he could move in that evening. 'I don't want to go back to Howe Street,' he said. 'If I go back there, even for one night, it'll raise her hopes. I don't want to do that.' He made a chopping movement with a hand. 'It's better to make a clean break, I think. Don't you?'

Nick agreed. He was for clean breaks too. And lucky ones. In fact, any sort of break suited him. 'That's fine then,' he said. 'We can go round there now and I'll show you the place. I have to go out a bit later, but you're welcome to tag along, if you've got nothing better to do. I'm going for a drink and bite to eat with some friends.'

'Suits me,' said Bruce.

They left the studio and made their way to Nick's car. Bruce noticed that it was a Porsche.

'I had one of these,' he said. 'But I got rid of it.'

'Why was that?'

'Noisy exhaust,' said Bruce.

They set off for Leith. Bruce felt the leather of the seat below him; very good. And the model was a better one than his had been; more powerful, more expensive. Talent pays, he thought. Talent pays. There's a slogan for you, he thought. And it cost nothing.

56. A Bit of a Poser

Nick McNair lived in a converted bonded warehouse in Leith. 'Very bijou,' remarked Bruce as they walked across the car park at the back of the warehouse. 'You forget that Edinburgh's got places like this. London's got all those new places along the river. All done up. But we've got this.'

Nick fished for the keys of the shared front door. 'A word of advice,' he said. 'We're not actually in Edinburgh here. People feel a bit sensitive about it – or some people do. It's Leith.'

Bruce smiled. 'Don't worry,' he said. 'I'm good at merging with my surroundings. Leith it is.'

They went into the hallway, which had been cleverly converted, using old whisky barrels as panelling. 'This was one of the biggest bonded warehouses in Scotland,' said Nick. 'They converted the old bit and added the new, high bit at the end. I'm right at the top – the eighth floor. You'll like it.'

Bruce threw an appreciative glance around the hall. 'Who lives here?' he asked. 'I mean, what sort of people?'

'Creative people,' said Nick. 'Advertising. Media. And money people. Fund managers. Actuaries. People like that.'

'You must feel at home,' said Bruce. And he felt at home too, instantly. Julia Donald's flat in Howe Street had been all very well, but it was hardly the epicentre of the New Edinburgh. This was far more like it, although he was not sure about the epicentre of Edinburgh being in Leith.

They got into a lift which was barely large enough for two people. Bruce felt slightly disconcerted to be standing in such close proximity to Nick. And from that distance, from within the photographer's personal space, he could not help but notice that his new flatmate had not shaved one side of his chin. He noticed the hairs, tiny black eruptions, emerging from the skin like little . . . like little spikes. And Nick had dandruff too; not very heavy, but small flakes of it on the collar of his jacket. Bruce found his eyes drawn compulsively to these as the lift moved slowly up between floors, and at the fifth floor, with three floors to go, he could no longer control himself, and he reached out to brush the dandruff off Nick's collar, a friendly gesture, but one which misfired, as the lift lurched slightly and he missed and stroked Nick's chin instead.

Nick looked at him in astonishment.

'Sorry,' said Bruce, immediately retracting his hand. 'I was going to . . .'

Nick brushed the apology aside. 'No, don't worry,' he said. 'It's just that . . .'

But he did not finish, as the lift had reached the eighth floor and was opening onto another hall.

'I didn't mean . . .' began Bruce, as they moved out. 'I didn't . . .'

'No, no worries,' said Nick.

'What I meant . . .'

'I said no worries,' repeated Nick pointedly. 'We all have different ways of expressing ourselves.' And then, changing the subject, he pointed to the view from the large plate-glass window at the end of the hall.

'We look all the way over to the Calton Hill on that side,' he said. 'And from the infinity pool we look all the way over to Fife.'

They entered the flat. 'I'll show you your room first,' said Nick. 'Then I'll show you the kitchen and where everything is. I've got two fridges and so you can keep your food in one and I'll keep mine in the other.'

'That's great,' said Bruce. 'Did you know that the biggest source of aggro in shared flats is food? People get seriously angry about people eating their food. They even write notes like: "I've licked my cheese" to put people off. And then somebody else writes: "And so have I".'

Nick grimaced. 'Mind you,' he said. 'Eating at home is so . . . so yesterday. I eat out most nights. I suppose you do too.'

'Always,' said Bruce.

'I thought that we could go and have a bite to eat at the place over the road,' said Nick. 'It's quite a good little bistro. Seafood. And not a bad wine list.'

'Perfect,' said Bruce.

'I was going to meet some of my friends there,' said Nick, glancing at his watch. 'But they don't mind putting another chair round the table. Meantime, take a look round. Make yourself at home. Where are your things, by the way?'

'Her old man is looking after them for me,' said Bruce. 'He's pretty disappointed that Julia and I aren't a numero any more.'

'Sometimes the parents take it worse than the girl herself,' mused Nick. 'They weigh the bloke up and decide that he's good son-in-law material and then suddenly it's all over. No more son-in-law. Back to square one.'

'Tough cheese,' said Bruce. 'But these things happen.' He paused. 'Tell me, what do we do next? Do I get to meet the agency people?'

'Sure,' said Nick. 'You can come along tomorrow, if you like. I'll show them a sheet of shots and they'll give me their reaction. I can't imagine that it will be anything other than a big yes. In fact, I know that's what they're going to say.'

'And then?'

Nick picked up an envelope from a table and slit it open with a forefinger. 'Bills,' he said. 'What happens then? Well, for a job this size they'll involve the owner of the agency. He's pretty hands-off, as he has lots of other businesses. But when there are hundreds of thousands of spondulicks at stake, then he likes to know what's going on. He'll probably want to meet you.'

'That's fine by me.'

'Good,' said Nick. 'He's actually quite good company. I've met him a few times. He owns a couple of wine bars in George Street and places like that. Mister Donald, as everybody calls him. Graeme Donald, I think. Yes, Graeme Donald. Big chap. Funny hairstyle, like Donald Trump's.'

Bruce stood absolutely still. Julia's father. If a few words can end a world, they can have no difficulty in ending a career. Although Nick was unaware of it, he had just disclosed the reason why Bruce would never be the face of Scotland. Unless . . . unless Graeme Donald was a fair-minded man who would not let personal factors influence a business decision. That was always possible.

'I know him,' said Bruce. 'I used to work for him.'

'Great,' said Nick. 'That means it's a walkover.'

57. Uncle Jack's Visit

Matthew and Elspeth returned to Edinburgh on a morning flight from Heathrow Airport. They had again broken their journey with two nights in Singapore, staying once more at Raffles. There, sitting before dinner in the Long Bar, under the swaying, hypnotic movement of the ceiling punkahs, Matthew had turned to Elspeth and said: 'I find this very strange. This is the one place in this country where you can drop things on the ground with impunity. And yet I can't do it. I just can't bring myself to do it.'

Elspeth glanced down at the layer of discarded peanut shells, inches deep in places, that covered the floor in every direction. At the far end of the room, a teenage boy in a sarong swept away at this detritus, a modern Sisyphus.

'It provides release,' she said. 'A lot of these people spend their day working in . . . what? Banks and trading firms and places like that.'

'I had an uncle who lived here,' said Matthew. 'He came out here when he was twenty-four and he only came back to Scotland once. My father came here to see him, but he wouldn't talk about it when he returned. I was about eight then. I remember it quite well.'

Elspeth was intrigued. 'He said nothing?'

'He talked to my mother about it. I heard them. But when they realised I was listening they stopped. You know how parents do that – and it only makes you all the more eager to hear what they were talking about.'

'What happened to him?'

'I forgot all about him. Until the time he came back. I was about thirteen then.'

Elspeth took a sip of her drink and reached for a few of the unshelled peanuts in the dish before her. She would only eat one or two, she thought; in that way she would not have to drop the shells on the floor. And yet she wondered why she and Matthew should feel inhibited about dropping the shells – everybody else was doing it. Was it something to do with coming from Edinburgh?

Were Edinburgh people the only people who held back from dropping peanut shells on the floor of the Long Bar?

She looked back at Matthew. 'And?'

'He turned up virtually without warning. My father suddenly said to me: "Your Uncle Jack's coming for dinner tonight." And he did. I went into the drawing room when I came back from school – I had been at a rugby practice – I remember that because a boy called Miller had tackled me and caused a nose-bleed. I had stuffed a bit of cotton wool into my nostril and it was still there. You know how blood dries and the cotton wool makes a sort of plug? It was like that.'

Elspeth knew about nose-bleeds. Occasionally the children had them – Hiawatha, in particular, had been susceptible – and she had been obliged to deal with them. 'You have to be careful about that,' she said. 'You can breathe the cotton wool in. I think it's better to let the blood form a natural plug.' She paused, struck by the intimacy of the conversation. And this, she supposed, was what marriage entailed – all sorts of intimate conversations – about nasal matters, for example – that one would not normally have with others. And yet there must be some barriers, she thought. There must be some things that married couples did not talk about between themselves; some areas of reticence. Or was that just Edinburgh again?

'But this uncle of yours,' she said. 'What happened when he came to dinner?'

Matthew closed his eyes. He had a good visual memory; he could not remember music, for some reason, but he could remember seeing things. And now he saw himself again, at thirteen, going into the drawing room of his parents' house. And he thought: My mother is still alive, and he felt a momentary twinge of regret. He had not loved her enough. He had been keen to cut the apron strings, to prove that he was his own person, and he had not returned her love. And then the apron strings had been cut for him, decisively and swiftly, by an aggressive tumour, and he had a lifetime to regret his unkindness.

He opened his eyes and reached for Elspeth's hand, which he held in his, gently. She looked surprised. 'Is something wrong?'

'Just remembering.' He let go of her hand. 'I went into the room, and my Uncle Jack was there. He was sitting in a chair near the window, and when I came in he stood up. He was unsteady on his feet, and I thought that he was going to fall over, but he had hold of the back of the chair and he straightened himself.

'He was a tall man and he seemed to me to be very thin. But what I really remember was his hair – he had very neatly brushed hair, parted down the middle, and slicked down, like those hair-styles you see on the men in black and white films. Thirties hairstyles. He was smoking – he had a cigarette holder, a short black cigarette holder with a mother-of-pearl band across it. I remember that so well.

'Then he said to me, "Come here, young man, so that I can get a good look at you." And he took hold of my arm and pulled me over towards the window. I looked down at the floor; I was embarrassed. When you're thirteen, and a boy, you're embarrassed about everything. And I had that bit of cotton wool in my nose, you see.

'He looked at me for what seemed like a very long time. I heard his breathing. And I smelled the nicotine that must have covered him. All those nicotine particles.'

Elspeth shivered. 'And then?'

'And then he let go of me and he turned to the window, without saying anything. And my father came in and whispered to me, "Your Uncle Jack gets very easily upset. He's a nice man. But he gets easily upset. Just leave him now."'

Matthew became silent.

'And that was all?' Elspeth asked.

'I had dinner in the kitchen. I didn't see him again.'

'And that's all you know about him?' asked Elspeth. It occurred to her that he might still be alive, might still be there in Singapore.

Matthew hesitated. 'I've just looked in the Singapore phone book up in the bedroom,' he said. 'While you were having your bath. I looked under his name.'

'And was he there?'

'Yes.'

They took a taxi from the front of Raffles, ushered into the car by the Sikh doorman with his large handlebar moustache.

'He reminds me of somebody,' said Elspeth. 'Somebody with a moustache . . .'

'The Duke of Johannesburg,' said Matthew. 'Remember – we had dinner at that restaurant near Holy Corner and then went to the Duke's house. Remember?'

Elspeth looked at him blankly. 'When?'

Matthew was astonished that she did not remember, and was about to express his astonishment. They had gone out to Single-Malt House and one of the Duke's sons had played the pipes and . . . Wrong woman. It had been Pat, not Elspeth.

His hand shot up to his mouth instinctively. 'Oh . . .'

'I really don't remember meeting a duke,' said Elspeth. 'I'm sure I've never met a duke. I would remember, surely. After all, it's not an everyday thing. There aren't all that many of them and it's the sort of thing one would remember – even if the duke himself was not particularly memorable. Some of them are quite dull, I understand.'

Matthew, keen to cover his mistake, was happy to move the conversation on to dukes in general. 'I suppose that some are. But then, there are some who are quite interesting. The Duke of Buccleuch, the one who died not all that long ago, was an interesting man. And a very nice man too. You wouldn't really have known that he was a duke, just to look at him. And he did a lot of good work.

'And then there was the Duke of Atholl. He was a very good bridge player. He had a private army, you know. A sort of ancient historical privilege. The only one in the country. But he never declared war on anybody. Not once.'

Elspeth stopped him. 'But the Duke of Johannesburg . . .'

'You would have thought,' Matthew continued quickly, 'that having a private army, one might want to use it. But he never did.

It's rather like having a nuclear weapon – you have it, but you can't really use it.'

'But, Matthew, who's the Duke of Johannesburg? I've never met him. I really haven't. Are you sure that we went there for dinner?'

Matthew realised that he was trapped. But at that exact moment, just when he was about to confess that he had made a mistake and that it was somebody else who had been with him that evening – and, after all, there was no shame in that – it was well before he had even met Elspeth and he was entitled, surely, to a past life – just at that moment the taxi-driver, who had been following the discussion with some interest in his rear-view mirror, chose to make a pronouncement.

'Maybe breakfast,' he said. 'Maybe breakfast, not dinner.'

Elspeth threw an amused glance at Matthew, who raised a finger to his lips.

'Maybe,' said Matthew to the driver. 'Maybe.'

The driver nodded. 'Anyway,' he said, 'we're nearly there. This is the Tanglin Club. See? This is a very good place.'

They drew up in front of an elaborate, wide-eaved building, surrounded by lush trees and shrubs, a small slice of jungle allowed to flourish in the middle of the gleaming city. Matthew paid the driver and they walked up to the front door.

'That dinner,' he said. 'That dinner. I'm sorry; I was getting things mixed up. I went with somebody else. It was Pat. My last girlfriend.'

Elspeth looked away. 'I knew,' she said. 'But I wish you'd told me.'

'I'm sorry,' said Matthew. 'I really am. I didn't want to hurt you. It's just that getting one's wife mixed up with one's girlfriend is not a very tactful thing to do . . . on one's honeymoon.'

Elspeth laughed. 'Oh, don't worry about that, Jamie. Let's just forget about it.'

They were almost at the door. Jamie? But there was no time to go into that.

'Will you recognise him?' Elspeth asked. 'If you haven't seen him for . . . what is it? Fourteen years? Something like that?'

'I think so,' said Matthew. 'He looks fairly like my old man. And if he's still got that middle parting then he should be pretty recognisable.'

They went through the wide entrance doors and found themselves standing in a broad, panelled lobby. At the far end, a staircase swept up to the first floor; to one side two young women sat demurely at a high mahogany reception desk. The overall feel was one of a solid opulence over which a blanket of deadening silence has descended.

Matthew walked over to the reception desk and announced himself. The women smiled. 'Your uncle is waiting for you in the Tavern,' said one of them. 'My colleague will show you the way.'

The Tavern was a fair imitation of what an outsize English pub might have looked like before the invasion of electronic gambling machines, muzak, and cheap, chilled lager (and the culture that went with that particular brew). It was entirely deserted, apart from one table in the centre of the room, where they saw a tall, dapperly dressed man with a centre parting in his thick head of slicked-down hair. Next to him was a small Chinese woman in a dark dress, a smart red leather handbag resting on her lap.

The waiting couple rose to their feet as Matthew and Elspeth made their way over to meet them. Matthew's uncle spoke quietly, his voice rather hoarse, like the voice of one who has just risen from his bed in the morning and not yet cleared his throat. Matthew saw a cigarette holder lying on the table, without a cigarette in it. It was the cigarette holder he remembered: black, with the mother-of-pearl band.

The woman was introduced as Jack's wife, Maria. 'My wife is Catholic,' said Jack. 'I, of course, am still Church of Scotland – after all these years. We have a number of Presbyterian churches here, you know. And a few Presbyterian schools, too. What's the name of that place, dear?'

'Pei Hwa,' said Maria, in a high-pitched rather sing-song voice. 'Pei Hwa Presbyterian Primary School.'

'That's it,' said Jack. 'And there's another one too. What's its name again?'

'Kuo Chan,' said Maria. 'It's a secondary school. Two schools. One primary. One secondary.'

'Oh yes,' said Matthew, and then, brightening, he said, 'Elspeth is a teacher. Or rather, was one. She taught at a Steiner school in Edinburgh. Then we got married.'

'Jolly good,' said Jack.

59. Cat People

Jack and Maria led Matthew and Elspeth into the Churchill Room. This was a large, wood-panelled dining room with a dance floor in the centre and tables arranged round the sides. A grand piano stood at the edge of the dance floor and a man in white tie and tails was playing this, while behind him two other musicians, a drummer and a guitarist, were fiddling with equipment.

'One of the nice things about this club,' said Jack, 'is the fact that you can always get a dance. Every night, more or less. And bridge too. We've got a jolly good card room. You can get a good game of bridge three days a week.'

'Four, sometimes,' corrected Maria. 'And Mah Jong one day a week.'

'She likes her Mah Jong,' said Jack, smiling at his wife. 'I don't care for it myself. All that click-clicking as you put the pieces down. Gets on my nerves.'

'Do you play Mah Jong?' asked Maria.

'No,' said Elspeth. 'I'm afraid I don't.'

'Nor me,' said Matthew.

There was a silence. Then Matthew spoke. 'Do you mind my asking, Uncle Jack,' he said. 'Do you mind my asking what it is that you do out here?'

'Import/export,' said Jack quickly. 'Goods in. Goods out. Not that we're sending as many goods out as we used to. China is seeing to that. They make everything these days. Everything. How can Singapore compete? You tell me that, Matthew. How can we compete?'

It appeared that he was waiting for an answer, and so Matthew shrugged.

'Precisely,' said Jack.

A further silence ensued, broken, at last, by Maria. 'Do you like cats?' she asked.

Matthew looked to Elspeth, who looked back at him. 'Yes, although I . . . we don't have one.'

'We like them a lot,' Jack said. 'And I'm actually president of the Cat Society of Singapore. Not the Singapore Cat Club – they're a different bunch. The Cat Society.' He looked down at the table in modesty.

'Jimmy Woo was the president before Jack,' explained Maria. 'He's one of the big Siamese breeders here in Singapore. His father, Arthur Woo, was the person who really got the breed going here.'

Jack cleared his throat. 'Well, that's a matter of opinion, my dear. Old Dr Wee was pretty influential in that regard. And there was Ginger Macdonald well before him. He shot his cats when the Japanese arrived, you know. Rather than let them fall into their hands.'

Maria looked grave, and cast her eyes downwards, as if observing a short silence for the Macdonald cats. Then she looked up. 'It's a pity that you're here this week rather than next,' she said. 'We've got our big show then. People come from all over. Kuala Lumpur. Lots of people come down from KL just to see the show. Henry Koo, for instance.'

'No, he's Penang. Not KL,' said Jack.

'Are you sure?'

'Pretty sure. The Koos have that big hotel up there. And they breed pretty much the finest Burmese show cats in south-east Asia. A whole dynasty of grand champions.'

Maria looked doubtful. 'Then it's another Koo,' she said. 'The

Koo I'm thinking of definitely came from KL. Maybe he was Harry Koo, not Henry.'

The conversation continued much in this vein throughout dinner. Jack was keen to discover what Matthew thought of Raffles and Maria came up with shopping recommendations for Elspeth. Then, just as coffee was being served, the small band struck up and several couples at the other tables went out onto the dance floor.

'I'd be delighted if you'd dance with me,' Jack said to Elspeth. He threw a glance at Matthew and then nodded in the direction of Maria. Matthew took the hint and asked her if she would care to dance with him.

Jack was a good dancer and Elspeth found herself led naturally and confidently around the dance floor. As they passed the other couples, polite smiles were exchanged, and Jack nodded to the men. 'I'm very glad that Matthew phoned,' he said. 'I've been out of touch, you know. It's like that out here. You get caught up in your own life and you forget about family back home.'

'You must have a busy time,' she said.

'Oh we do. There's never a dull moment. Especially when the show comes up.'

They returned to the table and Maria suggested that Elspeth might care to accompany her to attend to her make-up.

SINGAPORE CAT SOC'Y
·PAST PRESIDENTS·

1936-42	Ginger Macdonald
1942-45	Pacific War (*no President*)
1945-56	Ginger Macdonald
1956-70	Dr Wee
1970-84	Arthur Woo
1984-2006	Jimmy Woo
2006-	

'We'll meet you ladies back in the bar,' said Jack. 'I'll show Matthew the card room.'

The women went off, and Matthew walked with his uncle back through the lobby.

'What an enjoyable evening,' said Jack. 'A jolly good evening. Good of you to get in touch, Matthew.'

'I'm glad that we've met again,' said Matthew. 'I recall your last visit, you know. I remember your cigarette holder.'

Jack gave a chuckle. 'Yes. One remembers the little details. I find that too.' He paused. 'Tell me, Matthew, you'll have heard the talk, won't you?'

Matthew looked puzzled. 'The talk?'

'Yes,' said Jack. 'The talk. People said, you see . . . Well, you'll know what they said. About you being . . . being mine rather than your father's. That talk.'

They had almost crossed the lobby. Matthew stopped in his tracks. 'I'm not sure what you mean.'

Jack took the cigarette holder out of his pocket and started to fiddle with it. 'The talk was that you were my son. I heard some of it myself.'

Matthew found it difficult to speak. His throat felt tight; his mouth suddenly dry. 'I don't know what to say . . . I'm sorry. This is a bit of a surprise.'

Now Jack became apologetic. 'Oh, I'm terribly sorry, old chap. It never occurred to me that you wouldn't know. But I do assure you, there was never any truth in it. Idle gossip. That's all. Now, let's go and take a look at the card room. They might be playing bridge, but we can take a peek and won't disturb anybody. This way, old chap.'

Later, in the taxi on the way back to Raffles, Matthew sat quite silent.

'That didn't go well, did it?' said Elspeth, slipping her hand into his.

'Ghastly,' said Matthew.

'You're very quiet,' said Elspeth. 'Has it depressed you?'

Matthew nodded, mutely – miserably. He remembered the

discussion between his parents: why had they lowered their voices; why had the visit of Uncle Jack been such a fraught occasion? Why had Uncle Jack looked at him so closely – scrutinised him indeed – at their earlier meeting? Suddenly it all seemed so clear.

I am the son of the president of the Cat Society of Singapore, thought Matthew. That's what I really am.

60. Huddles, Guddles, Toil and Muddles

While Matthew and Elspeth were returning to Raffles Hotel, back in Scotland Street Domenica Macdonald, anthropologist and observer of humanity in all its forms, was hanging up a dish towel in her kitchen. Matthew and Elspeth had dined in the Tanglin Club, while Domenica had enjoyed more simple fare at her kitchen table: a couple of slices of smoked salmon given to her by Angus Lordie (rationed: Angus never gave her more than two slices of salmon) and a bowl of Tuscan Bean soup from Valvona & Crolla. She savoured every fragment of the smoked salmon, which was made in a small village outside Campbeltown by Archie Graham, according to a recipe of his own devising. Angus claimed that it was the finest smoked salmon in Scotland – a view with which Domenica readily agreed; she had tried to obtain Archie's address from Angus, but he had deliberately, if tactfully, declined to give it. Thus did Lucia protect the recipe for Lobster à la Riseholme in Benson's novels, Domenica thought, and look what happened to Lucia: her hoarding of the recipe had driven Mapp into rifling through the recipe books in her enemy's kitchen. She might perhaps mention that to Angus next time she asked; not, she suspected, that it would make any difference.

With her plates washed up and stored in the cupboard and her dish towel hung up on its hook, Domenica took her blue Spode teacup off its shelf and set it on the table. She would have a cup of tea, she decided, and then take a position on what to do that afternoon. She could possibly ... She stopped, realising that she actually had nothing to do. There was no housework to be done in the flat; there were no letters to be answered; there were no proofs of an academic paper to be corrected – there was, in short, nothing.

The realisation that time hung heavily on her hands was an unsettling one for Domenica. She had always been an active person, and the only time that she could recall having too little to do was during the years of her marriage when, as Mrs Varghese, she had lived in Kerala in a household dominated by her husband's difficult mother. She had wanted to busy herself there with projects, but had been prevented from doing so by the strong expectation that a woman in her position did no work. And so she had endured hour after hour of enforced idleness, putting up with the constant chatter of her garrulous and petulant mother-in-law, until in a terrible flash – an accident in her husband's small electricity factory – she had been propelled into widowhood.

After that, Domenica had not known boredom. The province of an anthropologist is mankind, and mankind offered itself in all its manifold peculiarities. There had been more field-work, including an interesting and productive period amongst the Nabuasa of Timor, which had led to the publication of the book on which her career had been based. But who now had read, or even had heard of *Ritual Exchanges as Indices of Power in a Nabuasa Sub-Clan*? Nobody, thought Domenica. I might as well have written those words on water.

This melancholy contemplation of the transience of academic distinction could have plunged Domenica into something akin to despair. But it was not in her nature to mope, and her realisation that she had nothing to do simply had the effect of galvanising her into action. My friends, she thought, are those whose advice I should take, even if they are not with me at this precise moment. And what would they say? She thought of James Holloway, who was most certainly not one to sit and do nothing. James would say to her: 'Get yourself a motorbike.' Indeed, he had once tried to convert her to biking and had taken her as a passenger on an outing to Falkland, where they had watched real tennis being played in a court in the gardens of the palace. Such a strange game, thought Domenica, with its curious cries and requirement that one should hit the ball off the roof. James had appeared to know the rules and had tried to explain them, but Domenica had a mental block about the rules of sports, and had not taken them in. It was every bit as complicated, she felt, as American football, which did not seem like a game at all, but an orchestrated fight. But that, of course, is what so many men want to do, or at least see done. They want to see conflict and competition, which was what sport was all about.

No, James could keep his motorbikes as far as Domenica was concerned. And what would Dilly Emslie advise her? Dilly, of course, had no truck with motorbikes, but would probably advise her to take on another piece of research. That was good advice, but Domenica did not relish the thought of going off into the field again. The Malacca Straits had been enjoyable, in their way, but somehow she did not see herself summoning up the energy to set up a long trip of that sort. What would be required, then, would be something much more local – anthropology did not have to be performed among distant others; it could be pursued in the anthropologist's back yard. Her friend, Tony Cohen, had gone to Shetland, which was not all that far away, and had written *Whalsay: Symbol, Segment and Boundary in a Shetland Island Community*. There were plenty of things worth studying in mainland Scotland or in its surrounding islands; enough to keep an anthropologist engaged for years. Something local, then, was the solution.

Cheered by the thought that she might find a project that could be embarked upon from home, Domenica rose to her feet and crossed the room to the cupboard in which she kept her notebooks. One of these she called her Projects Book and it contained the jottings of various ideas that she had had over the years. Some of these jottings dealt with Scottish themes, and it was possible that she might find something to follow up in there.

But that was not what she found. Rather, on opening the cupboard and reaching within for the pile of notebooks, her hand alighted on something smooth and cold to the touch; cold enough to chill the heart, with guilt, with sudden regret. A blue Spode teacup. The original one.

Domenica had sought to catch a thief. In so doing, she had become one.

61. *Portrait of a White Lie*

Of course, she thought of Angus, and turned to him. That was the right thing to do; not only did he know the full background to the whole issue of the blue Spode teacup, but he had been actively involved in it. It was Angus who had removed the cup from Antonia's flat, and that made him party to this unfortunate state of affairs; not that she would blame him for this in any way – he had merely acted on her instructions. She was not sure if she needed to reproach herself either – she had acted in good faith – but this absence of moral fault did not mean that she felt comfortable about the fact that she now had in her possession a teacup that did not belong to her. If one has in one's possession an item which one knows belongs to another, then there is a clear obligation to return it to the rightful owner; holding on to it is theft.

As Domenica wrestled with the moral implications of her unfortunate discovery, Angus Lordie settled down to an afternoon of painting. He had been looking forward to a spell of peace, he thought, as the previous few days had been unsettling in the extreme. There had been the business over the puppies – although he was trying to put that out of his mind; of course the puppies would be all right, why would they not be? Then there had been Big Lou's disclosure that she was sheltering the Pretender in her flat in Canonmills. That had been very disturbing, as Angus felt strongly protective of Big Lou. The Pretender, whoever he was, would almost certainly be a charlatan, determined to take maximum advantage of the kindness and hospitality of others. And Big Lou was kind to a fault; everybody knew that.

But what had unsettled Angus more than anything else was that curious meeting with Lard O'Connor in Glass and Thompson and the entrusting by Lard into his hands of the picture he had brought to show Matthew. The moment he had said goodbye to Lard, with a promise to telephone him once Matthew arrived home from his honeymoon, Angus had left Glass and Thompson and made his way back to his flat in Drummond Place, bearing the large wrapped parcel in which the painting was concealed. If people knew what I was carrying, he thought, how surprised they would be. A portrait by Sir Henry Raeburn no less; but not just any Raeburn . . .

He met nobody in Abercromby Place or Nelson Street, but when he turned into Drummond Place itself, and was only a few hundred yards away from home, he bumped into Magnus Linklater.

Magnus was clearly in the mood for a chat. 'Well, Angus,' he said. 'That's an interesting-looking parcel you've got there. One of your own?'

Angus thought quickly. He would have loved to reveal to somebody else – anybody else – what he thought he had, but Magnus was a newspaper editor and would it be a good idea to reveal to the world just yet that a Raeburn portrait of Burns had at last turned up? No, thought Angus, it would be premature. He could not be absolutely sure that this was Burns by Raeburn. He could not be absolutely sure even if this was anybody by Raeburn. There were plenty of Raeburn imitators, inferior artists who painted in the style of the master. Indeed, there were Russian factories, Angus believed, that would turn out a Raeburn today for a few hundred pounds. Could this, he wondered, be a Russian Raeburn?

He had to say something to Magnus, who was looking at him politely while at the same time glancing sideways at the painting. Angus noticed that the top of the wrapping had slipped and had revealed the upper edge of the frame.

'My own? Well, not really,' he replied vaguely. 'Somebody else's painting. I'm just . . . just looking after it for him.'

'Nice frame,' observed Magnus. 'What's the painting like? It's not a MacTaggart, by any chance?' He pointed to a door behind them; they were standing directly outside the house once owned by Sir William MacTaggart.

Angus laughed. 'No. Nothing like that. Nothing of any real consequence.' He felt himself blushing as he spoke; Angus, a direct speaker, had never found it easy to lie, and rarely did so.

'Well,' said Magnus. 'It's good to see Cyril. And how are Cyril's puppies? I haven't seen them in the gardens recently.'

Angus blushed again, more deeply this time. 'I'm sure that they're all right,' he said. 'They've gone off to a good home.'

Magnus smiled. 'Well, that's good news,' he said. 'I had been wondering how you would find homes for all of them. But you obviously did. And one can't be too careful, apparently. I was reading the other day about somebody whose puppies were stolen and sold to a restaurant. Would you believe it?'

Angus swallowed hard. 'That's bad,' he said. His voice sounded distant.

'Oh well,' said Magnus. 'I mustn't linger. And you've got your Raeburn to get back to the studio.'

Angus gave a start. 'Raeburn?'

'Oh, I'm sure it's not that,' said Magnus. 'But one might live in hope.'

Angus forced a laugh. 'I wish I owned a Raeburn,' he said. He did not blush this time; he did not own a Raeburn, even if he happened to be carrying one. He did not own this portrait of Burns; that was the important point. Lard O'Connor owned it, or . . . perhaps somebody else.

He completed his journey to the flat and carried the painting carefully into his studio. Then, setting it down against a wall, he carefully slit the paper down one side and removed it. For a few minutes he did nothing other than stand in front of the painting, absorbing every detail: the well-kent face, with its finely sculpted, intelligent features; the dark hair; the prominent eyebrows; the white, pleated neck stock. And behind it the colours: the dark reds, the rich blacks against which Raeburn painted his sitters, although in this painting there was a table behind the sitter and on this table there was a large decorated jardinière.

Angus dropped down to his knees and examined the jardinière at close quarters. He had seen a picture of it before somewhere; he was sure of that – somewhere, a jardinière, or a memory of a jardinière. He looked at Burns, and the poet stared back at him.

'Dear Rabbie,' he muttered. 'We're a parcel of rogues in a nation. I know that. But one day, maybe, that will all change. Maybe.'

62. The Marrying Kind of Man

'What on earth are you doing down on your hands and knees, Angus?' Domenica had knocked, but had not been heard. When Angus was in his studio, with the door closed, that could happen, and so, finding the front door ajar – Angus did not bother about security: 'Such a bourgeois notion,' he had said to Domenica – she pushed it further open and entered the flat.

Domenica wrinkled her nose. She had always found that Angus's flat had a strange smell to it – not an entirely disagreeable smell, it must be said, but a strange one none the less. It was a mixture of oil paint from the studio, kippers from the kitchen – Angus bought kippers each week from Creelers at the farmers' market – and dog. Domenica had been assured by Angus that Cyril was bathed regularly – at least twice a year – and that as dogs went he was not particularly smelly. But she could still detect his presence through the odour of slightly damp fur and gaminess that wafted about him.

She moved through the corridor, noticing that Angus had not opened his mail for a few days but had left it where the postie tossed it each morning, in a pile in the corner. If Angus were married – not that anybody would marry him, she thought – then all of this would be changed. The skylights, which she now looked up at, would be cleaned, the floorboards would be stripped and revarnished, Cyril would be shampooed once a week; everything would be sparkling.

And Angus himself would be spruced up. A wife could get rid of his clothes and march him round to Stewart, Christie for a complete new wardrobe. That Harris tweed jacket of his would be the first to go, although even a charity shop would draw the line at that. Perhaps the best thing would be to get the Council to come round for a special collection, in the way in which they came round to uplift old fridges and beds, if you booked them. The Council could come and take away all of Angus's clothes.

But all of this was completely hypothetical, Domenica reminded herself. Nobody would marry Angus; nobody could bear to take the whole project on. Certainly she would not . . . She stopped herself. It was all very well for her to say that she would never marry Angus, but could she really say that nobody else would? There were many desperate women in Edinburgh – legions of them – who would probably be quite happy to marry any man, even Angus, if a man were to ask them, which alas he had not. These women would do anything to secure a husband, and would overlook any defects in a man if needs be. Domenica herself was not in this position, but she knew many who were. Lack of inclination on the man's part to marry was a comparatively minor issue for such women. One friend of Domenica's had married a man of such talent and sensitivity in the field of interior decoration that it was widely felt that he was unlikely to have the time to marry. Single-minded pursuit, traps and – or so Domenica felt – sheer force on the woman's part had eventually settled that matter. Another friend, having despaired of finding a full-size husband, had settled for a man who was so thin as to be almost invisible when viewed from the side. He had himself been keen to marry, but had never found anybody, probably, Domenica thought, because nobody had ever actually seen him. 'Better than nothing,' her friend had said philosophically. And it had been a very happy marriage; from the merest scraps, from part of something, may something whole be made.

But then the thought occurred to Domenica: what if another woman, one of these desperate women, were to marry Angus? Would she resent this other woman taking her friend from her? Angus would presumably not be allowed to drop in on Scotland Street with the comfortable frequency of their current arrangement. Women did not like their husbands to have other women as friends, no matter how innocent the relationship. Angus had always been there in her life; without him, things would be quite different. Perhaps . . . But what was the point of marrying Angus, other than to look after him? Did she really want to be in his company all the time, or at least for as much time as being married to him would entail? She thought not.

She pushed open the studio door, and saw Angus on his hands and knees. He looked up, smiled and rose to his feet.

'I was inspecting a painting,' he said. 'A very beautiful – and, if I am proved right – a very important painting, too.'

Intrigued, Domenica crossed the floor of the studio to stand before the portrait.

'I see,' she began. 'Is it who I think it is?'

Angus brushed the dust off the knees of his trousers. 'It certainly is,' he said. 'Or rather, I think it is.'

'And who painted it, do you think?' asked Domenica.

Angus let the question hang in the air for a few moments. Then he said, 'Raeburn. Henry Raeburn.'

Domenica leaned forward and peered at the portrait. 'It has that feel, doesn't it? That richness.' She paused. 'Is it signed?'

Angus shook his head. 'Raeburn didn't sign. You decide these things on technique and on the documentary evidence.'

'And the technique in this painting is right?'

Angus opened his hands in a gesture of uncertainty. 'I think so,' he said. 'But then there are people who know more about these things than I do.'

'James Holloway?'

'Precisely. We'll obviously have to show it to him and see what he says.' He moved away from the painting and took an outsize, red-bound book from a shelf. 'This is Armstrong's book on Raeburn,' he said. 'There's a long list of his sitters at the back here. Look.'

'And is Burns mentioned?'

'No. But that doesn't mean too much. This list is not exhaustive.'

Domenica straightened up and took a few steps back to admire the painting from more of a distance.

'You know,' she said, 'I'm not sure why women found Burns attractive.'

Angus frowned. 'But Burns was handsome,' he protested. 'Look at him.'

'To an extent,' said Domenica. 'It's what one might call an easy face. Reasonably harmonious.'

'Perhaps women liked him because he liked them,' said Angus. 'Isn't that how women feel?'

'I've heard that said,' answered Domenica.

63. A Dug's a Dug for a' that

What happened next was to change Domenica's view of Angus and, indeed, of Cyril. It was in part a sudden moment of mystical insight, a vision of *agape*, a Cloud of Unknowing moment; but it was also a simple realisation on her part of the qualities of both man and dog. And the agent of this transformation was to be Robert Burns himself.

She was standing in the studio with Angus, looking at the Raeburn portrait of Burns. Cyril, who had been sitting on his blanket in another corner of the room, now joined them. He looked up at Domenica, whom he liked, and wagged his tail. Domenica, however, absorbed in the portrait, barely noticed this greeting and continued to talk to Angus. Cyril then sat down and looked about him. As a dog, he had that vague sense that all dogs possess that something was about to happen, although he was not sure what it was. A walk could be ruled out – he had already had that; and dinner-time, if it ever came, was hours away. So the most he could hope for was a word of encouragement or recognition, a pat on the head perhaps, some gesture which indicated to him that the human world was aware of his presence.

He looked about him, and it was at this point that he saw the portrait of Burns. Now dogs are usually insensitive to art. Even the dogs of great painters, whose existence has been footnoted by art historians, have been largely unaware of the artistic greatness of their masters. Botticelli's dog, Nuovolone, an example of the no longer extant breed of Renaissance Terrier, appeared to be indifferent to the large canvases that dominated his master's studio. And Vermeer's dog, Joost, who was of an even rarer breed, a Still-Life Retriever – dogs known for their ability to retrieve objects which had fallen from the still life table – even he paid no attention to the light which shone forth from his master's paintings. This is because dogs rely on smell, and for them a picture is an object with a single smell: a smell forged into one by the separate odours of stand oil, pigment, the hair of the paintbrush and so on. So if a dog comes into a studio, the smell of a painting bears no relation to the objects it depicts. Even a painting of something which would normally be expected to excite the attention of a dog – a hare hung up after the hunt, for example – will not be seen for what it is, but will just be something made of paint and a few other things. In this sense dogs are extreme reductionists.

But now Cyril, having failed to elicit a response from Domenica, turned and looked in the direction in which she and Angus were looking. And suddenly he saw Burns staring back at him. When this happened, he did nothing to begin with, but then he very slowly walked across the studio, approaching Burns as he would a stranger whose intentions he had not yet ascertained.

'Look,' said Angus, nodding in Cyril's direction. 'Cyril's interested.'

Domenica looked at Cyril and smiled. 'Surely not,' she said. 'Doesn't he only see in one dimension?'

'Watch,' whispered Angus.

Cyril was now crouching in front of the painting, his ears down, staring fixedly at the portrait. Then he wagged his tail, a quick backwards and forwards movement, like the motion of windscreen wipers in a storm. Angus now moved forward and went down on his haunches, next to Cyril.

'That's Robert Burns,' Domenica heard him say to the dog. 'Mr Burns, this is Cyril. A gash an' faithfu' tyke / As ever lap a sheugh or dyke / His honest, sonsie, bawsn't face / Ae gat him friends in ilka place / His breast was white, his touzie black / His gawsie tail wi' upward curl / Hung owre his hurdies wi' a swirl.'

Cyril looked up at Angus and smiled, as if acknowledging a compliment.

'Aye,' said Angus. 'You liked dugs, Rabbie. And this dug here is your Luath, or as close to him as you'll find these days. He's a good enough dog, I think. He's certainly been good enough for me.'

He placed a hand on Cyril's head and ruffled his fur gently. Cyril looked up at his master in appreciation, and then returned his gaze to Robert Burns.

Angus addressed Domenica over his shoulder. 'You'll remember Caesar and Luath, won't you, Domenica?'

Domenica did, but had not thought of the poem for years. But Burns was still there, engraved in her memory, drummed into her as a small child at school, in an age when children still learned poetry by heart, and took those lines as baggage, for comfort throughout their lives.

'I remember them,' she said.

'Caesar was the high-born dog,' Angus went on. 'And Luath was a bit like Cyril here. Nothing grand. And they talked about the cares of men and whether the rich or the poor had the better time of it.'

Cyril now advanced slowly towards the painting. He was making a strange snuffling sound, a whimpering, looking up at Robert Burns, as if in some sort of supplication. Then, very slowly, as if expecting a rebuff, he touched the surface of the painting with his tongue.

'Did you see that?' Angus said over his shoulder. 'That's the biggest compliment a dog can pay. That's his homage.'

Now Cyril had had enough; the moment was broken. With a final glance at Burns, he turned round and made his way back to his blanket on the other side of the room. And as he crossed the floor, he smiled at Domenica, the sunlight from the high studio windows glinting off his single gold tooth.

'I think he knew,' said Angus, rising back up to his feet. 'Don't you think he sensed that this was somebody special?'

In normal circumstances, Domenica would have dismissed this as sheer anthropomorphism. A dog could not appreciate Burns; to say otherwise would be to give in to the weak sentimentalism

·Vermeer's Still-Life Retriever·

that animal owners were so prone to and that she always found so ridiculous. But there was something infinitely touching about what she had observed. Cyril, the malodorous Cyril, who was just a dog, no more, had seen something in the painting and had been visibly affected by it. She could not be indifferent to that. She could not be.

'I think that Cyril has just authenticated this painting,' pronounced Angus.

64. Childhood Memories

They withdrew from the studio. Angus covered the Raeburn with an old blanket, a threadbare square of hodden grey, and called Cyril to heel. Then, with the studio door closed behind them, they made their way into the kitchen.

Domenica resisted the temptation to open a window. It is not generally considered polite, she reminded herself, to go into the house of another and open a window, there being an element of judgement in such an action. Nor, she thought, should one rearrange any of the items in a room, nor even turn on a light. She did not think that Angus would notice any of these things, but she had been strangely moved by what she had witnessed in the studio, and she did not want to compromise the almost mystical moment of insight that had been vouchsafed her.

And what precisely was that? It was difficult to be too specific – the whole point about a moment of insight is that it defies quotidian description – but she had suddenly appreciated the sheer otherness of Angus. Most of us go through life so absorbed in the cocoon of ourselves that we rarely stop to consider the other. Of course we think that we do; indeed we may pride ourselves on our capacity for empathy; we may be considerate and thoughtful in our dealings with others, but how often do we stand before them, so to speak, and experience what it is to be them? She asked herself this, and remembered, vaguely, something she had read somewhere, about the I-Thou encounter. Martin Buber? That sounded right, but now, in the kitchen of Angus Lordie's flat, the recollection was vague, and the moment, already, was passing.

She looked at Angus, at his paint-bespattered corduroy trousers; at his somewhat battered Harris Tweed jacket; at the Paisley handkerchief-cum-cravat that he had tied round his throat; at his shoes, old brown brogues which he obviously tended with care, for they were polished to a high shine. How often have I looked at him in this way? she asked herself. How often have I noticed or, indeed, listened to him? We talk, but do I actually listen, or is our conversation mainly a question of my waiting for him to stop and for it to be my turn to say something? For how many of us is that what conversation means – the setting up of our lines?

She looked at him as he moved over to the sink and filled his ancient kettle with water. She looked at the sink itself, at the tottering pile of pots that surely could not be added to any further without collapse. She looked beyond the sink at the window behind it, in need of a clean on both sides. She looked at the notice-board he had created for himself from a large square of dark cork; at the photographs tacked onto it; the notes to self; the bills paid and unpaid. This was Angus. This was another. This was another life.

While he busied himself with the kettle and the ladling into a jug of several spoonfuls of coffee, Domenica moved over to the notice-board and bent down to examine the photographs. She had never seen them before. The notice-board was nothing new to the room, but she had never seen it before, and she felt ashamed, because Angus was her friend, one of her closest friends, and she had never even bothered to look at his notice-board.

'Do you mind?' she asked. 'Do you mind if I take a look at these photographs?'

He half-turned from his position at the sink. 'No,' he said. 'I don't mind. Of course you can look at them. I'll tell you what they are, if you like.'

Domenica peered at the photographs. There were about a dozen of them, and they seemed to be of varying ages. Some, the older ones, had an almost sepia look to them, as if they had been taken from an old family album. Others were more vivid, the colours still there, even if fading slightly.

'I assume that's you,' she said. 'That's you as a boy.'

Angus, who was fetching cups from a cupboard, glanced over his shoulder. 'Yes. That's me. And a friend of mine. He came from Mull. His dad was a doctor over there. The doctor drove a Lagonda. I remember it. Beautiful car. We were at school together. He was called Johnnie.'

Domenica looked more closely. Two boys, aged twelve or so, stood in front of a dry-stane dyke, both wearing kilts and jerseys. She noticed that the shadows on the ground were long; it was after noon. Behind the dyke she could make out a field, a hillside, rising sharply to a high, empty sky. She closed her eyes, very briefly, and for some reason the words came into her mind, unexpected, unbidden, but from the region of the heart, from that very region: I love this country.

She became aware of Angus behind her. She heard his breathing.

'We had just started at Glenalmond,' he said. 'Our first year there, I think. It was quite tough in those days – and they turned us out to roam the hills on a Sunday. In the summer term, at least. Johnnie and I used to go all over the Sma' Glen. There was a farm called Connachan down towards Monzie where we used to go for tea when we were meant to be up at the top of the hill. The farmer had a couple of daughters our age and they'd tease us. We got on famously.

'And at the back of the farm,' Angus continued, 'there was the River Almond. You probably know it. Well, further up, along the road to Auchnafree, the farmer had a wire cable across the river with a basket suspended from it. You could pull yourself across in the basket. He and his shepherds used to use this to get across the river without getting their feet wet. The sheep-dogs too. Dogs like Cyril. The dogs loved it. Dogs love anything like that.

'We used to swim in the river too. It was always freezing, even in summer. And then we'd eat sandwiches on the rocks. Bully beef sandwiches. Remember bully beef? Do you think anybody eats it now?'

He paused. 'There are some lines,' he said quietly, 'that come to me when I look at that photograph. "We twa ha paidled in the burn / From morning sun til dine" . . .'

'"But seas between us braid hae roar'd" . . .' Domenica supplied.

'Exactly,' said Angus. 'Johnnie . . .'

He stopped. She waited for him to say something more, but he did not.

65. From Hero to Zero in One Simple Word

Bingo! thought Bruce. He was sitting in the small restaurant over the road from Nick McNair's flat in Leith, into which he had just moved. Then he thought: Julia Donald! That dim, dumb . . . zero. Yes, that's what she was. She was a zero, a minus quantity even. And to think that she had me believing that her baby – her stupid zero baby – was mine, when all the time she was seeing Watson Cooke, the Watsonian zero in that Clarence Street dump of his. Number Zero, Clarence Street, EHZero ZeroYS! What a narrow escape. And they deserved each other, just as they would deserve all those zero nappies for that dim baby of theirs. No thank you! Not *pour moi*!

Now, at the table in the restaurant, with seven of Nick's friends, Bruce felt much happier. There was a bit of an unresolved issue over the fact that the advertising agency for which Nick was working was owned by Julia Donald's father, but Bruce was beginning to think of a way out and he would deal with that later. There would be plenty of time. For the moment he would have to work out how to respond to the woman on the other side of the table who was looking at him. More than that; she was giving him the look. And that was when he said to himself, Bingo!

There was a slight problem, of course, and that was that Bruce had not caught her name when they had been introduced. Shelley? Sheila? It was something like that. Well, that was not a problem, really. If you don't know somebody's name, thought Bruce, then ask them. It was an excellent chat-up line, in fact. What's your name? is seriously romantic, he thought. It works every time.

He leaned across the table. 'What's your name?' he asked.

The young woman on the other side of the table smiled. She was undoubtedly attractive, and when she smiled she became even more so. 'Shauna,' she said. 'And you?'

Bruce returned the smile. 'Bruce. Just call me Bruce.'

There was no need to add the 'just call me' part, but Bruce found that it was another thing that worked every time. I work every time, he thought. It's not what I say, it's me!

'Do you work with Nick?' Bruce asked.

Shauna nodded. 'Yes,' she said. 'Now and then. I do shoots with him.'

She looked down the table and waved at Nick, who was seated at the other end. Nick winked back at her.

Bruce smiled. 'You're in an agency?' Everybody surrounding Nick, he had decided, seemed to work in some agency or another.

'Yes,' said Shauna, 'but I'm strictly advertising. Nick shoots for PR people. I'm very specialised. Just soaps, moisturisers, things like that. I do ads for the beauty industry.'

'Great,' said Bruce.

'You might have seen some of my work,' Shauna went on. 'Do you read the mags?'

Bruce thought for a moment. What mags was she talking about? The sort of magazines that Julia liked to read – those vacuous glossies?

'Sometimes,' he said.

Shauna was looking at him. 'Let me guess what you do,' she said, propping her chin on her hands in mock concentration. 'You're a model, right?'

Bruce sat back in his chair. 'Well . . .'

'I knew,' said Shauna. 'I could tell. You can always tell the clothes horses.'

Bruce was silent.

'No offence,' Shauna said. 'Some of my best friends are clothes horses.' She laughed.

Bruce bit his lip and looked away from her. He muttered something to himself, something unrepeatable. But she, too, had turned away and was talking to the man beside her, a thin man with a pair of round wire-framed spectacles; not a clothes horse, thought Bruce.

He looked about him. There was a man to his left, who was talking to somebody on his other side, but on his right was a woman, also attractive, but in different way from Shauna. She, though, was engaged in animated conversation with the man on her right. Bruce looked down at his hands. He suddenly felt very lonely.

He rose to his feet and looked about the restaurant. A small sign at the far end of the room pointed the direction: a picture of a man's hat and a pair of women's gloves. Bruce crossed the room, leaving the noise behind him. He pushed open the door of the lavatory and stood in the small space before the basin. There was a mirror. He looked in it.

'What do you think you're doing?' he whispered to the reflection. 'Just what do you think you're doing?'

There was no answer. He reached out and traced the line of his chin on the mirror.

'Is this it?' he asked. 'Is this all you are?'

He was suddenly aware of somebody pushing open the door behind him. He leaned forward to allow the person to pass.

'Bruce?'

It was Nick McNair. He was standing directly behind Bruce, and Bruce could see his expression in the mirror. He looked concerned.

'Are you all right, Bruce?' Nick asked. 'You got up and charged out. You looked sick to me.'

'I'm all right,' said Bruce. 'I just felt . . .'

Nick was staring at him. He shook his head. 'You're not all right, Bruce. You look really upset.' He paused. 'Is it the splitting up? Is that it?' He reached out and placed a hand on Bruce's shoulder. 'Listen,' he said. 'I know what it's like. You feel all raw inside. You just do. And you just have to wait for time to do its thing. It will. Eventually.'

Bruce looked down at the floor. 'I lied to you,' he said. 'I said that I left her. It was the other way round. She chucked me out. She'd been two-timing me.'

'Oh dear,' said Nick.

'Yes. And her old man took back the car he gave me. And he's Graeme Donald. Yes, that's him. The guy who owns the agency. He hates me, you know.'

Nick was silent. He took his hand off Bruce's shoulder. 'You're in a bad way, Bruce,' he said. 'I suspected that you'd been chucked out. That's why I offered you the room.'

'Why bother with me?'

Nick put his hand back on Bruce's shoulder, a gesture that Bruce found strangely comforting.

'Because I'm a Christian,' said Nick.

66. Greed All About It

The ending of a honeymoon is, in metaphorical terms, the ending of a period of charity during which the other is able to do no wrong or, rather, is able to do wrong but also able to get away with it. As we all know, politicians have a honeymoon period during which the electorate forgives if not everything, then at least rather a lot. Then, when the metaphorical honeymoon comes to an end, the mood shifts, and every slip, every ill-advised step, indeed every sign of simple human fallibility, is eagerly pounced upon. There! shouts the opposition in triumphant chorus. There! You see what he's like! Sleaze! Ineptitude! The very qualities that we ourselves so conspicuously lack! The end of a real honeymoon, one might hope, is not quite like that, even if one has discovered, on the honeymoon, perhaps, that one has married a sleazy and inept person. Even then, one's spouse does not typically become critical and unforgiving, as an electorate may be. Yet life is certainly different after the honeymoon.

To begin with, one has to work, and for Matthew that meant going in to the gallery on that first morning back – easier work, perhaps, than clocking in at a factory or a busy office, but work none the less. The mail, which had been moved from the doormat to his desk by a helpful friend, was stacked in neat piles: three weeks of catalogues, enquiries and bills. The bills had yet to turn red, but would require reasonably prompt attention; the catalogues would need to be perused; the enquiries answered. Three weeks may not be an overly long time in a slow-moving business, but it seemed to Matthew that his working life, there in the gallery, was part of an altogether different world – a world which was of course familiar, but which in some ways was now strange. That would pass, of course, but for the moment the world of Dundas Street, of Edinburgh, somehow felt very alien. The light was different – this attenuated, northern light; the colours, too – these subtle shades – greys, greens – everything was so much more muted than the bright tones, the strong light of Australia.

He sat at his desk and contemplated the piles of mail. He had left Edinburgh a newly married man, blissfully happy, excited beyond measure. Now he was back as a man who had faced death in shark-infested waters, who had been rescued by a dolphin – a rescue he could not bring himself to talk about because nobody would believe him; a man who had been wrongfully detained and threatened with psychiatric confinement; a man who had thought that he was his father's son, only to discover that he might well be the son of another man altogether, the president of the Cat Society of Singapore. Those were transforming events for anybody, but how much more so for one who had been on his honeymoon at the time?

He had left Elspeth behind in the flat, still in bed, still deep asleep in her state of unadjusted jet lag. He had looked at her fondly from the door of the bedroom, standing there gazing upon the form under the blankets: his wife. The word still came uneasily to his tongue; it was so new. And he, Matthew, who had thought that he would never find anybody, was now a husband; moreover he was a husband setting off to work. It was such a mundane, unexceptional situation, the great domestic cliché, but for Matthew it was something to be relished, and committed to memory.

They had not discussed what Elspeth was to do. She had said that she would no longer teach, but that she wanted to be occupied in some way. Matthew had suggested that she work in the gallery with him, but she had been reluctant to do that: a marriage, she thought, stood its best chance if both parties had their own areas of activity within it. Seeing one another all day and then again in the evening could become claustrophobic, Elspeth thought, even if one was head-over-heels in love with one's spouse. So the gallery would be Matthew's, and she would do something else.

'Something will turn up,' she said.

And he had agreed. She was the sort of person for whom something would always turn up.

Matthew thought of this as he sat at his desk in the gallery and worked through the pile of mail. Even if there were bills – and one of them, a bill from his framers, was quite large – there was good financial news from the managers of his portfolio. Some of his shares had done particularly well during his absence on honeymoon and the letter was bullish in tone. 'Even further gains can be anticipated,' it said, 'and we are inclined to advise against profit-taking at this point.' He was relieved that he was no poorer, but he was not sure if he necessarily wanted to be all that much richer. And he was convinced that he did not want to engage in profit-taking, either now or at some stage in the future. That sounded so greedy, he thought; the sort of thing that fat cats took, or the sellers of junk bonds, or speculators in currency. They took profits and gobbled them up in the way in which a greedy person cuts off the best part of a pie.

He laid aside the financial report and attended to the rest of the letters. One was a hand-written note in a script he recognised: that of Angus Lordie.

Dear Matthew,
Welcome back! Make sure you contact me the moment you get in as I have some extraordinary news for you. Remember Lard O'Connor, your somewhat dubious pal from Glasgow? He of the ample proportions? Well, he turned up while you were away – with a picture for you, which he consigned to my eager hands pro tem. You'll never guess what it is! A well-known Scottish portrait painter, Raeburn, no less! And his subject? A Scottish poet, from Ayrshire, to be precise. Yes! Contact me soonest for delivery of said masterpiece and chat about what can be done.

Matthew looked at his watch. If Angus came round shortly, they could go over the road for coffee, and Big Lou would welcome them warmly, as she always did. That was the reassuring thing about Edinburgh. It was always the same; nothing ever changed.

67. A Private View

Matthew's telephone call produced an assurance from Angus that he would be round at the gallery within half an hour. 'With the painting,' Angus added. 'It may as well have another outing, since it's been carried around the streets of Edinburgh ever since Mr O'Connor graced us with his presence. And he brought it over from Glasgow in the train. He probably put it in the guard's van.'

'There are no guard's vans any more,' Matthew pointed out. 'In fact, many of our trains don't even have seats any more. Look at the number of people who have to stand.'

Angus rang off and Matthew returned to his pile of mail. There was a sale of Scottish art coming up at Sotheby's, and he had been sent the catalogue. There was a Raeburn, but an undistinguished one, thought Matthew; one might walk right past it and not bother to enquire as to who the sitter was. But Robert Burns . . . One could not walk past him.

He was still looking at the catalogue when Angus arrived twenty minutes later. He was carrying a large, wrapped parcel, and Cyril was with him. On entering the gallery, Cyril, who liked Matthew, ran across the room to greet him, licking his hands appreciatively. Then he lay down at Matthew's feet and stared at his ankles.

Cyril had long wanted to bite Matthew's ankles. He did not want to do this out of hostility – quite the contrary: Cyril admired Matthew's ankles, which he thought presented the perfect target into which to sink one's teeth. Had he been able to articulate this desire, he would have had to resort to Mallory's famous explanation as to why he wanted to climb Everest: because it was there. Matthew's ankles were there, too, and the sight of them made Cyril drool as he rested his head on the carpet below Matthew's desk. Just one little nip, he wondered. If he was quick enough about it, they might not even notice. But it was not to be. Cyril knew that he was just a dog, and that it was not given to dogs to do all the things they might wish to do. There was neither rhyme nor reason for this limitation; it, again, was just there. Angus, who fed him and took him for walks, was a god; and in Cyril's theology, vaguely sensed, like some obscure article of faith handed down from a previous generation, it was the duty of dogs to do the bidding of their gods and to accept whatever small mercies they might be shown. Cyril's heart, therefore, was filled with gratitude: gratitude for Angus, for whom he would sacrifice his life if called upon to do so; gratitude for the smells which suffused his world, smells sometimes so strange and beguiling that they challenged even his acute olfactory memory; gratitude for being here with these two men rather than outside.

After a quick enquiry about Matthew's trip, Angus busied himself with the unwrapping of the painting. 'Your fat friend from Glasgow has surpassed himself,' he whispered. 'The missing Raeburn portrait of Burns. Absolutely beyond a shadow of a doubt. And he had it! Lard O'Connor had it!'

Matthew examined the painting carefully, crouching to do so, and exposing a further portion of ankle. Cyril watched, his eyes narrowing, focused on the glimpse of taut white flesh. His whiskers twitched.

'Well, it looks like Raeburn all right,' Matthew said, straightening up. 'Did Lard know what he had?'

'Not the first clue,' said Angus.

Matthew was thinking aloud. 'Of course there's the question of provenance,' he said. 'We can assume that it's stolen. Lard is a gangster, you know.'

Angus's face fell. 'Does that mean that we have to hand it in?'

Matthew sighed. 'Well, we can hardly ignore the fact that it probably belongs to somebody else.'

'But can't we just ask him where he got it from?' asked Angus. 'There may be an innocent explanation, for all you know. People sometimes have these old things in the family. They don't know what it is they have. Maybe the O'Connors had . . .'

Angus stopped in the face of Matthew's sceptical look.

'I doubt it. But we can certainly see. We can ask him.'

'And perhaps we should give him the benefit of the doubt,' said Angus.

Matthew conceded that this would be possible. He had begun to see the headlines: Edinburgh Art Dealer Discovers Missing

Raeburn. And there would be a quote from Sir Timothy Clifford, who would say, 'This is a major moment for Scottish art. The nation can be very grateful to this young dealer whose eye it was that unearthed this treat of Scottish portraiture.'

And the Culture Minister herself would say, 'Another piece of Scotland's artistic patrimony has today been brought home. Well done all concerned!'

'All right,' Matthew said. 'I'll get in touch with Lard and ask him to come over to speak to us about it.'

Angus agreed that this was the best way forward. But for Matthew there was another question to be resolved, and he now asked it of Angus: how could he be sure that this was what he said it was? Could authentication be based purely on the style in which the painting was executed?

Angus was aware that Matthew's knowledge of art was spotty, to say the least. He was learning, though, and this painting would let him learn further.

'Style may be the test,' he said. 'But there's the internal evidence of the painting itself. The sitter. The clothing, and so on.'

Matthew looked down at the painting. 'He's dressed the right way, isn't he? Burns wore those white neck thingies. And it looks like him, doesn't it?'

'It certainly looks like him,' agreed Angus. 'But there's something else. You see that jardinière there – in the background. You see it? It's very interesting. I've seen it somewhere before, I'm sure of it.'

'In another Raeburn?'

Angus stroked his chin. 'I don't know. Maybe. But take a look at it. It's ceramic, probably Chinese, or possibly Western chinoiserie. Lowestoft, for example, did some very Chinese-looking things. It could be from one of the English potteries.'

Matthew leaned forward to examine the painting more closely, and as he did so, Cyril gave a growl. Somebody was at the door of the gallery, peering in. A man of bulk; of stature. A Glaswegian. Cyril could tell, and he growled.

68. Entrances and Exits

'So youses have been looking efter ra picture?' Lard O'Connor said as he entered the gallery. Cyril growled again, and then lifted his head up and gave a bark.

'That's your dug, isn't it?' Lard said, looking at Cyril. 'I seen you wi' him last time, Angus? Remember? Up at that fancy chippie. That place doon the road.'

'Glass and Thompson,' said Angus. 'Indeed you have. Cyril was with me when you brought the painting over.'

'Cyril?' asked Lard. 'What sort of a name is that for a dug? Cyril! My weans have dugs, but I wouldnae let any o' them call a dug Cyril! Cyril's a name for . . .'

Lard hesitated, and glanced at Matthew. You never know in Edinburgh, he thought, and these days you had to be careful what you said.

'Well, be that as it may,' said Angus breezily, 'as you can see, Mr O'Connor, Matthew is back from Australia. From his honeymoon.'

Lard smiled. 'Honeymoon?' he asked. 'Did you get any sleep?'

Matthew smiled – nervously. 'We were in Perth, Mr O'Connor.'

'Perth's in Scotland,' said Lard. 'I was in . . . I knew some boys in the prison there. They've got a big prison up there.'

'Yes, I believe that's true,' said Matthew. 'But you were in Barlinnie, I assume . . . I mean, you must have known some boys in Barlinnie. Wrongly convicted, of course.'

Lard laughed. 'They werenae wrangly convicted,' he said. 'Naebody who's in ra Bar-L is wrangly convicted! Their problem was that they couldnae get Mr Beltrami to speak for them. If you get Mr Beltrami, then you get your story across, know what I mean?'

'Very interesting,' said Matthew. 'But, anyway, there's a Perth in Australia. That's where we were.'

Lard raised an eyebrow. 'I ken fine that Perth's in Australia,' he said, a note of irritation surfacing in his voice. 'You think that just because . . .'

'Not at all,' said Angus quickly. 'Now listen, Mr O'Connor, I think I can tell you something very interesting about this painting of yours.'

Lard gave Matthew a final warning look and transferred his gaze to Angus. 'Oh yes? What's it worth? Couple of hundred?'

Angus smiled. 'Considerably more than that. Very considerably. If it's what we think it is, then you're looking at a very large sum of money, Mr O'Connor. Many thousands.'

Lard was interested now. 'Do you mind if I have a wee sit-doon?' he said. 'Then you can tell me all about my . . . auntie's picture.'

He lowered himself onto the chair that Matthew had drawn up for him. The chair was of solid construction, but under Lard's weight, the strainers creaked.

'Your auntie?' asked Angus. 'So that's where the painting is from?'

'Aye,' said Lard. 'My auntie doon in Greenock. My mamie's sister so she was. Deid now. But she left me and my brothers all her wee knick-knacks, you know. She had some gallus stuff. China. A statue of the Virgin Mary this high from over in Knock. That went to the wumman who used to take her to church every Sunday. We would have offered it to Archbishop Conti, you know, if she hadn't taken it.' He was now warming to his theme and continued, 'And there was some Lladró. You know that stuff? A Lladró statue of a couple having a snog. I think that's what it was called. Really good stuff. My auntie had an eye, you see.'

'Like Mr Burrell,' interjected Matthew.

'Aye,' said Lard. 'Exactly. Like Mr Burrell hissel.'

Angus rubbed his hands together. 'Well, that's all very interesting,' he said. 'We can come back to that issue a bit later on. The important thing is to decide what you want us to do with this painting. I take it that you want to sell it? Or is it of emotional value, having been your auntie's?'

Lard looked up at the ceiling. 'I think . . . I think I might just sell it,' he said. 'I think that's what my auntie would have wanted me to do. She knew that I liked to sell things.'

Matthew watched him as he spoke. It was difficult, he thought, not to smile while the lies were told.

Lard turned to Matthew. 'You can sell it, son? We could go haufers. Or do you want to buy it yoursel? If you give me a good enough price, we can dae business together, nice and discreet, know what I mean?'

Angus glanced at Matthew. 'But why should you worry about discretion, Mr O'Connor? If it's your auntie's picture, as you tell us, than surely it doesn't matter how it's sold.'

'It's my auntie's memory,' said Lard angrily. 'I wouldnae want everybody to know that I was selling my auntie's picture. You know what folk are like.'

'Of course,' said Matthew. He looked at his watch. It was time for coffee and he wanted Lard O'Connor out of the gallery. If they went over to Big Lou's then they could leave him there when the time came. 'I suggest that the three of us leave the painting here – it will be perfectly safe— and go over to Big Lou's for coffee. You'll remember her, I think. Big Lou.'

Lard's face brightened. 'I remember her. That nice wumman. Aye, that's a good idea, Matthew. We can tak a dander over there and talk aboot it a'.'

They left the gallery, the Raeburn having been safely stored in Matthew's strongroom. Then with Angus and Cyril leading the way, followed by Lard, and then Matthew, they crossed Dundas Street towards the steps that led down to Big Lou's coffee house. And that is where Lard fell. There, on the very steps on which the late Hugh MacDiarmid had once stumbled, Lard fell forward; fell past Angus, who was immediately ahead of him, hit the stone with his head, and tumbled like a great, broken rag-doll, down to the bottom of the basement.

Matthew looked down. The sun was slanting across the street and fell in soft gold on the inert body below. In that curious moment of clarity that follows disaster, that moment of silence when the din of an accident is replaced by the quiet that preceded it, he saw that the angle of Lard's head in relation to his body was an unnatural one. Matthew saw, too, that the great sides of the fallen man, barely contained in the stretched fabric of his shirt, were not moving, as one would expect, if there was breath in the body. But there was none; just stillness.

69. Death of a Gangster

Later, Matthew was to have only a blurred recollection of the events that came in the immediate aftermath of the collapse of Lard O'Connor. He remembered standing at the top of the steps that led down to Big Lou's coffee bar; he remembered the sound of Lard's head hitting the stone, a sort of sharp crack, like a piece of wood being broken; and he remembered finding himself down at Lard's side, reaching for the great, heavy arm that was poking through the railings, and moving it to a more comfortable position. But Lard, by then, was beyond comfort.

For his part, Angus had a clearer memory of everything that happened, down to the smallest detail. He remembered the sound of Lard's breathing as the Glaswegian visitor followed him down the steps. Angus remembered stopping and half-turning to explain to Lard that the steps were hazardous and that it was in this precise spot that Scotland's most distinguished poet of the twentieth century had almost brought his literary career to a premature end. But he did not say any of this because, as he turned, he heard a strange sound emanating from Lard's mouth – a choking sound; the sound of one struggling for breath.

Then Angus saw that Lard's face was quite white and that his vast bulk was beginning to sway. He'll crush me if he falls, he thought, and moved to the side of the steps, pressing himself against the flimsy barrier of the badly maintained railings. That action saved him from sure and certain injury as Lard suddenly toppled forward and half-slid, half-bounced down the steep set of stone steps.

When Lard reached the bottom, Angus rushed forward, to be joined by Matthew at the side of the inert, prone figure.

'Tell Big Lou to call an ambulance,' said Angus quickly. 'And then come back out here and help me shift him. We don't want his head lower than his body. All the blood will drain down.'

Matthew stepped over Lard and dashed into the café. Big Lou had already abandoned the bar and was coming towards him. She had her cordless telephone in her hand.

'Call an ambulance,' shouted Matthew. 'Quick.'

Cyril barked. He was standing outside, staring at Lard on the ground and at Angus kneeling beside him. Something had happened in the world of men, but he was unsure what it was and if he was expected to do anything. To be on the safe side, he raised his head and gave a howl. That would cover an eventuality that was looking increasingly likely to him.

Matthew and Angus now manhandled Lard's trunk and legs down the last few steps so that they were at the same level as his head and chest. He lay there on the cold stone, his mouth open, his eyes staring up at the patch of sky above. There was no movement.

'Artificial respiration,' said Matthew. 'I'm going to apply mouth-to-mouth.'

Angus nodded. 'And shouldn't we thump his chest?' he asked.

'We could give it a try,' said Matthew. 'But he looks a goner to me.'

They did their best. At one point Matthew thought that he detected some movement within Lard, but it proved just to be a great belch, which came up from his stomach, a last protest against the Glaswegian diet that had been directed into that long-suffering organ. It was a posthumous belch, and it was followed by silence.

A few minutes later, the ambulance arrived, and two men, each carrying some sort of box, came dashing down the steps.

'All right, boys,' said one of the ambulance men. 'We'll take over.'

They worked on Lard for more than ten minutes, ventilating him and applying a defibrillator to his chest. When the current was switched on, Lard's body gave a twitch, but nothing more, and was once again still. They tried several times, looked at the heart tracing on the machine, and then exchanged glances.

'Did you see what happened?' asked one of the ambulance men, feeling for a pulse under Lard's chin and then shaking his head.

'He gasped,' said Angus. 'He was just above me on the steps and he gasped. It was a strange sound. Then he tumbled over and hit his head on the way down.'

The ambulance man nodded. 'His heart had probably stopped by the time he hit the ground,' he said. 'Big chap like this. That's the way they go.' He paused. 'Friend of yours?'

Angus hesitated. Was Lard his friend? He knew very little about him, and what little he knew was hardly favourable. But now he was mortal clay – that which we all become sooner or later. And if there is such a thing as an immortal soul – and Angus thought there was – then Lard had had such a one as the rest of us; a flawed one, perhaps, but a soul none the less. He had said something about his weans. So there were children. And a Mrs O'Connor. And a life of plans and ambitions and fears – just the same as the rest of us.

'Yes,' he said. 'He was a friend of mine.' He looked at Matthew. 'And of you too, Matthew?'

Matthew nodded. 'Yes, he was my friend too.'

'I'm very sorry,' said the ambulance man. 'But I can tell you, he won't have known what hit him. Out like a light. If that's any consolation.'

It was, and Angus thought of those words as he helped the ambulance men to roll Lard onto the stretcher and carry him up the stone steps. 'We're not meant to allow you to help,' said the other ambulance man. 'Health and safety regulations, you know. But you boys were his friends and maybe he would have liked it.'

'He would,' said Angus. 'He would have liked it.'

And he thought for a moment how stupid our society had become, that its nanny-like concern for risk should prevent one man helping another to take a dead friend up the steps of Big Lou's coffee bar. How silly; how petty; how dehumanising. And when they reached the top, he looked up at the sky, which had been overcast earlier on, but now was clearing. There was high cloud, white cloud banked up to wide expanses of blue, and Angus wondered, curiously, what an artist might have made of this scene, Bellini perhaps, or Moretto. The angels would descend – well-built, strong angels – to carry Lard upwards to his rest; a man who had been undeserving in this world welcomed into the next, where human wrongs are forgiven and the heaviest become light.

70. Life, Death and the Road to the Isles

Matthew and Angus gave lengthy statements to the police. Photographs were taken, measurements made, chalk marks scratched on the steps to trace the overweight Glaswegian's fatal plunge. And then the police, having been satisfied that they had all the necessary details, went on their way, leaving Matthew, Angus and Big Lou to comfort one another in the coffee bar.

At the end of an hour of going over what had happened, Big Lou announced that she did not wish to keep the coffee bar open that day. She wanted to go home, to recover from the shock. Matthew, looking at his watch, realised that he would have to go back to the gallery. The 'Back Soon' notice was mildly misleading even on a normal day; now it was extremely so.

'Come and have lunch with me,' said Big Lou to Angus. 'Come down to the flat. We can carry on talking there.'

This invitation was just what Angus wanted. He could not face going back to his own flat, to his empty studio; the witnessing of a tragedy, even a small one, makes us want the company of others, makes us want not to be alone.

'I'll come,' he said to Big Lou.

They said goodbye to Matthew and began to make their way down Dundas Street towards Canonmills. Everything seemed so normal, so everyday, thought Angus, and yet only few hours before they had seen a man snatched from this life without warning. In the midst of life we are in death. Angus remembered the words from the Book of Common Prayer – those grave, resonant words. 'Man that is born of a woman hath but a short time to live, and is full of misery. He cometh up, and is cut down, like a flower . . .' Lard had been cut down like a flower, before his very eyes. We brought nothing into this world, and it is certain we can carry nothing out. That was as true of Lard as it was of anyone. Such powerful words – such true words; language – and life – stripped to its bare essentials.

He looked at Big Lou, walking beside him; at that solid, reliable woman who had suffered so much.

'I feel very raw inside,' he said to her. 'I hardly knew him, but it's been such a shock.'

She reached over and touched him lightly on the arm. She had never done that before, but she did it now.

'I know what you mean,' she said. 'I couldn't carry on working today after I saw what happened to that poor man.'

They walked on in silence. Now they were at the bottom of Brandon Street and not far from Big Lou's flat. Angus had never been there before, but had imagined it. It was full of books, he believed – the stock that had been in the bookshop when she had bought it and turned it into a coffee bar.

'I'm looking forward to seeing your books, Lou,' he said, as they started to climb the stairs to her flat, which was on the top floor.

Lou nodded. 'There are a lot of them,' she said. She paused. 'I suppose, though, that the Pretender will be in. He hardly ever gets up until halfway through the afternoon.'

With all the morning's excitement, Angus had forgotten about the Pretender, whom Big Lou was sheltering on behalf of her Jacobite boyfriend.

'How long is he staying with you, Lou?' he asked. 'Surely they don't expect you to put him up for much longer?'

Big Lou sighed. She explained that she was not sure. Robbie had talked of a short time, but the Pretender seemed to have settled in and showed no signs of going off to rally his supporters, which is what she thought had been the original plan.

'He's awfully difficult, Angus,' said Lou, as she fished for her keys. 'He doesn't really speak any English, and so Robbie communicates with him in French. I have a bit of French too, but he seems to ignore me whenever I say anything to him. It's as if he doesn't understand what I'm saying.'

Big Lou opened her front door and ushered Angus into the flat. A light was on in the hall, and from the kitchen there came the sound of voices. She looked surprised.

'Robbie,' she whispered. 'Robbie and the Pretender.'

They crossed the hall and entered the kitchen. Angus saw Robbie first, sitting with his back to him, at the kitchen table. On the other side, a slighter figure, wearing a purple dressing gown, was gesticulating angrily. When Big Lou and Angus entered the kitchen, Robbie turned round and the Pretender stopped gesticulating.

'I've brought Angus back for lunch,' Big Lou explained. 'We saw a terrible thing outside the coffee bar. A man died.'

Robbie looked sympathetic. 'Oh. What happened?'

'Hah!' said the Pretender. '*Un homme est mort. Bof! Alors? Et moi? Ça ne me regarde pas.*' (Hah! A man died. Bof! And then? And me? That has nothing to do with me.)

Big Lou glanced at him and whispered to Angus. 'He's very self-centred.'

Robbie rose to his feet. 'There is a bit of a crisis here, Lou,' he said. 'The Pretender went out this morning.'

'That makes a change,' said Big Lou. 'Normally he spends the morning in bed.'

'Well, not this morning,' said Robbie. 'He went up to the High Street. And he got involved in an incident in one of those tourist shops that sell tartans. Some row about Royal Stuart tartan. They called the police and the Pretender ran away.'

Angus had difficulty not smiling. History, it seemed, had a way of repeating itself. 'So now he's on the run from the authorities,' he said.

'Yes,' said Robbie. 'And he wants to go up to the Outer Islands. He wants to get away and rally his supporters.'

'Well, that must be why he came in the first place,' said Angus. 'And it would have been rather disappointing if he had not become a wanted man. Hiding in the heather is all very well, but it must seem a bit pointless if one is not actually being pursued by anybody.'

Robbie glowered at Angus. 'It's not a joke,' he said reproachfully. 'This is dead serious. The Hanoverians will stop at nothing.'

Angus tried to look serious. 'I'm sorry. I shouldn't make light of these things.'

The Pretender now rose to his feet. He glared suspiciously at Angus and then addressed Robbie.

'*Aux îles,*' he said. '*Nous n'avons qu'une seule destination. Les îles.*' (To the Isles! We have a single destination. The Isles.) To the islands, thought Angus. Well, at least there were reliable ferries these days, which is more than could be said for the Scotland of Charles Edward Stuart.

"Aux îles"

71. *A Threat from Irene*

'Now then, Bertie,' said Irene Pollock, as they walked up the hill towards Queen Street. 'As you know, Dr Fairbairn has gone to Aberdeen.'

Bertie nodded gravely. He had been thrilled by the news that Dr Fairbairn was leaving, but his hopes of being released from psychotherapy had very quickly been dashed.

'But don't worry,' his mother went on. 'He has not left you floundering.'

Bertie thought that there was no danger of his floundering. He had never seen the point of his weekly psychotherapy session; nothing that Dr Fairbairn said had ever changed anything for Bertie, and now that he was going to see Dr Fairbairn's successor, the same would apply.

'Is Carstairs near Aberdeen, Mummy?' Bertie asked.

'Goodness me, Bertie,' said Irene, throwing him a curious glance. 'Why should you want to know about Carstairs?'

Bertie did not answer this question. He knew that the State Hospital was at Carstairs, and he knew too that this is where Dr Fairbairn was likely to end up. There was so much proof of his instability that it would not need any testimony of Bertie's to make the case for the psychotherapist's detention. You only have to listen to him for five minutes, thought Bertie, and you know that all is not right with Dr Fairbairn.

'They've made Dr Fairbairn a professor,' said Irene. 'That is a great honour for him, and so he felt that he had to leave Edinburgh to take it up.'

Bertie thought for a moment. 'You'll miss him, Mummy, won't you?'

'We shall all miss him, Bertie,' said Irene carefully. 'Dr Fairbairn's move is a great loss to the psychotherapeutic community here in Edinburgh.'

Bertie reflected on this. He would not miss Dr Fairbairn at all. But this was not a time, he thought, to be mean-spirited.

'And it's a pity that he won't get to know Ulysses,' said Bertie. 'Ulysses looks so like Dr Fairbairn, Mummy. Have you noticed that too?'

Irene brushed the question aside. 'Aren't you looking forward to meeting the therapist who's taken over from him?' she asked. 'I'm sure that you'll get on very well with him.'

Bertie looked down at the pavement. It was important to be careful not to step on any of the lines. Vigilance was all. One did not see the bears, but that did not mean that they were not there; the Queen Street Gardens provided an ideal habitat for bears, Bertie felt.

'Do I really need to see him, Mummy?' he asked. 'I've stopped doing naughty things. Wasn't that why you sent me to Dr Fairbairn in the first place? Because I'd set fire to Daddy's *Guardian* while he was reading it? Wasn't that the reason?'

Irene looked down at Bertie with disapproval. 'What's past is past, Bertie,' she said. 'We don't need to go over those old things. No, your psychotherapy sessions are designed to help you understand yourself.'

Bertie thought about this. 'But I do understand myself, Mummy,' he said. 'I don't see why I need psychotherapy for that.'

'Well, you do,' said Irene. 'There are some things that you need that you don't know you need. And it is Mummy's business to make sure you get those things. Later on, Bertie, you'll thank me.'

Bertie said nothing. In the most profound and hidden corners of his soul, he wished that his mother would just go away. But at the same time, he dreaded the prospect of losing her, and felt that even to entertain such thoughts was dangerous. It was like believing in Santa Claus after the time when such beliefs become untenable: one did not want to relinquish the belief lest the loss of belief had dire consequences, such as no presents. So one believed just that little bit longer.

But now they were on Queen Street and close to the door that led up to Dr Fairbairn's consulting rooms.

'Will Ulysses come for psychotherapy too?' asked Bertie, as they climbed the stairs. 'I think that he will really need to understand himself.'

Irene laughed. 'Why do you say that, Bertie?'

'Because when he gets bigger he might wonder why he looks different from me,' said Bertie.

'But that's nothing unusual,' said Irene. 'Members of families often look different from one another.'

Bertie conceded that this was true. Olive had a sister who looked quite unlike her, and Hiawatha and his brother certainly did not look remotely like one another. But was it not unusual, he pointed out, for a baby to look like the mummy's friend?

Irene stopped. She crouched down so that she was at eye-level with Bertie. 'Bertie, *carissimo*,' she whispered. 'Ulysses' daddy is Daddy. I've told you that before. It's just a coincidence that he looks like Dr Fairbairn. These things happen – and it doesn't make it very easy for the mummy if her little boy says things that some people might find a little bit strange. So, never, ever talk about it again, please.'

Bertie stared at his mother, wide-eyed.

'I mean it, Bertie,' she said severely. 'If you mention it once more, just once more, then . . .' She paused. Bertie was watching her closely. What sanction, he wondered, did his mother have? He had no treats that could be taken away. He received no pocket money that could be cut. There was nothing that his mother could do.

Irene glanced over her shoulder. 'If you say one more word about it,' she whispered, 'Mummy will smack you really hard. Understand?'

Bertie reeled under the shock of this threat. His parents had never raised a hand to him, not once, and now this. He was stunned into silence, just as Little Hans must have been when, as reported by Freud, his mother threatened to castrate him.

'So,' said Irene, standing up again. 'That puts an end to that.'

Nothing more was said as they made their way up the last flight of stairs and entered the consulting rooms. Bertie noticed that the brass plate, which had previously announced that these were the premises of Dr Hugo Fairbairn, had been replaced with one on which the name Dr Roger Sinclair PhD had been inscribed.

Bertie sat down in the waiting room while his mother rang the bell. He was still smarting from his mother's unexpected threat when Dr Sinclair appeared in the doorway and led Irene inside. Bertie reached for a copy of *Scottish Field* on the waiting room table. *Scottish Field* – his consolation, his reminder that there was a world in which psychotherapy, yoga and Italian lessons did not exist; where fishing and climbing hills and freedom thrived; a Scotland quite different from his own. Yes, it was there, but it was tantalisingly out of reach, and nothing seemed to bring it nearer.

72. The New Psychotherapist

It was fifteen minutes before Irene looked out of the door of the consulting room and called Bertie in. He set aside *Scottish Field*, sighed, and went to join his mother.

'Bertie,' said Irene, 'this is Dr Sinclair. He wants you to call him Roger.'

Bertie looked at the man on the other side of the desk. He was younger than Dr Fairbairn and he had a much nicer face, thought Bertie. It was a pity, he said to himself, that Ulysses did not look like him, rather than like Dr Fairbairn. Perhaps the next baby – if his mother had another one – would look like Dr Sinclair. Bertie wondered if he should say this to his mother, but decided that it would perhaps trigger another curious threat; for some reason she seemed very sensitive about these things. Poor Mummy – if only she had more to do with her time; if only she would get herself a hobby . . . he stopped. A depressing thought had occurred to him: I am her hobby.

Dr Sinclair was smiling – Dr Fairbairn very rarely smiled – and Bertie was pleased to see that his jacket was quite unlike Dr Fairbairn's blue linen one.

'So, Bertie,' the therapist began, signalling for Irene and Bertie to sit down. 'I'm Roger Sinclair and I'm going to be helping you in the same way as Dr Fairbairn did. I know, of course, that you'll be missing Dr Fairbairn.'

I'm not, thought Bertie, and was about to say that, as politely as he could, when Irene intervened.

'Yes, he is,' she said. 'But Bertie understands. And he's happy that Dr Fairbairn has got a chair at last.'

233

Bertie looked at his mother in astonishment. What was this? Had Dr Fairbairn not always had a chair?

Dr Sinclair nodded. 'Dr Fairbairn left some notes, Bertie,' he went on. 'So I know all about the little chats that you and he had. Did you find them helpful, Bertie?'

'Yes, he did,' said Irene. 'Bertie found them very helpful indeed.'

Dr Sinclair glanced at Irene. 'Good. But what do you think, Bertie?'

'He's very much looking forward to working with you,' said Irene. 'Aren't you, Bertie?'

Bertie nodded miserably. He looked out of the window. The tops of the trees in Queen Street were moving – there must be a strong wind; strong enough to fly a kite really high, if one had a kite, that is, and Bertie did not. He wanted a kite. And he wanted a balsawood aeroplane with a rubber band that you wound up and then, when you let go, it drove the propeller. Tofu had had one of those and had let Bertie look at it. He was very proud of it and cried when Larch stamped on it and broke it. Even Tofu could cry; Bertie had never seen Tofu cry before. He cried, and when Olive saw him crying she crowed; she jeered. Tofu spat at her. It was always like that, Bertie thought. People did unkind things to one another, and he did not like it.

Dr Sinclair was looking at Bertie. 'Your mummy tells me that you're at the Steiner School,' he said. 'I had a friend who was at a Steiner School, you know. He liked it a lot. Are you happy at school, Bertie? Have you got lots of friends there?'

'He's very happy,' said Irene. 'The Steiner School is an excellent school. And there are friends there, aren't there, Bertie? Olive, for example.'

Bertie looked at his mother. It was his mother's idea that Olive was his friend, not his. But he did not think that there was any point in trying to persuade her otherwise, and so he merely nodded, and then looked at the floor.

'Olive?' said Dr Sinclair, his voice rising in pitch. 'That's a nice name. Tell me about Olive, Bertie.'

'She's a very nice little girl,' said Irene. 'Bertie has her to play from time to time. I know her mother quite well. We go to lectures at the Institute of Human Relations together. You'll no doubt be in touch with them, once you get settled in.'

Dr Sinclair was silent. He looked at Bertie for a few moments, and while he did so he fiddled with a pen he was holding. Then he turned to Irene. 'I think that perhaps Bertie and I are ready to have a little chat, just the two of us,' he said evenly.

Irene frowned. 'I'm very happy to stay,' she said. 'This first time, you know. It may be better for me to stay. I'm sure that's what Bertie would like. Bertie . . .'

Dr Sinclair rose to his feet. 'That's very good of you,' he said. 'But I do think that it's important that we have that little chat *à deux*. So, if you don't mind, Mrs Pollock, you can sit in the waiting room. I'll call you if we need you.'

Irene had shown no sign of rising from her seat, but Dr Sinclair was now standing directly behind her, gently tugging at the back of the chair, as if to dislodge her.

'Very well,' said Irene, her voice rather strained. 'I shall wait outside.'

Once Irene was out of the room, Dr Sinclair returned to his chair and smiled encouragingly at Bertie.

'You know where I come from, Bertie?' he asked. 'Australia.'

'Oh,' said Bertie politely.

'Yes,' said Dr Sinclair. 'You'd love Australia, Bertie. Have you ever seen a kangaroo?'

Bertie had seen one at the zoo, when they had gone there on a school trip. Irene, who did not agree with zoos, had always refused to take him.

'I saw a kangaroo at the zoo,' he said. 'I really like them.'

'Yes,' said Dr Sinclair. 'I like them. But you have to be careful with roos, Bertie. The bigger ones can be quite dangerous.'

'I've heard that,' said Bertie. 'I've heard that they can kick you quite hard.'

Dr Sinclair looked at him with interest. This, he thought, is an articulate, likeable little boy.

'And this Olive?' said Dr Sinclair suddenly. 'I bet you don't really like her.'

'No,' said Bertie, and then, relenting, as he was a kind child, he said, 'Well, I like her a tiny little bit, but not very much.'

Dr Sinclair smiled. 'Some girls can be quite bossy, can't they?' he said.

Bertie relaxed. He was beginning to like Dr Sinclair. 'Yes, they can,' he said.

'And some mummies too,' said Dr Sinclair very quietly, but just loudly enough for Bertie to hear.

Bertie hesitated. Then he nodded.

Dr Sinclair looked at Bertie. You poor little boy, he thought. You haven't got a mother – you've got a personal trainer.

73. Of Men and Make-Up

The Braid Hills Hotel, the scene some years earlier of that disastrous South Edinburgh Conservative Ball at which numbers had been insufficient to make up an eightsome (but how things had changed), was now to be the setting of one of the strangest dramas to be enacted in Edinburgh for a considerable time. A few days after Angus had called at Big Lou's flat and had first met the Pretender, Lou announced to him that at long last her unwelcome guest was moving on and that there was to be a farewell ceremony for him that very night.

'It's a ceremony, not a party,' she told him when he and Matthew dropped in for mid-morning coffee. 'Robbie's quite particular about that. Historical occasions involve ceremonies, not parties.'

'Oh, I don't know about that, Lou,' said Matthew. 'There must have been some parties to mark big events. The millennium celebration down in London was a big one. They had a party in the Dome, didn't they?'

'That ridiculous tent,' said Angus. 'And can you imagine the sort of people they had at the party? Every exhibitionist, superficial crooner in the business. Football players, and worse.'

Matthew thought for a moment. He would rather have enjoyed being there, he decided, but he was not sure if he should say so. And anyway, Angus had marked views on these things and nothing that Matthew could say would change them.

'I knew somebody who went to it,' said Big Lou suddenly. 'A very senior civil servant. He sometimes comes in for coffee in the late afternoon. On his way home. He told me that he went to that party.'

'Poor man,' said Angus. 'But I suppose that duty called.'

'No,' said Big Lou. 'He enjoyed it. He shook hands with the Prime Minister of the time – and he was wearing make-up. He noticed it, close up.'

'Well, he was going to be on television,' said Matthew. 'He had to. He would have looked cadaverous otherwise.'

'I don't think men should wear make-up – ever,' said Angus.

Matthew raised his hand to his face, but dropped it immediately, as if in guilt. Big Lou glanced at him.

'Moisturiser?' she asked Angus. 'Can they use moisturiser?'

Angus shook his head. 'No,' he said. 'Not in my view.'

Matthew blushed. He had used moisturiser for two years now, and he had felt the benefits.

He looked at Angus's skin, which was very dry; leathery almost. It was probably too late for him to start wearing moisturiser. 'If you don't wear moisturiser,' he said quietly, 'then your skin can get all sorts of wrinkles in it.'

'Aye,' said Big Lou. 'Matthew's right there. Look at W. H. Auden. Look at his face. Have you seen pictures of it?'

'I have,' said Angus. 'But Auden, as I happen to have read, had some rare skin condition. Even moisturiser wouldn't have saved him. He said his face had undergone a geological catastrophe.'

'And ended up looking like a wedding cake that had been left out in the rain,' added Big Lou. She had a large collection of Auden in her flat; in the stock she had acquired from the former bookshop there had been a whole shelf of his work.

Angus now turned to Matthew. 'Tell me, Matthew, do you wear moisturiser yourself?'

Matthew shifted in his seat. He looked over towards Big Lou, who was standing behind her counter, her cloth poised in mid-wipe.

'Tell him it's none of his business,' she snorted.

Matthew shook his head. 'No, I don't mind. To be honest, Angus, I do. I wear moisturiser. I put it on in the morning, and then again at night. Elspeth and I use the same brand. We only discovered that when we got married.'

Angus stared at him. 'I see. And what did she say when she found that out?'

'She was pleased,' said Matthew. He paused. 'Actually, Angus, I hate to say this, but you're rather out of date. I can tell you of loads of prominent men in Scotland who use moisturiser and are not ashamed to say so. From every walk of life.'

Angus was interested. 'Politicians?'

'Yes, of course.' And Matthew now gave him the names of three prominent male figures in politics who used moisturiser.

'And the arts?'

'Hundreds,' said Matthew. 'In fact, name one man in the arts – one man who's any good, that is – who doesn't use moisturiser. You won't be able to.' He hesitated. 'Apart from you, of course, Angus.'

'And in business?' Angus asked.

'Naturally,' said Matthew. 'Not everyone does, of course. Some of them don't need to. But lots of businessmen use it, I promise you. I was in the New Club bar with my father once and all those financial types were talking about moisturiser.'

Angus looked thoughtful. 'So it's not . . . it's not effeminate to use it? Is that what you're telling me?'

Big Lou could not help but laugh. 'Oh, Angus,' she burst out, 'you're very old-fashioned. Nobody worries about being effemin-ate these days. Those things don't matter any more. If men want to wear make-up, they can. If they want to sit around talking about . . . about . . .'

'About moisturiser,' Matthew provided.

'Yes, about moisturiser, well they can. Nobody's going to stop them. Men have been liberated.'

Angus narrowed his eyes. 'They have? Are you sure?'

'Of course I'm sure,' said Big Lou. 'Men can be themselves now, without worrying about gender expectations. Those barriers came down years ago. You've been locked in that stuffy studio of yours and you've missed the news.'

Angus turned to Matthew. 'Could you advise me where to buy it?' he said. 'Or maybe you could go and get some for me.'

Matthew laughed. 'And say to the woman at the cash register, "This isn't for me, it's for a friend"?'

Angus nodded. 'Yes, something like that.'

They were silent. Matthew was thinking how sad it was that the news of the liberation of men should not have reached Angus before now; Angus was thinking of moisturiser, and wondering whether it would smell like shaving cream. And did one put it on before or after one shaved? And Big Lou's thoughts had returned to the Braid Hills Hotel, and the hills beyond, whence came the Jacobites' help.

74. *The Jacobite Rally*

The Braid Hills Hotel, of course, was more than a mere hotel – it was a symbol. Perched on the brow of a hill, it looked down over the rooftops of Morningside to the city and the hills of Fife beyond. It was solid, imperturbable, reassuring – always there, as was the Castle itself in the distance, and it spoke of the values that created the city that lay before it. Like the Dominion Cinema, it had not changed much – a fact that was much appreciated by those who used it. There was far too much change in the world, and fantoosh hotels and glitzy cinemas would come and go. What people wanted was places that had always been there, places they could trust, places that had become deeply embedded in the folk memory.

It had been the scene of many important events over the years: weddings, funeral teas, Rotary Club dinners and so on; and many people had individual memories of these occasions which would be triggered as they looked up at the hotel from the road below. For Betty Dunbarton, for instance, relict of the late Ramsey Dunbarton WS, the glimpse of the Braid Hills Hotel afforded her as she drove out each Friday to lunch with her friend, Peggy Feggie, in Fairmilehead, reminded her of the evening when she and Ramsey had dined there after the last performance of *The Gondoliers* at the Church Hill Theatre. Ramsey had played the role of the Duke of Plaza-Toro with great distinction and had ordered a bottle of champagne to mark the end of the run. And then, just as they embarked on their meal, the doors of the dining room had opened to admit the rest of the cast, who had decided to have their last-night dinner in the same place. Ramsey had looked surprised, and then embarrassed, and she had said, 'But my dear, did you not know that there would be a cast party?' Without hesitation he had replied, 'Of course I did, my dear. But I chose to dine with you instead.'

Later that evening, as they returned home, he had said, 'I have to tell you, my dear, that I have lied to you. I did not know that there was to be a party. They did not invite me. I did not want you to be hurt.'

It was only the second time he had lied to his wife – and on both occasions he had done so to avoid causing her hurt or embarrassment. The first occasion had been when they were engaged and they had gone for a walk down at Cramond. They had seen the

Gardyloo, the boat then used to take sewage out to sea, and she had asked, 'What is that odd-looking boat carrying, Ramsey?' And he had told her that it must be gravel, going over to Fife, in order that he should not have to tell her its true mission. Two white lies – both of which had been confessed, and both forgiven.

But the occasion to which the Braid Hills Hotel was now unwittingly playing host was of a very different nature. As Angus and Matthew arrived in the bar with Big Lou, a small group of Jacobites were already there. Lou recognised some of them as friends of Robbie, and nodded a greeting, but did not join them. Angus glanced at them with interest: strange specimens, he thought – that character Michael and his ridiculous spotty acolyte who hung on his every word; the odd woman who claimed to be able to trace her ancestry back to the sixth century or whenever; they were a very motley group.

'I must say this is a very peculiar occasion,' said Angus to Big Lou. 'Where's the Pretender?'

'He's going to arrive with Robbie,' explained Lou. 'Then they're going to set off from the car park. There'll be a piper, apparently.'

A few more Jacobites had now joined the other party, which had swollen to about thirty. They all had glasses of whisky in their hands and were toasting one another enthusiastically. There was a hubbub of noise, and it was growing louder when, from outside in the car park, there arose the wail of pipes. Clutching their whisky glasses, the Jacobites all headed for the door, followed by Angus, Matthew and Big Lou.

The Pretender arrived in the side-car of an old motorbike driven by Robbie. As it made its way up the hotel drive, the Jacobites all gave a roar of welcome. Saltires were unfurled and waved above heads, as were standards bearing the lion rampant. Several home-made flags appeared with a white rose stitched upon them. The pipes continued to wail.

As the motorbike came to a halt, the top of the side-car slid back and the Pretender gingerly rose to his feet. He was wearing a tartan jacket and trews, a great white ruff around his throat, and red shoes topped with large silver buckles. When he stood up, his supporters gave a great throaty roar which sounded as if it came from a hundred throats, rather than thirty. Then the Pretender opened his mouth and shouted something, but his words were snatched away by the stiff breeze that had blown up. Some of the Jacobites leaned forward, trying to make out what he said, others merely punched the air and shouted back. Then the Pretender sat down, gave a signal to Robbie, and half closed the top of the side-car. At this point, Robbie waved to Lou, and she waved back.

The piper began to play 'Will Ye No Come Back Again?' and the crowd took up the singing of the words: 'Bonnie Charlie's noo awa' . . .' and the motorbike moved off slowly, followed by several Jacobite children and an extraordinary tartan dog, who had appeared from nowhere. The tartan dog barked, and made a spirited attempt to bite the Pretender's arm, now waving out of the side-car. But he was pulled away by one of the children and the Pretender made his exit unharmed.

They did not go back into the hotel with the Jacobites, but walked slowly back to Matthew's car, which he had parked near the end of the drive.

Angus glanced at Big Lou. 'You'll miss Robbie,' he said gently. 'How long will he be away?'

She shrugged. 'He hasn't told me,' she said. 'And aye, I'll miss him.'

Matthew said nothing. He was thinking of what he had just seen. Was it real? Could such goings-on happen in a country other than Scotland? The answer was yes and no.

75. Bruce Discovers his Feminine Side

It was now a few days since Bruce had experienced his moment of insight in Leith. Thanks to the supportive presence of Nick McNair, the following day had been a productive one, in which he had further examined where things were going wrong – everywhere, it was decided – and who was to blame for this – nobody except him. Of course the defects in a personality are rarely entirely remedied by a bout of self-evaluation, but in some cases they may be; there are at least roads to Damascus on which astonishing moral progress may be made.

'Do you want me to go ahead with the project?' asked Nick, as they sat together in the kitchen of the flat. 'The Face of Scotland business?'

Bruce looked down at the floor. Did he want to see his face on billboards? The old Bruce would have said 'Yes' to that without hesitation; the new Bruce was not so sure.

Sensing his hesitation, Nick gave him a nudge. 'I think you're unhappy about it,' he said gently. 'Not everybody likes that sort of exposure. It takes a certain sort of personality.'

Bruce looked up. 'And you think I have it?'

Nick thought for a moment. 'I did. When I met you in The Bailie, I did. And then when we had the session in the studio, I still did. But now ... well, now I'm not so certain. Now I think that you're not like that at all. And frankly, I'm rather glad.'

Bruce wondered what to make of this. Was this Nick's way of letting him down gently? The photographer himself provided the answer to that. 'No,' he said. 'It's not that I don't think it would work. I think it would. It's just that if you went ahead with it, you'd make yourself more and more unhappy.'

'And you don't want that?'

Nick laughed and put an arm around Bruce's shoulder. Bruce stiffened, drew away, then stopped himself. Why should he reject this gesture of comfort?

'Sorry,' said Nick, and made to remove his arm.

'No,' said Bruce. 'Leave it there. I find it ... comforting.'

'We don't like to touch one another,' said Nick. 'Or men don't. Women are much more tactile, aren't they? They embrace their friends. They reach out to one another. They cry together. We don't. We don't allow ourselves.'

'We're so busy being strong,' Bruce said.

Nick nodded. 'Exactly.'

'And all the time we're weak.'

Nick smiled. 'Yes. Being human is being weak. Same thing.' He paused. 'Do you remember the last time you cried?'

It was not an easy question to answer. For many women, the answer will be found by remembering the last time they saw a moving film; for men there is no such easy landmark. Few men allow themselves to cry in films, even if they want to; they swallow hard, fight the tears, smile indulgently at the woman crying beside them. And Bruce had not cried for a long time.

'No. I can't remember. Years ago, I suppose.'

Nick shook his head. 'Bad. Really bad. Do you want to cry now?'

Bruce said nothing for a while. Did he? If he did cry, what would he be crying for? He asked Nick that, and got an answer.

'You might want to cry out of sheer regret,' said Nick. 'You might want to cry over the time you've wasted; over the hurt you've caused to others. Things like that. These are all good reasons for crying. Or you might want to cry simply because it's emotionally cathartic to do so.'

Bruce digested this. 'What about you? Do you cry?'

'Sure. Quite a lot. I sometimes cry from sheer frustration. When things go badly wrong with a set of photographs. Or sometimes when I get back to the flat and I realise that I'm on my own and I shouldn't have broken up with Colleen in the first place and it's too late to go back. When I realise that I really love her and that the way I speak about the bust-up is sheer bravado and nonsense and that if she appeared in the doorway over there and asked me whether we could try again I'd say, "Yes, oh yes, of course you can."' He stopped. 'But this isn't about me, Bruce. It's about you. What do you want to do?'

Bruce now knew what he wanted to say. 'No, I don't want to go ahead with it. I don't want to be the Face of Scotland. I don't want to carry on looking at myself in every available mirror. And anyway ...' he paused. 'You can't carry on looking good forever, can you? You get lines, don't you? The years catch up on you.'

Nick was looking at him intently. 'Yes, sure. But . . . you do use moisturiser, don't you?'

Bruce's hand went up to his face. 'I do. Not every day, though. Just when I remember.'

Nick shook his head in disapproval. 'You should use it every day, Bruce. Morning and evening. I've got some fantastic stuff. It's really good. Do you want to see it? I'll show it to you, if you like.'

'Please,' said Bruce.

And it was while Nick was out of the room fetching the jar of moisturiser from the bathroom that Bruce made his decision. He would go back to being a surveyor. He would forget about all his schemes and get back to some basic hard work. He would go back to Mr Todd, his former boss, and make a clean breast of it. He would ask for a job, and then he would do it well.

Nick came back with a jar. 'This is it,' he said. 'You can get it either in tubes or in jars. I prefer jars.'

Bruce opened the lid and sniffed at the oily cream. 'Nice smell,' he said.

'Yes,' said Nick. 'Try some. Look, I'll show you.'

Nick took the jar from Bruce and dipped his fingers into the cream. Then he smeared a thin layer across Bruce's forehead and began to rub it in. Next, he applied some to the cheeks. Bruce closed his eyes. He began to cry. Small sobs at first, and then louder.

'That's the spirit,' said Nick quietly. 'That's it, Bruce. Have a good cry. Let the tears come.' He replaced the lid on the jar of moisturiser and put it down on the table. Moisturiser and a good cry: two things for modern men to think about.

76. A Changed Man

Raeburn Todd, generally known as Todd, joint senior partner of the firm of Macaulay Holmes Richardson Black, Chartered Surveyors, had not expected that morning to see Bruce sitting in the reception room of the firm's new offices at the Fountainbridge end of the Union Canal. The architect who had designed these offices was of the school that did not believe in walls, except where utterly necessary to prevent the ceiling from falling down. As a result, it was possible from anywhere within the firm's premises to see clients who came into the waiting room as they entered it; just as it was possible for everybody in the office to observe who was doing what in the coffee room, or indeed anywhere, except, of course, the washrooms, where the architect had reluctantly agreed to provide walls of smoked glass. Even so, with the light in a certain direction . . .

Todd and his brother, Gordon, had talked about this matter of walls and dividers with the landlords' designers, who had been responsible for the internal arrangements of the office, but these designers had simply become glassy-eyed, as designers do when confronted with people who clearly know nothing about design. They had got nowhere. The designers knew that people eventually became accustomed to open plan arrangements and stopped complaining. Of course there were some clients afflicted with a nostalgia for walls, but for the most part they knuckled under; which Todd and his brother eventually did, although they reflected on what both Macaulay and Richardson would have thought, had they still been in harness. If old-fashioned Edinburgh had enjoyed a reputation for being tight and closed, then Macaulay embodied those qualities to a striking degree. He always kept his coat on in the office, and indeed Todd had been in the firm for some months before he finally saw Macaulay's face, which had until that point been largely concealed behind scarves, screens and newspapers. And as for Richardson, he locked himself into his room at the office and had to unlock the door to admit anybody to the room. Edinburgh in those days was not an inclusive place.

But it was not with such thoughts that Todd now occupied himself. He frowned. Was that not the obnoxious young man he had fired? Anderson? Bruce Anderson. It was! That chin, that peculiar hair which for some reason always smelled of cloves; it was definitely Anderson.

Now he was talking to the receptionist; flirting with her, no doubt. He was always doing that, and Todd remembered having to talk to him about a complaint from one of the secretaries. He was incorrigible.

And then Todd saw the receptionist rising to her feet to bring Bruce over to his glass cubicle. He felt irritated, but at the same time intrigued. It took some nerve to come back to a place from which one had been decisively thrown out.

'Mr Todd?'

Todd nodded.

'You remember me, perhaps? Bruce Anderson.'

Todd reluctantly took the outstretched hand and shook it. He was Edinburgh; he was polite. 'Yes. I remember you. How are things going for you? You went to London, I hear.'

Bruce was invited to sit down. Todd was civil and there seemed to him to be less cockiness in Bruce's attitude.

Bruce swallowed. He had decided to be direct, but it was difficult. Todd was staring at him; he was civil but unsmiling.

'I've changed,' said Bruce simply.

Todd raised an eyebrow. 'Changed jobs? Not a surveyor any more?'

Bruce blinked. 'Changed inside. I'm a changed man.'

Todd looked nervously over Bruce's shoulder. Had this young man converted to something?

'If you let me,' said Bruce, 'I'd like to explain. When I worked for you, I let you down. I was sloppy in my work. And then there was that incident with your wife, in the restaurant . . .'

Todd stopped him. 'I don't want to go into that, if you don't mind.'

'But you must let me explain,' said Bruce. 'I know what you think of me – and I deserved everything that came my way. But when it came to that, I was innocent. There was nothing going on. It was just lunch. We had met in the bookshop in George Street and it was lunchtime. Purely social.'

He finished, and looked at the floor. 'I'm sorry,' he went on. 'I really am. I was a bad employee. I was full of myself. I was a real

247

pain. But now I'm sorry.' He paused. 'And I want you to give me another chance. If you'll have me back.'

For a while Todd said nothing, but looked directly at Bruce. Bruce held his stare. He did not look away.

Todd thought: he never spoke like this before. He's a young man. Everybody makes mistakes. And he remembered, years before, when he was barely qualified, how he himself had . . . no, it was best not to think of that again.

He made his decision. 'So, you're telling me you've turned over a new leaf? Is that what you're saying?'

Bruce nodded. 'Yes. I have. And I'm not just saying it. I really have.' He paused. 'Do you have any openings at the moment?'

Todd spoke reluctantly. 'As it happens, we do.'

'Well, would you consider me?'

Todd pursed his lips. 'What have you been doing since . . . since you left us?'

Bruce opened his mouth to speak, but closed it again. Then: 'Wasting my time.'

Todd's eyes widened, but then he suddenly laughed. 'That's an honest answer.'

'I've started to be honest,' said Bruce.

'Well, it's good to hear that,' said Todd. He hesitated, but only for a moment. 'All right, Anderson, we'll take you back.'

Bruce rose to his feet and took a step forward. He seized Todd's hand. 'I won't let you down, Mr Todd. I promise you. It'll be different.'

'I hope so,' said Todd, smiling.

'Thank you so much,' said Bruce. 'And now: how are you doing? You're looking in great shape, by the way.'

Todd inclined his head.

'No, I mean it,' said Bruce. 'You don't look a day older.'

Todd was pleased. 'Well, I'm still playing a lot of golf. It's good to get out on the golf course and get the wind into one's lungs.'

'But do you use moisturiser?' asked Bruce.

Todd looked puzzled. 'On the greens?'

'No,' said Bruce. 'It's just you said something about the wind on the golf course. It dries out the skin.'

Todd shook his head. He was not interested in such things.

77. *Up for the Cup*

Angus was just about to telephone Domenica that morning when her call came through. 'I take it that you are up and about,' she began. 'Up and about and at your easel?'

Angus looked at the breakfast things on his table – the jar of marmalade, the crumbs from the toast, the plate that had contained his muesli, now scraped clean. Breakfast things were not a good subject for still life, he decided; they were just too prosaic.

'I was just about to phone you,' he said. 'I wanted to tell you about what happened at the Braid Hills Hotel yesterday. Vintage stuff.'

'The Jacobites?'

'Yes, indeed. Big Lou's Pretender set off for the Highlands.'

'So he's noo awa?'

'Precisely. In the side-car of a motorbike.'

There was silence while Domenica digested this piece of historical detail. 'Well, that's very interesting,' she said. 'And we must assume that Government forces are combing the hills even as we speak. But, listen, Angus, I need you down here mid-morning. Coffee time. Something has cropped up. What we may call a window of opportunity.'

Angus agreed, and after a short morning of rather unsatisfactory work in his studio he attached Cyril to his leash and walked round the square to Scotland Street. Cyril was glad to be out and about, and strained at his lead, sniffing the breeze wafting up Scotland Street. Such a breeze contained valuable intelligence for a dog: it let everybody know which other dogs were having a walk at the time; which dogs had been that way earlier on and had made territorial claims; and it carried news, too, of human activities. For an urban dog, each area of town has its particular smell when it comes to human scents. In some areas of town, for example, the people themselves smell somewhat high; this is very rare in Edinburgh, of course, but occurs in some other places. In other areas, kitchen activities are the prevailing note: sun-dried tomatoes are prevalent in the New Town, a hint of quiche, notes of Medoc; Morningside dogs, by contrast, pick up the unmistakable odour of scones, that dry, slightly floury smell, and the smell, too, of cologne.

Scotland Street that morning, however, smelled only of cat, and Cyril let out a precautionary bark. He detested the cats of Scotland Street; unpleasant, arrogant creatures who taunted him over his leashed state, parading themselves within feet of him in the knowledge that the lead prevented him from meting out immediate justice. Cyril growled, but he realised that Angus was not in a mood to linger, and he had no alternative but to make his way without any attempt at a show-down.

Domenica had heard them coming up the stair and greeted them at her front door. Unusually, she admitted Cyril to the flat rather than suggesting that he stay out on the landing. Cyril stepped forward to give her an appreciative lick, which he felt was not adequately appreciated. She was a strange woman, this, he thought, but infinitely preferable, from the canine point of view, to that woman below, the one with the little boy he liked so much.

'Don't make yourself too comfortable, Angus,' Domenica began. 'We have work to do. Then I shall make you coffee.'

Angus raised an eyebrow. 'Please explain.'

'Well,' said Domenica, 'by a marvellous bit of serendipity, Antonia has announced that the gas people are coming to read her meter this morning. She's overpaid, she says, and they are having a big argument over it. So she doesn't want to miss the appointment.'

'I see.'

Domenica rubbed her hands together enthusiastically. 'She has to go out, and has left me the key to let the gas men in. So this gives us our chance to replace the blue Spode teacup.'

Angus looked at her blankly. 'Replace it? But we've just liberated it.'

Domenica explained, and Angus started to smile as the story unfolded. 'You're in a mess,' he said, at the end. 'You shouldn't have taken it in the first place.'

'Well, we can sort the whole thing out now,' said Domenica. 'You can take it back.'

Angus was prepared to help his friend, but he now began to feel slightly used. 'Well, frankly, Domenica, I don't see why you can't do it yourself. You've got her key.'

Domenica sighed. 'Of course I could take it back, Angus,' she said. 'But the point is this: I don't know where it came from.'

'From the kitchen,' Angus supplied.

'Yes, yes. But where in the kitchen? If I go and put it back in some odd place then she'll know, won't she? She will assume that I've been in the flat, using her key – or, rather, misusing her key. If you go, you can put it back in exactly the place you found it.' She paused, looking intently at Angus. 'You do remember where you found it, don't you?'

Angus had to admit that he did. 'It was in a small cupboard above the sink,' he said. 'There were one or two other teacups there. Nothing very good, I'm afraid. An old chipped Minton Haddon Hall cup, I think.'

'Those can be quite nice,' said Domenica.

'Yes, they can,' said Angus. 'William Crosbie had a set, as I recall.

I was in his studio down south once, and we drank tea out of Minton cups. I remember, because he was painting one at the time. It was in a still life that he had set up.'

He stared at Domenica. 'You could put it back in that cupboard, now that I've told you where it is.'

Domenica brushed the suggestion aside. 'Far better for you to do it.'

Angus decided not to argue: Domenica had made up her mind, and he would be the loser in any argument. Women always win, he thought. They just always win.

'All right,' he said. 'I'll take it. Are you sure that she's out?'

'She dropped the key in when she went,' said Domenica. 'She said that she'd be out for several hours. You're perfectly safe.'

Angus rose to his feet and took the key from Domenica. Then she passed him a plastic bag containing the blue Spode teacup.

'I feel a bit like a burglar,' he said.

Domenica was dismissive. 'Burglars don't return property,' he said. 'They take it. You're returning it.'

'But what if a person who was returning property, clandestinely, were to be caught?' asked Angus. 'Wouldn't he then look, to all intents and purposes, exactly like a burglar?'

'Appearances can be deceptive, Angus,' said Domenica. 'Now let's not waste any more time.'

78. *Antonia's Big Secret*

Domenica opened the door of her flat and Angus slipped out. He looked about him furtively, which was ridiculous, he thought; there was nobody about and he could open Domenica's door with complete impunity. His errand was a simple one and would take a minute at the most. And it was a just one, he reminded himself: he had nothing to reproach himself for about returning to Antonia that which belonged to her.

He turned the key in the door and pushed it open. Something was hindering it, and he had to push quite firmly in order to shift the obstruction: the post. Once the door was open, he looked down and saw that a letter had become trapped under the opening door and was slightly torn. He picked it up, examined it, and then put it down again in its original position. Then he closed the door behind him and began to make his way through the hall.

He stopped. A painting had caught his eye; a small painting, a collection of objects against a bright background. Was it? He moved forward to peer at the painting and he saw the signature. Elizabeth Blackadder. Well, thought Angus, Antonia may have bad taste in men, as Domenica had reported to him, but she had good taste in painting. A Blackadder. Interesting. And what was this? A small pencil study of a boy's head. By? He looked more closely and realised that he was looking at a sketch by James Cowie – the style was unmistakable. That was even more interesting. Cowie in his Hospitalfield days, probably. Well, well . . . Antonia must have a bit of money, he thought. Where would she get that from? Her estranged husband, he supposed. He was one of these Perthshire types; they often had funds.

He moved out of the hall and went into the kitchen. Taking the blue Spode teacup out of its bag, he put it down on the draining board next to the sink. Then he opened the cupboard above the sink. There was the Minton, and there was the space in which the blue Spode teacup had stood, now unoccupied. Surely Antonia would have noticed that, he thought. And when she opened the cupboard the next time, there it would be. The poor woman would think that she was hallucinating. He smiled. It was a childish pleasure, and a silly one, but it was rather amusing to think of her confusion.

He replaced the cup, closed the cupboard, and was sticking the empty bag into his pocket when he heard the front door open. He froze. Was this the gas man coming to read the meter? No, because he had the key that Antonia had given to Domenica. So it was Antonia, coming back.

Angus did not have time to think. He looked about him wildly. There was only one door, and that led into the hall. He heard another door open and shut. The bathroom: she was going in there, and that at least gave him a few moments. He could dash out of the hall, open the door, and be gone by the time she emerged. But then, almost immediately, he heard the bathroom door opening again. The cupboard. There was a large broom cupboard at the end of the kitchen – Domenica had a very similar one in her kitchen. He would hide in that.

Fortunately the cupboard was virtually empty, and Angus had no difficulty in fitting in and closing the door behind him. He was just in time: from the darkness of his hiding place he heard Antonia enter the kitchen. He heard a tap being turned on and something – presumably a kettle – being filled with water. She's making tea, he thought, and that means that she'll soon make the discovery.

He heard her open the cupboard above the sink and then there was a silence. After a few moments it was broken by a muttering. In spite of his circumstances, Angus found himself grinning. That had been her making the discovery and wondering how she could possibly have missed the cup.

The kettle boiled quickly and there was the sound of water being poured. Then a further silence and a rather different noise, a clicking. The telephone: Antonia was making a telephone call. I wish she would get on with it and go back into her study, thought Angus. Then I could make my escape.

He heard Antonia's voice quite clearly through the door of his hiding place.

'Maeve? This is me. Yes, fine. I was going out to get my hair done but my hairdresser was ill. One of the assistants offered to do me but I never trust those girls. Most of them look as if they're straight out of school. They don't have the experience, if you ask me.'

There was a silence as the other person spoke.

'Yes, I know that they have to get experience somehow, but not on my hair, if you don't mind. I like my own person. He's called James. He's got really long fingers and he goes snip, snip with tremendous panache. Quite the lad. He comes from Lochgelly, of all places. You don't expect hairdressers to come from Lochgelly, for some reason, but there you are. He tells me that a lot goes on in Lochgelly.

'But listen, Maeve. Listen. Have you got the stuff?'

Angus stiffened. Got the stuff? The person at the other end of the line was saying something and Antonia was silent.

'Can you get me a decent amount this time?' Antonia went on. 'And good quality. I've got quite a few people waiting for theirs. And, tell me, is it cut the way I like it?'

Angus drew in his breath, almost unable to believe what he had just heard. But there was more to come.

'And be careful about the law,' Antonia said. 'Be discreet. We don't want to end up in prison.'

Something was said at the other end of the line, and then the receiver was put down. This was followed by footsteps leaving the kitchen and the slamming of a door in the distance. Very gingerly Angus pushed the door of the cupboard open and peered out into the kitchen. She had gone into her study, he decided, and he could safely leave.

Within a minute he was back in Domenica's flat.

'Thank heavens you're back,' said Domenica. 'I saw her coming up the stair. Did she see you?'

Angus shook his head. 'She's a drug-dealer,' he said, his voice lowered. 'A big-time drug-dealer.'

79. *On the Way to a Funeral*

Feeling uncomfortable in his dark suit – the trousers were a bit tight – Angus sat back in the seat of the ten-thirty ScotRail express to Glasgow. He had never felt at ease in suits, apart from the generously built one he had inherited from his father. That suit, a voluminous green affair made of tweed woven on the hand-pedalled loom of a Harris weaver, had eventually fallen to bits from sheer old age, and was greatly regretted. The suit he was wearing now, by contrast, was sparing in its use of cloth, and felt like it.

'This suit of mine,' he said to Matthew, who was seated opposite him on the train, 'is mean-spirited. Just like the age we live in.'

Matthew glanced at his friend's outfit. 'You could have it let out. You could speak to Mr Low at Stewart, Christie.'

Angus shook his head. 'I'd be ashamed to show it to Mr Low,' he said. 'I bought this suit on Princes Street about ten years ago. And you know how awful Princes Street is now. It's like some muckle grand souk. It really souks.'

When Angus burst out laughing at his own joke, a few other people in the carriage threw glances. They were both so obviously going to a funeral, with their dark suits and black ties: laughter, surely, was unseemly.

'You drew a few disapproving looks, there,' said Matthew sotto voce. 'You're not meant to laugh on your way to these solemn occasions.'

Angus made a dismissive gesture. 'Talking of Princes Street,' he said, fishing for a silver hip-flask from his pocket, 'Domenica was up to high doh the other day over the price of scones in Jenners tea room doubling overnight. She hadn't actually been there for tea for some time, but she had bumped into Stuart Brown who works round the corner and drops in there from time to time. He told her.'

'That's serious,' said Matthew, nodding his head in the direction of the hip-flask. 'Dutch courage?'

Angus smiled. 'I always take a dram to these occasions, Matthew. They're so bleak otherwise.'

Matthew understood, but politely declined the flask when Angus offered him a swig.

'It's Glenmorangie,' said Angus. 'I have a couple of bottles in the house. The old stuff. Have you seen the new bottles? They're making a whisky called Nectar d'Òr now. Apparently òr is a Gaelic word. But the whole thing looks somewhat French to me. I don't know why. I just get that impression.'

'Perhaps they want the French to drink it?' suggested Matthew. 'The whisky people are very interested in their image. They don't want people to associate whisky with people like . . .' He stopped himself, just in time. He had intended to say people like you.

Angus looked at him sharply. 'With people like me, Matthew? Is that what you mean?'

Matthew smiled. 'I suppose so.' And then he added hurriedly: 'Not that there's anything wrong with people like you, Angus. It's just that we can't continue to be all tweedy and fusty, you know. Not if we want to sell our whisky.'

'But isn't this meant to be a tweedy and fusty country?' asked Angus. 'And isn't that what people like? Isn't that why they come to visit us and buy our whisky and so on? Precisely because we're not like everyone else?'

Matthew did not reply. But Angus was warming to his theme. 'That slogan that you see, "One Scotland, Many Cultures". If it's meant to be directed at tourists – and surely they don't intend to spend our money telling us what to think – then what a bit of nonsense! Do they seriously think that anybody is going to come to Scotland to see multiculturalism? What pious nonsense! People come to Scotland to see traditional Scottish things. That's why they come. They come to see our scenery.' He pointed out of the window. They were passing through Falkirk. 'They come to get a sense of our history. Old buildings. Mists. All that stuff, which we do rather well.' He paused, and took a sip from his flask. 'They don't come to see our social engineering programmes.'

Matthew thought about this. Angus had outspoken views, often wrong, but he was probably right about visitors. Any visitor he had met had wanted the tartan myths to be true. And they were always proud of having Scots blood way back in the mists of time. A great-grandfather who had come from Aberdeen, or something like that. It was powerful, simply because people wanted some sense of belonging, of being from somewhere. And the modern world, he supposed, with its shifting, dislocated urban populations was the antithesis of that.

Angus adjusted his tie uncomfortably. 'Glasgow,' he said, looking thoughtfully out of the window. They were not there yet, but then he muttered, 'The dear green place.'

'Yes,' said Matthew. 'It's a great place. Great people. But then you get characters like Lard . . .'

'If they wanted a slogan,' mused Angus, 'they could have said, "One Country, Two Cities".' How about that, Matthew? Wouldn't that have said it all?'

Matthew reflected on this. 'Poor Lard,' he said.

Angus nodded. 'He'll get a good send-off, though. They go in for those things in Glasgow. Big flowers.'

'And a wake?'

Angus brightened. 'Oh yes, that'll be quite an occasion,' he said. 'Mind you, I'm not sure if we should attend. I'm not being stand-offish, but do you realise who'll be there, Matthew? All those big Glasgow gangsters. Ice cream franchise people. I rather suspect that you and I will be out of our depth. This won't be like an opening at your gallery, you know.'

'Let's wait and see.'

There followed a long period of silence. Then, as they neared Glasgow, Angus remarked, 'It must be difficult for the minister. Or in Lard's case, the priest. He must know the score. He must know what Lard was like.'

Matthew agreed. And yet, was that not the whole point? That sins were forgiven? That each of us, whoever we were, however imperfect, was loved? And was that not what he and Angus were saying, in going across to Glasgow in these suits, these black ties; were we not saying that ultimately we are all brothers and sisters, united in our humanity? He was imperfect; Angus was imperfect (and fusty too); Lard was imperfect. But was it not all these flaws, manifold and diverse, that united us all, made us one?

The Edinburgh to Glasgow train is a place of many thoughts; these were Matthew's as they drew slowly into Queen Street Station.

80. Let us now Praise a Rather Infamous Man

Angus, crammed into a crowded pew with Matthew and eight other people, watched as an elderly man in a black suit walked up to a lectern and cleared his throat.

'I have been asked,' said the man, 'to say a few words about the man to whom we have all come to say farewell: Aloysius Ignatius Xavier O'Connor. RIP.

'I was Aloysius's teacher and that is why I am standing here talking to you today. It is not something, I should point out, that any teacher relishes – that he should speak at the funeral of one of his pupils. It should be the other way round. But life has a way of turning things on their heads, and the old may on occasion have to say goodbye to the young.

'Young Lard – I mean, Aloysius – well, perhaps I should call him by the name that everybody knew him by. And I don't think that he would mind unduly. So I shall call him Lard. Young Lard was a funny wee boy when I first taught him. He had that look in his eye that you get to know as a teacher – the look that says: I'm going to be out of the ordinary. Many of you will remember Father Joe, such a character himself, and a good man. I remember his saying to me, "That wee boy will make his mark, so he will." And he did, of course.

'Lard was not always easy when he was a wee boy – and I think he'd be the first to admit that. He was very keen on borrowing things, and I often had to go round to the O'Connor house and remind him to return things he had borrowed from the school. But he always helped me to carry them back to the school, and his mother always made me a fine cup of tea when I called on those errands.

'He was very popular with the other boys, and he remained well-liked by others for the rest of his life. When he was at Polmont, he always helped the younger boys find their way about the place and settle in. He could not abide bullying, and there was many a bully who was hospitalised by Lard. But he always took them flowers in the hospital afterwards, which shows the sort of man he was. In that great frame of his there beat a generous heart.

'And how many people benefited from Lard's generosity? When I retired from the school, years after Lard had left it, he came round to the school office and left me a present. It was a set of keys to a car, which he wanted me to have for my retirement. What a gesture that was. And the fact that there was a small dispute later about that car in no way took away from his thoughtfulness and his generosity. That was Lard all over.

'Some people may have had their differences with Lard over the years. There are some who say he cut corners. All that may be true, but on a day like this, we should not remember the bad things a man may have done, but we should remember the good. If Lard has anything to answer for – and, like the rest of us, he was not perfect – then he will answer for it in another place. He will no doubt ask for forgiveness and he will receive it, for that is what we are taught, and that is what we believe. So let none of us go from this place thinking ill of Aloysius Ignatius Xavier O'Connor, but thinking rather of his many acts of kindness, his humour, the joy he brought to those who loved him. And may there grow on his grave spring flowers from those memories. Spring flowers.'

There was complete silence as the teacher stepped away from the lectern and made his way back to his seat. At the back of the church, which was filled to the very last pew, a man cleared his throat, coughed. The priest stood up, and the rustle of his vestments was amplified by the microphone he wore attached to his front. Angus looked at Matthew; both had been moved by this oration. Matthew thought: what a kind man that teacher is, and Angus thought: that is what makes this city.

They stood to sing a hymn, and the priest said a final prayer.

Then it was over, and Lard, resting on a trolley bedecked with flowers, was wheeled out of the church, out into the light.

Waiting while the crowd of mourners filed out of the church, Matthew looked at the faces. There were a number of scars: scars across cheeks, nicks across the forehead. There were signs of all the hardness to which parts of Glasgow were well accustomed; which it joked about and made light of, even if in a perverse way; but which had cut deep, deep into its soul. This was the funeral of a gangster who happened to be Catholic; the funeral of a Protestant gangster would have involved the same sort of people: no difference.

And outside, people stood and chatted, shook hands, comforted one another. The light was bright; shafts of sunlight shone through clouds that had parted to bathe the city in patches of silver and gold. In a few minutes rain might drift in over the Atlantic, veils of it falling over this place, but for now it was dry.

Lard lay in glory in a glass-sided hearse to which a black, plumed horse had been yoked. He lay surrounded by flowers, great wreaths spelling out messages from friends and family. LARD said one; and another, BIG MAN, and QUALITY. And then there was the biggest wreath of all, which simply said: DEID.

'I think that we should get back to Queen Street,' said Angus.

Matthew agreed. He had been strangely moved by the service and he did not want to break the spell.

They started to move down the path that led from the church to the road, but they were stopped by a squat man in a black overcoat.

'Youse ra boys frae Edinburgh?' he asked.

'We are,' said Angus.

'Youse still got Lardie's painting?'

Matthew glanced at Angus. 'Yes, I suppose we have.'

The squat man seemed relieved. 'Well I'm Frankie O'Connor, Lard's wee brother. I'll come through and pick it up next week, if that's all right wi' youse. Better be.'

'Of course,' said Matthew. 'And I'm sorry about your brother.'

'Thank you,' said Frankie. 'But he had it coming to him, so he did.'

81. Best-Laid Plans

By unspoken agreement, Angus and Matthew did not talk about Lard O'Connor's painting in the taxi back to Queen Street station. They had been moved by Lard's obsequies, and by the eulogy delivered by his former teacher. And, as is always the case on such occasions, they had been reminded of their own mortality. I must paint my great painting, thought Angus; time is running out. And perhaps I should get married too, if anyone will have me. Domenica? She would be ideal – at least she knows what I'm like – but there's the problem with Cyril, which is irresolvable. Could he live on the landing, in some sort of heated kennel? Antonia would veto that, although with her drug-dealing she's hardly in a position to criticise anybody for anything.

'You know that woman,' he said to Matthew, once their train journey had started. 'You know that woman who lives opposite Domenica?'

'Not really,' said Matthew. 'Domenica introduced me to her once at the end of Cumberland Street. She said something about saints.'

'She's meant to be writing a book about Scottish saints,' said Angus. 'She goes on about them. All these peculiar saints who lived in places like Whithorn. Apparently virtually everyone was called a saint in those days. You just had to put a few stones together, call it a church, and you became a saint.'

Matthew did not think it was that easy. Nothing was easy in those days. 'Life was pretty hard,' he said. 'There was a great deal of darkness. In the metaphorical sense, of course.'

'And now?' asked Angus. 'No darkness?'

'Oh, there's darkness,' said Matthew. 'We happen to live in a country where there isn't – at the moment. But it could change. All that would be needed would be for people to become ignorant again. And they are.'

Angus looked around the carriage. Virtually everybody was reading. 'I don't know,' he said.

'Well,' said Matthew, 'did you see that survey published in the papers the other day where people were asked if they believed Winston Churchill ever existed? A quarter of them said they thought he was mythical.'

Angus reflected on this for a moment. There had also been the question of Scottish history. There were surveys all the time which showed that people had no idea who they were or why they were there. Perhaps he should execute a great painting – a great allegorical painting – entitled *Who Am I?* which would show the link between past and present. But nobody painted like that any more. He would be laughed at in the Royal Scottish Academy. He would be ridiculed. Paintings today had to reflect nothingness and confusion, not order and intellectual coherence.

He decided to return to the subject of Antonia. 'That woman may be writing about saints, but . . .' He leaned forward to address Matthew confidentially. 'She's a drug-dealer. A big one.'

Matthew looked startled. 'In Scotland Street? Under Domenica's nose?'

'Yes,' said Angus. 'I overheard her placing a big order. She talked about the stuff being cut to her satisfaction. She talked about being careful as she did not want to go to prison. It was perfectly obvious what was going on.'

For a few moments Matthew said nothing. Then, 'The problem in these cases is always: what do you do?'

Angus snorted. 'That's the problem in life in general, surely.'

'Perhaps. But do you go to the police? And what about us, Angus? What do we do about Lard's painting?'

Angus sat back in his seat. 'I don't know. I really don't know. But first things first: should we really call it Lard's painting? Was it ever his?'

'He brought it to us.'

'Of course. But do you think for one moment that it belonged to that aunt of his in Greenock?'

Matthew had to agree that this was unlikely.

'So it's stolen property,' said Angus. 'Every bit as stolen as the Duke of Buccleuch's da Vinci was – before they recovered it.' He paused. 'And you can't just sit on stolen property.'

Matthew took the point. 'So what do we do? We know that the painting must have been stolen. Do we take it to the police?'

'I see no alternative,' said Angus. 'They'll see if it's on their list of stolen paintings.'

'And if it isn't?'

Angus shrugged. 'I suppose they give it back to the O'Connor family. To Frankie O'Connor.'

Matthew greeted this with silence.

'And yet,' Angus conceded. 'And yet. The painting isn't theirs. It really belongs to the nation, in my view – that is, if no proper owner comes forward.'

Matthew was thinking. 'If we give it to the police, we still have a problem. Frankie O'Connor. He's not going to take kindly to that. And those people, you know what they're like ... We're in danger, Angus.'

Angus had to agree: Frankie O'Connor would certainly not take kindly to hearing that the painting had been given to the police. Unless ... 'He's only expecting a painting,' Angus said suddenly. 'He won't have the first clue which painting. The old switcheroo, Matthew!'

Matthew waited for further explanation.

'I have plenty of portraits in my studio,' said Angus. 'We merely put one of these in the frame that currently holds the Raeburn. Mr Francis O'Connor will be perfectly happy. In fact, we can offer to buy it from him. The new Raeburn, that is.'

Matthew was not immediately convinced, but as their journey continued, Angus managed to persuade him that this was their best course of action. 'I have the perfect candidate for the switch,' he said. 'I have a portrait of Ramsey Dunbarton in the studio that I really don't know what to do with. His widow, Betty, didn't want it – she claimed that she didn't want her memories of Ramsey to be disturbed by a painting. So we'll pass that on to Frankie.'

'But does he look at all like Burns?'

'No,' said Angus. 'But I'll touch it up a bit. I'll use acrylic. Dries in an instant. I'll give him the Robert Burns treatment. Poor old Ramsey.'

'Who was he?' asked Matthew.

WHO AM I?

'He was a lawyer in Edinburgh. A very fine man, in his way. He was terrifically proud of having played the Duke of Plaza-Toro in *The Gondoliers* at the Church Hill Theatre.'

'We all have something,' mused Matthew. And what, he wondered, was he proud of? Elspeth Harmony, he decided. He was proud that he had married Elspeth Harmony, that she had thought him worthy of her. And Edinburgh. He was proud of Edinburgh too, and of Scotland; and why not? Why should one not be proud of one's country – for a change?

82. Lessons in Leadership

Bertie had now attended two sessions of the First Morningside Cub Scouts in their meeting place in the Episcopal church hall at Holy Corner. The first session had involved a bitter disappointment, when Olive had turned up too. That was bad enough, but her immediate promotion to sixer had made things far worse.

'It's very unfair,' Bertie had observed to Tofu. 'She knows nothing about cub scouts. In fact, Olive knows nothing about anything. She's the one who said that Glasgow was in Ireland. I remember her saying it.'

'Stupid girl,' said Tofu. He himself was not sure about the location of Glasgow, but he was not going to reveal that. 'Girls are really stupid, Bertie. Particularly Olive.'

Bertie, who was fair-minded, felt that he could not let this pass. 'They're not all stupid,' he said. 'Look at Miss Harmony. She used to be a girl. And she's not stupid.'

Tofu looked pensive. 'Maybe. But then, look at your mother, Bertie. Look at her.'

Bertie changed the subject. 'And she's going to throw her weight around, now that she's a sixer. She said that we're going to have to pull up our socks.'

Olive had issued this warning at an early stage. Indeed, no sooner had Akela gone to deal with another preliminary administrative matter than Olive had turned to Bertie and Tofu and delivered a stern admonition.

'Let's get one thing clear right at the beginning,' she said. 'My six is going to be the best-run and most successful six in the pack. Understand?'

Tofu had glowered. Bertie had looked at the floor.

'So,' Olive continued, 'I don't want any arguing. If I say something is to be done, then it is to be done. And here's another thing. From now on, you don't call me by my name, you call me "Sixer". Is that quite clear?'

Bertie and Tofu had remained silent, but an extremely small boy, diminutive indeed, who had been allocated to their six, nodded enthusiastically. 'Yes, Sixer,' he said.

Olive turned to this small boy. 'What's your name?' she asked.

'Ranald,' said the boy in a thin, piping voice. 'Ranald Braveheart McPherson.'

Bertie and Tofu looked at him in astonishment, but Olive merely nodded. 'You can be my assistant, Ranald,' she said.

'You can't just choose your assistant like that,' protested Tofu. 'Akela has to choose.'

'I think Tofu's right,' agreed Bertie. 'I don't think that sixers have all that much power, Olive.'

Ranald stepped forward, on spindly legs. 'We mustn't argue,' he said. 'We mustn't argue with the sixer.'

This discussion on constitutional arrangements might have continued, but it was time for activities, and for the rest of the session the issue of Olive's power did not arise. Fortunately, the games played were such as to take Bertie's mind off the Olive problem, and at the end he decided that it might be possible largely to avoid Olive by simply ignoring her. This expedient, however, did not work so well at the second session, the following week, when Olive had watched Bertie and Tofu closely, criticising their every step and saying that they would have to do better.

'We don't need to be quite so critical, Olive,' Akela had warned. 'A good sixer encourages the others. So you should praise people as well as tell them where they're going wrong.'

Olive had listened, but her expression was resentful, and Bertie wondered if she had internalised the message. He had read about internalising messages, and he decided that this was something that Olive was not very good at. But such reflections were soon to be abandoned when it was announced that the following Saturday afternoon the entire pack would decamp to the Meadows in order to practise map-reading and navigation skills. Compasses were issued and a fascinating hour was spent in learning how to hold a compass and how to read a map.

Akela explained that each six would be divided into two, so that the members would work in groups of three: one cub would be in charge, and would hold the map, and another would be entrusted with the compass. Bertie glanced at Tofu, who looked back at him in perfect understanding, the unspoken anxiety being: would they be with Olive?

They were not. Olive was allocated to two others, a disconsolate-looking boy and a girl with a startled expression and pigtails, who had not said anything from the moment of her enrolment. Bertie and Tofu both heaved a sigh of relief. But when Akela turned to them, they were informed that Ranald McPherson was to be in charge.

'What about me, Akela?' protested Tofu. 'I'm much bigger than he is. Look. He only comes up to here. And look at his stupid legs. He's too small to be the leader.'

'Tofu dear,' explained Akela. 'Leadership is not about size; nor indeed about legs. You don't have to be big to lead. Look at the Queen. She's not all that tall and yet she's a very good leader. Leadership comes from inside.'

'That's right,' said Olive.

Akela threw a glance at Olive. 'And leaders must earn respect,' she continued. 'A good leader doesn't try to push people around too much.'

'See,' said Olive, looking directly at Tofu. 'That's why some people are leaders and some people aren't.'

There was no time for further discussion, as final arrangements had to be made. When the time came, they would all walk together down Bruntsfield Place and then cross the Links. Once they were safely away from the traffic, on the other side of the Meadows, they would split up into their respective groups and use the maps which had been prepared for them to negotiate their way round the University Library, through the George Square Gardens and back to the Meadows. On their way they would have to note certain features of the landscape and answer questions about them on their return.

That evening, Bertie explained to his mother what was planned. Irene listened grimly.

'A somewhat old-fashioned exercise,' she said when Bertie had finished his account. 'In these days of satellite navigation.'

83. A Shot in the Park

They walked along Bruntsfield Place, the whole cub scout pack in an ordered line, past George Hughes & Sons Fishmongers, past the Yoga Centre, the antique shop, the Himalayan Restaurant and Hasta Mañana. Olive, at the head of her six, commented loudly on each landmark as they passed it. 'That,' she said, 'is Mr Hughes's fish shop. I have been there twice. Mr Hughes catches all those fish himself.'

Bertie frowned. 'I don't think he does, Olive. I think that he goes down to the harbour and buys them. I saw his van going down the hill once.'

Ranald Braveheart McPherson, trotting behind Olive, rallied to her support. 'You mustn't argue with the sixer, Bertie.'

'That's right,' said Olive. 'And you mustn't argue with your girlfriend. There's nothing worse than a boyfriend who argues with his girlfriend.'

'You're Olive's boyfriend?' asked Ranald. 'You're lucky, Bertie.'

Bertie blushed deep red. 'I'm not,' he muttered. 'I never said . . .'

'Oh yes you did, Bertie Pollock!' snapped Olive. 'You've been my boyfriend for ages. Everybody knows that.'

'Then why does he never go out with you?' Tofu challenged. 'Boyfriends take their girlfriends to the cinema. When did Bertie last take you to the cinema, Olive?'

'I'm not really allowed to go,' he said. 'My mother . . .'

'I'll take you to the cinema, Olive,' said Ranald, adding, 'you can come with me and my mummy.'

'Hah!' shouted Tofu. 'Mummies don't go on dates, Ranald.'

'Thank you,' said Olive. 'Did you hear that, Bertie? Did you hear what Ranald said?'

Such pleasantries continued, and it was not long before they reached Bruntsfield Links and saw, in the distance, the tree-lined paths of the Meadows. Now a buzz of excitement arose. Compasses, which had been issued to each team, were grasped in small, damp hands; woggles tightened; laces tied up. And then minutes later, when they had walked across to the other side, they were divided into their groups, maps were issued, and the challenge began. Everybody dispersed.

Bertie and Tofu stood in a huddle with Ranald Braveheart McPherson.

Tofu addressed Ranald. 'You're meant to be the leader,' he said. 'So tell us where to go.'

Ranald looked anxiously at the map. 'I think that we go that way,' he said.

'No,' said Bertie. 'Look. That's a picture of the tennis courts. That's them over there. See? And there's Arthur's Seat. That big hill. So that means that the map goes this way.'

They consulted the compass. The needle, wobbling on its base, spun round indecisively.

'If we watch where the sun goes down,' said Tofu, 'that'll show us where west is.'

'But it's only two o'clock,' said Ranald.

'Then we wait,' said Tofu. 'Best to get things right.'

'I don't think so,' said Bertie. 'If we wait here until the sun goes down, then it'll be dark.'

They looked at Ranald.

'You're the leader,' said Tofu. 'You decide.'

Ranald Braveheart McPherson shivered. A chill breeze had sprung up, and his knees, small, bony protuberances on thin legs, were turning red. In the absence of Olive, his authority seemed a slender, insubstantial thing. He had no idea where they were, nor where they should go. Perhaps it was not such a good idea to be a cub scout after all; perhaps he should have stayed inside.

Bertie assumed leadership. 'That way,' he said, pointing in the direction of Arthur's Seat, glimpsed above the tree tops. 'We'll go that way to begin with, and then we'll turn up there and follow that path. Agree?'

Tofu and Ranald were both pleased that Bertie was taking over, and Ranald quickly passed him the map. Then they set off. But it so happened that at exactly that time, the Royal Company of Archers was holding its annual ceremonial competition shoot – for the Edinburgh Arrow, a trophy awarded to the member who actually hit the target. On years when nobody hit it – and this was a not uncommon occurrence – then the arrow was awarded to the archer who came closest.

Dressed in their fine green uniforms, feathers protruding proudly from their bonnets, the archers stood in ranks near the corporation tennis courts. A few arrows had already been fired, including a wildly inaccurate shot from one of the brigadiers, in which the arrow had slithered along the grass in the direction of the Royal (Dick) Veterinary College, to be intercepted by a playful dog, who had seized it and carried it away in the direction of the Sick Kids' Hospital.

Bertie, Tofu and Ranald, standing by a hedge, watched the competition with great interest.

'They're the Queen's bodyguard in Scotland,' explained Bertie. 'They're very important.'

They watched as one of the archers stepped up to the plate and fitted an arrow to his bow. He was a powerfully built man and he drew the string well back. Then, taking aim at the distant target, a large, straw circle, he let the arrow fly which it did, convincingly so, but not in the direction anticipated by the bowman. Caught in the breeze, the arrow curved a slow arc across the sky and fell to earth at exactly the point where a man was walking along the perimeter of the park. Although its force was largely spent by that stage of its flight, there was enough velocity in it to pierce the sleeve of his jacket and lodge in the fabric.

The archers had now finished their shoot, and were packing up to leave, to return to Archers' Hall, their fine headquarters off Buccleuch Place. The archer who had fired the last shot looked furtively about him, and slipped off at a fast walk.

'Did you see that?' whispered Bertie. 'Did you see him shoot that man?'

Ranald shivered. 'Let's go home before they shoot us,' he said miserably.

'No,' said Bertie. 'We must get on with what we're meant to be doing.'

He looked at the map and pointed out the route they should take. This led them past the place where the victim of the misfired arrow, a handsome-looking man dressed in black, was still standing indignantly, wrestling with the arrow that was protruding from his sleeve. He had pulled it out of its resting place, but its tip had become caught in the material and was proving difficult to extricate.

'We saw who did it, mister,' said Tofu. 'We saw him.'

The man greeted this information with interest. 'Could you point him out to me?'

'I think so,' said Bertie. 'But they've all walked away.'

'I know who they are,' said the man. 'It's that Royal Company of Archers. They've got a clubhouse of some sort back there. That's where they'll be heading.'

84. Meet the Archers

Bertie looked at the man who had been shot by the arrow. He looked familiar for some reason, but he could not remember why. Then he remembered: he had seen his picture on a book his father had been reading and he had asked him who it was. 'Ian Rankin,' Stuart had replied.

'Excuse me,' Bertie now said. 'Excuse me, but aren't you Mr Rankin?'

'Yes, I am. And you are?'

'Bertie Pollock, sir. I'm a member of the First Morningside Cub Scouts and ...'

Tofu interrupted him. 'And my name is Tofu,' he said. 'It's an Irish name meaning ...'

'Vegetable paste,' offered Bertie.

Tofu scowled. 'Chieftain,' he said. 'It means chieftain.'

Ian Rankin turned to the third member of the party. 'And you, young man?'

'Ranald Braveheart McPherson,' came the squeaky voice.

'Well then,' said Ian Rankin. 'I suggest that you three help me to solve the mystery of who shot me. Shall we go round to the Archers' Hall?'

They made their way round the edge of the Meadows. Ian Rankin passed the arrow to Bertie to look after. 'Evidence,' he said. 'We must keep the evidence.'

'Will they try to run away again?' asked Tofu.

'We'll see,' said Ian Rankin. 'I don't think they could run very fast – most of them. But we'll see. We must realise that we're dealing with some pretty desperate characters here. Earls and people of that sort. You never know what people like that will do.'

They continued along Buccleuch Place and then turned the corner at the second-hand bookshop.

'There's one of your books in the window there, Mr Rankin,' Bertie pointed out. 'Look. And, look, it's only one pound.'

They turned another corner and began to make their way down a small lane. At the end of the lane was a handsome building, in the eighteenth-century style, the front door of which was surmounted by a large coat of arms executed in stone. The door seemed firmly closed, but there was a light within indicating that the hall was in use.

Ian Rankin knocked firmly on the door and he, and his three uniformed assistants, to all intents and purposes Baker Street Irregulars, waited for a response.

Inside the hall, one of the archers, a brigadier, peered out of a small peep-hole.

'Oh no,' he muttered to somebody behind him. 'That chap you shot by mistake. He's outside with a gang of helpers.'

The other archer moved forward and looked through the peep-hole. 'Oh dear,' he said. 'But at least he's still alive. And, do you know what? I think it's that Rankin chap. What are we going to do?'

'Get the form,' said an archer behind him. 'The usual form. It works every time.'

There was a general scurrying among the archers and a piece of paper was produced from a drawer in a bureau at the back of the hall. This was a waiver of liability form, drafted years ago by one of the lawyer members of the company, and it offered membership of the Royal Company of Archers in return for an agreement by the injured party not to pursue the matter.

'It's saved an awful lot of trouble in the past,' said the brigadier, blowing the dust off the form. 'Many years ago one of the then governors of the Bank of Scotland hit a city councillor in the leg when he let off an arrow at the Garden Party. Fortunately we had the form, and it did the trick. They're thrilled to be invited, you see, and they sign it, in almost every case. Then we tell them what the uniform costs, and they go away. Works every time.'

With form in hand, the brigadier opened the door. 'Yes?' he said, quite politely.

Ian Rankin turned to Bertie. 'Was it him?' he asked.

Bertie shook his head. He could see the guilty archer, standing in the shadows, and he pointed to him. 'It was that man over there, Mr Rankin,' he said.

'All right,' said the brigadier. 'Sorry about that. Some of the chaps are a little bit wonky in their shooting. Terribly sorry. But, here's an idea. If you would care to forget about the matter, then we'll make you a member! We have great fun and, as you see, we've got this marvellous hall! That picture over there is by Allan Ramsay, for example. It shows the Earl of Wemyss in his archer's kit.'

He thrust the piece of paper into Ian Rankin's hands.

'You should join, Mr Rankin,' said Tofu. 'It looks fun.'

'Ask them how much it costs first,' whispered Bertie.

The brigadier glowered at Bertie. 'Just sign there,' he said.

Ian Rankin hesitated. There was no harm in this, he thought, and he was a kind man. He had received his apology and this very generous offer of membership. He signed.

'Good,' said the brigadier. 'Now we'll send you the details of

274

the annual dues and the cost of the uniform. You can get it made up for just under five thousand.'

'Pounds?' said an astonished Ian Rankin.

'Yes,' said the brigadier. 'Frightfully expensive. Sorry about that. But there we are. Sorry you won't be joining us after all!'

And with that he shut the door. 'I should have listened to you, Bertie,' said Ian Rankin. 'That's the way the establishment operates in this city, of course. They assimilate critics. It's an old trick.' They walked back to Buccleuch Place.

'We'd better get on with our map-reading exercise,' said Bertie.

'And I should get on with my walk,' said Ian Rankin. 'But I must thank you three young men for being such excellent detectives. I think that we solved that mystery really rather satisfactorily.'

They bade farewell to each other, and the three boys made their way back in the direction of the University Library. They were back on course now, and with some good navigation from Bertie, they soon succeeded in completing the task. Twenty minutes or so later, they found themselves reunited with Akela and the other cubs. Everybody was accounted for, except for one or two stragglers, who would probably turn up later on, Akela thought.

85. Gangsters, Drugs, Dreams – and Dogs

With the need to deal quickly with the late Lard O'Connor's painting, before the much regretted Glaswegian gangster's younger brother, Frankie O'Connor, travelled to Edinburgh to reclaim it, Angus had invited James Holloway to his studio to inspect the portrait of Burns.

'I'm pretty sure that this painting is what you think it is,' said James. 'There's so much evidence now. But the jardinière really clinches it.'

Angus had raised with James the issue of the jardinière which appeared in the background of the painting. He had been convinced that he had seen it somewhere before, and had wondered whether it had appeared in any other paintings of the period. James thought that it had not, but had taken the matter further and had eventually identified it as the Chinese jardinière belonging to Lord Monboddo, the famous eighteenth-century philosopher, linguist and lawyer.

'Here's a recent photograph of that very jardinière,' said James, passing a glossy print to Angus. 'You see, it's the same in every particular.'

Angus took the photograph and held it alongside the jardinière in the Raeburn. There could be no doubt: the two were the same.

'So what that suggests,' James went on, 'is that Raeburn painted Burns's portrait when the poet was visiting Edinburgh. We know that he was received by Monboddo, who ran a salon in his house at 13 St John's Street. It was quite a salon, of course: not only Burns attended what Monboddo called his "learned suppers", but all the leading intellectual lights of the day.

'I thought,' James went on, 'that if we ever found a Raeburn portrait of Burns it would have been painted at Dr Fergusson's house in Sciennes, but there we are. This is definitely in Monboddo's house.'

Angus smiled in pleasure. 'That makes it even more exciting,' he said. 'I have a lot of time for Monboddo.'

'Of course,' said James. 'He was a most remarkable man. And yet people made fun of him. The portrait of him by John Kay, for instance, depicts him against a framed picture of a group of tailed men dancing round in a circle.'

'Well, he did say that men used to have tails,' Angus pointed out.

'Didn't Darwin have something rather similar to say?' retorted James.

Angus nodded. 'Oh, I agree. He was in some respects a Darwinian before his time. But, moving on from Monboddo, we have an immediate problem on our hands.'

'This Glasgow gangster?' asked James. 'Or rather, his brother?'

'Yes. We must do everything we can to stop them getting this picture. They have no right to it – they obviously stole it.'

James thought about this. 'Fair enough. But in those circumstances, it will have to go to the police, won't it?'

Angus stroked the frame of the painting lovingly. 'Yes, but I can tell them, quite honestly, that it was brought in by somebody who has now disappeared and can't be traced, and that in these circumstances I would propose donating it to the nation if they can find no lawful owner from whom it has been stolen.'

'A very sound idea,' agreed James. 'And a perfectly legal and morally correct one too. And, on behalf of the nation, I accept.'

With the broad policy agreed, James and Angus set about prising the Raeburn from its frame. Once removed, the painting seemed a somehow diminished thing, naked and vulnerable – a mere creature of canvas and wooden stretchers. But even with this, it glowed with that wonderful muted light that infused each Raeburn, and one could tell that this was from the hand of a master.

Next, Angus fetched the redundant portrait of Ramsey Dunbarton and measured it against the frame that the Raeburn had just vacated. Some adjustment would be required to Ramsey's portrait, but nothing excessive, and it was while he was marking this with chalk on the surface of the canvas that a telephone call came through from Domenica.

James could tell that the call was an important one. 'No!' exclaimed Angus down the line, his eyes widening. 'Is there no end to her brass neck?' And, 'She'll be wanting to keep her distance from the actual transaction – that's what she'll be wanting!' followed by, 'We'll come down to Scotland Street immediately. Stay where you are, and keep calm.'

'Trouble?' asked James when Angus had replaced the receiver.

Angus rolled his eyes. 'Serious trouble,' he said. 'We shall have to go to Domenica's flat without delay, James. I shall explain on our way.'

With Cyril trotting beside them, Angus and James set off on the short walk to Scotland Street. Angus gave James an account of the conversation that he had overheard in Antonia's flat when he was returning the blue Spode teacup. 'And now Domenica says that Antonia has asked her to take another delivery for her,' he said.

'She claims to be going to the hairdresser again and said that there would be what she called a "very delicate" delivery while she was out. Could Domenica take it for her? She's always doing that, of course, expecting Domenica to sign for all sorts of things, but never a consignment of drugs!'

James listened to this and gave a whistle. 'She'll be wanting Domenica to do the dangerous work for her,' he said. 'Receiving these things is presumably the most perilous part of the transaction. She'll want to keep well clear of that. Has she given her money to hand over?'

'Domenica said that there's an envelope that feels as if it's full of money,' answered Angus.

'I find it quite despicable,' said James. 'It's bad enough that she's involved in the whole sordid business, but to implicate an innocent neighbour is dreadful. It's like those people who use unwitting so-called mules to do their dirty work for them.'

Angus agreed with this assessment. 'We shall see what Domenica proposes,' he said. 'But in my view we should immediately involve the police. They can be waiting for the delivery and they can make their arrests.'

'Yes,' said James. He paused. 'And how long do you think Antonia will get for this?'

'It depends on the quantity of drugs,' said Angus. 'She talked about it being cut when I heard her, but it may still be quite an amount. Five years perhaps.'

The question made Angus think. If Antonia were to be sent to prison – as looked likely – then her flat would presumably be confiscated, on the grounds that it was purchased with illicitly obtained money. That would mean that it would come onto the market, and if that happened, he might consider buying it. It would be very pleasant living next to Domenica and . . . and if Domenica ever thought about marrying him, he could move in with her and Cyril could be kept in the next-door flat. That would remove Domenica's anxieties about having Cyril in the house. It was a brilliant idea, and with the arrest of Antonia imminent, it seemed like a perfectly feasible one.

He allowed himself to daydream. Cyril could have his own brass plate on his front door. Cyril Lordie, it would say, Beware of the Owner.

CYRIL LORDIE

CYRIL

BEWARE OF
THE OWNER

86. To Catch a Dealer

No sooner had Angus pressed Domenica's bell than the door was opened from within. 'It's always a bit disconcerting,' he said, 'to have a door fly open immediately one presses the bell. Not that I'm criticising you, Domenica – I'm merely making an observation.'

'I see,' she said. 'So you'd prefer to wait?'

She turned to James. 'Good morning, James. I take it that you're not disconcerted?'

James smiled in embarrassment. He had heard Domenica and Angus sparring with one another in the past, a pursuit they no doubt found enjoyable, but which could make others feel awkward. 'I don't think it really matters,' he said. 'The important thing is that the door is opened. That's what counts, surely.'

Domenica ushered them into the flat, Cyril being allowed in as well. The well-mannered dog looked around appreciatively and sniffed the air. There was a rug, and he moved to this and sat down, his mouth slightly open, showing his single gold tooth, awaiting instructions. Much of the life of a dog is spent awaiting

279

instructions; any instruction will do – a command to sit, even when sitting will serve no purpose, is appreciated; or a command to fetch, even when there is no reason for anything to be fetched. With instructions, a dog feels that he is contributing to the human world that he sees going on about him, a world which is so often opaque and confusing – for dogs, and indeed often for humans; a world of frantic activity, of people going backwards and forwards, entering rooms and then leaving them, sitting down and then standing up, and to what end?

Domenica's mind, though, was still on the question of when to open the door. She was not going to have Angus getting away with a remark she regarded as undermining. 'I must say that I find it very irritating to be kept waiting,' she said firmly. 'In my view, if the door is not opened within one minute of the bell being rung, there is a need for an apology or explanation. Anything longer than that and the message is clear: the caller is not important.'

'Yes,' said Angus. 'But you do need a little time to compose yourself once you've rung a bell. That's all I was saying. Composition time. It's the same with telephones. If the other person picks up the phone immediately it rings, you get a bit of a shock. You expect a few rings at the other end.'

'That's true,' agreed James. 'It's a rather abrupt start to a telephone call otherwise.'

They went into the kitchen. Angus sniffed the air, just as Cyril had done: the smell of Domenica's coffee always seemed so much more delicious than the smell of the coffee he made for himself. Why, he wondered, does somebody not make a perfume, or an aftershave lotion perhaps, that mimicked that smell? Perfumes could be so overwhelming, so cloying by comparison; a person who brought with him or her some wafting reminder of coffee would surely be much appreciated.

The pouring of the coffee was the signal for the topic of conversation to move on. Domenica now related to her guests how Antonia had rung her doorbell – she did not reveal how quickly she answered it – earlier that morning and asked her, again, to take a delivery. 'She was as cool as a cucumber,' she said. 'Standing there, utterly without scruple. And do you know what she said to me? She said: please be discreet.'

'That clinches it,' said Angus. 'This is . . . what do they call it? The drop?'

James shook his head. 'I don't think so. The drop is a term used purely in espionage. It's when you drop the papers or the microfilm in a dead tree and somebody comes along and picks them up. Half the secrets of the Cold War were exchanged in that way.'

'How bizarre,' said Domenica. 'Men don't ever really grow up, do they?'

Angus and James were both silent for a while. Then Angus spoke. 'Many intelligence people were women, you know. Daphne Park, for example. She worked for MI5, I believe. I had lunch with her down in London once after they put her in the House of Lords. She's a very remarkable woman.'

'Women make rather good spies because we're observant,' said Domenica. 'But, listen, this is not the point. The point is that at any moment Antonia's consignment is going to arrive. What are we going to do?'

'We call the police,' said Angus.

Domenica shook her head. 'I really don't think we have time. If I phoned the police now, they would simply send somebody round to check up on my story. And that could frighten the dealers off. They'd see a police car parked outside.'

Angus conceded that this was likely. 'So what do we do?' he asked. 'Do we simply take delivery?'

'Why don't we do that?' James said. 'Domenica takes delivery, and one of us nips downstairs and takes the number of the person's car. Then that's the stage that we call the police. They then come – we tell them the full story . . .'

'We can't,' said Angus. 'I'm not going to tell them about getting into Antonia's flat and hiding in the cupboard. That's probably an offence in itself. I'm not going to tell them that.'

Domenica intervened. 'We don't need to say anything about that. All we need to tell them is that I was asked to take delivery by Antonia. I can then say that my suspicions were aroused – which will be true – and that we investigated the box or packet or whatever it is and discovered that it was full of drugs. Then we hand the whole thing over, and Antonia goes to jail.'

The mention of jail made Angus think again of Antonia's flat. 'If she goes to prison,' he said, 'and there can be no doubt that it's about time that she did, then I wonder what will happen to her flat? It's very nicely situated. One of the rooms, I've always felt, would make a very fine studio. It's that one with the skylight, which gives a good northern light.'

He watched her for signs of a reaction. If she said, 'Well, Angus, why don't you think of buying it?' it would be a good sign. That would show that she would like him to be her neighbour. And if she would like him to be her neighbour, then perhaps she would like him to be something more than that.

But Domenica said nothing. She let the remark pass, as if nobody had said anything of the remotest interest or consequence.

87. Deceptive Appearances

The hands of the clock moved slowly. Everybody was too nervous now to talk very much and so for a while they sat in silence as they waited for the arrival of Antonia's supplier. Angus found himself wondering what this person would look like. Lard O'Connor had been such an obvious figure – a gangster of the old school, almost loveable, from a distance, while Antonia's supplier would come from a totally different end of the criminal spectrum. Such people were callous and psychopathic, indifferent to the chaos and misery their wares caused in the lives of those who consumed them. And yet, here was Antonia, outwardly respectable, quite congenial company – at times, and in her way – implicated in precisely the same trade, even if a lowly link in the chain. But if one passed her in the street it would never occur to one that she was a drug-dealer; one might even see her in Jenners and think nothing of it.

'What was the name of that Italian?' he suddenly asked Domenica.

'Which Italian?'

'The one who said that he could identify criminals by their appearance?'

James provided the answer. 'Cesare Lombroso.'

Domenica nodded. She knew all about Lombroso. 'You're thinking of Antonia, I take it,' she said. 'You're reflecting on her lack of a criminal appearance?'

'Well, I was,' admitted Angus. 'And you have to admit, she doesn't exactly look the part of the drug-dealer, does she?'

'Lombroso was interested in the face and the shape of the head,' Domenica said. 'If you look at the illustrations in his book, you'll see that it was all about low foreheads and the eyes being too close together. He had those wonderfully frightening pictures of Murderer – typical Sicilian type and so on.'

'Well, they did rather look the part, didn't they?'

Domenica laughed. 'Have you seen the photographs of Dr Shipman? The one who bumped off half his patients. Would you have been worried if he came to give you an injection?' She answered her own question. 'I doubt it, Angus. There have been plenty of mild-looking murderers.'

Angus looked thoughtful. 'Undoubtedly. But at the end of the day, there's still some connection between the look on a face and what's going on in the mind. The old saw that the eyes are the window of the soul has some truth in it. Take Richard Nixon. And then compare him with, say, Bill Clinton. What do the faces say to you?'

'Nixon had a . . .'

'Tricky face?' Angus interjected. 'Paranoid? Couldn't you look at that face and say, "That's a man who has an enemies list"?'

'Whereas William Jefferson Clinton . . .'

Angus made a gesture to indicate the obvious. 'An open, friendly face. Sympathetic. Warm.'

'And in each case what you saw on the outside is what you got on the inside?'

Angus nodded. 'Exactly.' He turned to James. 'And in portraiture,

James, would you not agree that character can shine through the face?'

'Oh yes. Although it might depend on whether there was any flattery going on. Portrait painters are not above flattery, Angus, as I'm sure you are well aware.'

Angus laughed. 'I am. That is, I am aware. And I hope that I'm above flattery – most of the time. I suppose there are occasions when I feel that I have to be kind. But being kind to somebody is different, surely, from flattering them.'

They were silent again, each thinking, perhaps, of Antonia and any display in her physiognomy of her secret. Had there been signs that people had missed? Angus remembered seeing the moderately expensive pictures on her wall; for a successful drug-dealer, those would have been easily affordable. Well, that at least answered the question of how she could buy them. It would also explain how she managed to live without working, if one did not count the writing of a novel about the Scottish saints as working, which he did not. And there was a further mystery, the answer to which would soon be revealed: what sort of drugs would she be dealing in? The most likely answer to that, he thought, was cocaine. Antonia would be providing cocaine to the upmarket dinner parties where such things were consumed. She was perfectly placed for that in the New Town, with its elegant flats and wealthy inhabitants. He shook his head, almost wistfully. He had never been invited to one of these fashionable dinner parties, possibly because of Cyril, he thought. Or the clothes he wore. Or even his age.

It was while Angus was entertaining these thoughts that Domenica's doorbell rang. At the sudden, shrill sound all three of them gave a start and looked anxiously at one another.

'I'm going to answer,' whispered Domenica. 'You stay in here. Don't do anything.'

She left the kitchen and went into the hall. Angus and James could still see her, though, from the kitchen table, and they watched her every step.

Domenica opened her door. There, immediately outside on the

landing, was a tall woman somewhere in her forties, wearing a green Barbour jacket and tight-fitting corduroy jeans.

'Domenica Macdonald?'

Domenica nodded. This was not what she had expected. The voice was commanding, confident.

'Antonia telephoned me and said that I could leave something with you while she was out.' She gestured to a large cardboard box, which she had laid down on the ground behind her. 'I've howked this up from downstairs and I've got another one in the Land Rover. Could I pop this inside and then I'll go and fetch the other one?'

The woman did not wait for an answer, but lifted up the card-board box and virtually pushed her way past Domenica, who was still standing in the doorway in what appeared to be a degree of shock.

'In the kitchen?' asked the woman. 'Can I dump it through there?'

Again she did not wait for an answer, and made her way across the hall and through the kitchen door. Once in the kitchen she put the box down on the table and straightened up, to look at the two astonished men.

'Angus Lordie!' the woman exclaimed. 'Now this is a surprise! Of course you live round here, don't you. Jimmy said he'd bumped into you in Drummond Place five or six years ago.'

Angus struggled to his feet. 'Maeve,' he said weakly. 'I had no idea ...'

'Of course you didn't,' she said briskly.

'I ... I ...' stuttered Angus.

'Look,' she said. 'Don't worry about all that. It's ages ago. And I've been happily married for years. Don't worry about a thing. Water under the Forth Bridge. Lots of it.'

88. Illicit Skills

James and Domenica exchanged glances: the confusion which now so clearly covered Angus Lordie had extended to them too, though to a lesser degree. They, at least, knew where to look, which was at Angus; he, however, was staring firmly at the floor, as if it might reveal the solution to what was evidently a situation of considerable personal embarrassment. Domenica felt sympathetic. It is awkward enough, she thought, even in ordinary circumstances to encounter a former lover whom one has mistreated; how much more difficult must it be to do so in circumstances such as these, where the former lover reveals herself as a master criminal.

And there were loyalty issues too, she thought. The decision to report a neighbour to the authorities was one thing; it was quite another to report at the same time, in a single grand denunciation, both a neighbour and a former love. As she looked with some pity on Angus, he blushed red and stuttered, and she speculated further on what had happened between the portrait painter and this somewhat unlikely drug-dealer. For a few heady and ridiculous moments she imagined that this woman might have been his model; that these long limbs, now encased in sexless corduroy, might once have been bared and draped across some stylised couch in Angus's studio; that from that sultry scene a torrid romance might have developed. It was possible, but her thoughts were interrupted by the model herself, if that is what she had been, who now addressed Angus again, in a perfectly matter-of-fact way, and not as one discovered in flagrante delicto.

'The traffic across the bridge was as bad as ever,' she remarked. 'It's all very well abolishing tolls, but that just encourages people to drive.'

Angus looked up. 'It's the trains,' he said. 'If we had a decent rail service, then people would come in by train. But compare what we've got with any other European city . . .'

The woman nodded. Then she turned to Domenica. 'You must think me terribly rude,' she said. 'I've barged in without introducing myself.' She glanced at Angus, as if to censure him for his failure to make the introduction. He noticed, and effected it, introducing Maeve Ross to both Domenica and James. 'Maeve,' he said, rather lamely, 'is an old friend.'

'Well, that's one way of putting it,' said Maeve cheerfully. 'But yes, Angus and I go back some time. Youthful ardour.' She laughed. 'Youthful ardour followed, in each case, by more mature reflection. What would you say to that, Angus?'

Angus laughed nervously. 'Well put, Maeve.' He paused. 'But I must say that I'm rather surprised to . . . to find you mixed up in all this.'

Maeve frowned. 'In what?' She tapped the cardboard box. 'In this? In this stuff?'

Angus nodded, almost apologetically. 'Yes. This business with Antonia. Is it wise? What if you were caught?'

Maeve gave a dismissive snort. 'You can't go through life worrying about being caught. And anyway, I see nothing wrong with this at all. Willing seller, willing buyer.'

Angus drew in his breath sharply. 'But what about the misery?' he asked. 'This stuff ruins lives.'

Maeve looked at him in astonishment. 'Only if you have too much of it. Not that I've ever encountered anybody doing that.'

Maeve's insouciant attitude seemed to give Angus the courage to argue. 'You've never encountered anything like that? How can you say that? People overdose all the time. They get addicted. Their lives – their whole lives – are directed to getting more. How can you ignore that?'

As he spoke, Maeve looked at him as if she was struggling to make sense of what he said. 'I'm really not with you,' she said.

'And then there's the law,' Angus continued. 'It's a criminal offence, you know. Or maybe you've never encountered that side of it either.'

James and Domenica, watching like tennis umpires, their gaze fixed first on one and then on the other, now looked at Maeve to see how she would react.

'Oh, I don't care about the law,' she said. 'The law has become ridiculous. It's become oppressive. Those bureaucrats in Brussels with their unending desire to regulate us out of existence – resistance is the only answer to that. And resist we shall . . .' She paused, judging the effect of her words. Then she leaned forward and opened the top of the cardboard box. Three pairs of astonished eyes watched in fascination as she extracted a jar from within.

'This marmalade,' she announced, 'is utterly harmless. And yet those meddlers – yes, I repeat, those meddlers – in Brussels would prevent us from making it and selling it to our friends. And we in the Scottish Rural Women's Institute (Provisional Wing) are not going to lie back and let that happen. Oh no! We shall not.'

She passed the jar to Domenica. 'Look. Isn't that a beautiful, rich colour? The finest Seville oranges, roughly cut. Marvellous stuff – a hundred times tastier than the watery rubbish that passes for marmalade in the supermarkets. And yet that's all that many people can get these days, now that the home-made stuff has been driven underground.'

Domenica prised open the lid of the jar and sniffed at the contents. 'One could certainly get addicted to this,' she said, smiling.

'Indeed you could,' Maeve agreed. 'And if people weren't prepared to run this stuff over from places like Fife and Perthshire, then I can assure you there would be many in Edinburgh who would be like addicts deprived.'

'Would you mind if I sampled some?' Domenica asked. 'I have some oatcakes in the cupboard.'

'Delighted,' said Maeve. 'I always pop a few extra jars in for Antonia. I'm sure that she won't mind.'

The oatcakes were produced and plates were distributed.

'Ah,' said Maeve. 'Blue Spode. I have a particular liking for Spode. Antonia has a similar pattern, if I remember correctly.'

Domenica avoided Angus's eye. Life was full of connections – and coincidences. Love, blue Spode, marmalade – these were all things that worked away in the background, binding people to one another in invisible nets. She suddenly thought of a piece of seventeenth-century music – was it seventeenth century? – that had haunted her since first she heard it. 'In Nets of Golden Wires' – that was what it had been called. In nets of golden wires – such a lovely image of how life, and love, may ensnare us, and now she took a small bite out of the oatcake Maeve passed her. It was a sharing – almost sacramental in its solemnity – and it had for her an evocative power every bit as strong as that which had been exerted upon Proust by those small madeleine cakes, years ago, in a very different world.

89. Confession Time

At more or less the same time that the illicit home-made marmalade, spread generously on Nairn's low-salt oatcakes, was being tasted in Scotland Street, Matthew crossed Dundas Street to have his morning coffee at Big Lou's. It had been an unusual morning for him in that he had sold a painting before ten-thirty, the time when he normally slipped across the road for coffee. Most of his business, such as it was, was done at lunchtime or in the late afternoon, but on this occasion a man had come in, glanced around the gallery, and immediately bought a small nineteenth-century watercolour which Matthew had only recently acquired. It was a satisfactory sale from Matthew's point of view, unless . . . and as he crossed the road he began to have his doubts. The purchase had been so quick, so decisive, that it was possible that the man had recognised the painting and Matthew had not.

By the time he reached the coffee bar and had negotiated his way carefully down Big Lou's dubious stairs – the very stairs down which Lard O'Connor had tumbled out of this world – Matthew had decided that he had made a grave mistake.

'I think I've just undersold something,' he remarked miserably. 'I had this little watercolour, you see, Lou, and this man came in and bought it.'

From behind her counter, Big Lou listened politely. 'Well,' she said, 'that's what you do, isn't it, Matthew? You're an art dealer, are you not? You can no more get emotionally involved with your paintings than I can with my coffee beans. Both have to go some time or other.'

Matthew attempted a smile. 'It's not funny, Lou. He took such a quick look round I should have realised that he was just skimming the place for bargains. Then he saw the watercolour and bought it immediately.'

Big Lou smiled. 'Then that means that he didn't recognise it as something else.'

Matthew did not see how that followed, but Big Lou went on to explain. 'If he had thought that it was really . . . what, a Turner, he would have pretended to think about it. He would have hummed and hawed and then eventually he would have tried to beat you down. Swooping on something like that is not usually a signal for the seller himself to have doubts and to delay the sale.'

This observation, which Matthew had to acknowledge was reasonable enough, served to put him in a better mood. 'You're probably right, Lou,' he said. 'And anyway, even if it is something special, should I begrudge him his find? I can afford to lose money.'

'Just as well,' muttered Big Lou. She had always had her doubts about Matthew's ability to run a business, although now, with Elspeth in the background, she felt more confident. Back home, when she was a mere girl, her mother – and her aunts, for that matter – had drummed into her that old Arbroath saying, 'A man on his own is a farm heading for disaster'. She had heard it so often, sometimes apropos of nothing at all, that she had come to accept it as unquestioned truth. Indeed one of her aunts had the words worked into a sampler that hung on the kitchen wall, along-side other aged samplers with equally pithy sentiments. 'The last ewe is the one you dinnae see' was one such message; opaque, perhaps, but obviously redolent of something in the mind of the female relative who had worked the stitches.

Big Lou turned the tap of the steam pipe on her coffee machine. It was the part of the process that she liked the most, and it made her feel, in a small way, like a ship's engineer opening a valve, or the driver of an old steam train. She liked the hiss; she liked the agitation of the milk; and she liked the small cloud of steam that arose if the nozzle emerged for a second or two above the level of the foam.

'You never told me much about Perth,' she said. 'You liked it well enough, I take it?'

Matthew watched her pour the foamed milk into his cup. His reply was terse. 'Yes, I liked it.'

She picked up the hesitation, and glanced at him. That girl Pat, the one he used to employ, she had been to Perth, Big Lou recalled, and something had happened there; something that she never explained. Had something similar happened to Matthew?

'You don't sound enthusiastic,' she said. 'Did something happen, Matthew?'

Matthew looked up at her. He had not wanted to talk about it, but standing now at Big Lou's coffee bar, with nobody else about but this strong, sympathetic woman, his resolve broke.

'I was washed out to sea,' he said. 'It happened so quickly. I was washed out to sea and then . . .'

'Well you obviously survived.'

'Yes. I did. I was saved . . . I was saved by a dolphin.'

He looked at her, expecting her to ridicule him, but she did not. 'That's happened before,' she said.

He looked at her with gratitude. 'Does that mean you believe me?'

'Of course,' said Big Lou. 'I know you well enough to know that you don't make things up. If you say that you were saved by a dolphin, then as far as I'm concerned you were saved by a dolphin. And why not? They like us, though heaven knows why.'

Matthew felt the relief flood over him. The fact that he had been able to tell Big Lou about his experience and not be laughed at made things much easier for him.

'I don't know why it means so much to be able to tell you that,' he said. 'But it does.'

'Of course it does,' said Big Lou. 'You've had a traumatic experience. We need to talk about things like that. And this dolphin business – well, that's an extraordinary thing that happened and you need to be able to speak to somebody about it. Otherwise you'd begin to wonder if it ever really happened.'

'Thank you, Lou. Thank you very much.' He paused. Big Lou was still frowning, and had started to rub briskly at the surface of the coffee bar with her towel. Matthew knew the signs: when Big Lou did that, she was troubled. 'And you, Lou,' he said gently. 'You need to tell me something too.'

'Oh, Matthew,' Lou burst out. 'It's Robbie. Robbie and that wretched Pretender.'

Of course it is, thought Matthew. At the heart of every woman's distress there always lay a man. Or, as in this case, two.

90. Transvestites Rescued in the Minch

'Tell me about it, Lou,' said Matthew. And she did, standing there at her coffee bar, her familiar, well-used polishing towel in hand. There was nobody else present, just Matthew, but it probably would not have made much difference had there been strangers there; Big Lou would still have spoken. And anybody, even one who did not know her, who knew nothing of her history of involvement with feckless or downright peculiar men, would have been moved by her story.

'Well,' began Big Lou, 'after Robbie and the Pretender left the Braid Hills Hotel that day, they drove up north on the Stirling motorway. Robbie phoned me that evening from that hotel up in Glencoe, you know, the one in the middle of nowhere. They planned to stay there that night. He phoned from the bar.'

'The Pretender likes a drink, doesn't he?'

'Yes,' said Big Lou. 'And when Robbie phoned he said that there had just been a major row in the bar. Apparently the Pretender had started to create a bit of a fuss over some remark that the barman passed as to his outfit. He threw a glass of whisky at him and was chucked out for his pains. So they had to move on. It was misty and Robbie was worried about riding the motorbike in the dark because the lights didn't work very well.'

Matthew's eyes widened. 'Of course, he was always talking about being out in the heather, like his illustrious predecessor.'

'Aye,' said Big Lou bitterly. 'Always talking more or less sums it up. Anyway, they eventually got to Fort William and Robbie suggested that they stay there and the Pretender said that he did not want to stay anywhere where there were likely to be troops.'

Matthew burst out laughing. 'Well, really! What century does he think he's in? And, anyway, there are no troops in Fort William. There's the mountain rescue people, I suppose, but that's about it.'

'I think that Robbie had to put his foot down,' continued Big Lou. 'So they stayed there overnight in some bed and breakfast. The owner wasn't pleased to be woken up, I gather, but took them in anyway. But they were thrown out the next morning when the Pretender tried to recruit the owner. He tried to get him to rise up against the English. But the owner was English himself and did not take too well to this.

'So they went on. And eventually they got up to Skye and caught the Uig ferry over to North Uist.'

Matthew was listening attentively. 'To meet up with Flora Macdonald?'

Big Lou shrugged. 'I don't know what they thought they were doing. But that's where he wanted to be. Robbie telephoned me from Benbecula, which is the last I heard from him. He said that the Pretender had met up with somebody or other and had got drunk with him. He was trying to sober him up. And then the battery on Robbie's mobile ran out and that was it. They were on their own.'

'So they're still there?' Matthew asked. 'Still on Benbecula?'

Big Lou shook her head. 'No. They were probably there for a few days. That was Thursday I heard that, and that was when I heard from him last.' And she reached under the counter for a half page cut from a newspaper. She unfolded the clipping and laid it on the counter so that Matthew could read it.

He picked up the newspaper article. Above the text was a photograph of a smallish rowing boat being towed behind what looked like a rescue lifeboat. There were two figures in the rowing boat: two women, both wearing rather old-fashioned bonnets. The face of the lifeboat's skipper could be made out quite clearly; he was smiling.

He read out loud the text below. 'Dramatic rescue in the Minch,' the article said. 'The Uig lifeboat was called out yesterday to deal with a small craft which had been spotted in trouble in the Minch. Reports had reached Uig of a rowing boat crewed by what appeared to be two transvestites getting into difficulty and moving in circles in increasingly high seas. The lifeboat's efforts were at first resisted but eventually the occupants of the boat were persuaded to accept a line and they were brought in safely to Uig.

'The two occupants of the boat were interviewed by police on landing and a doctor was called. The doctor subsequently detained two men under the Mental Health (Scotland) Act and the two have been taken to Glasgow for further psychiatric examination. The crew of the lifeboat declined to go into further details, but were reported to have been amused by what they regard as a highly unusual rescue. "It reminds me very strongly of something," said the lifeboat skipper. "But I can't quite put my finger on it."'

Matthew stopped reading. 'Oh dear, Lou. That's not so good, is it? Have you heard from Robbie since they . . . since they took him away?'

Big Lou shook her head. 'I haven't, Matthew,' she said quietly. 'And you know something? I don't want to hear from him. I've decided that this is the end. I've put up with all this Jacobite business for long enough because I realised how important it was to him. But now I can't take any more of it. I've had it up to here. I really have.'

She paused, lowering her voice. 'And here's another thing, Matthew: I think the Hanoverians were more democratic. They didn't have that divine right of kings obsession that the Stuarts had. They were simply better.'

Matthew reached out and touched her lightly on the arm. What words of comfort could he provide? What could he say about Robbie, and the man before, and the man before that? Every one of Big Lou's men had been hopeless in one way or another. She deserved better – anybody who knew her would agree on that. But love, it seemed, was not a matter of desert. It was random and unpredictable. Unworthy men were taken on by good women, and the other way round. There was no justice in the way in which the patterns of love arranged themselves.

He would have liked to say to Big Lou: 'Don't worry, Lou. The next one will be better.' But he could not say that, because it would not be true. So they stood there, neither saying anything, and then, after a few minutes, Matthew looked at his watch and told her that it was time for him to get back to the gallery.

91. Fathers and Sons

Dr Roger Sinclair, clinical psychologist, inheritor of the mantle of the recently enchaired Professor Hugo Fairbairn, was standing close to the large sash window of his consulting room in Queen Street. Outside, above the distant hills of Fife, wisps of cloud played chase across the sky. He watched these through the glass; the sky here was so different, he thought, from that other sky under which he had grown up. This one was constantly changing, was washed out; at times covered with curtains of rain, at times made of an attenuated blue that was gentle, like the surface of a milky sea; the sky of his boyhood had been high, and wide, empty and intensely blue, like lapis lazuli; filled with light, too; a great theatre for the sun.

He took a step forward, so that his nose almost touched the glass.

Somebody had said to him once that in France window-shopping was called *lèche vitrine*, the licking of the window; a wonderful expression that somehow conveyed the longing felt by those who wanted the goods within but could not buy them. Orality, he thought, of course it was orality: the infant within wishes to incorporate the world through his mouth; to swallow the goods in the window.

He noticed that his breath had created a small patch of condensation on the glass, an island shape, dense and opaque in the middle, fainter at the edge; the rest of the glass was the sea, liquid, pure. He stood back an inch or two and saw that the island was exactly the shape of Australia – home – and using the tip of his little finger, he traced a line in the moisture, a route from Brisbane to Melbourne. My journey, he thought, or the start of it.

He had been born in Brisbane, and had spent his childhood in Toowoomba, where his father had been the accountant of a large firm of cattle exporters. His father's face came to him now; his father who had started his own voyage in Kelso and had always spoken of it to his son as if it were some sort of Eden, a place where everything was somehow more valid than the world of the smoky office from which he looked out onto the great cattle pens with their patient victims, their attendant clouds of flies. His father had hated the expression 'ten pound Pom' and had said: 'If they want to call me a ten pound Scot, I'm happy with that, but don't call me a ten pound Pom.' As a small boy Roger had been puzzled. Who had paid ten pounds for his father? Was that all that he was worth?

And now I've come back, he thought, just like a salmon that remembers where it was spawned. But do I really belong to this place? He had driven down to Kelso shortly after his arrival, as an act of homage induced entirely by guilt, and had looked for the house that his father had talked about. He found it, and had stood outside and gazed at its modest façade, at the windows giving immediately onto the street, and had thought how mean and small can be our holy places.

He stared at the fading map and at the place where Toowoomba would have been. Then he closed his eyes and saw a block of the boys' boarding school where he had been sent, together with the sons of the owners of the big cattle stations, and where he had been so unhappy. He saw the place near the door where he had been pushed to the ground hard by a large muscular boy from the Cape York Peninsula who had then sat on him and winded him so thoroughly that he thought that he would die. And he saw his mother, the pillar of the Anglican Bridge Club, drinking endless cups of weak tea with her friend on the front veranda and saying to her, 'I'm dying of boredom, you know, Lill. A slow death. Pure boredom.'

He, at least, had escaped to Melbourne, and to university, and had discovered psychology, against the will of his father, who had wanted him to follow him into business. He had left home on the understanding that he was to register for a bachelor of commerce degree at Monash, and had done so. But a week after registration, and after attending the first three orientation lectures, he had changed his registration to psychology.

He did well, although he never told his parents of the change in his course. His mother would hardly have been concerned; her mind was on the affairs of the Anglican Bridge Club, and the difference between a bachelor of commerce degree and a degree in psychology would not have struck her as being very great. Anyway, she was proud of him, and of anything he did; his father was the problem.

When he graduated, his parents came down to Melbourne for the ceremony.

His father was bemused. 'Look, Rog,' he said. 'They've made a mistake on the programme. They've put you under psychology rather than commerce. Better get that sorted out!'

'No, I don't think we should make a fuss, Dad. I'll just go through with it. We can sort it all out later.'

His father had been appalled. 'You can't do that, Rog! You can't go and get the wrong bit of paper. Heavens no. I'll speak to them myself, if you like.'

He swallowed. 'Actually, Dad, I changed courses. I meant to tell you, seeing how you were paying for the whole thing, but you know how it is . . . I kind of forgot. It's a very good degree, and they've accepted me for a master's in analytical child psychology. That's quite a thing, you know. The competition is very stiff.'

His father had looked at him in wide-eyed horror. 'You forgot to tell me . . .'

And Roger thought: all my life you've wanted me to be just like you, to do the things you like to do, to be a smaller version of you. You thought I wasn't tough enough. You sent me to that school. You said that I should stand up for myself, be a man, be an ordinary Aussie bloke, just like you. But that's not who I am.

His father looked at him, and then looked at his mother. She looked away. This was male business, father and son business. She did not want them to fight. She wanted them to be friends, just as the husbands and sons of the other women at the Anglican Bridge Club were friends.

92. A Complex Complex

Bertie sat in the waiting room while his mother was inside, talking to Dr Sinclair. They had been ten minutes already and, with any luck, it would be another ten before Dr Sinclair called him through.

Sometimes, in the days when he came to see Dr Fairbairn, the two adults had talked for forty-five minutes before Bertie was admitted, which meant that he had only fifteen minutes of the psychotherapist's bizarre questions. In Bertie's mind, Dr Sinclair, or Roger as he had asked to be called, was not nearly so bad but, even so, it would be nice if their sessions were shortened by his mother's interventions.

He searched the pile of magazines on the waiting room table to see if there was a new copy of *Scottish Field*. There was, and he seized it eagerly. There was an eagle on the cover this time, and Bertie studied the plumage and claws with some interest. Tofu had said that he had seen an eagle in a tree in his garden, but Bertie doubted this.

Tofu lied about most things when it suited him, and it usually suited him to impress other people. He lied about his father, saying that he was a private detective, when Bertie knew that he was really a writer of books on vegetarian matters. He lied about his mother, who he claimed had been eaten by a lion while on safari in Africa, but who was, according to Olive, locked up in prison. Olive herself, of course, was not above lying. She had misled Akela with entirely false claims of previous scouting experience, but much more importantly she had deceived everybody at school with claims that Bertie was her boyfriend, which, as far as he was concerned, was most certainly not the case.

He opened *Scottish Field* and turned the pages. There was an article on a man who had turned an old byre into a house. There was an article about a man who restored old cars, and one about wolves and whether they should be reintroduced into Scotland. Bertie thought this would be a good idea, but that it would be best to reintroduce them into Glasgow first before they started to reintroduce them into Edinburgh. If the wolves did well in Glasgow, and didn't bite too many people, then they could start by reintroducing them into Queen Street Gardens before they allowed them to make their lairs elsewhere.

He paused, and looked up at the ceiling. What would happen, he wondered, if they reintroduced wolves into Queen Street Gardens but did not tell his mother? And what would happen if he, Bertie, read about this in *Scottish Field*? Would he have to warn his mother if she told him that she was taking Ulysses for a walk in the gardens – as she sometimes did? If the wolves ate his mother, of course, they might take pity on Ulysses and raise him as one of them. Bertie had read about this happening, about feral children being brought up by wolves and such creatures, and he thought it would be fun to have a brother who lived with wolves, like Romulus and Remus.

Bertie skimmed through the article on wolves and reached the pages at the back where there were pictures of the latest parties and dances. This was the part of the magazine that he liked the most, as he now recognised some of the people in the pictures, and it made him feel part of everything to see them enjoying themselves.

He would go to these parties and dances himself when he was eighteen; he was sure of that; he would go without his mother. There had been a dinner at Prestonfield House, he read, and there had been hundreds of people there. He scrutinised the pictures and saw some faces he knew: Mr Charlie Maclean, in a kilt, talking to Mr Humphrey Holmes; Mr Roddy Martine talking to a lady in a white dress with a tartan shawl about her shoulders. Bertie's eye moved over the captions. Annabel Goldie talking to Mr Alex Salmond, and both smiling. He had read about them in the papers and he knew who they were. He was telling her a joke, Bertie thought, and it must have been very funny, because she was laughing a lot. And there were pictures of a band. Mr David Todd playing the fiddle in his tartan trousers while a group of people danced. Bertie sighed; he had only ever been to one party, and that was Tofu's, at the bowling alley in Fountainbridge. There were never any photographs of parties like that in *Scottish Field*.

Irene did not take forty-five minutes. Within ten minutes of going in, she came out again.

'You can go in to see Dr Sinclair now, Bertie,' she said, rather tersely. 'Mummy's popping out to Valvona & Crolla, but will be back at the end of your session.'

Bertie went in and sat in the chair in front of Dr Sinclair's desk.

There was a silence, and out of politeness Bertie thought he would make a remark. 'Do you ever think about wolves, Dr Sinclair?'

The psychotherapist, who had been scribbling a note on his pad of paper, looked up sharply.

'Wolves, Bertie? No, I can't say I think about wolves very often.' He paused. 'Do you?'

Bertie nodded. 'I think that wolves are going to come back,' he said.

Dr Sinclair stared at him. 'That's interesting, Bertie. Does that worry you?'

Bertie thought for a moment. 'A little bit. I wouldn't like to be bitten by one.'

Dr Sinclair said nothing. Freud's Little Hans, he thought; he had been worried about being bitten by the dray horses. And then there was Freud's wolf man. How strange that young Bertie should . . .

Bertie interrupted this disturbing train of thought. 'Of course, we could always get the Archers to deal with them if they became too much of a problem in Edinburgh.'

Dr Sinclair looked puzzled. '"The Archers", Bertie? Who are these archers?'

'They wear a green uniform,' explained Bertie. 'And they have a hide-out on the edge of the Meadows. I'm not sure if they'd be able to hit the wolves, though . . .'

Dr Sinclair made a note on his pad, but kept his gaze on Bertie. I almost made a major mistake, he thought. I was on the point on discharging this poor little boy, on the grounds that he did not need therapy. And now this . . . a complicated neurotic structure, complete with wolf and archer fantasies, and I missed it entirely, until it revealed itself, unfolded before my eyes.

I owe his mother an apology, he thought. It just goes to show how professional arrogance and its attendant assumptions can lead one up entirely the wrong path.

93. A Dinner Invitation

Bruce's invitation to dinner at the Todds' house in Braid Hills had been delivered to him by Todd's secretary. It was written on a correspondence card tucked into a white envelope: 'Dear Bruce, Sasha and I would love to have you round for dinner next Saturday. Free? I hope so. Raeburn.'

Bruce spent some time analysing the precise wording of this message, and the mode of its delivery. The fact the envelope had been brought to him by Todd's secretary was significant, but he could not yet work out exactly what that significance was. Was Todd embarrassed to ask him face to face? Was he concerned Bruce would find it easier to refuse if he delivered the invitation personally? Or was it a case of his not being overly enthusiastic and therefore issuing the invitation as a casual note, dashed off and tossed across the desk to his secretary? It was hard to tell.

And then there was the wording, which was capable of as many readings as there were words. 'Sasha and I': did that mean Sasha was the originator of the invitation, with Todd being added merely for politeness's sake? He could hardly have written: 'Sasha would love to have you round for dinner', as that would have made clear his own indifference, or indeed antipathy, to the idea of entertaining him.

The words 'would love to have you round' were also problematic. Todd would never say he would love anything to happen; that did not sound at all like him. He would say, 'I would like to have you round', or, possibly, 'Would you care to come round for dinner?' He would not say, 'I would love you to have you round.' That was the language of the thespian, the man in touch with his feminine side; it was not the language of men like Todd. So this meant, perhaps, that the wife was the real author of the note.

But then, just a word or two further on, the presumption changed. 'Free'? had the ring of the authentic Todd: he was always saying things like that. 'See?' 'Agree?' 'Problem?' He liked single-word sentences with a question mark at the end. And 'I hope so' was also quintessential Todd. It was an expression he used when he wanted to preclude further discussion. 'Free? I hope so' meant: you had better be.

So Bruce concluded this invitation was the work of two minds. The words used at the beginning were those dictated by Sasha; those at the end were Todd's. They both wanted him to come to dinner then. And Bruce, still grateful to Todd for his kindness in giving him his job back, had written a note saying he would be delighted to accept. 'Saturday great,' he wrote. 'Can't wait. Bruce.'

Even if he had not expected to be invited for dinner quite so soon, Bruce had anticipated some gesture from Todd. Since he had started in the firm once more, Bruce had been assiduous in the performance of his duties. His reports had all been models of their type: hedged about with all manner of exclusion clauses, as was standard surveyor practice, but clear and concise, and, what was most important, delivered well on time. One client, in fact, had been so pleased by the speed with which Bruce had completed a survey that he had specially drawn Todd's attention to it and asked him to compliment Bruce.

Bruce accepted Todd's words of praise with modesty. 'I do my best,' he said. 'It was an unusual place.'

'Oh yes?'

'Yes,' said Bruce. 'It underlined how heated the market's become: a quarter of a million for a very small studio apartment in Great King Street.'

Todd shrugged. 'Fashionable area.'

'I know that,' said Bruce. 'But this was actually a converted cupboard. A large one, but still a cupboard.'

'That's taking it a bit far,' said Todd.

Bruce nodded. 'They had a very clever architect. He managed to get a mezzanine floor in and a sunken bath. Pretty amazing.'

'And windows?'

'No,' said Bruce. 'The original cupboard had no windows. It was just a cupboard, you see. But they put in really good hidden lighting. Quite a place.'

'It's often the address that counts,' mused Todd. 'A cupboard in Great King Street is worth a three-bedroom flat in Easter Road.

But well done, anyway. They seem pleased with what they've got.'

'I hope there's only one of them,' said Bruce. 'I don't think there would be room for two.'

Now, standing before Todd's house, glancing at his wristwatch to check he was neither too early nor too late, Bruce took a deep breath. It would not be easy seeing Sasha again, after that unfortunate misunderstanding, and as for the daughter . . . Had Todd said anything about her?

Todd answered the doorbell. 'It's you,' he said.

'Yes,' said Bruce. 'Me.'

Todd ushered him into the hall. It had been all of four years – maybe a bit longer – since Bruce had last been in the house, but as he stood there, it all seemed remarkably familiar. The views of the Edinburgh skyline, which could be seen from the front windows, were reproduced in prints on the wall. And then there were the golfing prints: 'Hole in One', 'The Old Course at St Andrews', 'On Course for a Birdie' and so on.

'The ladies are through here,' said Todd, indicating the door that led into the living room. 'You'll remember my daughter, Lizzie, won't you? That dance we all went to?'

Bruce tried to ensure that his expression did not give him away. Lizzie Todd! There had been nothing about her on Todd's invitation, and had there been Bruce would not have been standing there that evening. What a disaster she was, Bruce started to think, and then stopped himself. That was the old Bruce; the new Bruce said: 'Lizzie? Of course I remember her. How nice.'

They entered the room. Sasha stood by the window, while Lizzie sat on a sofa, her shoes on the carpet below her, her feet tucked under her. They both looked at Bruce as if he had interrupted a conversation.

'There you are,' said Sasha, moving to shake Bruce's hand. 'You remember Lizzie, don't you?'

Bruce swallowed. It was eight o'clock. If dinner was served reasonably quickly he could be away by eleven-thirty at the latest. But then . . . The new Bruce smiled. 'Lizzie,' he said. 'It's been a long time.'

She was looking up at him he as he spoke. He remembered her sneering, but she did not do so now. And her face, from this angle at least, was extremely beautiful, like that of a Madonna in the first blossom of pregnancy; full, satisfied, expectant.

94. Bruce Amazes Himself

'So,' said Bruce to Lizzie Todd. 'What are you doing these days?' A strand of blonde hair had fallen over Lizzie Todd's brow and she swept it aside before she answered. Bruce wondered: had she been a blonde when he had met her last? He had a vague memory to the contrary, but it had been years ago. His eyes, though, followed the strand of hair. It was highlighted, he thought; highlighted, at the least.

'Me?' said Lizzie. 'I left Glasgow last year and came back through here. I've got a flat in Woodburn Terrace. You know that place just after the Dominion Cinema?'

'Of course,' said Bruce. 'I surveyed a flat there once. It was rather a nice flat – ground floor. But the people had cats, and you know what they can do to a place. And there were student neighbours.'

'Not all students make a noise,' said Lizzie. 'I've got some students in the flat next to me, and I hardly ever hear them.' She paused. 'Mind you, we made a noise in our student flat over in Glasgow. You could probably hear us in Edinburgh.'

Bruce laughed. 'Who didn't? I suppose that it's because you're selfish at that stage.' He heard himself speaking; selfish – he was not selfish any more. Not since four weeks ago.

He looked at her. I could do worse, he thought; a lot worse. But did he want to get involved? There had been no girlfriend since he had split up with . . . at first he could not bring himself to mention the name, but then he thought – new Bruce, and he uttered it silently: Julia Donald.

'What did you study at uni again?' he asked.

'Indeterminate studies,' she said. 'It was a great course. You could design a lot of it yourself – hence the name. You had parameters, of course.'

Bruce nodded. He had never been out with a girl who understood the word parameters. It was useful word for a girl, he thought, especially at the beginning of a relationship. Now here are the parameters . . .

'You're smiling.'

He looked at Lizzie. 'I was just thinking of something,' he said.

In the background there was the sound of ice being taken from an ice bucket and put into a glass.

'Was it something I said?'

He smiled, more openly now. 'Yes. The word parameter. It's a great word. Like perambulator. That's all.'

Lizzie looked amused. 'We had a lecturer called Steve. He used to talk about parameters all the time. I saw him once in Byres Road with his wife and baby. He looked so . . . so defeated.'

'Was the baby in a parameter?' asked Bruce.

Lizzie reached out and gave him a playful nudge. Bruce watched her hand, and willed it to stay where it was, but she withdrew it. His gaze moved up; she had a dimple in her cheek – he had never noticed it before, but it was there now, now that she smiled. And she was wearing a perfume that he had smelled before; one that he liked. Perhaps it had been in one of those fold-over and sniff pages in a magazine.

'I like your perfume,' he said. 'What is it?'

She looked slightly surprised. 'Something my mother gave me. She bought it in the duty free. Want some?'

Bruce arched an eyebrow. 'Not for me,' he said.

'You wouldn't use one of those fragrances for men, or whatever they call them?'

'I wouldn't mind those. Some of them are great.'

'But you don't use anything at the moment?'

He shook his head. Then, 'Actually, I use a moisturiser. My flatmate talked to me about it. It's a men's moisturiser.'

306

Lizzie approved. 'It's about time that more men used moisturiser,' she said. 'You've got skin, same as all of us. You need to look after it.'

Sasha, who had been attending to something in the kitchen, now returned. Todd had been busying himself at the drinks trolley while Bruce and Lizzie chatted; he now threw Sasha a glance, one of those signals between married people. She came to his side.

'Raeburn, could you give me a hand with something?' Her voice was loud enough to be heard by Bruce and Lizzie. Lizzie's eyes narrowed as she looked at her mother, but only briefly.

'Certainly,' said Todd. 'Just let me give everybody their drink. Here.' He brought glasses over and placed them on a small table at each end of the sofa on which Bruce and Lizzie were sitting. Then he and Sasha left the room.

Bruce reached for the gin and tonic that Todd had mixed him. He was not very fond of gin and tonic, but had asked for it when he came in because he had been feeling ill at ease and a gin and tonic was a simple request. The glass was cold to the touch, little drops of condensation on the outside, wet against his hand.

He put the glass down and then turned to Lizzie. The strand of hair had fallen over her brow again. He reached out. 'Let me attend to that,' he said.

'My hair,' she said. 'I need one of those hair bands, but they look so silly.'

'They don't,' he said. 'Or they wouldn't . . . on you.'

She smiled at him. He saw her teeth. He leaned forward, across the sofa, and kissed her. He almost overbalanced, but checked himself. Then he pulled back and looked at her. She was staring at him in astonishment.

'I'm sorry,' he mumbled, half-looking over his shoulder, at the door through which Sasha and Todd had disappeared. 'I just felt that I had to do that. Sorry.'

She reached forward, as she had done before; this time she left her hand on his forearm.

'Don't be sorry about that. In fact . . . do it again.'

'What about your folks?' he asked.

'They're in the kitchen.' She paused. 'And anyway, I think they like you.'

Bruce hesitated. What he was about to say was not just for effect; new Bruce, he thought. 'And do you?'

'Of course. I think you're . . . Of course I like you.'

He did not know why he said it, but the words emerged anyway. 'Enough to marry me?'

He almost made himself gasp. He sat back and smacked his head with the palm of his hand, the gesture of one who has said something profoundly stupid.

'Well, that's a bit sudden, isn't it?' Lizzie said. 'But I like you enough to go to the Dominion Cinema with you. That's a start.'

95. The Deepest Secret Edinburgh Has to Offer

Domenica's lunch with Dilly Emslie was long overdue. The two friends had made several attempts at meeting, but on each occasion life had intervened, as Domenica put it. One lunch had to be cancelled because Domenica developed an abscess under a tooth and required to be under the dental surgeon's knife at the time. On another occasion Dilly found herself in a committee meeting that overran its allotted time by several hours, and was still going strong at three in the afternoon. This time, though, the table at Glass and Thompson was booked well in advance and diaries were cleared several hours on either side of lunchtime.

Not that Domenica found she had much to clear: she had nothing on in the morning, she noticed, and nothing on in the afternoon. And the evening, too, was blank. And that, she decided, was one of the issues she needed to discuss over lunch: she needed a project and could think of none. There had, of course, been some excitement, which had given some salience to her days – there had been the business over the blue Spode teacup, which had run for some months, and then there had been the issue of Antonia's marmalade. That had provided excitement for others as well, but its denouement had been very tame indeed. Now there was no prospect of Antonia's arrest – marmalade, she expected, was beneath the notice of the police, although one should never over-estimate, she felt, the potential pettiness of officials. Scotland was not France, where the diktats of Brussels were routinely ignored; Scotland was a law-abiding country, and there was always the possibility somebody somewhere would take it upon himself to make a fuss about illegal marmalade. But even if that happened, Antonia was unlikely to be sent to prison.

So, with that prospect precluded, what was there to look forward to?

'I need to do something,' Domenica said to Dilly as they settled at their window table in Glass and Thompson. 'I feel rather . . . rather useless at the moment.'

Dilly looked at her with concern. 'You're not depressed, are you?'

Domenica shook her head. 'No, I don't think so. I know what depression feels like. I was depressed for a while after my husband was electrocuted.' She looked thoughtful. 'You know, I had the most extraordinarily tactless medical advice on that occasion.'

'I suppose doctors can be tactless, like the rest of us,' said Dilly.

'In this case even more so,' said Domenica. 'We were in Cochin then, which was where we lived at the time. I went to see my normal doctor and he referred me to a colleague – a psychiatrist, I suppose. I thought that this man would put me on a course of anti-depressants, but no. You know what he suggested? Electric shock treatment.'

Dilly tried not to laugh, but could not help herself. 'Unfortunate,' she said.

'Yes,' said Domenica. 'In the particular circumstances. And anyway, I recovered once I had made my booking to come home. The prospect of saying goodbye to my mother-in-law cheered me up immensely. The depression lifted more or less immediately.'

Domenica looked about her. The café was busy, but she did not recognise anybody in it. That could change, and probably would; Edinburgh was still sufficiently intimate for there to be no real anonymity.

Dilly looked at her friend. 'Yes, you need a project, Domenica. A person like you can't sit around. But . . .' She was being very careful. The last time they had had this conversation, Domenica had embarked on a highly dangerous field trip to the pirate communities of the Malacca Straits. Providence had already been tempted once, and might not allow for a satisfactory ending if tried again.

Domenica, who had been looking out of the window as if expecting inspiration from that quarter, suddenly turned round. 'Do you ever get the feeling that there's something going on in Edinburgh? Something that you can't quite put your finger on?'

Dilly thought about this and was about to answer when Domenica continued: 'Remember that book by Italo Calvino, *Invisible Cities*? Marco Polo tells Kubla Khan all about those cities that the Emperor has never visited. The cities aren't real, of course, but he gives the most wonderful descriptions of them.'

'I remember it,' said Dilly. And she recalled, for a brief moment, that haunting line, 'In Xanadu did Kubla Khan a stately pleasure dome decree . . .' And did Willy Dalrymple not entitle his first book *In Xanadu*? But if she said anything about Kubla Khan, or

Xanadu, or even Willy Dalrymple, then she would be a person from Porlock, and so she waited for Domenica to go on.

'I think there's something going on in Edinburgh,' Domenica said. 'There's an invisible city just underneath the surface. Every so often we get a glimpse of it; somebody makes an unguarded remark, begins a sentence and then fails to finish it. But it's there. What we anthropologists would call a realm of social meaning.' She paused. 'Have you noticed how so many people in Edinburgh seem to know one another? How when you go to a do of some sort, everybody smiles and nods? Have you noticed how in conversation too there is an automatic assumption that you know the people the other person is talking about?'

Dilly shrugged. 'I suppose . . .'

'There's a whole network,' Domenica went on.

Dilly looked at her friend. Domenica was always so rational, so balanced. Had she become a tiny bit . . . a tiny bit paranoid? Surely not.

'A network of what?' she asked.

Domenica hesitated. Then she leaned forward. 'Watsonians,' she whispered.

At that moment, a bank of cloud, which had been building up in the east, moved across the sky, obscuring the sun that had been streaming down upon Dundas Street. The familiar suddenly became unfamiliar; the friendly, threatening.

Dilly raised an eyebrow. 'But of course,' she said. 'We all know that.'

'But do we know how it works?' Domenica asked. 'We know that they're there. But how do they operate? That would make a really interesting anthropological study. "Power and Association in a Scottish City" – I can see the title of the paper already!'

Dilly had to agree. It would make fascinating reading. But how would Domenica penetrate the closed circles of Watsonians? She posed the question, and waited for a reply as Domenica sat back in her seat, a smile spreading across her face. 'There will be no difficulty,' she said. 'I have the perfect cover.' She paused, and then delivered her bombshell. 'I'm one myself.'

96. A Scorched-Earth Wardrobe

Elspeth Harmony sat at the kitchen table in the flat in India Street and contemplated her situation. It was not one of those stock-takings that follows upon a personal crisis, it was, rather, a leisurely dwelling on where she was and how she had got there. Unlike Dante, she did not find herself in the middle of a dark wood; such woods might lie ahead, but she was not yet old enough to feel them pressing in on her. Nor did she feel that she had lost Dante's straight path, even if she had, within the space of a few months, sold her flat, left her job and married Matthew. Even her name had changed – for some purposes at least – although she still thought of herself as Elspeth Harmony, and would use that name for professional purposes. But what professional purposes? she asked herself. She was no longer a teacher, and that she missed.

My life, thought Elspeth Harmony, has been totally transformed. How many months ago was it that I said goodbye to the children at the Steiner School? Five? Six? That had not been easy, as she had gone back specially to see them after her suspension – for pinching Olive, under severe provocation – had been rescinded. The children had been puzzled by her sudden replacement by a new teacher. One afternoon Miss Harmony had been there, and then the next morning they had Mr Bing welcoming them into the classroom, with no sign of Miss Harmony.

There had been speculation in the playground, of course. 'She's been kidnapped,' announced Tofu. 'You just wait. There'll be a note from the kidnappers asking for ransom. And we'll all have to give up our pocket money for months, just to get her back.'

Bertie did not think that this was a very credible theory, but said nothing. He thought that Miss Harmony would be back; she would not leave them like that; she would not desert them. And a few days later he was overjoyed when she did come back, not perman-ently, but at least to say goodbye properly. 'I'm getting married,' she said. 'I'm very happy, but I shall miss all of you so much.'

'Even Tofu?' asked Olive. 'Will you even miss him, Miss Harmony?'

If Miss Harmony hesitated, it was only for the briefest of moments before she replied. 'But of course I'll miss Tofu, Olive! I shall miss all of you.'

Olive looked doubtful.

'Will you have children yourself, Miss Harmony?' asked Skye, and added, 'Are you already pregnant?'

'Goodness no,' said Miss Harmony. 'I mean, I'm not expecting a baby just yet, but I would certainly like one.'

'Does your husband know how to make you pregnant, Miss Harmony?' Skye persisted. 'Will you be able to teach him?'

Miss Harmony blushed, and laughed. 'Let's not talk about me,' she said. 'Let's talk about what fun you're going to have with Mr Bing as your new teacher.'

And then, after that conversation, there had been the leave-taking. Many of the children had cried, and Elspeth Harmony had found herself weeping too, and had been obliged to stop her car in Spylaw Road and compose herself before she could drive on. It had been a good school in which to teach, and she had loved the children, for all their little ways. Love: the quality in a school-teacher which no training can instil; it must be there, in the heart, ready to be discovered, poured out.

Now love would find a different focus in her life. She had a husband, and a home to make out of this rather austere bachelor establishment into which she had moved. Of course that required tact; Matthew was proud of his flat and of the things it contained. He had shown her his British aviation prints in the bathroom and his framed batik from Bali. Neither of these, she felt, had a long-term future in the flat, but she had refrained from saying anything just yet. And as for the kitchen, the only possible approach, she felt, was a scorched-earth one. She had seen pictures of Clive Christian kitchens and she thought one of those would fit very well in India Street; it was not the sort of street to have Clive Christian kitchens at present, but all that could change.

Then there was the question of Matthew's wardrobe. On the second day after their return from their honeymoon, while Matthew had gone off to the gallery, Elspeth, still clad in the silk dressing gown she had bought in Singapore, had looked through Matthew's wardrobe and bedroom cupboard, examining his clothes. It had felt a bit strange at first, to be looking through the clothing of another like that, but she had reminded herself that they were married now and married people had no secrets from one another, or should have no secrets. And surely the most obvious place to start in this policy of sharing was the wardrobe.

She started with his sock drawer. There were no surprises there – in that few of the socks seemed to match. She smiled: that was a universal problem, connected in some way with the Bermuda Triangle which most washing machines seemed to possess and which swallowed socks, flushing them away to some unknown destination somewhere. She had the solution to that, though – those small rubber rings through which socks could be threaded in pairs, thus keeping them together in the wash, like swimmers sharing the same lifebelt.

She opened the drawer below that, and closed it again quickly. She was not ready for underpants. Not yet. After years of marriage perhaps, but not now. So she moved on: a sweater in a curious beige colour – Matthew's distressed oatmeal sweater, as it happened. That would have to go. And folded underneath it a pair of crushed strawberry corduroy trousers. She took these out and examined them. Here and there the corduroy was worn; surely they could be thrown out now. She put them on the floor. Now for the jackets.

But by the end of her survey, Elspeth had made a large pile of Matthew's clothes in the middle of the floor. The distressed oatmeal sweater; the crushed strawberry trousers; four jackets which looked as if they had lost all shape and will to live; three pairs of shoes in which the leather was wrinkled and cracked.

She went into the hall and looked up a number in the local directory. Deceased houses respectfully cleared, said the advertisement. Well, this was not a deceased house, but these were obviously people who would know how to get rid of old clothes. She dialled the number and was answered by a man who spoke respectfully, almost in sepulchral tones. Yes, they could come that morning, and yes, they could take anything.

She went into the kitchen and made herself a cup of coffee. It was a very satisfying thing, she felt, this looking after a man. Men were so vulnerable, she thought; they need us so badly, poor dears. And think what they would look like without us. Just think.

97. Olive is Outraged

Bertie walked across the Meadows with his father after an eventful evening at the First Morningside Cub Scouts. Stuart had travelled up to collect him on the 23 bus, but had decided they should walk back to Scotland Street. It was a warm evening, and Bertie, it seemed, was still full of energy. The walk might use up some of that, though that was by no means certain: small boys, he had discovered, were possessed of a boundless reserve of energy barely sapped by even lengthy periods of exercise. Where does it go? Stuart asked himself. Why does it drain away as the years go past, to the point where even the decision to walk from Scotland Street to the Mound involves a certain determination, a supererogatory commitment? And, more worryingly, at what point am I on that inevitable entropic curve?

Bertie wanted to talk to his father about what had happened at cubs, but was still going over it in his mind, rehearsing the extraordinary sequence of events that had suddenly blown up and then played itself out with astonishing speed. It had all started when the various sixers were busy preparing trays of items for Kim's Game. They had been told the basic rules – items were set out on a tray in random order. The tray was then covered with a cloth, which was then removed for a minute, during which time the contender had to try to memorise all the items that the tray contained. 'It's called Kim's Game, boys and girls,' said Akela.

Bertie put up his hand. 'That's after the novel by Rudyard

Kipling,' he said politely. 'Kim was a little boy who got caught up in the Great Game.'

Akela looked at him with surprise. 'That's quite correct,' she said. 'Well done, Bertie. And have you read *Kim*?'

Bertie nodded. 'I like Mr Kipling's books,' he said. 'And I've read the *Just So Stories* and *The Jungle Book*, and one or two others. But my mummy doesn't like them. She says Mr Kipling was a reactionary.'

'And I bet Mr Kipling would say your mother's a cow,' whispered Tofu. 'Only joking, Bertie.'

Olive's hand shot up. 'Akela,' she called out. 'I have something to report. Tofu's just called Bertie's mummy a cow. Yes you did, Tofu! I heard you!'

Akela frowned. 'Well, let's not argue,' she said. 'I'm sure that Tofu would never say a thing like that, would you, Tofu?' She clapped her hands. 'Now each six has its tray, so you can all start.'

Olive took control of their tray and began to set out the random articles that had been provided. Old dominoes, a comb, a key ring and so on; all were laid out on the tray ready for memorising. The boys watched her intently, none more so than Tofu, who was glaring at her through narrowed eyes.

'Why did you clype on me?' he hissed.

'I don't know what you mean,' said Olive airily, as she continued

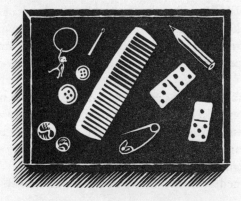

to arrange the items. 'If you're asking me why I told Akela about that horrid thing you said about Bertie's mummy, then it was because it was my duty as a sixer. And anyway, it's not Bertie's mummy's fault, is it, Bertie? Your mummy can't help being a cow, can she?'

Bertie looked down at the floor. He wanted only to play Kim's Game; he did not want to discuss his mother. And it was then that Tofu, who had been sucking his cheeks in and out in a suspicious manner, suddenly spat at Olive, the spittle hitting her on the bridge of the nose, directly between the eyes. Had it been a bullet, it would have been a fatal shot.

Olive screamed and leapt to her feet, desperately wiping her face. Then she started to cry. Akela heard the commotion from the other end of the room and came running across to see what had happened. 'Olive,' she cried, putting an arm around the sobbing girl. 'Are you all right? What on earth happened?'

Between her sobs, Olive explained that Tofu had spat at her.

'Tofu!' said Akela. 'What is this? Cubs do not spit. Nor do they fight.'

'She started it,' said Tofu. 'She scratched me really badly. I had to defend myself, Akela.'

Nobody had seen the quick work Tofu had done with a safety pin that had been among the things on the tray. Now he held up his arm and showed Akela the thin, red line of blood that he had discreetly gouged with the point of the pin. Akela gasped. 'Olive! Did you do that?'

Olive looked outraged. 'I didn't, Akela! I didn't.'

Akela turned to Ranald Braveheart McPherson, who was watching proceedings in astonishment. 'Ranald? You tell me. Who started this?'

Ranald looked about in desperation. He glanced at Olive, who was glowering at him, and then at Tofu, who made a quick cutting motion across the front of his throat. Ranald made his choice. 'Olive,' he said. 'Olive started it, Akela.'

'There,' crowed Tofu. 'I told you.'

Akela looked at Olive. 'Now, Olive,' she said. 'I've noticed that ever since you became the sixer, you've thrown your weight around. I've heard you criticising the boys. And now this. That is not the way I expect a sixer to act. So I'm afraid I'm going to have to demote you and appoint a new sixer.'

Olive stared in crumpled disbelief as Akela turned to the boys. 'Now, one of you boys will have to be sixer.'

'Me,' said Tofu.

Akela shook her head. 'Thank you for offering, Tofu, but I'm not sure that you're quite ready for that. So I think I shall appoint you, Ranald. You be the sixer.'

Ranald Braveheart McPherson looked startled. He did not want high office, particularly with this group of unpredictable people; the only person he was not afraid of was Bertie. But there was to be no further discussion; Akela had returned to the other side of the room.

Those were the events that Bertie wanted to relate to his father, but it all seemed to him to be too recent, and so he kept silent as they walked along Forrest Road and then past the statue of Greyfriars Bobby.

'That's a wonderful statue,' said Stuart. 'You do know the story of that dog, don't you, Bertie?'

Bertie nodded. Greyfriars Bobby had been a great dog; a loyal, true friend to his master. Loyalty, truth and friendship: those were the things that Bertie admired, and that he wanted to find in the world. But it seemed to him that they were qualities that were in short supply: desiderata that one could only hope would one day come into their own, find their place. Until then he had Tofu and Olive and his mother, and the rest of the imperfect world.

98. The Lightness of Scones

Matthew and Angus walked smiling into Big Lou's café. They were slightly earlier than normal, and they found Big Lou, her sleeves rolled up, washing the floor with mop and pail. Cyril, who had entered the café discreetly, always being worried about being made by Big Lou to sit outside, slunk off to find his favourite spot under his master's favourite chair. Big Lou, to his relief, ignored him.

'You're looking very pleased with yourselves,' Lou said to the two men.

Matthew and Angus exchanged mutually congratulatory glances. 'Well,' said Matthew, 'there are occasions when one may feel a certain . . . how shall I put it? A certain satisfaction with the way things have worked out.'

Big Lou squeezed her mop into the pail. 'You mean you've just sold a painting. For twice what it's worth, no doubt.'

'Nothing as simple as that, Lou,' said Matthew.

'We have pulled off a major coup . . . for the nation,' said Angus. 'Not that we wish to trumpet that from the rooftops. It's just that you asked, Lou. And we're telling you.'

Big Lou snorted. 'I cannae imagine either of you doing anything for the nation,' she said.

Angus smiled. 'Well, that's where you're wrong, Lou. Sorry to be the one to point it out, but you're wrong.'

Big Lou picked up the pail and put it behind the counter before washing her hands at the sink. 'You tell me all about it then, boys,' she said. 'And I'll let you know what I think of it.'

Angus and Matthew sat down at their table. 'We'll have scones with our coffee this morning, Lou,' Angus said. 'A couple of those rather sturdy scones of yours, please.'

'Sturdy?' snapped Big Lou. 'And what do you mean by that?'

'I mean that they're not perhaps the lightest of scones,' said Angus. 'Not that I'm criticising you, Lou. It's just that . . . well, those scones might go down well in Arbroath, but here in Edinburgh . . . people prefer, perhaps, a slightly lighter scone.'

'Nonsense,' said Lou. 'Light scones are all air and nothingness. You can get your teeth into my scones.'

'A scone can never be too light,' said Angus. 'Read the cookery books, Lou. They all say that.'

'Not where I come from,' retorted Lou. 'But anyway, what's this thing you're so pleased about?'

Angus looked at Matthew, who indicated with a nod of his head that he should go on to tell the tale. 'It's all about Burns,' he said, 'and a Raeburn portrait.'

He told Lou what had happened. Frankie O'Connor, younger brother of the late Lard O'Connor, had arrived from Glasgow, as he had threatened to do. Not only had he come, though, but so had two of his friends.

'You should have seen them, Lou,' said Matthew. 'They were straight from Central Casting. Glasgow hoods. Frankie's pals.'

Matthew went on to narrate how Frankie had shown no interest in seeing his brother's painting, but had said he was perfectly willing to sell it for GBP 200. Matthew had readily agreed, but asked, as he paid, about the painting's provenance.

'He claimed Lard had been given it in return for cutting a hedge,' he said. 'Such a wonderful explanation that it may even have been true. There was no mention of the aunt in Greenock or Gourock or wherever it was.'

'Otherwise obtained,' said Angus. 'As we thought.'

'So now?' asked Lou.

'Now we hand it over,' said Angus. 'And the powers that be let us know if it's on their list of stolen paintings. Nobody has come forward, so it probably isn't. So it goes to the Scottish National Portrait Gallery.'

As this conversation proceeded, Cyril dozed beneath the table. As a dog, human speech was a mystery to him – a babble of sounds that was so hard to interpret, no matter how hard he strained. Tone of voice, though, provided a key: when the sounds were low and constant, all was well; when the pitch was raised, something was happening, and that might have consequences for dogs. Then there were the few words he really did understand – words laden with meaning, from the canine point of view. 'Walks', that rich and promising word, was of immense importance in the canine vocabulary; a word that activated every pleasure centre in a dog's brain. 'Good dog', a more complicated phrase, standing, in its complexity, at the very outer limits of canine understanding, as obscure as the rules of quantum physics. That two words should combine to produce a single meaning – that was the conceptual challenge for a dog. So the canine brain ignored the word dog as a superfluous complication, and focused, instead, on 'good'.

But when Cyril awoke from his brief nap, the problem that confronted him was not one of understanding what was being said over the table, but what he saw underneath, down at dog level, close to the floor. For there before him, only inches away, were Matthew's ankles; half clad in socks, half exposed. It was a sight of which Cyril had dreamed, and in some of his dreams he had acted. This was Cyril's temptation, and it was an immensely strong one. Indeed, had Mephistopheles himself concocted a challenge for Cyril, he could not have come up with a stronger, more tempting entice-ment. Matthew's ankles were Sirens, and they beckoned from the rocks of his ruination.

He could not resist. For years he had gazed upon these ankles and restrained himself. But now he knew he could do that no longer. His life would soon be over; dogs did not last all that long, and he wanted to do this before he passed beyond tempta-tion. So, suddenly, and without giving Matthew any warning, Cyril moved forward and nipped Matthew's right ankle; not too hard – he liked Matthew – but enough for Matthew to give a start and look down.

Cyril looked up, his jaws still loosely fixed around the ankle; he looked up into Matthew's surprised eyes. This was the end; Cyril knew there would be shouting and he would be beaten with a rolled up copy of *The Scotsman*. He would be in disgrace, perhaps forever. This was truly the end.

Matthew stared at Cyril. He opened his mouth, ready to say something, to shout out in outrage even, but he did not. He looked down upon Cyril and then, reaching down, he gently pushed him away. He did not want Cyril to be punished. He said nothing.

Thus we forgive one another; thus reconciliation and healing begin.

99. A Civilised Menu

Domenica rose early that Saturday and dressed with care. She liked the idea of dressing with care, a notion she had come across in a Michael Longley poem addressed to Emily Dickinson, in which he described her as 'dressing with care for the act of poetry'. She would dress with care for the social act that lay before her: the entertaining of her friends to dinner.

The choice of courses was an important one. Domenica was not an enthusiastic cook, in the sense that she did not derive a great deal of pleasure from cooking; but she was a good one. And the meal her guests would be given that evening would give them no cause for complaint. It would have an Italian flavour, of course; that was the cuisine with which she felt most comfortable and the one for which the ingredients were the most readily available in Valvona & Crolla.

And the guest list was chosen with equal care. There were several invitations that had to be repaid, and others that would be allocated purely on the basis of merit. James Holloway would come, of course; and Judith McClure and Roger Collins; and Michael and Mona Shea; and the Duke of Johannesburg; Pippa and Hugh Lockhart from round the corner; and Andrew and Susanna Kerr; and . . . She paused. She had noted down on a piece of paper the names of those who were invited and hoped that she had forgotten nobody; Angus, of course – no dinner party in Scotland Street would be complete without him; and Matthew and Elspeth. That would be enough; her table in the kitchen, when extended at each end with the addition of a bridge table, could seat up to sixteen in conditions of elbow proximity.

She had arranged to meet Angus in Valvona & Crolla that morning.

'I shall help you to choose the wine,' he had said. 'Not that you can't choose it yourself, it's just that one can make so many mistakes when it comes to wine.'

She had accepted his offer. Wine was something Angus knew about, and she trusted his judgement. At Valvona & Crolla, though, when inspecting a range of obscure Puglian wines, Angus turned to her suddenly and said, 'Domenica, why are we doing this? Why are we having all these people round to dinner?'

It might have been another occasion on which Mallory's reply would have been called for: because they're there, but she said instead: 'Friendship.'

He had not expected that answer. 'Just that?'

'Yes. Because a dinner party provides the ideal opportunity to sit with people. To talk to them.'

'You don't think, then, that it's simply a bourgeois ritual?'

Domenica smiled. 'I might have thought that in the past,' she said. 'No more, though. I now realise, I think, how important these bourgeois rituals are. Or all rituals, for that matter, bourgeois or not.' She reached out and took from him the bottle he had extracted from the shelf to show her. 'Bari, I see. Do you know what you can find in Bari, Angus?'

Angus shrugged. He knew little of the Italian south, even if he liked its wines.

'The bones of Father Christmas,' said Domenica. 'Santa Claus, no less, or Saint Nicholas of Myra, to give him his full title. He was the basis of the Santa Claus legend, and they keep his relics in a candy-striped box in the Church of San' Nicolo in Bari.'

Angus was busy examining the wines; only half-listening.

'There is so much to see in Italy,' Domenica continued. 'The Holy House in Loreto, for example. That's the Virgin Mary's house. It was carried over from the Holy Land by angels, I believe.'

'How very remarkable,' said Angus, moving along the shelf to examine a small selection of Tuscan wines.

'But to return to rituals,' said Domenica. 'In the Sixties we thought we could get rid of everything. Rituals were exposed as meaningless. Restraint was taken as a sign of inhibition. Personal authenticity was all. Behave as you wanted to. Liberate yourself.'

Angus nodded. Domenica was right about these things, he felt, and he was prepared to go along with her.

'Of course, we're now finding out the consequences of all that,' said Domenica. 'Look at the way people behave in the streets at night. Look at the rudeness, the discourtesy, the ugliness and violence of our public space.'

'Yes,' said Angus. 'It's very bad. Very bad indeed.'

'Yet anybody who points it out is laughed at. It's very uncool, isn't it, to point out that we are a society in dissolution?'

Angus nodded. His eye had been caught by a jar of artichoke hearts. 'Yes,' he said. 'Quite so.'

'And as for that Government minister who attacked the Proms,' said Domenica. 'Don't you despair? She said the audience was not inclusive. Since when, may I ask, has it become mandatory to have an audience which is representative of society at large? What an absurd idea. Sinister, too.'

'There are some very unsettling people around these days,' agreed Angus. 'People who tell us what to think. People who have no understanding of the concept of artistic freedom.' He paused. 'Have you thought, Domenica, of doing a first course of tagliatelle with white truffle sauce? Look, here is some of that truffle paste. It's not at all expensive, and it tastes delicious. It really does.'

'And then?'

'And then you can follow it with a fish stew. One of those strong Neapolitan ones. Octopus and the like.'

'I could,' said Domenica. 'But returning to rituals, Angus – don't you think they are the absolute cement of any society? Rituals and key institutions. And when you destabilise them, when you point out the emperor has no clothes, you find you've got a void where society used to be. Just a whole lot of individuals, all strangers to one another.'

'Undoubtedly,' said Angus. He looked at her. 'But what are we going to do, Domenica? What's the solution?'

'We have to recivilise society,' said Domenica quietly. 'The whole of Britain: England, Scotland, the works, everything has to be recivilised. We have to rebuild. We have to recreate the civilisation we have so casually destroyed.'

Angus knew she was right. But the task of recivilising seemed

324

so daunting, so extensive, that he wondered if he and Domenica were up to it, especially when one had to cook dinner as well.

100. A World Put Back in Balance with Love

James Holloway was the first to arrive, that is if one did not count Angus, who had spent most of the day in Domenica's flat, helping her with preparations. While James and Angus talked together about the Raeburn portrait of Burns, she attended to the laying of the table in the kitchen. Then others arrived, let in by Angus who, as usual on these occasions, was acting as host. How pleasant it would be, thought Domenica, to have Angus here all the time, helping about the place, doing the sorts of things he was doing this evening. But no, she dismissed the thought; Angus came with baggage – there was Cyril, and there was all that paint and turpentine and mess. There were few men, she reflected, who came without clutter.

After she had finished in the kitchen she went through to the drawing room to meet her guests. Almost everybody had arrived now, and the din of conversation had risen markedly. Angus had opened a window, not only to ventilate the room, but also to allow some of the noise to escape. Domenica imagined the sentences spoken by her guests drifting out of the window and over Drummond Place Gardens, rising slowly, like Buddhist prayer slips, and then floating out over the Forth: little snippets of conversation, observations, small asides. Marconi had said, she recalled, that sound never dies – it merely gets fainter and fainter. And that meant that somewhere out there, floating above the cold plains of the Atlantic, was the ever-fainter sound of the *Titanic*'s band playing 'Nearer My God to Thee'. Such a strange thought . . .

And then she thought: I should have invited Antonia. The unsettling thought distracted her and she crossed the room to where Angus was talking to Susanna Kerr.

'Yes,' said Susanna, 'it will be marvellous if that is the real Raeburn portrait of Burns.'

'It is,' said Angus. 'I'm absolutely convinced of it.'

He was drawn aside by Domenica. 'We forgot to invite Antonia,' she whispered. 'Should I go and see if she's in?'

Angus thought for a moment. This was not a time to nurse a grudge. 'I shall go and get her,' he said. 'I'll tell her the truth. We forgot.'

Angus was dispatched to deliver Antonia's invitation and returned a few minutes later saying that Antonia had accepted, and would join them shortly. 'I suspect that she had already eaten,' he said. 'But she accepted none the less. It's rather greedy, don't you think, to have two dinners?'

'Not if you do it out of politeness,' said Domenica. 'What appears to be greed in such a case becomes an act of courtesy. And we must be more charitable towards Antonia. She is, I fear, one of the weaker brethren and needs our help.'

After a while, they moved through to the kitchen and seated themselves around the extended table. Angus sat at one end, and Domenica at the other: host and hostess, with their guests ranged between them. The conversation, which started the moment they sat down, rose in a hubbub of opinion, conjecture and friendly refutation. Elspeth, seated next to Matthew, took his hand under the table and pressed it gently. He looked at her fondly and smiled. 'It doesn't matter about the clothes,' he whispered. 'I can get new ones.' Relieved at his forgiveness, she pressed his hand again.

Each had his or her thoughts: pleasure at being in company – and such good company too; delight at the pungent smell of the white truffle sauce and the texture of the tagliatelle; eager anticipation of the course, and discourse, yet to come. For her part, looking down the table, Domenica caught Angus's eye and raised her glass to him, a private toast, which he responded to with a toast of his own. And then, halfway through the meal, Domenica tapped her now empty glass with a spoon. It was the right moment, she thought; any later and people might feel maudlin, or tired. It was just the right moment.

'Every year,' she said, 'Angus kindly recites a poem of his own composition. The time for that poem has now arrived.'

'We would not have it otherwise,' said Roger Collins.

'No indeed,' agreed Hugh Lockhart.

Angus looked down, in modesty. 'Dear friends,' he said. 'My heart is full . . .'

And he continued:

> *But not so full that I cannot speak of love;*
> *For that, you know, is the truest of words*
> *Most profoundly spoken, in any tongue,*
> *And in any circumstances.*
> *May we who are blessed in friendship*
> *Find it always in our hearts*
> *To speak that word and make it the fulcrum*
> *Of all our acts; proclaim it, too,*
> *Our guiding light in moral gloaming.*
> *Love heals, makes whole,*
> *Restores the delicate balance*
> *That so long ago went out of kilter,*
> *When hatred and suspicion first*
> *Uttered their beguiling, primeval snarl.*
> *I am a Scot, and a patriot;*
> *I love this country, for all its ways,*
> *I am as moved as any when I see*
> *That landscape of quiet glens,*
> *Those pure burns and rivers,*
> *Those blue seas and islands*
> *Half blue. I love all that,*
> *And the people who dwell therein;*
> *But I love, too, our neighbours*
> *And those who are not our neighbours;*
> *I shall never relish their defeats,*
> *Nor celebrate their human difficulties;*
> *For, frankly, what is the alternative?*
> *I see no other way.*

I see no other way but that;
I see no other way but love.

He finished. He may have had more words, but he could not utter them; not now. And nobody had anything to add to what he had said; no words of dispute or disagreement, for what he had said was all true, every word of it.

Now you can order superb titles directly from Abacus

☐ 44 Scotland Street	Alexander McCall Smith	£7.99
☐ Espresso Tales	Alexander McCall Smith	£7.99
☐ Love Over Scotland	Alexander McCall Smith	£7.99
☐ The World According to Bertie	Alexander McCall Smith	£6.99
☐ The Sunday Philosophy Club	Alexander McCall Smith	£7.99
☐ Friends, Lovers, Chocolate	Alexander McCall Smith	£6.99
☐ The Right Attitude to Rain	Alexander McCall Smith	£6.99
☐ The Careful Use of Compliments	Alexander McCall Smith	£6.99

The prices shown above are correct at time of going to press. However, the publishers reserve the right to increase prices on covers from those previously advertised, without further notice.

────────────────── ⟨ABACUS⟩ ──────────────────

Please allow for postage and packing: **Free UK delivery.**
Europe; add 25% of retail price; Rest of World; 45% of retail price.

To order any of the above or any other Abacus titles, please call our credit card orderline or fill in this coupon and send/fax it to:

Abacus, P.O. Box 121, Kettering, Northants NN14 4ZQ
Fax: 01832 733076   Tel: 01832 737526
Email: aspenhouse@FSBDial.co.uk

☐ I enclose a UK bank cheque made payable to Abacus for £ . . . .
☐ Please charge £ . . . . . . to my Visa, Delta, Maestro.

☐☐☐☐☐☐☐☐☐☐☐☐☐☐☐☐☐☐

Expiry Date ☐☐☐☐   Maestro Issue No.   ☐☐

NAME (BLOCK LETTERS please) . . . .

ADDRESS . . . .

. . . .

. . . .

Postcode . . . . Telephone . . . .

Signature . . . .

Please allow 28 days for delivery within the UK. Offer subject to price and availability.